SHEILA GRAY ONCE SAID,

PSEUDONYM

"I'D GIVE MY LIFE TO BECOME A BEST-SELLING NOVELIST..."

AND THAT'S EXACTLY WHAT IT COST HER.

DENNIS E. HENSLEY & DIANA SAVAGE

WHITAKER

Publisher's Note:
This novel is a work of fiction. References to real events, organizations, or places are used in a fictional context. Any resemblances to actual persons, living or dead, are entirely coincidental.

Pseudonym

Dr. Dennis E. Hensley
www.DocHensley.com
dennis@dochensley.com

Diana Savage
www.DianaSavage.com
www.facebook.com/diana.savage.7
Twitter: @DianaESavage

ISBN: 978-1-62911-614-3
eBook ISBN: 978-1-62911-615-0
Printed in the United States of America

Whitaker House
1030 Hunt Valley Circle
New Kensington, PA 15068
www.whitakerhouse.com

Library of Congress Cataloging-in-Publication Data (Pending)

1 2 3 4 5 6 7 8 9 10 11 w 23 22 21 20 19 18 17 16

Dedication

Dennis E. Hensley dedicates this novel to Lorine A. Parks, his former English professor at Saginaw Valley State University, and the woman who in many ways served as a model for the fictional character of Laureen in this book.

Diana Savage dedicates this novel to her daughter, Aimee Joy Lenger—a loving, compassionate, and creative woman of God.

Acknowledgments

Dennis E. Hensley wishes to thank his literary agent, Jerry "Chip" MacGregor, for another excellent liaison with a quality publishing house, and extends a continuous note of love and thanks to Rose for being a wife who encourages, nudges, and tolerates a writer as a husband.

Diana Savage wishes to thank the special people in her life who have helped her to recover and grow after she experienced the difficulties that gave her insight into this story's protagonist.

CHAPTER 1

The morning did not start well for Sheila Gray. Not only was turning thirty-three tantamount to announcing to the world, "I'm now officially a lost cause," but at 8:45 AM, someone rang her doorbell.

She frowned at the interruption. She wasn't expecting any packages, so it must be either an eager door-to-door salesperson or a pair of religious busybodies getting a head start on their daily quota of souls. Normally, she would have already left for work, but her employer, Reynolds Heating and Air-Conditioning, had given her the day off for her birthday. Her plan was to make practical use of it.

She jerked open the front door, but no one was on the porch. Then she spied a white envelope, her name printed in bold letters on the front, propped against the screen door. From the size, she assumed that it contained a greeting card. Her dark mood lifted slightly, and she smiled. Someone had remembered her birthday! She retrieved the envelope and tore it open.

Gracing the front of the card was a cartoonish bowlegged woman with straggly hair, a missing tooth, and an oversized posterior. The caption read, "You ain't getting better, gal, you're just getting older." On the inside of the card was the message, "Welcome to the backside of 30... and, oh, what a BIG backside it is!"

The card bore the signatures of all three administrative assistants at Reynolds.

Sheila's smile faded, and she stood nearly motionless, scarcely aware that her hand was crumpling the card and envelope. She sagged against the doorframe.

She knew that her friends had intended only good-natured teasing, but this was no joke to her. Indeed, she *was* thirty-three, and they were absolutely right: She truly wasn't getting any better. Her life was going downhill, in many ways.

Every birthday forced her to face the reality she somehow managed to suppress the other 364 days of the year—that she had failed to fulfill the sense of destiny she'd once felt so strongly. This year, she also had to admit that she was trapped in an untenable situation.

A tear fell on the hand holding the crumpled card, startling her. At that moment, clouds scudded in front of the sun, and a chilly breeze blew through the screen. She backed up slowly and shut the door on the outside world. Her errands would have to wait awhile.

An hour later, Sheila decided to make another attempt at facing the day. Of course, she couldn't count on Dan to make her feel any better. He wasn't the type of husband to come home with a cake or a gift of jewelry. He would never make dinner reservations at a fancy restaurant and then send her a text message telling her to wear shoes fit for dancing. No, not Dan. He'd just come home expecting his supper served on time. Oh, once or twice, he'd brought her some birthday flowers, but those times had been too long ago to remember.

He'd never made any fuss about their anniversary, either. His only gift of any significance had been her set of gold wedding rings—one plain band, the other with a small solitaire diamond—on their second anniversary. When they first got married, they didn't have money for a car, let alone luxuries such as rings. After Sheila could no longer hide her disappointment, Dan eventually brought home a mail-order catalog with three of the least expensive styles circled and told her to choose a set. She was grateful to get the rings finally, but she'd always wondered how much of Dan's uncharacteristic decision to spend money on her had stemmed from his possessive, jealous nature.

She glanced at her reflection in the bedroom mirror. She used to feel prettier, when she'd worn her brown hair long—not in this outdated style that Dan preferred. Now, bags had formed under her eyes from too many sleepless nights. As she stepped back and caught her full reflection, she had to admit that the one thing she still felt halfway good about was her figure. Remaining childless had helped her physically, if not emotionally.

Making her way to the kitchen, she found Dan's daily honey-do list still stuck to the refrigerator door, along with three lottery tickets, all held in place by a pineapple magnet. She scanned the tasks he'd scribbled, most of them things to pick up: his jacket at the dry cleaner, his latest list of titles he'd reserved at the library, the items she'd forgotten on her last trip to the grocery store.

At least those errands wouldn't take too much time. And since she had the whole day off work, she wouldn't have to squeeze them in during her lunch hour or on her way home from the office. Perhaps that afternoon, she'd do some pleasure reading or watch a movie from their collection. She might even treat herself to a store-bought brownie and a dish of ice cream. "Happy birthday to me, doggone it," she sang.

Well, since it *was* her birthday, maybe she should fix herself up a little before going into town—color her cheeks with some blush, highlight her green eyes with a dusting of eye shadow. In the bathroom again, she opened a drawer and pulled out a small bag. Then, frowning, she slowly returned the bag and shut the drawer. Why even bother? Dan objected whenever she used too much makeup. To keep the peace, she'd have to wash her face before he came home, so she decided she might as well wear her usual washed-out look to town.

She drove to the dry cleaner first. As she walked through the door, the strong odor of chemicals assaulted her sinuses. Just her luck, no one was at the counter. What a way to spend her birthday—breathing in carcinogens. But wait, here was the proprietor now. Sheila presented her claim tag, then began rummaging in her purse for her debit card.

"Sheila Davis? Is that you, Sheila?"

Turning around, she saw an elderly woman with silver hair.

"It's Sheila *Gray* now," she replied instinctively, "but, yes, I'm...." Then she realized who was standing before her. "Mrs. Parks! I don't believe this. I haven't seen you in...has it been fifteen years?" Sheila dropped her purse on the counter, opened her arms, and enveloped the woman in an embrace. "What are you doing back in Brissenden? I thought you'd left Indiana for good. This is wonderful!" As she held her former teacher close, Sheila noticed how thin the woman had become. Age had certainly caught up with her.

Then worry fired Sheila's imagination. As her teacher and mentor, Laureen Parks had played a vital role in her life. What if...? But, no. Sheila wouldn't allow herself to entertain any what-ifs right now. Instead, she leaned back and studied the woman before her. Mrs. Parks's face was pale and drawn, and the skin of her neck hung loosely in a sort of wattle.

"Please, call me Laureen." A slight flush of pink momentarily replaced her pallor. "When I saw you walk in here as I drove by, I recognized you immediately. You surely haven't changed much. Do you have time to go for coffee?"

Sheila smiled. "Nothing could make me happier. Today is my birthday, and I have the day off from work. In fact, why don't you follow me to my home? I live nearby. Oh, I can't believe how long it's been since I last saw you."

"It *has* been a long time," Laureen agreed. "Since that summer I drove you to college."

Sheila flinched, but she recovered quickly. Turning back to the counter, she paid her bill and picked up Dan's jacket, then led Laureen outside. They reached the Grays' in five minutes.

In the entryway, after Sheila had taken her coat, Laureen lingered in front of the small framed print that read, *"Wives, submit yourselves unto your own husbands." —Ephesians* 5:22. She raised an eyebrow, then moved on to the portrait of the couple that hung just below.

"So," she said, "this must be your husband. Nice-looking man. Are the pictures of your children someplace el—" She caught herself. "Oh, I *am* sorry. I didn't mean to be nosy."

Sheila finished hanging her guest's coat in the hall closet. "That's all right. We're just a twosome. I wouldn't have minded having a family, but Dan never felt the time was quite right."

Laureen hesitated, as if pondering what to say next. "So...so, you're a career woman, I take it?"

To delay her response, Sheila slipped into the kitchen, placed a pre-measured pod into the coffeemaker, and pushed the start button. Then, raising her voice, she responded, "I don't think you could call working as an office manager at a small-town heating and air-conditioning company much of a career." She shrugged. "It's a job. But I work with nice folks, and I get my birthday off with pay. I'm thirty-three today."

"Oh, yes! You said something about that at the dry cleaner. Happy birthday! If I had known ahead of time, I'd have brought you a cake."

"Thank you," said Sheila. "I have some cookies we can enjoy." She removed the lid from an airtight plastic container filled with homemade peanut-butter cookies—Dan's favorite. She hesitated only briefly before arranging a handful on a plate. She would simply not eat her share, so she could return enough of them to the container that Dan wouldn't notice any were missing.

When both mugs of coffee were brewed, she placed them on a tray, along with the cookie plate, and carried the refreshments into the living room. "So, what brings you back to Brissenden?" she asked as she handed Laureen a mug. "Since it's still only April, I'm sure you're not here to attend a class reunion, as those are usually in the summer."

Laureen took a sip of her coffee, then set the cup on the side table and straightened her skirt somewhat primly before stating, "Actually, I've come here to die."

Sheila nodded. So, Mrs. Parks—Laureen—was planning ahead, getting prepared for her later years. That was just like the organized teacher she remembered. "You're moving back for retirement?"

"I'm sorry if I am confusing you, my dear. But, no, there won't be a retirement. I have terminal cancer. The doctors have given me between five and ten months to live, depending on the success of the treatments I opt to undergo. So, as you see, it won't be long before I die."

Sheila gasped. "Surely, you can't mean that! I've just found you again. You were my favorite teacher, my role model, my...." Her eyes filled with tears, and the room went blurry.

Laureen reached over and squeezed Sheila's hand with her own blue-veined one. "Well, I'm not dead yet. And nothing would please me more than to spend time with you during my final months. I've moved back into the home my husband and I shared during my teaching days. After Herbert died, six years ago, I stayed in Houston. Then, one day, Bernice Stone called me."

"The Mrs. Stone who used to teach world history at Brissenden High?"

"Yes. We kept in touch after Herbert's job transferred us to Texas. At any rate, she told me she had noticed a for-sale sign in front of our former Brissenden home. She wondered if I had any interest in returning here. I won't bore you with the details, except to say that things worked out, and I'm back."

"But *why?*" asked Sheila. "I'm happy to have you in the area, of course, but wouldn't your new friendships and connections in Texas be reason enough to remain there?"

"Not really," said the older woman, leaning back against the couch cushions as if she were too tired to sit up straight. "I'm a Midwesterner at heart, and some of my distant family members live in this part of the country. Besides, I wanted to see Hoosier cornfields and rolled hay bales again before I died. If that makes me sound like a hick, then so be it." She grinned. "I'm old and dying, so I can say and do what I want."

At the repeated reference to death, Sheila shuddered. "And...the doctors are...?"

"After three physicians presented me with identical findings and prognoses, I have accepted my fate. I'm not hanging on to false hope. I've always been a pragmatist, Sheila. The fact is, I'm dying. That's that." She picked up her coffee and drank deeply, as if hoping the caffeine would give her a temporary surge of energy.

Sheila stared at the black and dark-brown swirls decorating her mug. They seemed to echo the downward spiral toward oblivion that had engulfed her life. A long time ago, she, too, had accepted her fate and relinquished all false hope. Death could overshadow one's life in more ways than just through a terminal-cancer diagnosis.

"I know the feeling," she murmured—suddenly horrified at what she had said aloud. "I...I mean, I can only *imagine* how...how you...." She looked down again, embarrassed.

"Sheila?" Laureen said softly. "Is everything all right?"

"Sure," Sheila responded hastily. "I don't know *what* could have made me say such a thing. I'm sorry. I didn't mean to imply that I understood everything you've been going though." Silence fell as she groped for something to do or to say to put things right again.

"It's your birthday, but you're desperately sad, aren't you?" Laureen said, her voice full of compassion. "I see it in your eyes, and I hear it in your voice. This house is a reflection of sadness." She gave Sheila a tender smile. "What has happened to you?"

The older woman's compassion touched a nerve. Desperate to put on a good front, Sheila forced a laugh. "Oh, you know how we women are. Birthdays make us nostalgic." She shrugged. "I'm fine. I was just shocked to hear your news." She rose abruptly and returned to the kitchen.

Laureen followed her. "It's more than that. Is it something we can talk about? I've always been a good listener."

Sheila opened the box of coffee pods. "Really, I'm fine. Let me fix you a fresh cup. What flavor would you like this time?"

Laureen chose a hazelnut blend and then sat at the kitchen table rather than return to the living room. She motioned for Sheila to join her. "May I confess something to you?"

"Confess?" said Sheila, frowning. "What do you mean?"

Laureen smiled demurely. "I didn't bump into you just by chance this morning. I've been looking for an opportunity to reconnect with you." She shifted her thin frame slightly, as if trying to get comfortable on the unpadded kitchen chair. "You're actually one of the main reasons

I came back to Brissenden, but I've been afraid to confront you directly. For the past week, I've been keeping an eye on you, from a distance. Today, I finally summoned the courage to make my move."

Sheila laughed nervously. "You're putting me on."

"Nothing of the sort. For a long time, I've wanted to have a private chat with you. I just didn't know if your life...your *schedule*...would have room for an old woman like me."

"Don't be silly." Sheila rose to check the coffeemaker's progress and soon returned to the table with her guest's refilled mug. "You know I've always put you on a pedestal."

Laureen smiled at the compliment and the refill. "Thank you." Then she added, "I've had two major regrets in my life. It is much too late to do anything about the first regret, but there still may be a chance to rectify the second one."

Sheila watched her beloved former teacher expectantly, glad that Dan wasn't due home for several more hours.

"When I attended Ball State University, it was assumed that I would become a teacher," Laureen said. "But what I really wanted was to be a writer. The next Pearl S. Buck or Catherine Marshall or Dorothy Sayers, only better! I plastered the walls of my college dorm room with black-and-white magazine photos of Willa Cather and Margaret Mitchell and Harper Lee. I thought that if they could be successful writers, then so could I."

At the recollection of her early determination, the older woman's crease-lined eyes brightened briefly. "Heaven knows I tried. At first, I thought I was making some headway. The college literary magazine accepted a couple of little poems I'd written, and the school paper published some of my book reviews. But, try as I might, I couldn't sell anything to the national magazines. I submitted short stories and poetry, interviews and articles, and even a short play...all of them, rejected. Not even a note of encouragement came back. I was heartbroken."

"I'm so sorry," Sheila said quietly.

"I am, too," Laureen declared. "Even a little success would have lessened the pain of rejection. But I finally had to face the facts—I just didn't have the gift of writing. I could critique and review and edit and evaluate the works of others, but I couldn't create any original writings worth reading. So, in a fit of either rage or shame, I burned the entire box of rejected manuscripts, pursued teacher certification, and accepted a job teaching English here in Brissenden." She paused to take a sip of her coffee.

"And you never tried to write professionally again?"

"Never," she confirmed. "I decided to invest my efforts in teaching young people to appreciate good literature and training them to write well. And I set a new goal for myself: to discover a gifted young writer whom I would mentor all the way to publication. If I couldn't be published myself, then I wanted to help someone else who eventually would be."

"You helped so many of us become better writers," Sheila said. "You set high expectations of all your students, and we improved because of it."

"I like to think so, and I appreciate your kind words, but I still have unfinished business. And time is running out." She folded her hands in front of her on the table. "I have no time for tact, Sheila. The simple fact is, I had one student—*only* one student—who possessed the potential to become a professional writer under my tutelage. That student was *you*. I knew it from the first essay you submitted, and all your writing samples—stories, poems, plays—confirmed it. You had that creative gift I had so yearned for. That's why, before I had to leave Brissenden, I did everything I could think of to nurture your talent."

Sheila felt the almost imperceptible flicker of a long-dormant dream returning to life. Could it be a sign that now was the time to confront what had been holding her back all these years? She glanced at the clock. *Please, God, keep Dan from being overly angry if I don't finish his to-do list today.*

Laureen took a deep breath. "Now, I've returned to Brissenden, only to discover that you have done *nothing* to fulfill your destiny as a writer.

I need some answers, Sheila...details! I can't leave here today until you answer one question: What have you been doing with your life for the past fifteen years?"

Sheila swallowed hard as the memories flooded back.

CHAPTER 2

"If Neva Bradshaw gets the drama department trophy, she'll act like it's an Academy Award," said Sarah Vestal, putting a finger in her mouth as if to gag. "Back in second grade, she started crying when our teacher read us *Bambi,* and she hasn't stopped since."

Seated with three of her friends in the high-school auditorium, Sheila Davis tried to tune out the chatter around her so she could focus on reading the paperback novel she'd brought. This was the last boring awards assembly she would ever have to endure. One month from now, June 3, she would graduate and be out of here.

"They should offer awards for drawing or piano so that some of us could be up on that stage," Jenny Leverett complained, taking a compact out of her purse. "I mean, can we be serious for a moment here? Home economics awards? That stuff went out with my grandmother. Puh-lease!" She looked in the mirror and whispered, "Gino Butonni is just three rows behind us, Mari. Are you getting all hot and bothered?"

"Shut up!" said Maricela Montero. "He's just my chemistry lab partner. That's all."

"Oooooh, and what a wonderful chemistry there *is* between you," Jenny continued. "He's fine, girl, and I can tell that he likes what he sees in you. I heard him tell Tim that he prefers girls who are 'stacked.' You must have him drooling. He'll ask you out. You'll see."

"You're so crude," Maricela said. After a short pause, she whispered, "You really think he likes me?"

Sheila heard someone tap twice on the microphone to get everyone's attention. She looked up and saw the principal, Mr. O'Neill, in the center of the stage. Then she noticed that her English teacher, Mrs. Laureen Parks, was also on stage. That was odd. Mrs. Parks had nothing to do with any of the departments that usually dominated every awards assembly.

She liked Mrs. Parks a lot. Having lost her mother as an infant, being left with only her father and two brothers as family, Sheila appreciated being able to talk confidentially with an older woman from time to time. More than just a teacher, Mrs. Parks had become a mentor and even, in some ways, a mother figure to Sheila, encouraging her in her educational goals and sharing her enjoyment of reading.

After delivering his opening remarks, Mr. O'Neill departed slightly from the predictable schedule they usually followed at these assemblies. Sheila decided to close her book and focus on what he was saying.

"We have numerous school letters and trophies to present," he announced, "but, to start today's program, one special award—a first for our school—will be given out by Mrs. Parks." Then the principal stepped back and nodded across the stage.

Mrs. Parks, with her sleek black hair, stylish skirt suit, and confident walk, approached the microphone carrying a large manila envelope and a small cardboard box, which she set on the small table nearby.

She thanked the principal, then explained that in her seventeen years of teaching at Brissenden High, it had been her desire to discover a writer worthy of bringing statewide attention to the school.

"This year," she announced with enthusiasm, "that has finally happened. The Indiana College Newspaper Affiliation sponsors an annual essay competition for high-school seniors. The winners receive a U.S. savings bond worth one hundred dollars, a check for five hundred dollars, and a scholarship to attend a six-week pre-college summer writing program at a participating college or university."

Mrs. Parks picked up the manila envelope, opened the flap, and extracted a folded letter and a large certificate. "Earlier this year, I submitted an essay written by one of my senior English students, but I didn't tell the student I did so. Two weeks ago, I learned that this student had received one of the first-place awards. The judges called this student's essay"—she looked down at the letter—"'well-organized, insightful, and mature.' And I couldn't agree more."

From the small box, Mrs. Parks lifted a trophy consisting of a golden quill mounted on a wooden plaque made to resemble a writing tablet. "Allow me to present the ICNA award for our district to...Sheila Davis! Please come up, Sheila, and accept your certificate, bond, check, and trophy, and acceptance letter."

Sheila couldn't believe it. An award? A scholarship? For writing? For *her*? She was too numb to move.

Sarah, Jenny, and Maricela jostled her into action, virtually lifting her from her seat and pushing her toward the stage. As Sheila made her way up the steps, her schoolmates applauded loudly, and several even whistled. All the teachers seated on the platform stood to shake her hand.

After handing the trophy to Sheila, Mrs. Parks gave her a big hug. "I'm very proud of you!" Mrs. Parks said in her ear.

With the spotlights blinding her, Sheila stammered into the microphone, "I never dreamed Mrs. Parks was talking about me. I want to thank her for entering my essay, and...and...."

And then, as though she were Neva Bradshaw, she began to cry. But these were genuine tears of joy and amazement. Truly, this had to be the greatest day of her life. A writer! She was being proclaimed as a writer. An award-winning writer. She waved the trophy in the air, then descended from the stage as her classmates offered another round of applause.

The rest of the day seemed a blur. By the time she was riding the school bus home, all Sheila knew for sure was that Mrs. Parks had told her to talk to her father about the scholarship and to get him to sign the application, indicating his approval of her participation.

Sheila's father had never favored college for girls. Or for boys, for that matter, although he'd admitted he wouldn't stand in the way of his two sons' pursuing a college education, provided they put themselves through school. Sheila, however, needed to set her sights on landing a man, settling down, and starting a family.

Even so, she'd tried on numerous occasions to talk her dad into letting her go to college. It had been like trying to have a conversation with one of the animals in the barn. But this time was different. This time, she had a scholarship and some spare money, to boot. She could attend the six-week college writing course without having to beg her father for financial assistance. And after that…? Well, after that, she'd figure out how to *continue* with college, some way, somehow.

She smiled as the bus bumped along a back road toward her house. Just a couple of hours earlier, her friends had been scoffing at their high school for continuing to award students for "excellence in home economics." And yet, here they were, eighteen years old and riding big yellow school buses and living on farms. Were they really all that different from their moms and grandmas? Sheila, of course, could not know for sure, since she had no recollection of her mother or her grandmothers, all of whom had passed over to glory before she had even started school. Still, the irony was not lost on her. Maybe someday she would write about that, too.

Her writer's journal and personal diaries were filled with story ideas, fantasies, recorded dreams, notes about novels she'd read, and promises to herself of places she would visit, cities she would see, and goals she would reach. She was a dreamer, but she was also very practical. If living on a farm had taught her nothing else, it had taught her all about hard work and discipline. The problem was, her father had a one-track mind when it came to girls: *Get 'em married and get 'em gone.*

Well, she wouldn't mind the "get 'em gone" part so much. She was ready for new pastures. But the "get 'em married" part could wait. College would come first—and her writing. The award she'd received today had verified that her dreams of becoming an author weren't all that far-fetched.

The trick would be convincing Daddy to let her participate in the summer writing session. At eighteen years of age, she technically didn't need his permission, as far as the school was concerned. But if she wanted to continue having a place to call home, she knew better than to go against his rules.

She stepped off the bus and made her way straight to the barn, carefully avoiding mud puddles and pungent cow pies. She stood just inside the door to let her eyes adjust to the darkness and could hear her father's pitchfork in the loft as he tossed down feed for the livestock in their stalls. The sweet aroma of hay filled the air.

"Daddy, I'm home."

"The boys ain't back from the fields yet," came his voice from above. "Better get yerself changed and supper started. They'll be plenty hungry. Me, too."

"I have something to show you, Daddy," Sheila answered. "It's an award I got today at school. Can you come down and look at it?"

Her father continued his work. "Award fer what?"

"For writing. At our school assembly today, my English teacher, Mrs. Parks, told everybody that she submitted one of my essays to a contest, and I was one of the winners. I got a really nice trophy. Can't you come down and look at it?"

"Trophy for *writin'*? What good's it for?"

"It's really nice, Daddy. Look, I'll hold it up. Lean over so you can see it." She removed the Golden Quill trophy from its box and raised it above her head.

Her father stepped forward and glanced down before returning to his work. "Writin' won't put food on yer table the way gardenin' and cannin' will. Head on up to the house and get supper started."

So, the trophy hadn't impressed her father. She'd try again. "I'll tell you what *will* put food on a table," she said loudly. "Cash money. That'll work every time. It wasn't just a trophy, Daddy. They gave me a U.S. savings bond and a check for five hundred dollars." She held up the manila envelope containing her certificate and the scholarship paperwork. "I've got it all right here. There's the check, the bond, my award certificate, and a letter saying I'm entitled to a six-week college writing program this summer."

Her father stepped forward again, stared at the envelope, then dropped the pitchfork and hurried down the side ladder. He grabbed the envelope from her and removed the contents, surveying the check and the bond. Sheila could tell he was amazed that his daughter actually had earned money for something she had written. Then his eyes narrowed in suspicion. "What's the catch?"

"No catch, Daddy. It was a contest. They run it every year, trying to find good writers among high-school students. It's just that no one from my school had ever won it before. They made a big deal about it at the assembly. I went up on stage and gave a little acceptance speech, and later a man from the city newspaper took my picture and said they were going to run a story about me. It was really exciting. The money's mine. No strings attached."

"Don't have to buy no encyclopedias or nothin' like that?"

Sheila frowned. "Of course not, Daddy. It's an award—a prize. Mr. O'Neill and Mrs. Parks are really proud of me. I can attend a six-week college-level writing program this summer. The award pays for everything."

Her father rubbed a hand over his unshaven face, then shook his head and handed the papers back to her. "Yep, I knowed there was a catch. Trying to get ya to sign up fer some expensive college lessons, are they? I seen it before. They give ya the first book free, then they tell ya that ya signed up for the whole encyclopedia. Trust me, ain't nothing free in this life. If anybody says so, they're lyin' to ya. Always a catch... always a catch."

"Not this time, Daddy. I'm telling you, it's all legitimate. Look. This is a real savings bond, isn't it? It's got my name on it. And if you'll let me use the car, I'll go down to the bank and cash this check and bring back the money and wave it in your face."

Her father's face flushed red. "Don't ya get smart-mouthed with me, gal."

Sheila bit her lip. Had she just blown her chances at getting his permission? She lowered her eyes and softened her voice to say, "I'm sorry, Daddy. I didn't mean any disrespect. I was just scared you wouldn't let me go to summer school. I warned Mrs. Parks you might react this way. She assured me that I could live on campus at Brissenden College, right here in town. You could come and see me anytime you wanted to...*if* you wanted to. Classes won't start until the middle of June, and I'd be done by the end of July. That would give me all of August to be back here to help you on the farm."

Her father grunted. "Just who's gonna take care of the garden and put up the produce meantime? Who's gonna fix meals and keep house while we men are gettin' in the field crops? Summer's our busiest time of year. Ya can't just go traipsin' off and playin' school anytime ya feel like it."

Sheila took a step closer. "I'll come home on weekends and work extra hard. Please don't say no, Daddy. I'm not asking you to spend any money on me for college. I've got the scholarship and this check. I can pay my own way." She looked at him pleadingly. "I've never asked you for anything except for a chance to go to college. I've worked hard doing all the woman's duties here since I was a little girl. I've certainly pulled my weight all these years, and you've always known I'd leave the farm someday. Please grant me this one favor. If I go to college for six weeks, and it turns out I'm not suited for it, then I promise I'll come right back here and pick up where I left off."

Her father leaned against a post. The look on his face reminded Sheila of a cornered dog. She knew that after her mother died, her father had felt guilty for not being able to give Sheila a better life than her own mother had had as a girl back on her own family's farm.

Then Sheila's father straightened slightly. "Well, I s'pose I can give ya a few weeks to play at this silly college notion. Maybe it'll get it out of yer head once and for all." Then his voice grew stronger. "But I ain't spendin' no money on this college thing, I'll tell ya that. You can go for six weeks if ya stay at the local college and come home Saturdays to work and stay through Sunday fer church and afternoon dinner. Then I want ya back here soon's it's over. Hear me?"

Sheila gave him a brilliant smile. "Oh, yes, Daddy! I promise! Thank you, thank you!" She kissed him on the cheek so quickly, he didn't have time to wave her off. Then, clutching her trophy and paperwork, she raced to the house.

CHAPTER 3

By the time Sheila came downstairs with her pillow and sleeping bag and set them beside her book bag and suitcase near the front door, her father had already finished his early morning barn chores and was drinking a cup of coffee.

"Need help with your luggage?" asked her redheaded, freckle-faced older brother JD.

"That'd be great. I was so worried about being late, here I am, ready for Mrs. Parks, at least ten minutes early." She smiled nervously as she adjusted the hair tie around her ponytail. Then she looked at her father, who was glancing through the day's headlines. "Daddy, will you be able to come out and meet my teacher?"

He grunted from behind the newspaper.

JD removed his John Deere ball cap and tossed it on an end table, where it landed next to a worn Bible. "Dad, this is a big day for Sheila, you know."

The older man scowled. "Don't need no teacher tellin' me what's good fer my own girl," he responded, as if Sheila weren't in the room. "Fillin' her head with notions that got nothin' to do with what she should be doin' in life."

Sheila's stomach knotted as she turned to face her father. The knowledge that she'd be out of the house for the better part of six weeks gave her an unaccustomed boldness. "What I should be doing in life?

Cook, make beds, collect eggs, work in the garden, and mend clothes? I want something more than that. Mrs. Parks says I've got talent. And the folks who awarded me that scholarship say so, too." She glanced at her father pleadingly, but he refused to look in her direction.

"That's all a bunch of play-pretties, as far as I'm concerned. They gave ya some trinket fer playin' school the way they wanted ya to. Well, life just ain't that easy."

JD let out a long breath. "It wasn't *just* a trophy, Dad. You saw it. They gave her money, too."

"Ya call that money? Coulda raised a calf and gotten *twice* that much at the fair next month. But yer sister wouldn't have a thing to do with that idea. Had to have her head in a book all the time. I don't know why I ever agreed to let her waste six weeks at that college."

"I'm not going to stay here the rest of my life," Sheila said, inserting herself into the conversation again. "You did the right thing. And, besides, I'm going only eight miles away. It's not like I'll be off in Europe or Asia."

"Might as well be," said her father. "You just don't understand, neither of ya. Just don't understand." He folded the newspaper and slapped it on his lap.

"What's to understand?" asked JD. "You like having Sheila here, but she's all grown up and out of high school now. You want her to stick around the farm, but she wants to make her own way. No mystery in that."

Harold Davis looked sharply at his son. "Ya got that all wrong. Ya think I want to keep her around here just so I can get some work outta her? Well, it ain't about that at all!"

JD straddled a hassock and sat directly in front of his father. "Then, for Pete's sake, what *is* it about, Dad? Tell us both."

The older man turned his gaze toward the fireplace. On the mantel, framed in vintage wooden latticework, a faded photo of Sheila's mother sat next to a sampler that read "Trust and Obey." "Ya don't remember much of yer ma, do ya, boy?" he said softly.

JD shook his head.

"Well, she was just about the finest person anyone could ever meet. I worked summers fer her daddy when I was seventeen. Clarissa wasn't but fourteen back then, but I never seen anything so pretty. And she was nice, too. Sweetest smile and sweetest disposition ya ever saw. Her old man died later that year, and their family fell on hard times. That Christmas, I started callin' on yer ma, and after she turned fifteen, I asked her mama to sign the papers so we could get married."

Sheila nodded along with JD. They knew most of the story already.

"We lived with them fer a while, and I helped get their farm back on an even keel," their father continued. "But I wanted somethin' better fer yer ma. Eventually, I got us a little land, and we worked it hard. Every time we got a few hundred dollars ahead, we bought more acres around us. We put up this front part of the house and moved out on our own after Spencer was born. You came along a year later, JD. It was probably too soon. Still, it made us happy to have two boys. Yer ma was tired, though, I could tell."

For a moment, he paused, looking once again at the picture. It was as though staring at it served to organize his memories. "We didn't plan on havin' no more babies. But then, Sheila, you come along three years after JD. Yer ma wasn't strong. It broke her health. My sister—yer aunt May—come to live with us fer a time, takin' care of you children."

Sheila didn't remember Aunt May at all, but JD said, "Aunt May was always nice to us." He paused, then added, "I don't remember Mom ever getting out of bed."

Their father shook his head. "She didn't have the strength. Took her meals—what little she could eat—in bed. Couldn't even nurse the baby. That broke her heart, I'll tell ya. I had the doc out here twice. He give her some pain medicine but said there wasn't much else he could do."

"Was it cancer?" asked Sheila.

"Naw. Leastwise, not that he ever said to me or her. He just said she was weak. I'd sit by her bed, and we'd watch the TV nights until she got too tired, and I'd have to turn it off. Hard to believe how fast she went downhill. Fer years, she was able to work the farm all day, then go to a revival meetin' till midnight, and be back up at five to go at it again. But then, all of a sudden, there she was, just wastin' away."

Silence hung in the room for a full minute as the older man struggled to keep his composure. Sheila could tell that her father was still in love with her mother, even after all these years.

Harold Davis cleared his throat. "When winter was comin' on, she had an inklin she wouldn't see spring again. She would say to me, night after night, 'Hal, I know you gonna show them boys everything you know 'bout runnin' a farm. But you can't forget little Sheila. She'll need trainin', too. You got to promise me you'll show her everything I would have if I'd been there for her. Your sister and the neighborhood women can teach her to cook and sew. I can't die peaceful if I don't think she'll become a God-fearin' woman when she's growed up and be able to get a man of her own. Promise me, now.' So, sure enough, I'd promise her." He turned to Sheila. "And I've done my best to keep that promise. But it won't be finished till I see ya married to some fella who has a nice place like ours. I owe that to yer ma."

Sheila stared at her father a moment, then said, "Daddy, you've never told me before about your promise to Mother."

"No, 'course not. You don't remember nothin' 'bout yer ma."

"My memories have nothing to do with it. You raised me just the way she asked you to. But times are different now. Women can do more today than they could back then."

"That's right," JD added. "Sheila's got a better chance of finding a husband at college than just by going to church or entering a calf at the county fair."

"Yer ma didn't say nothin' 'bout college fer Sheila. You wasn't there. You don't know what she said to me."

JD grinned slightly. "Dad, you're reminding me of what the pastor said a couple of weeks ago about people who stick so close to the letter of the law, they forget the spirit of the law. Remember his illustrations of David feeding his men from the altar food, and Jesus letting His disciples pick and eat grain before washing? When they were criticized, the answer was that people need to use some common sense sometimes. And this is one of those times. I don't think Mom meant that you ought to make Sheila into a farm wife. Maybe she was just saying that you should help her love God, be a good worker, and be the kind of woman who could marry a good provider. And you've done all that."

The older Davis seemed to ponder JD's words, but his twisted facial expression revealed he wasn't totally buying into the argument.

JD raced on. "Suppose the roles had been reversed, and you'd been the one dying. You might have told Mom to be sure that somebody showed Spencer and me how to work a farm. But what if, after I grew up, I came in the back door one day and told Mom that I'd struck oil on the lower twenty acres, and I'd like to set up a pump? I don't think she would have said, 'No, your pa specifically said the only thing you and your brother could do is plant the fields and harvest them. Don't go digging any oil wells out there, Son.'"

Harold Davis gave a hint of a smile. "You be a bit of a preacher yerself, Boy." Then he became serious again. "Ya think yer sister has struck oil with this writin' of hers?"

"I don't know, Dad. A well can come in a gusher, or it can come up dry. The point is, you never know what you've got below the surface until you dig down into it. I think that's all Sheila wants—just a chance to see what's down inside her." JD glanced at her. "Am I right, Sis?" He looked back at their dad. "If it's nothing, then at least she'll know that. She can come home and turn her hand to something else."

Harold rubbed his chin as he appeared to weigh his son's words. Slowly, he returned his gaze to the framed photo of his wife. Her countenance reflected all the kindness, patience, and faith that she'd shown to Harold Davis, even when he was a young man of limited experience trying to make his way. Yes, thought Sheila, her father knew that JD was talking straight and that their mother would have wanted her to have a chance at something better.

"Spirit of the law, eh?" Harold mused aloud. He rose slowly from the chair. "Okay, Sheila. I'll meet ya halfway on this. I won't say nothin' bad about this college of yers, and I won't hold ya back."

For a moment, Sheila's spirit swelled with happiness at her father's change of heart. Then a question occurred to her. "What do you mean, meet me halfway?"

"I mean that I won't hold ya back from goin' to that college in the fall *if* ya find a way of goin' on yer own. I won't be spendin' money on college that we got set aside to buy that new tractor. Uh-uh. That's as far as I'll bend on this matter. Either ya find a way to pay yer own costs, or ya come back here to the farm."

The crunch of tires on gravel outside alerted them that Mrs. Parks had arrived. JD grabbed Sheila's suitcase and book bag and was out the door. Sheila stepped over to her father and gave him a hug. "Well, thank you for that. I'll find a way. You'll see."

"Now, don't fergit. JD'll pick ya up Saturday mornin' and then take ya back after Sunday dinner...." His voice had turned gruff, as if something were caught in his throat. "Lord help us, I don't know how the meals are gonna taste with JD and Spence doin' the cookin'."

Sheila smiled. "I'm sure whatever they put on the table will be fine. I've left plenty of prepared food in the freezer. Bye, Daddy." She gathered her sleeping bag and pillow, went out the door, and said a quick good-bye to JD before getting in the car for the short ride to the college.

When Mrs. Parks and Sheila arrived at room 213 in Upton Hall, luggage and bedding in hand, the door was opened before they had a chance to use the key. A short young woman, whose blonde-with-black-roots hair fell over her forehead in beach waves, stared at them. The strong smell of exotic perfume swirled into the hall, causing Mrs. Parks to cough. Black liner encircled the young woman's brown eyes. Her lips were the shade of black currants, and all her fingernails, as well as the toenails on her bare feet, were painted as if to match. Her long beaded earrings dangled down so far, they nearly touched the straps of her tank top, and her faded blue jeans sported an irregular line of ragged holes up the front on each leg.

"Hey!" she said. "What's up?"

Mrs. Parks stared a moment before saying, "This is Sheila Davis. We're looking for her room."

"Found it," said the young woman. "Her name's on the cards taped to the desk and bed right here."

Obviously apprehensive, Mrs. Parks asked, "And you would be?"

"Liz-Liz," the young woman answered, popping her gum and stepping to one side. "From East Chicago." She waved them inside.

"Your name is Liz, Liz?" Mrs. Parks asked, frowning slightly.

"Liz-Liz Baldossi," the young woman repeated. "Legally, it's Elizabeth Eliza, but we all need a gimmick. Am I right, or am I right?" She popped her gum again.

Sheila suddenly felt as if she were Rebecca of Sunnybrook Farm, and she'd been assigned to room with Courtney Love. But she wasn't about to back out now and go crawling home to her father with nothing more to look forward to than a life of farm chores. It was do-or-die time.

She walked past her teacher, set down her belongings, and extended her hand. "Hi, Liz-Liz. I'm Sheila. I'm eighteen, and I live right here in Brissenden, but I won a scholarship in an essay contest, so I'm moving here to the campus for six weeks. This is my English teacher, Mrs. Parks. She's the one who entered my essay in the contest, but it was a surprise to me, because she did it on her own. I can't tell you how much I've been looking forward to this program ever since school let out."

Liz-Liz held up her hands. "Whoa, whoa, sister. I don't need your whole life story in the first two minutes." Turning to Mrs. Parks, Liz-Liz whispered, "She on something?"

Mrs. Parks blinked. "I beg your pardon, young lady?"

"Look," said Liz-Liz, stepping into the hallway. "I'm going to clear out of here for a while...give you two a little space and all. You put your things away. There's an information packet on your desk. Dinner's at six. Maybe I'll catch you in the dining hall."

"Oh!" called Mrs. Parks. "You forgot your shoes."

Liz-Liz turned back slowly and stared at the woman as if she'd grown a second nose. Finally, she shook her head and walked away, still barefoot.

As the door closed, Mrs. Parks sighed. "Well, if you came to college to gain new experiences, you are certainly off to a quick start." She looked at Sheila, and the two broke into laughter.

"She thinks I'm a hick, doesn't she?" said Sheila, still smiling.

"I certainly wouldn't worry much about *that* one's opinion of you," said Mrs. Parks. "Liz-Liz may think you are from the sticks, but *she* looks like something from outer space."

"I'm sure we'll get along…in time," said Sheila. "I'd better get unpacked. Would you help me by unrolling my sleeping bag?"

Mrs. Parks sat on Sheila's bed and patted the spot next to her. "In a minute. First, while we have a moment or two to ourselves, I need to talk to you." She reached into her large woven-straw handbag and extracted a small jewelry box. "I have some news that I've been rather dreading to share with you," Mrs. Parks began. "I didn't mention it before because I didn't want to put a damper on your excitement about this new adventure. But, after thinking it over, I realize it may prove to be good news, after all. Maybe not at first, but probably in the long run."

Sheila felt slightly apprehensive. "What do you mean?"

Mrs. Parks smiled. "My husband has been offered a very important promotion with his company…and it requires relocating to Houston. He's worked hard and deserves this chance for advancement. We've already found a buyer for our house here in Brissenden, and so, in two weeks' time, we'll be moving to Texas."

Sheila felt as if she'd been slapped in the face. "Moving? To Texas? In two weeks?"

Mrs. Parks nodded. "I knew this would come as a shock to you, and I debated telling you earlier. But today is your day of new beginnings. It's appropriate that you start thinking more and more for yourself now that you're in college."

Sheila's eyes pooled with tears. "I can't believe you won't be here anymore. After all, you're the one who got me this opportunity."

"No." Mrs. Parks shook her head. "You got yourself into college by writing well and by winning the state competition. I merely brought your talent to the attention of the judges. Besides, I'll still be here for two more weeks."

"And phone calls after that?"

"Yes, and plenty of phone calls after that. Mail, too. I'll expect to see some of the writing you've done here in college. You haven't escaped my red pen yet!"

Sheila relaxed and even smiled slightly.

"I didn't give you a high-school graduation present," said Mrs. Parks, "because I wanted to give you a 'college beginning' present instead. I had something made just for you that can become a keepsake—if you want it to." She opened the small jewelry box, extracted a gold necklace, and presented it to Sheila.

"It's beautiful!" Sheila said with a gasp. "You had it made especially for me? But you've already done so much...I don't know what to say." She held the necklace reverently.

"It...." Mrs. Parks's voice had become a bit husky, and she paused a second before continuing. "It has three charms, each one representing a shared memory *and* a dream of mine for you. The little quill stands for your scholarship award, and it's meant to help you remember that you can use your writing talent to earn a college degree. The little book is to remind you of all the great literature we studied together and of your potential to become an author yourself one day. And the little clock face will not only help you to recall the good 'times' you and I spent working on your essays and stories but will also warn you continually that *time* is something that should not be wasted, only *invested*."

"I'll wear it always," Sheila promised, leaning forward to hug Mrs. Parks. Then she turned around so her teacher could help fasten the clasp.

Mrs. Parks stood. "Now, I'll unroll your sleeping bag as you requested." She quickly loosened the ties and unfurled the bag. "There. I'll leave now. You can unpack and set things up. It'll be good for you to have an hour or so alone to adjust to your new surroundings. I...." Her faced clouded, and she paused a moment before continuing in a strained voice.

"I have high confidence in you, Sheila. You are intelligent and hard-working, and you have a good heart. You've told me many times you want to be like me. I'm flattered, but let me tell you that, right now, I wish I could be you. You're young, and you have a natural gift for writing...." Mrs. Parks hurried to the window, as if she suddenly found something of interest outside.

"Mrs. Parks?" Sheila wasn't sure what to do. In the past, her teacher had always been the strong one.

The older woman took a tissue from her purse and daubed her eyes. "Forgive me for becoming emotional. This day is about you, not me. To be perfectly honest, I guess I've been feeling a tiny bit sorry for myself—for my own lost dreams. Being in this dorm room brings back memories I haven't thought of for decades: all those fantasies of seeing my name on the best-seller list...the autograph parties in major cities...the lecture circuit at college campuses...the radio interviews...the hope of being able to produce something that would enlighten and encourage readers for generations to come."

Sheila stepped closer to her teacher, feeling the need to say something, anything. "I...I'm sure you gave it your best shot."

"Oh, I did! I tried so hard! I simply didn't have the gift." Mrs. Parks looked at Sheila. "But I recognize the gift in you. I take great comfort in knowing that my secondary goal might yet be reached—that I might be instrumental in helping you have the chance to succeed."

"I'll give it my best effort, I promise you."

"I know you will, Sheila." Mrs. Parks hesitated, then said, "I realize you don't have a lot of support at home. I truly hope nothing sabotages this remarkable opportunity. But we've just begun a new millennium. You have a marvelous future ahead of you. Enjoy yourself. This is your big chance. Take advantage of it."

"I won't let you down," Sheila assured her. "And thank you so much for the necklace. If I ever get discouraged, the reminder of all you've taught me will buoy my spirits, I'm sure."

Mrs. Parks smiled. "Good. You *must* succeed. This means *everything* to me!"

They hugged once more, and then Mrs. Parks slid her purse strap over her shoulder, turned, and strode out the door.

CHAPTER 4

After Mrs. Parks left the dorm room, Sheila stood motionless for several minutes, unsure what she wanted to do more: laugh or cry. It was a fantasy fulfilled to be on her own for the first time in her life. Still, the news of Mrs. Parks's upcoming move was more than a little disconcerting.

Without Mrs. Parks's original encouragement, Sheila wouldn't have had the confidence to write about the feelings and thoughts she'd long kept hidden. And now, although her teacher had the best of intentions, chances were good that she wouldn't be directly involved in Sheila's life anymore. *Well, Mrs. Parks, you got me this far. I won't let you down.*

Sheila put away her belongings, then plopped on top of her sleeping bag on the bed closest to the door, and she absentmindedly fingered her new necklace. Ever since the fifth grade, she had dreamed of going to college, but, given her dad's attitude, she hadn't really believed it would ever happen. Now, here she was. Should she pinch herself?

The door opened, and Liz-Liz poked her head inside. "Hey!" she shouted, startling Sheila. "Is Mary Poppins gone? Good! You ready to chow down? I've scoped the place out, and the food looks okay. I'm starving."

As Sheila's pounding heart began to calm down, she managed to say, "Sure. I'm hungry, too. Lead the way."

The two roommates took off down the hall, joined by several other young women who were also heading downstairs to the cafeteria. Liz-Liz introduced herself and Sheila as the ever-growing group moved toward the elevators. By the time they reached the first floor, the eight young women wedged inside had learned that they were the eight female winners of the essay contest. One of them had already discovered that the eight male winners were staying on the fifth floor—very valuable information, indeed.

After making her selections from the wide variety of chilled salads and steaming-hot dinner offerings, Sheila sat down between Kim from Indianapolis and Annette from Connersville. Everyone at the long table talked at once about current boyfriends, former boyfriends, and prospective boyfriends. From time to time, someone would veer off into a discussion about books or writing, but it never took long to get back on the male track. During the course of a splintered conversation, Sheila learned that Annette was from a small school, too, and had also grown up on a farm.

By the end of the meal, a spirit of camaraderie and the anticipation of fun lessened whatever sense of trepidation or homesickness Sheila had suffered. She and her new friends left the dining hall in groups of three or four to walk around campus or to return to their rooms. Liz-Liz invited them to a nearby hall where she had made friends with a few of the male summer-school students, but Sheila declined.

Annette turned to Sheila. "I don't know anything about the campus," she confessed.

"Then why don't we go on a walking tour?" Sheila suggested. "I've been here a few times before, so I'm sure we won't get lost."

When they returned to the dorm two hours later, Sheila was surprised to see Liz-Liz already in their room. She'd expected her somewhat eccentric roommate to be out half the night. Instead, she hardly recognized the woman reading on the bed next to the window. Without the heavy makeup, Liz-Liz looked more like a middle schooler than a college student.

"Hey, girl," said Liz-Liz. "You and Annette got the lay of the land, did you?"

"Yeah." Sheila smiled. "It was fun. It's beautiful out tonight. Want to leave the window open for some fresh air?"

Creases of concern etched Liz-Liz's forehead. "You mean, leave it open while we sleep?"

"Sure."

"Is it safe to do that? I mean, we're only on the third floor."

Sheila looked at her curiously. "Well, of course it's safe. What are you afraid of?"

"We could get raped, robbed, beaten—any number of things. What planet do you live on?"

"Oh, Liz-Liz, this is Brissenden, not East Chicago. We're safe here. In fact, we don't even lock our doors at home."

"You're kidding! Man, at my house, we lock the doors, the windows, even the doghouse. Leave it open, if you want, but that means we're switching beds. I'm not sleeping beside an open window." She stood, picked up her sleeping bag and pillow, and swapped them with Sheila's. "I'm for safety over the 'fresh country air' bit anytime."

Sheila laughed as she cracked open the window, then gathered her toothbrush, towel, and toiletries. "I'm going to the restroom, but I'll be right back. Try not to be scared while I'm gone, okay?"

"I'll be here, cuddled up with Jack."

Sheila stopped in her tracks. "Excuse me?"

Liz-Liz pointed to the book she was reading. "Jack Kerouac. He's my absolute favorite."

"Jack who? I've never heard of him."

"Never heard of Jack Kerouac? What do they call that farm you live on? Isolated Acres? Go on. We'll talk when you get back."

Sheila hurried down the hall.

Once they were both settled in bed, and Sheila had set her alarm, Liz-Liz began, "Jack Kerouac was like the icon of the Beat generation.

You *have* heard of that, haven't you? Beats were the forerunners of the hippies. Anyway, Jack was an *amazing* writer. Can you believe my father actually met him one time in Greenwich Village? He told me the story so many times, I could repeat it to you in my sleep. Here's what happened...."

As Liz-Liz talked, Sheila realized that Kerouac was an icon to the entire Baldossi family. She wondered what her own father would think of Jack Kerouac. He'd probably consider him a bum instead of an icon. That gave her pause. If her dad, an upstanding deacon in their church, wouldn't approve of the famous writer, should she be listening to Liz-Liz's intriguing tale? Sheila watched her roommate's animated gestures and saw her face flush with excitement. Having grown up in a somber home, Sheila couldn't remember ever enjoying any experience such as Liz-Liz was relating. She loved the feeling of her spirit coming alive. It reminded her of times she'd spent with Mrs. Parks, discussing literature and brainstorming ways to improve her writing.

Before long, Liz-Liz was reading aloud from Kerouac, and Sheila found herself laughing hysterically at one moment, then being greatly moved the next. After a while, Sheila shared about some of her favorite works of literature, especially those of John Steinbeck, her favorite author. The two roommates, worlds apart in regard to many of their preferences, found a common love for the written word and the expression of ideas. Neither of them fell asleep until well past midnight.

The alarm jolted them awake at 9:45 AM. Knowing that all the scholarship students were to meet at the journalism building at 10:30, Sheila slowly forced herself into an upright position.

"Man, I'd love to catch a few more hours," said Liz-Liz with a moan. "S'pose they'd miss me?"

Sheila got to her feet and stretched. "Come on. If I can do it, you can do it."

"Yeah, but you're used to getting up with the roosters. I'm not."

Sheila laughed. "A quarter to ten is hardly dawn. Tonight, we'll have to shut up a little earlier if we want to get enough sleep."

Liz-Liz crawled out of her sleeping bag and sat cross-legged on her bed. "That's okay. It was worth it. You really know your lit. I guess even out here in nowhereland they have some pretty smart chicks. And I don't mean the little yellow kind, either."

"Thanks…I think," said Sheila, gathering the items she needed for a shower. "You're not going back to sleep, are you?"

"Nope. It'll take me a while to fix my face and hair."

Sheila smiled as she went down the hall. It was too bad Liz-Liz had to cover up her natural beauty with the armor of all those cosmetics and hair products. Then Sheila remembered a comment Mrs. Parks had once made about a girl in a short story who sported an outlandish appearance. She had asked Sheila to consider what kinds of wounds the girl might be trying to hide. Was Liz-Liz doing the same thing?

At 10:22, Sheila coaxed Liz-Liz out the door, reminding her to grab some shoes. Once inside the assigned room in the journalism building, they joined the other six female scholarship winners, taking up an entire row of seats.

At exactly 10:30, a man walked in the door and went straight to the lectern. "Welcome!" he said, speaking into the microphone. "I'm Dr. Peter Zonakis, chair of the Journalism Department. We're excited to have so many talented students with us this summer."

After giving them an overview of the college program and providing some general campus information, he waved several individuals to the front who had been standing along the back wall. Each wore a name tag. "Also attending summer school are these Brissenden College students and recent graduates who have agreed to be your mentors and guides during the summer workshop. If you have any questions or need assistance, feel free to approach them. The first class session will begin at one o'clock this afternoon. Enjoy your stay at Brissenden College."

With that, Dr. Zonakis left the podium and went out the door. Most of the students milled around in the room, introducing themselves to the student and alumni helpers. Liz-Liz went straight to a young man with a long ponytail, a sparse goatee, a pair of Birkenstocks, and cutoff jeans. The name tag on his surgical scrub shirt read "Sean Hagan."

"Hey," said Liz-Liz. "What's shakin', Hagan? We want to get some lunch. Got any suggestions for us—the campus cafeteria or a local fast-food joint?"

Sean Hagan slowly checked her out before responding. "Sure, I'll make a suggestion. Any special preferences? Vegetarian, maybe?"

"That's doubtful," replied Liz-Liz. "We've got at least two milkmaids from down on the farm. I'm pretty sure they're carnivores. Vegetarianism is bad for business, you know."

Annette nudged Sheila and rolled her eyes. "Your roommate thinks she's so much better than everybody else," she whispered. "I can't stand her!"

The previous evening's literary discussion had won Sheila over. "Oh, Annette, forget it. She doesn't mean anything by her mannerisms. That's just Liz-Liz's way of joking around. You'll see when you get to know her better."

Annette shrugged. "Frankly, I don't know that I *want* to know her better. I'm going to the restroom. Want to come, too? Or shall we meet at the front doors?"

"I'll catch up with you in a few minutes by the doors."

After discussing the pros and cons of the cafeteria lunch options, the group decided to remain on campus for pizza. Liz-Liz invited Sean to join them while Sheila hurried to meet up with Annette on their way out of the building.

At the dining hall, the students split into groups. Annette, Kim, and Sheila shared a table with a fourth student named Kelly. Being from Madison, near the Indiana-Kentucky border, Kelly had a slight Southern accent. Sheila loved to hear her speak and kept her engaged in conversation all during lunch.

Around twelve thirty, Sheila and Annette started clearing their table. As Annette was throwing away a leftover piece of sausage pizza, Sean and Liz-Liz walked past.

"How can you do that?" Sean asked.

Annette blinked. "What?"

"Don't act stupid," said Sean. "You know what I mean. How can you eat something that was once a living being?"

Annette's cheeks turned pink, but she said calmly, "Eating meat is my personal choice, Sean. I live on a farm where we raise veal."

"Veal!" he exclaimed. "You mean, you take baby calves away from their mothers, shut them up in four-foot stalls in a dark, airless barn to fatten them up, and then kill them? How sick is that?"

During his tirade, Annette had been biting her lip. Now she opened her mouth to reply, but in a flash Liz-Liz, was standing between her and Sean.

"Back off, Sean. Part of being a nonconformist is not judging everyone else by your own standards. Or don't you get that part of it? Besides, Einstein, where do you think the leather came from on those sandals you're wearing?" Liz-Liz took Annette's arm and directed her toward the front door. "Come on, girls. Let's blow this joint."

Sheila didn't move. Sean's judgmental rant had resurrected disturbing memories of her father's frequent reprimands. Especially vivid was a scene that took place after she and a girlfriend had gone to a summer carnival, an activity her father had deemed "too worldly."

"Remember just who yer pa is, girl. While you was at the carneevil, pro'bly flirtin' with boys runnin' the midway, if one of them church women woulda seen you, what then? They'd a gossiped about it all over town. Mighta even tried to get me kicked off the deacon board. Besides, no self-respectin' boy wants a loose gal fer a wife. From now on, you stick close to home and tend to keepin' outta trouble, ya hear?"

Sheila suddenly became aware of her name being called. She looked up to see Liz-Liz and Annette waiting for her by the door.

She quickly caught up with them and fell into step beside Liz-Liz as they exited the cafeteria "Thanks for standing up for Annette back there. Actually, for both of us."

"Yeah," Annette added, her voice still shaking. "I was so mad, I couldn't even think of a reply. All I could focus on was trying not to cry. I appreciate what you did."

"No problem," said Liz-Liz. "He was being a jerk. I may not be the picture of traditionalism, but if there's one thing I cannot stand, it's a guy who gets off by pushing women around."

The teacher in Sheila's first class that afternoon was interesting and inspiring. Sheila took copious notes, lest she miss something important. Her first assignment, due the next day, was to compose a short essay contrasting her most positive attribute with her most negative. As Sheila walked to her next class, she was already making a mental outline.

"Hey, Sheila!" Kim called as they passed in the hallway. "We're all meeting at six thirty in the dining hall. Can you join us?"

"Sure thing!" Sheila looked forward to hearing about the other classes and sharing some laughs with her new friends.

After her class on manuscript marketing, she lingered a few minutes to question the teacher about scholarship opportunities at Brissenden.

The professor looked at her kindly over the top of his reading glasses. "We do have scholarships available"—he paused a second to peer at her name tag—"Sheila. But if you're looking for funding assistance in time for the fall semester, you're a little late, I'm afraid. The application deadline was last spring."

At Sheila's crestfallen expression, he smiled encouragingly. "I do hope you can find another option. We'd love to have you as a student here at Brissenden."

"Th-thanks."

Sheila turned quickly to find someone to walk with, but the rest of the students had left, so she made her way to the dorm alone. Dark clouds roiled on the western horizon, and a humid breeze ruffled her hair. She knew her father and brothers would likely be making preparations to protect their livestock and equipment from the impending storm.

Life on the farm was so predictable, she knew pretty much where her father and brothers would be at any given time of the day. Their basic schedule changed only with the seasons. It perplexed Sheila to realize that the observation both comforted and terrified her. Routine did bring a sense of security. There were no floating parameters. One always knew the expectations. Yet, on the other hand, sameness was stifling. So were her father's rigid rules. She knew she didn't want to live like that forever. She wanted to do things, learn things. She wanted to *be* somebody.

One way or another, Sheila simply *had* to find a way to start college as a full-time student in the fall. She had an obligation to Mrs. Parks and, more important, to herself. Her former teacher had helped her to recognize the gift that she had. It was up to her to make something of that gift and fulfill her destiny. She smiled and looked toward the sky. *Mom, I wish you were here to share this with me. I'm going to do it!*

Sheila knew that part of fulfilling her destiny was succeeding in her classes; so, after dinner, she decided to go to the library to work on her assignments. Liz-Liz good-naturedly called her a party pooper and waved her on her way.

Entering the library through the front doors, Sheila was captivated by the muted sounds, the smell of books, and the dozens of cubbyholes available for working and reading. It was much more impressive than the Brissenden branch of the county library system.

The atmosphere didn't seem to help with her short essay, however. The exercise proved to be more difficult than she had anticipated. Mrs. Parks's encouragement, along with winning the scholarship, had helped identify her writing ability as her most positive attribute. She had to ponder several of her negative attributes before eventually settling on one she was willing to confess on paper.

When she was finally satisfied with her essay, she gathered her belongings and headed for the front doors. Along the way, she noticed a student arranging a display of new books. That gave her an idea. Maybe, when she became a full-time college student, she could get a job at the library. It would be wonderful to be surrounded by so many great works of literature.

She was still watching the student worker when she suddenly collided with a tall, warm mass and heard an umbrella clatter to the floor. She jumped back in horror. Oh, no! She'd just run into a fellow library patron. How embarrassing! As she glanced at his light-brown hair and steel-blue eyes, she thought he looked somewhat familiar. Where had she seen him before? Ah, he was wearing a student-volunteer name tag. *Dan Gray.*

"Oh, my goodness! I'm terribly sorry." Feeling like a complete klutz, Sheila bent to pick up the umbrella. When she mustered the courage to look at him again, she saw amusement on his face instead of the judgment she feared. What a relief! Then she remembered how well her bold approach had worked to cover her nervousness when she'd first met Liz-Liz. Maybe she would try that again.

She handed the young man his umbrella and stuck out her hand. "I'm Sheila Davis. I guess I need to watch where I'm going. Are you okay?"

He set down his briefcase and shook her hand. "Glad to meet you, Sheila. I'm Dan Gray. And, yes, I'm fine. You're the one who's probably going to be sore. I hope you didn't get hurt."

He was actually concerned about her! "No, I'm not hurt at all," she said, smiling. "I see you're a student volunteer with the summer writing program. I'm one of the participants."

He smiled. "Delighted to meet you. Welcome to Brissenden College. I'm director of the student newspaper for the summer honors program here."

"Really!" said Sheila. "How exciting!"

At her enthusiastic reply, Dan seemed to stand a little taller as he nodded toward the exit. "I was just leaving, and it looks like you are, too. Did you bring an umbrella?"

She glanced through the glass doors and saw a torrential downpour pounding the front steps. "No. I didn't even pack one."

"Well then, allow me to provide a little protection on your way back to Upton Hall." He swept open the door and unfurled his large umbrella.

Sheila smiled gratefully as she fell into step at his side. He was so much more polite and attentive than the guys in high school.

Rain splattered up from the sidewalk, splashing her legs; but, thanks to Dan, her head and shoulders were well protected as they hurried along. Whenever a wind gust knocked the umbrella askew, he stooped closer to ensure that she remained covered. And each time that happened, she could smell his English Leather aftershave.

All too soon, the dorm came into sight. Sheila suddenly realized she didn't want the walk to end, despite the rain. Hadn't Dan said he was director of the student newspaper? She should find out about his writing interests, the genres he enjoyed, his favorite authors. No doubt he knew all about Jack Kerouac and John Steinbeck.

As they stepped off a curb onto the main street running through campus, Sheila turned to Dan, wanting to ask him to name his favorite author. But before she could utter a word, his arm snaked around her waist, and he jerked her back to the sidewalk as a car whizzed by, only inches from where Sheila otherwise would have been standing. Its tires sent a wave of cold water onto the curb, drenching her and Dan from the knees down.

"That car nearly hit me!" Sheila shrieked, clutching Dan's arm in a death grip.

Dan patted her shoulder comfortingly. "But you're okay now, right? I didn't hurt you when I grabbed you, did I? When I saw the car coming, I didn't think I could warn you quickly enough."

"I...I'm fine," Sheila stammered, trembling. "That was a close one, though."

Dan didn't leave her side until she was safely inside the dorm lobby. "Be sure to change out of those wet shoes right away," he said. Then he smiled. "We don't want any of our writing students catching pneumonia."

His concern touched Sheila. At home, her father would have merely fussed about a delay in supper. She smiled at Dan. "Thanks for walking me here. Oh, yeah, *and* for saving my life."

He looked gratified. "Believe me, it was my pleasure. Say, I'm scheduled to help lead a summer session tomorrow afternoon. It's a special workshop on layout and design. Do you plan to be there, by any chance?"

"Yes, definitely."

"Good deal. I'll look forward to seeing you, then. Good night. I'm glad we 'ran into' each other."

Sheila laughed. "Me too, Dan. Me, too."

She watched Dan hurry down the sidewalk, jumping over puddles. The area of her waist that his arm had touched still felt warm. She liked the sensation of being cared for and protected. She liked it a lot.

On the way to her room, her shoes squishing as she walked, she passed the student lounge where most of the other scholarship winners had gathered. Liz-Liz caught sight of her and motioned her over. As Sheila approached, a pretzel flew out of nowhere and hit her in the head.

"We're playing high-stakes poker," Liz-Liz explained. "If you have pretzel sticks burning a hole in your pocket, step on up to the table." She stopped as she caught sight of Sheila's drenched legs and feet. "What happened to you? Fall in somewhere?"

"Got splashed by a car, that's all. I'll put my books in the room and change into something dry, then come back out here. Only as a spectator, though. I work too hard for my snack food to throw it all away gambling."

Liz-Liz groaned as Sheila turned on her soggy heel and left the lounge.

Just as Sheila had finished changing her clothes, the telephone rang, startling her. She lifted the receiver. "Hello?"

"Sheila? Is that you?"

"Mrs. Parks! Hi. How are you?"

"I'm doing fine, dear. The question is, how are you?"

"Great. I'm doing just great. It's wonderful here."

"I'm so glad. I've been worried about you ever since I left. That roommate seems so very different from you. Is everything really okay?"

"Liz-Liz? Yes. She's nice. Everything's fine. I've met lots of great girls, and I love the courses. We've had only one day of classes, but I've already learned a lot."

"I'm truly happy to hear that. I shouldn't have worried. You've always had a good head on your shoulders."

"Thanks."

"There's something else, Sheila. My husband's company has had some sort of minor catastrophe in Houston, and they want him there immediately to help straighten things out. So, we're heading there tomorrow, and the movers will arrive the next day to load all of our belongings. That means I won't have a chance to see you again before I leave town. I'm disappointed, I really am. Since you'll be home on weekends, I'll send a letter there with my new address and telephone number. Please, let's stay in touch."

"Of course we will. I'll write you often, just as soon as I get that letter."

"I'm very proud of you, Sheila. You're a bright and capable young woman. You have all you need to make your dreams come true. Just don't let yourself get sidetracked from the bright future you deserve."

"I won't." Sheila swallowed. "Thanks for everything. You've been wonderful."

"Study hard and keep focused. I'll write to you soon."

After Sheila hung up the phone, she sat on her bed for several minutes and reflected on flashbacks of moments with Mrs. Parks. She had come to care a great deal for her teacher. Now, realizing she might never see Mrs. Parks again, she felt cold and empty. She hugged her arms around her chest.

It was clear that Mrs. Parks cared for her, too, almost the way a mother might. That thought brought Sheila's own mother to mind. She had always wondered what her life would have been like had her mother lived. She'd always told herself, *You can't miss someone you've never known.* But now, that sounded ridiculous. Of course, she had missed her mother. She always would. For a time, Mrs. Parks had filled that void for Sheila. But now there was no one.

Sheila blinked away the memories and picked up a brush. As she smoothed her long brown hair, she thought, *Someday, I'll write a best seller. Then I'll take Mrs. Parks on a whirlwind book tour with me. We'll have the time of our lives!*

When Sheila got back to the lounge, a pizza had been delivered, and Kim had collected enough change to get everyone a can of soda pop from a vending machine down the hall. The group stayed up eating, drinking, and being oh-so-merry until after one in the morning.

Annette was the first to give in to fatigue. "I don't know about the rest of you, but I've got to get some sleep, or I'll be nodding off in class tomorrow. That is surely one way *not* to impress anyone here at the college."

The rest of the girls murmured their agreement and got busy cleaning up after themselves. When the last pretzel stick had been deposited in the trash, they made their ways to their rooms to settle down at last.

After Liz-Liz climbed into bed, she looked at Sheila. "So…did someone walk you back from the library?"

Sheila stared at her roommate.

"I don't miss much," said Liz-Liz. "See, when you came in tonight, you looked like you'd been wading somewhere, but your head and shoulders were as dry as Dr. Zonakis's opening lecture yesterday. And you didn't have an umbrella." She tapped her temple. "Elementary, Watson. Somebody shared an umbrella with you."

Sheila saw no reason to lie. "Yeah." She shrugged. "Some guy I ran into at the library was leaving at the same time. He offered to share his umbrella. He's one of the program volunteers."

Liz-Liz grinned. "Figured it was something like that." She turned off her reading lamp. "G'night."

By the next morning, the storm clouds had been banished by a brilliant sun blazing in a robin's-egg-blue sky. Sheila awoke even before the alarm went off, but she stayed in bed, replaying video-like memories of her chance encounter the previous evening. The boys in high school had always seemed to think of her as being a bit too serious. She'd gone on a fair share of dates, but not with anyone who really mattered. Her friends had often teased her, saying that her intelligence scared the boys away. They may have been right. It also didn't help that each boy who came to pick her up received the third degree from her father.

Sheila hoped that Dan Gray would not be put off easily. He seemed to be totally comfortable with her, as well as confident in himself. The thought of seeing him that afternoon made her heart beat faster. She threw back the sleeping-bag cover and hopped out of bed, eager to start the day.

After getting ready, Sheila hurried to the dining hall for breakfast. Annette greeted her with a cheery "Good morning" as she poured herself a cup of coffee.

"Hi, Annette. You look wide-awake. I guess our late night didn't do too much damage."

"Nah. Since our classes don't start until ten, I got plenty of rest. You look like you did, too. How's your roommate?"

"She's bemoaning the fact that she has to choose between doing her hair and makeup and eating breakfast," Sheila replied with a grin. "Personally, I prefer a low-maintenance look, but you know Liz-Liz. She's her own woman."

"Definitely so," Annette agreed. "But I'm warming up to her."

Throughout the morning and all through lunch, Sheila eagerly anticipated being in Dan Gray's workshop. Only two other students were in the assigned room when she arrived.

Dan looked up from the large table in front where he was arranging some materials. "Hi, Sheila."

"Hello, Dan."

His gaze lingered on her a few seconds longer than necessary. Feeling her face warming, she glanced down at the table, embarrassed that the two other students in the room, as well as the group she could hear entering, were probably watching them. Dan, however, quickly turned his attention to the rest, diffusing the momentary awkwardness.

Dan proved to be very knowledgeable about layout and design, as well as computers in general. His presentation included some innovative concepts, which Sheila found exciting, and she gave him her rapt attention. She found the courage to speak up a couple of times and share ideas she'd gathered while working on her high-school yearbook. Dan responded positively and even sought her opinion once or twice.

All too soon, the workshop was over, and the students started heading for the door. Not wanting to leave without speaking privately with Dan, Sheila deliberately dropped her notebook, then stopped and slowly retrieved it. When she stood upright again, Dan was in front of her.

"I enjoyed having you here today, Sheila. You really know your stuff."

"Thanks," she replied. "But you're the expert."

He smiled at the compliment. "I've had a lot of experience." Then he added, "Listen, I'd be happy to give you some more pointers and to share some more of my ideas with you over dinner tonight."

Sheila's breath quickened, and her mouth went dry. "Tonight? Well...I guess that would be okay."

"Great. I have another class to teach and then a meeting with the newspaper staff. How about I pick you up at the entrance to your dorm around seven?"

"Sure," Sheila answered. "I...I guess I'll see you then."

"It's a date."

Sheila almost floated to her next class. Although the instructor spoke informatively about an interesting topic, Sheila heard hardly a word. Instead, she mentally went over every article of clothing she had brought with her to Brissenden College. None of her casual outfits seemed quite right for a date with a guy like Dan. That left the one dress she'd packed—a white fabric with a pastel floral print. She would wear white sandals and bring along a white cotton cardigan, in case the restaurant's air-conditioning was too chilly. For a finishing touch, she would gather her hair in a side braid.

Rather than wait around for her friends after the last afternoon session, Sheila hurried toward the dorm. She wanted plenty of time to shower and do her hair and makeup before Dan came to call. Just as she was about to open the lobby door, Liz-Liz grabbed her by the sleeve.

"Geez, are you training for a marathon, or what? I practically had to sprint to catch up with you." Liz-Liz paused to gulp deep breaths of air.

"I didn't know you were behind me," said Sheila. "How were your afternoon sessions?"

"The first one was pretty good, but I wasn't that impressed by your layout-and-design friend. I think he's pretty full of himself."

Sheila bristled. Was Liz-Liz jealous because Dan had showed an interest in Sheila and not her? "Oh, you do, do you? Well, I think you may be wrong. Besides, you don't even know him."

Liz-Liz held up her hands. "Whoa! I didn't mean to make you mad. You're right, I don't know the guy." She opened the door for Sheila, then stepped into the lobby herself and added, "But then, neither do you."

They continued to their room in silence. Once inside, Sheila began gathering her toiletries.

"A bunch of us thought we might ask the scholarship boys if they wanted to go see a movie tonight," Liz-Liz told her. "You interested?"

"No, thanks," answered Sheila. "Actually, I've got a date."

"Oh, I see. You're going out with that guy tonight, aren't you?"

"Yes. And 'that guy's' name is Dan." Sheila saw a look of distaste cross her roommate's face. "What's the big deal?" she demanded.

"Look, I know it's none of my business...but something about him bothers me."

Sheila put her hands on her hips. "Something bothers *you*, and that means *I* shouldn't go out with him? I might not be as sophisticated as you are, but I'm not stupid, either. Give me a little credit."

"You know I don't think you're stupid," said Liz-Liz. "In fact, in the short time we've been together, I've come to see you as one of the sharpest people I know...in book learning. But even you have got to admit you've been a little sheltered."

"Stop worrying," Sheila told her. "You're worse than an old mother hen. It's just a date. Trust me, I know what I'm doing."

"Oh, I trust *you*. It's Danny-boy I'm not going with the house odds on. I've seen his type before."

"What's that supposed to mean?"

"It means he's just a wannabe, Sheila. He's trying to convince you he's somebody special, because, if he can make you believe it, it might actually come true."

Sheila fought to control her anger. "I don't know why you have it in for Dan, but I happen to think he's a nice guy, and I'm going out with him tonight. So, let's just drop it, okay?" Grabbing her towel and her toiletry bag, Sheila stalked out of the room and headed down the hall.

CHAPTER 5

That evening, when Sheila walked through the dorm lobby at 7 PM sharp, Dan was waiting at the entrance. He opened the door and gave her a scan from head to toe. Hopefully, he was admiring the way her dress showed off her slender waist and flowed smoothly over her hips.

"Hey, Sheila. You look great."

"Thanks," she said, noting his blue button-down Oxford shirt and charcoal slacks. "You, too."

"It's a nice evening for a walk. I thought we'd go to a little Chinese place I know. It's only eight blocks from here. You like Chinese food?"

"Sure," Sheila answered quickly, hoping Dan wouldn't ask what her favorite dish was. The closest she'd come to Chinese cuisine was opening a can of chop suey vegetables.

Dan slipped his hand into hers and guided her along the sidewalk. "I don't have a car right now. I haven't really needed one while working and studying on campus. I'll probably buy a new one after I graduate and get a full-time job."

Sheila listened intently to Dan as he opened up to her about his family, his years in high school and college, and his hard work—and the respect he'd earned for it—throughout his academic career. She asked an occasional question, but, for the most part, he carried the conversation. His long list of accomplishments impressed her deeply and caused her to want, more than ever, to make a good impression on him.

"I could have gone the jock route, if I'd really wanted to," Dan said nonchalantly. "I was a good baseball player. But I figured anybody could hit a ball with a stick. I preferred to focus on more intellectual matters."

"I'm not really into sports, either," Sheila said. "Some of my best friends from high school were on various teams, but I've never been athletically inclined."

"Well," Dan said, straightening his shoulders, "my choice to forgo sports had nothing to do with a lack of ability. I simply chose to direct my energies elsewhere. I could have been on any team I wanted to."

Feeling a little out of her depth with someone so gifted, Sheila tried changing the subject to a topic she knew more about—literature. But in the next moment, they reached the restaurant, and Dan opened the door for her to enter. The host led them past an enormous bubbling fish tank and seated them at a table beneath an orange paper lantern decorated with gold tassels.

A server brought them a steaming teapot and two porcelain cups. Dan poured tea for Sheila and then some for himself before opening his menu. "What sounds good to you?"

Sheila had no idea what to order. Her face grew warm as she quickly scanned the page, searching for something that sounded familiar. In her mild panic, however, none of the words seemed to make sense. "You've been here before. What can you recommend?"

"I'm going to start off with some wonton soup," Dan replied. "Then I'll have some shrimp lo mein with fried rice."

"That sounds great!" Sheila said, trying to hide her relief. "Let's double the order." Even though she wasn't a seafood lover, she was determined to make the most of the meal. She would have eaten snails, if necessary, to make a positive impression on Dan.

After they had placed their orders, Dan picked up the conversation. "Yes, I'm blessed to be able to do a lot of things well. My plan is to earn my doctorate and teach at a university."

Sheila had never known anyone with those kinds of aspirations. Certainly none of the boys in high school had been so focused and ambitious. And to think that Dan had asked her out on a date, when he could have had his pick of practically any girl on campus. Well, anyone except for Liz-Liz. Sheila wasn't sure why her roommate had such a bad attitude toward this outstanding young man.

The server returned, and while he set two bowls of steaming wonton soup on the table, Sheila said to Dan, "I've always dreamed of attending college. Coming to Brissenden for the summer session has been like a fantasy come true for me. But I don't know how I'll manage to return full-time."

"Why not?" asked Dan. "Aren't your grades good enough?"

"Oh, my grades are fine. That's not the problem."

"What, then?"

"It's my father." She sighed. "He doesn't have a lot of money, and college is expensive, especially a private school like Brissenden. Besides, my dad doesn't really believe higher education is necessary for girls. He thinks I should be content to find a job somewhere in town until I get married. I wouldn't be here now if it weren't for my English teacher, Mrs. Parks. She entered my essay in the contest that awarded me a scholarship to participate."

Dan looked thoughtful. "What about your mother?"

"My mom died when I was a baby. I don't even remember her. Mrs. Parks has become sort of a surrogate mother to me, but now she's moved away." Sheila absentmindedly touched the charms on the gold chain around her neck.

Dan stared at Sheila for a moment, then asked, "So, what are you going to do this fall?"

Sheila picked up her spoon and stirred her soup to cool it a little. "I don't know. I'd hoped to get a scholarship or something, but I found out it's too late to apply. I wish I could talk my dad into paying my way, at least for a year." She shook her head. "He'll never go along with that idea."

Dan reached across the table and took Sheila's free hand, threading his bigger fingers through her smaller ones and squeezing gently to massage them. "Keep your chin up, Sheila. Something will work out for you. If I can help in any way, you know you can count on me."

Sheila warmed to Dan's touch, as well as to his concern for her situation. She loved the way his hand covered hers. She'd always dreamed of finding someone who understood her, loved her for who she was, and would take care of her. Dan was quickly becoming a sort of knight in shining armor. She wanted him to know how much his offer of support meant, but when she tried to speak, she could only whisper, "Thanks, Dan."

He smiled and patted her hand before letting go. "You're sweet. I want to help you get everything you deserve. Speaking of that, tell me about your own writing. Maybe something you've written would be suitable for the student newspaper."

Sheila worked hard not to gasp with excitement at the prospect of getting published so soon. Leaving her hand on the table, in case Dan decided to reach for it again, Sheila told him about several pieces she'd written under Mrs. Parks's guidance. "In fact," she said, "I can show them to you this week. All my writing samples are back at the dorm."

"Great. I want to see them soon. But in the meantime, you'd better get busy with that soup, or it's going to get cold."

Sheila followed his suggestion, and soon the main course arrived. She was relieved to find that she liked the dish, but she was full after finishing only half her food. When Dan encouraged her to finish it, she patted her stomach and smiled. "I can't possibly eat another bite. It was really good, though. Thanks."

When they left the restaurant, the temperature was perfect for an evening stroll. The pleasant aroma of freshly cut grass wafted on the breeze, and overhead, the velvet sky seemed to hold an endless number of sparkling stars. At the first street corner, Sheila stopped and tipped her head back to get a full view of the magnificent starlight. Dan stepped behind her and put his arms around her waist, pulling her close. Sheila's breath quickened as she leaned back against his chest. In his arms, she felt warm and safe and desirable.

"It's incredible, isn't it?" she said, still looking at the sky. "It almost takes my breath away."

"*You* take my breath away," Dan replied. He slowly turned her around until they were standing face-to-face. Then he placed his hand on the back of her head and brought his lips to hers. Sheila wanted the moment to go on forever. She slid her arms around his neck and stood on tiptoe so he wouldn't have to bend so low. She felt the smoothness of his lips and the slight roughness of his whiskered face, which smelled wonderfully of English Leather, reminding her of his chivalry on their walk to her dorm from the library when they'd just met.

Then Dan's kisses became more aggressive, and Sheila's knees went wobbly. As if Dan sensed what was happening to her, he tightened his grip and seemed to hold her up with no effort at all.

Footsteps sounded behind them. They quickly parted and crossed the street. Dan took hold of Sheila's hand again. One block later, just after they passed a neighborhood market and entered the shadows again, Dan stopped and pulled Sheila toward him. He kissed her on the forehead, then said, "We're not far from my apartment. Would you like to stop there? We can listen to music and talk about books for a while."

Sheila hesitated. She knew what she should say, but she also wanted to be able to enjoy Dan's company without the worry of being interrupted. Her father would never find out, anyway. She wasn't sure what Dan would expect if she agreed to go to his place, but he had been a gentleman from the moment they'd met. And she would be careful. Still....

"Sheila?"

"Um, I'm not sure. I mean, I don't know if Liz-Liz will worry."

Dan stood very close and said softly, "There's nothing to be afraid of. I just want to hold you in my arms for a little bit."

Sheila felt her resolve weaken. More than anything else in the world, she desired the same thing. "Okay. But I really can't stay out too late."

Dan put his arm around her shoulders and propelled her forward. "Don't worry, Cinderella. I'll have you home by midnight. We won't give your ugly stepsister anything to complain about."

Was the edge to Dan's voice a result of her mentioning Liz-Liz? Sheila couldn't tell. But, in the comfort and warmth of his arm, she decided it didn't matter.

Dan glanced up at the sky again as they walked. "I've always felt that one of those twinkling lights up there had my name on it, almost as though I was born under a lucky star. I have this feeling that someday, something big is going to happen in my life." Then he smiled down at Sheila, as if to suggest that she might possibly be part of the "something big."

When they came to a drugstore, Dan turned from the sidewalk and led her up two flights of outside stairs to a door, which he unlocked. Inside his apartment, there was a small kitchenette and a living area, sparsely furnished with brick-and-board bookshelves, a produce-crate coffee table, and a couple of beanbag chairs. On the floor in the far corner lay a mattress next to a dilapidated nightstand.

"I'm sure you've heard about the living conditions of starving artists," Dan said. "Now you get a chance to witness them firsthand."

Sheila was intrigued by the romantic concept of living simply while working hard to become recognized for one's genius. "I like it," she said with a shrug. "It looks as if you have everything you need."

"I'm not sure I'd go that far," Dan said. "But it's inexpensive, and it beats putting up with all those bozos in the dorms."

"Really?" she asked. "I'm having a lot of fun staying in a dorm."

He smiled indulgently. "You're still young. Besides, this is a new experience for you. Believe me, after a while, you'll get sick of all those snobs. They think they're so cool, with their teams and their fraternities."

"I haven't met anyone here like that," Sheila said. "But then, I've hardly met anyone besides the other scholarship winners and the student helpers."

"Oh, they're here, all right," Dan said as he rolled his eyes. "Believe me, they're everywhere. All they care about is getting ahead, no matter what. Even if that means taking credit for someone else's work."

"That's awful!"

"Yeah, it is. And it's happened to me here, more than once. But that's enough about them." He stepped close and put his arms on her shoulders. "I'd rather focus on the beautiful girl I had the luck of running into yesterday." He lowered his head and gave her a gentle kiss.

Sheila could hardly believe how completely at home she felt in Dan's presence. He was the kind of guy she had always dreamed of meeting.

They talked for the next hour, cuddled together in a beanbag chair. Then Dan suddenly stood, reached for Sheila's hand, and pulled her up. "It's getting late. I think I'd better return you to your dorm now."

Although Sheila was far from ready to leave him, she said, "You're right. We'd better start back."

When they reached Upton Hall, Dan stopped at the front door. "I'll be busy leading one of your scholarship groups in the morning," he said, "but how about meeting for lunch?"

Sheila was thrilled that Dan wanted to see her again so soon. "I'd like that. Where should I meet you?"

"How about in front of the J-building at noon? We can decide then where we want to eat."

"Great! I'll look forward to it. Thanks for a wonderful evening."

"Sweet dreams, Sheila." Dan kissed her good night, then disappeared into the dark.

Liz-Liz was already asleep when Sheila let herself into the room. Sheila quickly undressed and slipped quietly into bed, so as to not disturb her. Although she was not the least bit sleepy and would have loved to have stayed up and chatted about Dan, she didn't think Liz-Liz would be too receptive to that idea.

In spite of the few hours' sleep she'd gotten, Sheila was awake before the alarm went off the next morning. She lay in bed, reliving every moment of the previous evening, from when she'd first seen Dan waiting for her outside the dorm to when he'd given her the final kiss good night. She mentally replayed certain phrases he had spoken, analyzing them for their implications. Then, feeling wonderfully energized, Sheila showered and returned to her room to dress for the day. She was already counting down the minutes until her lunch with Dan.

Liz-Liz was sitting up in bed. "Hey, girlfriend. How was the big date?"

Sheila broke into a grin. "It was fine."

"By the looks of you, it was more than fine."

Sheila laughed. "You're right." She shared the highlights of the evening while Liz-Liz dressed and applied her makeup, but she didn't mention the "ugly stepsister" comment. Nor did she feel comfortable mentioning Dan's assessment of dorm life, although she wasn't sure why.

"It sounds like Danny-boy showed you a really nice time. Even gave you the grand tour of his digs, eh? Anything major happen there that you forgot to mention?"

Sheila felt herself blush. "No! Nothing 'major' happened. We just had a great time *talking*."

"Have you ever had anything 'major' happen with a guy?"

Sheila looked down in embarrassment. "Well, no. Not really."

"That's what I figured. I know you really like this guy. Just be careful, okay?"

"Quit worrying," said Sheila, glancing up again. "Dan's a good guy. He really is."

"Okay, chickie. Whatever you say."

During Sheila's first morning session—a class focused on interview techniques—she sat next to Annette. On their way out the door after class, Annette said, "That was good, wasn't it?"

"Very good," Sheila agreed. "There's so much to learn. It's really exciting, but kind of depressing, too: I can't figure out a way to return in the fall. How about you?"

"Nope." Annette shook her head. "There's no way my parents can afford for me to come here. I'll be going to either community college or a satellite of Indiana University, in Connersville or Richmond."

"And you're okay with that?"

Annette shrugged. "What choice do I have? My parents feel bad enough already. I'm not going to make them feel worse by throwing a fit. I have to face reality. A real pain, of course, but it is what it is."

Sheila sighed. "You're right, I guess. My dad can't afford to send me here, either, but what really hurts is that he doesn't *want* to send me here. He's dead set against furthering my education at all. He wants to keep me stuck on the farm. It's really frustrating."

"Wow," said Annette. "Our situations are different, but I guess the end result is the same. Neither of us will be back in the fall."

Sheila set her jaw with determination. "I haven't given up all hope yet."

"Well, I've gotta go upstairs for my next class," Annette said. "See you at lunch?"

"Actually, I have other plans today. I'll be back at the dorm later, though. Bye."

"Okay, later!"

After her second class of the morning, Sheila dashed to the front entrance of the J-building to wait for Dan. A few minutes later, she felt someone touch her elbow.

Sheila whirled around.

"Hi, there, pretty girl," Dan said.

She beamed. "Hey, Dan. How was your morning?"

"Great. The sessions went well. I presented a lot of great information, and the students ate it up. They asked good questions, and I had all the answers. They loved me!"

Sheila laughed out loud at his enthusiasm. "Of course, they did. What's not to love?"

Dan smiled at her reply, then took her hand. "Let's go to lunch. What are you hungry for?"

"You choose. I'm easy to please."

"How about we split a sub?" he asked.

"Sounds great. Lead the way."

During lunch, Sheila handed Dan a folder of her writing samples. He glanced through the articles and selected one. "This shows real promise. Why don't we meet after dinner tonight, and I'll give you a few tips on slanting it for our student readers?"

Sheila was so excited, she could hardly finish her half of the sub.

Dan ate his lunch quickly and then talked at length about the class offerings at Brissenden, giving his opinion about the capabilities and strengths of the professors who taught those particular classes. Then he told Sheila again of his plans to continue his education so he could eventually teach at the university level.

"Frankly," Dan said as he cleared the trash from their table, "I'm sure that I can do a better job of teaching than almost any prof here. Some of them are really good, but I can be great."

Sheila marveled at Dan's knowledge and confidence. "You *are* great, Dan."

Dan smiled and held Sheila's gaze for several seconds. Then he put his arm around her and guided her out the door. On their way back to the J-building, they made plans to meet that evening after dinner. Sheila strolled to her first afternoon class slightly dazed. For the rest of the day, she struggled to pay attention to the instructors. All she could think about was seeing Dan that night.

"Hey, roomie! What's up?"

Sheila turned around, having just left her final class of the day. "Hey, Liz-Liz. Ready to go back to the dorm?"

"Sure am, girlfriend. I'm starved. I want to hit the chow line early. Are you going to grace us with your presence this evening, or will you be dining with Danny-boy?"

"I'm eating in the cafeteria," answered Sheila, "but Dan and I are getting together later. He's interested in running one of my features in the student newspaper, so we're going to do some work on it together. Pretty exciting, huh?"

Liz-Liz hesitated for a few seconds before answering. "Yeah…great."

"That's all you've got to say? I thought you'd be happy for me."

"Sheila, I was in another workshop with Danny-boy this afternoon, and I have to be honest: He's not as good as you seem to think he is. He claimed sole credit for a project that I know another student—one of the assistants in another of my classes—helped him on. I can understand why you're happy about the prospect of being published in the student paper, but I can't help worrying you might get hurt, eventually. He has an inflated ego, and the fact that you look up to him helps him fight his insecurities."

Sheila glared. "Dan already told me what happened with that other student, and you've got the story all wrong. Dan wasn't the one who stole credit. Besides, he isn't insecure at all. He's completely confident. You don't know what you're talking about."

Liz-Liz gave Sheila a look of concern. "You're a bright gal with a lot on the ball, but, as I pointed out before, you haven't had much experience with guys. I'm afraid Dan might not be interested in you for the reasons you think. When I questioned something he said in our workshop today, he nearly came unglued. He feels threatened whenever someone questions him or his creativity. If that's not a sign of insecurity, then I don't know what is."

"Look," said Sheila. "I know you guys don't mesh well, but that's just a personality conflict. You're not going to pretend that this is the first time you've disagreed with someone, are you?"

"Of course not. But it's more than that. The student I mentioned has known Dan for a while, and he told me what he's really like—an ordinary, average guy who wants to convince people he's extraordinarily gifted. He's alienated most of the other students on campus by always trying to one-up them."

"It sounds to me like your new friend is just jealous."

"I really wish it were that simple," Liz-Liz said. "But I think Dan Gray is bad news. In fact, I wouldn't be surprised if he's looking for some way to use your gifts and intelligence to his own advantage."

Sheila put up her hand. "That's enough! You're my roommate, not my mother. I don't want to hear one more criticism of Dan. I can evaluate him for myself, and I don't need your distorted interpretation of his abilities or his motives to do it. Now, in the interest of maintaining our friendship, I suggest we drop this subject…for good!"

"Okay." Liz-Liz lifted her shoulders in a shrug of surrender. "I tried."

The two continued their walk to the dorm in silence.

During dinner, although she was still upset, Sheila tried to put Liz-Liz's comments out of her mind so she could relax as much as possible. She truly enjoyed the group's camaraderie and didn't want to allow any negative feelings to diminish the fun of their time together.

After the meal, several of her friends decided to take the city bus to a local shopping mall. They invited Sheila to come with them, but she politely declined, explaining that she already had plans.

Liz-Liz joined her on the walk back to the dorm room. "Look, I'm sorry if I got on your bad side," she said. "I just don't want you to get hurt, that's all."

"I realize that," Sheila replied. "But I can handle this. In spite of what you think, Dan cares for me, and I truly care for him. We have a lot in common, and he believes in my work. You just don't understand how much that means to me. It's different for you. Your parents are educated. They support your interests. Never in my life have I had anyone near my own age I could really talk to about what I'm interested in. Dan's the best thing that's ever happened to me."

Liz-Liz shook her head as she opened the door to their room. "I know I can't relate to the life you've led, but…well, all I was trying to say is that you deserve better. You're bright and attractive. Believe me, there are lots of really great guys who would go for you in a big way. You just need to get out of Brissenden and live a little."

Sheila forced herself to remain calm as she stepped into the room. "You're wrong. As far as I'm concerned, guys don't come any better than Dan Gray. I don't have to look any farther."

"Okay. I won't say another word about him. I value our friendship, and I respect your decisions. Still friends?" Liz-Liz turned around and held out her arms.

Sheila smiled as she returned her roommate's embrace. "Of course. In fact, friends forever."

Later, as Sheila walked to the library to meet Dan, she mentally reviewed her roommate's concerns. They didn't make any sense. Dan hadn't had an easy life. He had shared with her about his family, including his father's excessive drinking, but he didn't appear to harbor any resentment toward anyone. Dan was simply more serious than most college boys. And that was part of what attracted Sheila to him. She had always been more grown-up than her friends at Brissenden High. At last, she had found someone with whom she could easily relate.

Sheila and Dan spent the better part of two hours working on the feature article she had written. Dan wanted her to shorten it by 175 words so that it would fit the allotted space in the student newspaper. At first, Sheila didn't think it was possible to cut that much material without losing vital content. However, with Dan's help, she managed to meet the desired word count. In fact, they both decided the shortened version was better than the original.

"Thanks," Sheila said. "I couldn't have done it without you. I'm really excited about getting one of my pieces published in the paper. Are you sure it's good enough? I mean, that's the reason you'll be running it, right? I want you to use it because it's well-written, not because of any feelings you might have for me."

"Don't worry," he assured her. "I'm a professional. I do care for you, but that's not why I'm using the piece. I wouldn't be a competent editor if that were the case. And, make no mistake: I'm very competent. This feature was good to begin with, but, with my input, it's even better. So, it's a great move for both of us. Now that we've got it in tip-top shape, let's go celebrate at Dairy Queen."

As they finished their hot fudge sundaes and were getting up from the table to leave, another patron, carrying two large ice-cream cones, backed into Dan.

"Whoa!" the man exclaimed. "Sorry about that. I was tryin' to side-step this big wet spot on the floor." He turned around with a look of recognition. "Hey, Dan-O. I didn't realize it was you. What are you doin' here? I thought you'd be long gone from Brissenden by now, running some big newspaper or teaching at Yale."

"Hi, Troy," Dan said without enthusiasm. "I'm working here at the college this summer. I'm in charge of the student newspaper."

"Really? I thought Dr. Yesler was the faculty adviser. What happened to her?"

Dan lifted his chin as his face grew red. "Dr. Yesler is still the faculty adviser, but that's just a formality. I'm the one who's really in charge. Anyway, I'll be here only one more year. I'm planning to start my master's program next fall."

"Yeah?" Troy's tone was tinged with sarcasm. "Well, good luck at whatever you end up doing, Dan-O, even if it's peddling newspapers instead of publishing them." He went out the door and walked over to a sports car, where he handed one of the cones to the young woman waiting in the passenger's seat.

"Come on, Sheila," Dan said gruffly. "Let's get out of here. That loser thinks he's somebody because his old man's got a big company with a cushy, ready-made job for him. Just wait until my novel gets published. He'll be laughing out of the other side of his mouth."

Sheila glimpsed the insecurity that Liz-Liz had observed in Dan, and her heart went out to him. Sheila knew what it was like to receive no parental support for one's ambitions. She also knew that Dan was working very hard to put himself through school. She realized with new clarity what an important friend she could be to him. He needed someone who truly believed in him. And Sheila resolved to be that someone.

CHAPTER 6

Darkness fell as they walked to Dan's apartment. By the time they reached the wooden steps, it was too dark to see well. Dan held Sheila's arm so she could navigate the stairs. Once inside, he pulled her close, kissing her long and hard.

In the dark room, Sheila felt rivers of pleasure rush through her entire being. *He could be with anyone he wanted to, and he's choosing to be with me!* She'd never kissed a guy like this before, and she wasn't quite sure of the "experienced" way to respond. All she could do was hope she was reacting correctly. So far, at least, Dan hadn't scolded her for doing anything stupid. She was so used to walking on eggshells around her dad, she'd learned to keep her antennae up at all times, so she could change course whenever necessary.

But Dan didn't seem inclined to find fault with anything she was doing, and they remained entwined in a passionate embrace for several minutes. Then Dan released her and moved to the stereo to put on some music. He returned to Sheila, took her by the hand, and gently tugged in the direction of the mattress.

Sheila's heart raced. Part of her longed to give in to his desires—her desires, too—but her lifelong training in biblical morals wouldn't allow her to surrender. "N-no, Dan. Please. Just...no."

There. She'd done it. Now Dan would probably lose interest in her. But, as afraid as she was of being rejected, she was even more afraid of the shame she would feel if she gave in.

Dan stopped tugging. To her great relief, he said, "That's all right. You're not ready yet. I just want so much to be with you. Let's just sit here for a few minutes before I walk you back to the dorm." He nodded toward the stereo. "Do you like this group? Their music is a favorite of mine." He sat in a beanbag chair and held out his arms. Sheila sank into them gratefully.

Dan began to talk to Sheila again about his goals and aspirations, including his desire to be a best-selling novelist. He paused a moment, then asked, "What about your own dreams, Sheila?"

She sat up, looked Dan directly in the face, and began to tell him her innermost desires. She shared about certain aspects of her life, including her relationship with Mrs. Parks and its dramatic influence on her. While she talked, she fingered her gold necklace.

"What is it with that necklace?" Dan asked finally. "I've noticed you wear it all the time."

Sheila smiled. "Mrs. Parks gave it to me, and I never want to take it off. It's almost like a good-luck charm. When I touch it, I'm reminded of her influence and her expectations of me. She was the first person to believe in me, and she convinced me that I had talent as a writer. I didn't even know my own dreams until she helped me recognize them. She's been an incredibly important person in my life."

Dan stared off into space. Sheila wondered if she'd said something wrong.

But, a moment later, everything seemed fine again, and he began to massage her back. "Sheila, have you ever thought about getting your hair cut?" he asked.

"Why? Don't you like my hair long?"

"Oh, sure. But you always seem to wear it up in a ponytail, or something. If your hair was shorter, you wouldn't need to do that." He moved his hands down her back and then up again in a gentle caress, ending at the base of her neck. "And then I could run my fingers through your hair without messing it up," he added softly.

A thrill ran through Sheila again. His touch and his words both relaxed and exhilarated her. "I'd be happy to change my hairstyle for you," she said. "I don't know how soon I can make a salon appointment, but I'll wear my hair down meanwhile."

"Good girl. That means a lot to me." He continued the back rub for a few more minutes, then whispered, "We'd better get you back to the dorm now, sweetie."

Regret washed over Sheila. Why did time have to go by so fast when she was with Dan?

As if noticing her disappointment, he added, "We won't be apart for long. I'll meet you for lunch again tomorrow."

The following Saturday, JD arrived to pick up Sheila at eight o'clock in the morning, as promised. When it was approaching dinnertime, she learned that her brothers had experienced so many failures in the kitchen that week, they'd resorted to fixing peanut-butter-and-jam sandwiches for several suppers in a row.

"We didn't realize how lucky we were until you weren't here to cook for us," said JD.

"Well, your luck's about to change," she said. "Get ready for your first cooking lesson."

Spencer suddenly remembered some "urgent" chores that needed to be done in the barn, but JD good-naturedly washed his hands and then listened to her instructions as, together, they prepared a big pot of spaghetti using homemade sauce from the freezer, a microwaved dish of home-canned green beans with bacon, and piping-hot garlicky butter-biscuit sticks made from scratch. Soon, the kitchen was filled with the mouth-watering aromas of cured pork, garlic, and Italian spices.

While the men gobbled down large helpings of everything, Sheila told them about her classes, dorm life, and the friends she had made on campus.

"Glad to hear all that," said Spencer. "We're proud of you, Sis."

Sheila glanced at her father. He merely reached across the table for a third helping of spaghetti.

She cleared her throat. "By the way, has any mail come for me that has a Houston postmark? Mrs. Parks promised to send me a letter with her new address and phone number."

JD and Spencer shook their heads.

"Haven't seen anything like that," JD said. "Maybe it's too soon, and something will come this week."

Sheila nodded. That made sense. But then, she noticed that her father was staring intently at his plate of spaghetti, his face flushed. How strange! Was he holding a grudge against her teacher for helping Sheila attend the summer program?

Each subsequent weekend, in between canning and freezing produce from the large vegetable garden and the fruit trees surrounding the house, Sheila did mountains of laundry, cooked hearty meals for the men, and cleaned house as best she could, taking a break from work on Sunday morning to attend church with her family.

Most every weekday, she met Dan for lunch and also spent the evening hours with him, mostly collaborating on projects for the student newspaper. When Dan let her know that he disapproved of several of the female students and didn't want Sheila hanging out with them, she spent even more of her time with him.

One evening, she paused from editing an article they were working on together. "I'm grateful for everything you're teaching me."

Looking a little surprised, he replied, "You're welcome. You have real editing talent. All you needed was someone to show you the ropes. Glad I could do it."

Sheila smiled. What a great team they made! She hoped Dan felt the same.

On Friday night of the fourth week of the summer program, Dan told her he had an important phone call to make from his apartment, so he'd be late picking her up at the dorm to go grab a bite to eat.

"No problem," Sheila assured him. "I could even walk to your place by myself to save a little time. It's not that far."

She didn't mind walking, but she did worry about all the dining-out expenses Dan had covered for both of them ever since they'd met. At the farm the previous Sunday, while cooking for her family, she'd found herself wishing Dan could have been there to witness her prowess in the kitchen. He was so good at what he did, sometimes she felt as if she could never measure up. Now, this slight schedule change gave her an idea. On her way to the apartment, she stopped at the little neighborhood market she'd noticed on their first date.

Dan had left his door unlocked, and when she entered his apartment, he was just hanging up the phone. He pointed to the grocery sack in her hands. "What do you have there?"

She grinned. "I thought it was time to show you I can do more than put subjects and predicates together. Do you have some butter and a skillet?" From the sack, she pulled out a pre-sliced loaf of French bread, a small container of grated Parmesan cheese, a package of shredded mozzarella, a jar of basil pesto, and a large cluster of black grapes.

Dan looked pleased as he got out the items she'd requested. "What are you making?"

"One of my specialties—Parmesan-crusted pesto grilled-cheese sandwiches. They're to die for." She removed four slices of bread and buttered one side of each, then spread pesto on the opposite side. She covered the pesto with mozzarella cheese, assembled the sandwiches, and sprinkled the tops of the buttered slices with grated Parmesan. "Now the magic begins," she said, setting the sandwiches upside down in the hot skillet.

She quickly washed the grapes and divided them between two plates. Then it was time to flip the sandwiches and sprinkle the rest of the Parmesan on top of the browned sides. The aromas of garlic and basil filled the small apartment.

"Mmm! That smells wonderful," Dan said.

"You can make yourself useful by setting the table over there." She nodded toward the produce crate he used as a coffee table. "I don't know where you keep your flatware or plates."

Five minutes later, they were enjoying the simple but savory meal. After Dan popped the last of the grapes into his mouth, he gazed at her admiringly. "You are quite a woman, Sheila Davis. You're beautiful, and you're a great cook, all in one package."

Sheila smiled. Liz-Liz simply had no idea how badly she'd misjudged Dan.

On Sunday after church, Sheila gave JD another cooking lesson as she prepared supper. In between instructing him on how to make the perfect mashed potatoes and how to keep baked pork chops from drying out, she told him about Dan. "I'm considering inviting him to church and for dinner next Sunday. What do you think?"

JD nodded. "I think you should. You've never seemed to care this much for anyone before. I figure we ought to meet him sooner than later, to give him the once-over. Of course, Dad might not be too cordial. You know how he is. He wants to make sure you end up with the right guy. But don't let him upset you."

Sheila smiled and thought of Liz-Liz, almost laughing out loud at the mental picture of her roommate and her dad agreeing on something. "Okay," she told JD. "I'll give it some thought this week and then decide. Thanks for listening."

After the meal, Sheila cleared the table, did the dishes, and finished folding her final load of weekend laundry before riding back to campus with JD.

"I know you're enjoying your time here," JD said as she unfastened her seat belt, "and that's great. But remember, Dad isn't going to let you come back in the fall. I realize how much it means to you, and I've tried to talk to him, but he won't change his mind, so you need to face the fact that it isn't going to happen. Just don't get your hopes up, okay?"

Tears stung Sheila's eyes. "I won't. Thanks for trying, though. Maybe I can figure out a solution in these final two weeks."

JD nodded. "Anyway, you call me if you want to bring that new boyfriend home next Sunday. That'll give me some time to get Dad warmed up to the idea."

She leaned over and gave him a hug. "Thanks for everything. You're the best."

When Sheila returned to her room, she found Liz-Liz and Annette eating pizza and playing cards with Marylou Habecker and Juanita Bivens.

"Hi, Daisy Mae," said Liz-Liz, handing Sheila a can of Pepsi. "How's everything down on the farm?"

"Oh, you know. Pretty much the same old, same old," answered Sheila. "I spent yesterday cleaning and canning and cooking and doing laundry. Then, first thing today was church, followed by more cooking, cleaning, and laundry. A grand time, I assure you."

"Do I detect a note of bitterness?" asked Annette. "Is something wrong?"

Sheila sat on her bed. "No. Yes. I don't know. I'm just frustrated, I guess. When I'm here at school, I feel alive and invigorated, like I'm on the brink of the rest of my life. But when I go back home on the weekends, it's as if nothing has changed. Everyone still sees the same old me doing the same old things. I couldn't wait to get back here tonight. I'm just a little freaked out that we have only two weeks left in the program."

Annette patted Sheila on the shoulder. "It's okay. I understand. This six-week course is like a fantasy for us. We know reality looms on the horizon. But don't let it ruin the time you have left here. That would be a real shame."

"Yeah, Sheila," Liz-Liz added. "Who knows what could happen in the coming days? I say, while you're here, live it up, baby!"

"Hear, hear!" said Annette.

Sheila smiled for the first time since her return. She knew Liz-Liz and Annette were right. Rather than be miserable about what she couldn't control, she should focus on enjoying the opportunities she *did* have. "Amen," she said. "I'll drink to that!"

The others dissolved into fits of laughter at Sheila's response and nearly missed hearing the phone ring.

Liz-Liz was the first to notice. She grabbed the receiver. "Hey, what's up?" she said into the phone. "What? Oh, hi, Dan. Yeah, she's back. I'll let you talk to her." She handed the phone to Sheila. *Danny-boy,* she mouthed.

Dan invited Sheila to a movie being shown in another dorm that night.

"Okay," she agreed. "I'll see you in thirty minutes." After hanging up the phone, she went to the mirror to freshen up her makeup and brush her hair.

"You're leaving us *again?*" Annette said with exaggerated disappointment. "How can you do that when we're having so much fun?"

"I know, I know," said Sheila. "But I haven't seen Dan all weekend, and he really wants to see this movie."

"What!" Liz-Liz gasped. "You haven't seen him for *two days?* How have you survived?"

"Okay, I get the point," said Sheila with a grin. "Later this week, we'll all get together for a girls' night. Okay?" She just wouldn't tell Dan about it, so he needn't worry about her being with people he disapproved of.

"Sure," answered Annette. "Go on, Sheila. And have a good time."

After the movie, Dan took Sheila to his apartment. She settled in a beanbag chair while he turned on a lamp. "What did you think of the movie?" she asked.

"The same thing I thought the first two times I saw it," he replied, settling in beside her. "The dialogue was stilted, and the director should have used more close-ups in the restaurant scene. Don't you agree?"

"I…uh, sure, now that you mention it. I hadn't seen the movie before, so I was too caught up in trying to figure out 'who done it,' I guess."

"You'd never seen it? What planet are you from?" he teased. "It was nominated for a Golden Globe two years ago."

Sheila looked away and said quietly, "Daddy doesn't believe in 'worldly' entertainment. The only movies he lets me watch are the ones they air on television, because that means the language has been cleaned up and the sex scenes eliminated. Well, a few times, I did manage to get him to sign a permission slip so I could go on a field trip to the local cinema with my English class. I just loved Kenneth Branagh in *Hamlet*."

"So, your dad's pretty religious?"

Sheila nodded. "I know he's tried to raise me right. But sometimes I feel so out of step with what's going on in mainstream culture, I'm afraid to open my mouth around people and show them how ignorant I am."

Dan seemed lost in thought for a moment. Then he asked, "Do you believe everything you've been taught in church?"

"Most of it, I guess. Why?"

"Well, I was wondering about all the traditional teachings, such as…well, that wives should obey their husbands. Stuff like that."

She eyed him curiously. "That's what the Bible says, doesn't it? Scripture doesn't address movies or carnivals or other forms of entertainment, so I struggle with Daddy's views on those types of things, but I can't argue with basic truth. Doesn't your family believe that way? Or don't you go to church?"

"Of course we go to church," he replied smoothly. "Although, when I'm at college, the academic schedule sometimes interferes. But one's faith doesn't depend on entering a church building every week. It's important to know when to be flexible if you want to get ahead." He stroked her hair. "Your dad expects you to attend church with your family every Sunday, doesn't he?"

"Yes, and thanks for reminding me. I wanted to invite you to come to church with us this Sunday morning. And to our house afterward for dinner, of course. I know you'll hit it off with JD and Spence. As for Daddy…well, I doubt even the apostle Paul would please him. Wait! I don't think Paul ever had a girlfriend, did he?" She giggled.

Dan merely stared at her with half a smile, as if his mind were somewhere else.

"Well? Will you come?"

He blinked. "Uh, sure. I'll come." Then he stood. "Wait right here. I have something for you." He walked over to the nightstand, opened the drawer, and took out a long, narrow box, which he handed to Sheila.

She carefully lifted the lid. In the soft lamplight gleamed a heart-shaped gold locket and a matching gold chain.

"Oh, Dan!" she exclaimed. "It's beautiful. Thank you so much!" She gave him a big kiss, then handed the box back to him. "Here, put it on for me." She turned her shoulders and lifted her long hair to expose the nape of her neck.

Dan removed the necklace Mrs. Parks had given her and laid it on the floor. Then Sheila felt the coolness of the metal chain encircling her neck and the warmth of Dan's fingers as he fastened the clasp. Before she had a chance to let go of her hair, Dan kissed the back of her neck. "It looks great on you."

"It's a beautiful necklace," she said again, turning to him. "I absolutely adore it."

"It's even more beautiful now that you're wearing it." He slipped his arm around her again. "There's one thing I want you to promise me, okay?"

"Of course, Dan. Anything." She laid her head on his shoulder.

"Get rid of that necklace from your teacher."

Sheila sat up straight again. "Get rid of it? But...but why?"

"Don't you like the one I just gave you?"

"Of course! You know I do."

"Then prove it to me by wearing that one exclusively. I'd like you to remember me when you touch it, the way you thought about Mrs. Parks when you fingered hers. Of course, if that's asking too much...." His face took on a sad, dejected look.

"No, it's not. I can get rid of it if it'll make you happy." Sheila picked up the necklace and the box the new necklace had come in, then dropped both into her purse that lay slightly open beside the chair.

Dan kissed her again. "Good. That makes me happy."

Sheila felt relieved that she had made the right choice. She wanted Dan to be pleased with her at all times.

"Now," Dan said, his tone serious, "I have something very important to talk to you about."

Oh, dear. What was the matter now? It couldn't be that Dan was having doubts about their relationship, or he wouldn't have given her a beautiful necklace. She looked at him, puzzled. "What's wrong?"

"Honey, nothing's wrong. I just want your full attention, that's all." He turned toward her, as much as the beanbag chair would allow, and held both her hands in his. "Sheila, you're beautiful and talented, and you deserve the chance to pursue your dreams. I want you to listen very carefully to what I have to say."

She basked in his compliments—*beautiful. Talented.* What a wonderful guy Dan was! "I'm listening."

"I want us to be together. Not just in a dating relationship, but all the time. I know it's your desire to return to the college this fall, but it doesn't look like that will happen if you're still living with your dad. So, I've come up with a plan. Sweetheart, if you get a job and help support us while I finish my senior year, then I'll get a teaching job, and you can go to college."

Sheila stared at Dan. "Help support 'us'? What do you mean, exactly?"

Dan gazed intently into her eyes. "Sheila, I want you to marry me. We make a good team. I promise that this plan will give you a chance to be the writer you want to be. Once I start teaching, you'll get your turn." He pressed his cheek against hers. "I love you," he whispered.

Sheila's heart soared. Not only had she found someone who truly loved her, but she had also discovered a way to pursue her dream to be a writer—with just a slight detour. "Yes, I'll marry you. Yes!"

Dan eagerly sought her lips and kissed her long and hard. Then he pulled back slightly and touched one finger to the golden locket. "This gift is a special reminder that we belong to each other. Forever."

"Yes," she said dreamily.

"I love you," he said again.

"I love you, too, Dan. I'd do anything for you."

He stood, took her by the hand, and helped her to her feet. Then he led her in the direction of the mattress in the corner. This time, she barely heard the inner warning bells. She was engaged to be married to this sweet, generous man, wasn't she? Why wait for the formality of a piece of paper? She'd already determined to be whatever Dan needed in his life, and he had declared his love to her. They belonged to each other now, and she had the golden locket as a tangible symbol. With a heart filled to overflowing and with stars in her eyes, she followed him.

Dan stopped at the edge of the mattress and guided her down to sit next to him. Then he carefully moved the locket aside and bent to kiss the skin beneath it. Soon, Sheila lost all sense of time and place. As their lovemaking progressed, she felt herself responding in ways she never imagined. All she knew, all she cared about, was loving Dan and his loving her.

Nearly at the moment of no return, Dan sat up and opened the nightstand drawer.

"What are you doing?" she asked.

He tore open a small square foil packet.

Sheila suddenly went cold. "Why on earth do you have that?" she demanded, sitting up and pulling the sheet around her. "Are you afraid you'll catch some disease from me? Or are you the one who's infected? Just who else do you bring up here when I'm busy at school? Or when I'm home on weekends?" She started to grab for her blouse, but Dan stopped her.

"No, sweetheart!" he insisted. "Trust me, there's no one in my life but you. I'm doing this for us—for you. I'm so in love with you, I've looked forward to this night for a long time. It's just that I can't stand the thought of you finding yourself pregnant and not being able to pursue your writing dreams." He slipped his arm around her bare shoulders. "Remember, babe, it's just you and me against the world, now. Nobody will ever love you as much as I do. I want to take care of you for the rest of your life." He touched his lips to her forehead and then planted a row of light kisses down the side of her face to her earlobe.

She pulled away and picked up her blouse. "I want to wait."

Wearing the expression of someone who'd just realized he had made a serious staging error, Dan said smoothly, "Okay. There's no hurry. We can just relax together in bed."

Sheila recoiled even more. "I can't do this, Dan. I...I need to go back to the dorm. Now." She tried to move toward the edge of the mattress, but her feet became tangled in the rumpled sheets. She struggled to free herself.

Dan's brow creased as he eased away from her. But then, as if expending great effort to remain calm, he smiled indulgently. "Hey, we have a lifetime for this, right? No need to rush. Once we're married, we can spend the rest of our nights together. It'll be great."

Sheila stopped wriggling for a moment, and her racing heart calmed slightly. "You...I...you still love me? Still want to marry me?"

"Of course," said Dan, still smiling. "We were meant to be together. I mean, Prince Charming would never give up on his Sleeping Beauty, would he?"

CHAPTER 7

When JD and Sheila picked up Dan at his apartment on Sunday morning, nothing was said about the engagement. Dan and Sheila had agreed to wait until that afternoon to share the news, first with her father and then with her brothers. They would phone Dan's family that night, and then Sheila could tell Liz-Liz and the rest of her fellow students when she returned to the dorm.

On the short, quiet ride to the farm, Sheila worried what Dan would think of Clear Creek Christian Church. Her parents had gotten married there, and Sheila and her brothers had never been given the choice to attend anywhere else. Her father even served on the deacon board. It was his firm habit to oppose any changes. He believed the sanctuary décor and the style of worship should remain as they had been when his Clarissa was alive.

JD pulled into the lane leading up to the farmhouse, and Sheila felt a jolt of nervousness. Her knees trembled as she climbed out of the car.

Given the fact that Sheila had never felt at ease talking to her father, she was only too happy to let Dan be the point person. They walked hand in hand through the front gate up to the porch, where Harold Davis was sitting in a rocker waiting for them. Spencer stood leaning against the side of the house. Sheila introduced Dan to her father and brother, then started for the porch swing.

"No need to get comfortable, girl." Her father stood. "If we don't leave for church directly, we'll be late, and you know how I feel about latecomers to a worship service." He walked down the steps and out the gate to the car, trailed by Sheila's brothers. Sheila and Dan exchanged a brief look and then followed them.

Little conversation took place on the short ride to the church. Sheila, JD, and Spencer made small talk, but their father remained silent. To Sheila's surprise, Dan seemed impassive in the face of her father's cold demeanor. He responded when spoken to, but he didn't go out of his way to ingratiate himself to any of the Davis men.

Sheila had always felt obligated to please her father—and her brothers, too, for that matter—and so Dan's reaction both amazed and relieved her. It gave her a new sense of freedom. After all, she and Dan were now partners.

As they crossed the church parking lot, she felt proud to have Dan at her side. She knew they would be the center of attention. It was always that way when someone new visited. No doubt every woman in the congregation would be speculating about Sheila's relationship with this unfamiliar man. *Well,* thought Sheila, *they'll all know soon enough!*

Her father led the procession up the center aisle to the fourth pew from the front, the same spot he had occupied for the past thirty years. Along the way, he nodded to a few fellow farmers and several other male congregants. When he reached "his" pew, he stepped aside to let his entourage enter, then took his place on the aisle.

Pastor James Miller had been preaching at Clear Creek Christian Church for the past two years. Even so, Sheila's father still referred to him as the "brand-new" pastor. It was no secret that he thought this preacher's approach to religion was a little too warm and fuzzy. Sheila, on the other hand, found Pastor Miller's perspective refreshing.

As the service began, Sheila's mind wandered to her upcoming wedding. She thought it would be great to have Pastor Miller officiate the ceremony. She imagined herself in a flowing wedding gown with its train trailing behind her down the aisle. Soft candlelight would reflect off the warm wood of the altar. Her friends would radiate with joy at the happy occasion. And then she and Dan would cut the cake together....

With a start, she realized that the announcements were over, and Pastor Miller had begun to preach.

"The sermon this morning is on recognizing our gifts and returning them to God," he announced. "It is the duty of every Christian to fulfill his or her God-given potential. In fact, doing so is a legitimate form of worship that honors the very Creator who has gifted each one of us with these talents."

Sheila thought about her gift of writing—one she needed to nurture by pursuing an education. She reached for Dan's hand, more sure than ever that she had made the right decision in accepting his proposal of marriage.

At the conclusion of the service, the congregation filed out slowly, each person stopping at the door to greet and shake hands with Pastor Miller. When her turn came, Sheila introduced Dan to the minister.

"Welcome, Dan," said Pastor Miller. "I'm always pleased when our young people bring their friends to church. I hope you'll visit us again soon."

Dan smiled politely. "It's nice to meet you."

They walked out onto the grassy yard, where many of the families customarily visited after service. However, Sheila's father always went directly to the car. Like a trail of ducklings, Sheila, Dan, and her brothers followed.

On the way home, Sheila tried to end the strained silence. "I enjoyed Pastor Miller's sermon this morning," she commented.

"All this candy-coatin' and feelin' good about yerself ain't real religion," her father spat, taking issue with a remark she'd hoped would be innocuous. "God don't care what ya do fer a livin' or whether you can paint a pretty picture. Religion ain't about people. It's about God—respectin' His commandments and fearin' His wrath."

"Dad, I don't think Pastor Miller meant that religion was only about feeling good," JD ventured calmly. "Maybe he meant that following the Lord isn't supposed to make us miserable."

Sheila nodded. "I agree. Anything a person can do well is a gift from God. If you have a special gift and don't use it, it's almost like saying God made a mistake, or that you don't appreciate what He gave you."

Harold Davis scowled. "I don't see nothin' 'bout that in the Bible, even if the reverend thinks *he* does. Obeyin' the commandments is what's important. That's why we have religion—to make it clear."

They rode the rest of the way home in silence.

Sheila took Dan on a quick tour of the big farmhouse, ending in the kitchen. "Now, I'll fix dinner while you visit with Daddy and the boys on the porch," she told him.

Dan frowned. "Your dad doesn't seem like he's in the mood to visit."

"Actually, he's expecting you. They all are," Sheila explained. She didn't mention that she'd called JD on Wednesday to ask him to run interference anytime her father was involved in a conversation with Dan. JD had agreed, pretending to be disappointed that he would have to miss out on a cooking lesson.

Sheila tried to keep her mind on preparing the meal instead of fretting about what might be going on outside. Fortunately, she had enough experience in the kitchen to be able to put together a satisfying dinner without concentrating very hard. In no time at all, she had potatoes boiling on the stove and a large chicken cut up, floured, and in the frying pan. Then she assembled a salad of homegrown lettuce, cucumbers, and tomatoes. She peeled a pound of carrots and sliced them into a casserole dish, which she then placed in the microwave. Meanwhile, baking in the oven was a cherry pie she'd prepared and frozen months before.

When she had a spare moment, she grabbed her purse from the entryway and ran upstairs to her bedroom. She closed the door behind her, set her purse on the bed, and withdrew a small box tightly wrapped in aluminum foil—the box that had originally contained her locket from Dan.

When she'd promised Dan to get rid of the necklace from Mrs. Parks, she hadn't known exactly how she would do so. She couldn't bring herself to throw away such a special keepsake. But an idea had eventually occurred to her. Years before, she had discovered a loose floorboard in her bedroom closet and had turned the space beneath it into a secret hiding place. It would be the perfect spot to keep the necklace. Dan would never know.

She lifted the box to her lips for a farewell kiss. "I'm so sorry, Mrs. Parks," she whispered, "but this is all part of my plan for making my dream—*our* dream—come true. If you knew the circumstances, I'm sure you'd understand."

She tucked the box inside the opening, replaced the floorboard, and hurried downstairs in time to turn the chicken pieces in the skillet before they got too brown. Then she gathered five place settings and went to the dining room.

As she set the table, her mind conjured up snatches of imagined dialogue going on just out of earshot. She knew her father wouldn't make it easy for Dan. JD would do his best to keep the tone of the conversation light and friendly, and Spencer probably wouldn't say anything. *Dan is smart, educated, and confident,* she reminded herself. *He won't be intimidated.*

Once the table was ready, Sheila returned to the kitchen. She stirred the carrots and set the microwave to cook another three minutes, turned off the heat under the potatoes, and then headed to the pantry for the colander.

When she pulled the string to turn on the bare lightbulb overhead, she caught sight of a small brown teapot on the lowest shelf.

The teapot had belonged to her mother when she was a girl herself. Growing up, Sheila had spent hours playing with it in the pantry. Once she was safely tucked inside the small room with the door closed, she would pretend that the space was a cabin where she lived with her mother.

Now, Sheila dropped to her knees and picked up the teapot, gently rubbing a chipped spot on the tiny lid. She suddenly realized that she would have a new home soon—one with no connection whatsoever to her mother. She fought back the urge to cry as she returned the teapot to the shelf.

Sheila stood and smoothed her skirt, thinking about Mrs. Parks and how she had substituted in many ways for the mother Sheila had never known. It didn't seem right that Sheila couldn't share the news with Mrs. Parks of her upcoming union with Dan, but she was still waiting to receive her former teacher's new contact information. Maybe it was taking her longer to get settled than she had planned. Sheila only hoped she would be able to invite Mrs. Parks to the wedding.

Just then, Sheila heard the front screen door slam. She grabbed the colander and hurried back to the stove. A few seconds later, as she was draining the potatoes, Dan and JD came into the kitchen.

"It smells great in here," Dan said. "Need any help?"

"No, thanks," she said. "Everything's just about ready. All that's left to do is mash these potatoes and put everything else in serving dishes."

"I'll take the salad and the dressing to the table," said JD.

Sheila smiled. It was great having a couple of helpful men around.

When the five of them were gathered around the table, Harold Davis offered a prayer of thanks for the meal. Then he served himself before passing each dish to JD, on his left. As was their habit, the Davis men said little during the meal. Dan followed their example and ate in silence. Sheila picked at her food, too nervous to eat much. She couldn't stop worrying about the conversation that she and Dan were about to have with her father.

When she served dessert, the men made short work of the cherry pie. In the lazy quiet that followed the satisfying meal, Dan finally said, "Mr. Davis, Sheila and I would like to speak with you privately for a moment."

JD and Spencer excused themselves from the table and went to the barn.

Harold Davis sat perfectly still, a resolute expression hardening his face. Dan cleared his throat, and Sheila squeezed his hand under the table, willing the butterflies in her stomach to flit away for good.

"Mr. Davis," Dan began, "I realize that I've known your daughter only for a short time. But, in that short time, I've come to love her. We share many interests and goals, and I think that's important in a partnership. I know Sheila's young, but I've asked her to be my wife. We hope to have your blessing"—he paused for only a second—"but we're going to marry, with or without it."

Sheila nearly gasped out loud. If only he had left off those last few words! Her father wouldn't take kindly to the implication that he had lost control of the situation.

Harold Davis looked at Sheila. "Girl, you got anything to say 'bout this?"

"Y-yes." Sheila spoke barely above a whisper. "I love Dan, and I want to marry him."

Harold Davis turned back to Dan. "What exactly is it that ya do fer a livin'?"

"I'm not working full-time right now," Dan said. "Our plan is for Sheila to work to help support us while I finish my last year of college. While doing some computer tech work at Reynolds Heating and Air-Conditioning this summer, I learned that they're looking for a full-time receptionist. I'm confident I can call in a favor and get Sheila's name at the top of the applicant list. Plus, I can give her a glowing reference due to her work on the student newspaper at Brissenden College. Of course, I'll keep my part-time job at the school and continue taking classes. Then I'll get a job teaching, and Sheila can pursue her college degree and the writing career she dreams of. Eventually, I plan to teach at the university level, as well as to be a successful novelist."

Sheila's father snorted and shook his head. "Sounds to me like my daughter marryin' ya would work out great—fer you! Why should I give my blessin' fer her to marry a man who's got no income, no job, and, so far as I'm concerned, no prospects?"

"Daddy, that's not fair," said Sheila. "Dan's extremely talented. You don't understand."

"I understand plenty," her father barked. "This fella sees his chance to marry and have a woman support him while he bums around playin' at bein' a writer. Well, that woman ain't gonna be my daughter." Then he stood and pushed his chair back from the table. "No self-respectin' man lets a woman support him, mister. If ya want to talk to me about marryin' my girl, then buckle down and get yerself a real job. Until then, I don't want to hear another word about it."

Sheila sat motionless in her chair, but a tornado of emotions churned inside her. This was exactly the negative response she had feared. Why had Dan felt it necessary to aggravate her father by telling him flat-out that his opinion didn't matter? It had taken Sheila eighteen years to figure out the best ways to approach her father, and this certainly wasn't one of them. But the damage had been done. There was no going back. She either had to ride the crest of the wave or be crushed by it.

She stood. "Daddy, I'm sorry to have to say it this way, but Dan and I are getting married, whether or not you give us your blessing. I'm eighteen now. I'm not your little girl anymore. Dan actually listens to me and supports my dream to write. That's far more than I've ever gotten from you."

Her father stared at her in disbelief. "Ya mean you'd defy me by goin' against my wishes?"

By now, Sheila was trembling, but she summoned all her strength to keep her voice as steady as possible. "Daddy, I've lived my whole life by your rules. It's time for a change. I don't want to spend the rest of my days stuck on this farm. I love to write, and I'm good at it. Mrs. Parks convinced me of that. I want to pursue a writing career, but you wouldn't even entertain the thought of sending me to college so I could further my education. Dan understands my dreams, and he wants what's best for me. It's time I started living for myself instead of for everyone else."

Her father glared at her for a full ten seconds, then turned and headed for the front door. When he reached it, he stopped and faced Sheila again. "All I can say is, I'm sure glad yer ma ain't here to see this." Then he left the house.

Sheila collapsed in the nearest chair, buried her face in her hands, and sobbed.

Dan, still seated in his chair, leaned forward and put his arms around her. "It's going to be okay, Sheila. He'll come around, sooner or later. I'm sure he will. He's wrong, you know. I want to marry you because I love you. And I do believe in you. He doesn't understand what you need. You have talent, and you need someone who recognizes that. We'll show him. Just wait."

Sheila blinked away her tears and forced a smile. Dan kissed her forehead and wiped her wet cheeks with his thumb.

"I love you, Dan," she whispered. "But, even more than that, I need you."

"It's okay, babe. I'm here. I'll always be here for you. I'm going to be somebody someday. You'll see. You won't regret marrying me."

"You're already somebody special to me, and I know I won't have any regrets." She sniffed. "Now, let's clean up this mess and get out of here. All I want is to be back in your arms at your apartment."

"Aye, aye, Captain. That sounds good to me. I can't wait to have you there." Dan quickly stood and started gathering the dirty plates and silverware.

JD entered the kitchen as Sheila and Dan were putting away the last of the washed dishes. "So, I hear you got some ideas about getting married, Sheila."

"We've decided, JD," Dan replied. "It's not something we're just considering."

"That's right," Sheila added. "We hoped to get Dad's blessing today, but, of course, that didn't happen. Typical. He's never really cared about me or my happiness. The only person he thinks of is himself."

JD winced. "Now, Sis, I'm sorry things didn't go so good today, but you have to remember, you're still young. Dad's not ready to let go of you just yet. Maybe he never will be."

"Well, that's just too bad," said Sheila. "He's never been willing to listen to me. Why should I keep on doing what he wants? To be honest, I think my very existence has been nothing more than a thorn in his side. All I ever wanted from him was a little understanding. I wanted him to see me as someone worthwhile. Someone whose value goes beyond her ability to cook and clean. And now...I just don't care."

JD looked stricken at her harsh words. "Come on, Sheila. That's just not true. You've never been a thorn in anyone's side. Remember Dad's promise to Mom before she died—that he'd teach you the things a woman needed to know and would bring you up right? Sure, he's made some mistakes, but he's only done what he thought was best. I know it hasn't been easy, but he loves you, in his own way. I know he does."

Sheila fought hard not to start crying again as she hung the dish towel over the oven-door handle. "It doesn't really matter anymore. That's all in the past now. I'm finally going to have a future. That future is with Dan. Now, if you don't mind, I think we're ready to head back to campus."

JD looked as if he were about to argue but then changed his mind. "Okay, Sis. I'll pull the car around."

When Sheila and Dan followed JD outside, neither her father nor Spencer was anywhere in sight. She glanced toward the barn but still saw no sign of them. Perhaps it was just as well she didn't have to face them again. As the car moved slowly down the lane, Sheila looked back one more time. She wasn't sure whether she would ever return to the only home she'd ever known, but, at that moment, she truly didn't care.

The trio didn't talk much on the way back to Brissenden, although JD tried to make polite conversation. Dan responded civilly to JD's comments and questions, but Sheila was too exhausted to do anything except sit and stare at the road ahead of them. She knew there was no turning back now. Her father wasn't the kind of man who accepted defiance from anyone, least of all his daughter.

When JD pulled to the curb outside Upton Hall, all three of them got out. While Dan was removing a bag of Sheila's clean laundry, JD took Sheila's hand, leaned toward her, and kissed her cheek. "You call me in a few days, and we'll talk about this a little more. You know I love you, and I want you to be happy." When he pulled his hand away, he left a $100 bill in Sheila's palm. She started to protest, but JD put his finger to her lips. "Go on, now. Get on outta here so I can get home."

Sheila hugged her brother tightly, then shoved the bill into the pocket of her skirt and turned toward Dan. "Please wait for me while I take my things to my room," she told him. "Then let's go to your apartment. I just want to be with you. Okay?"

"Sure, honey. Whatever you want. I know it was really hard for you today, but you're doing the right thing. Sooner or later, your dad will see how wrong he is."

Sheila hurried inside. She was thankful that none of her friends was around, because she didn't feel like explaining anything to Liz-Liz and the others.

She and Dan held hands for the duration of the walk to his apartment. The waning afternoon sun spilled a pink glow across the neighborhood, making the landscape more beautiful than Sheila had ever seen it.

"Oh, Dan," she said, "I can't believe this is all happening. I'm really glad we're together. I can't believe that in one short year, I'll be a student here. Am I dreaming?"

Dan playfully pinched her. "You're not dreaming, Mrs. Gray. You're finally starting to live a little, that's all. From now on, things are going to go our way. I'll make sure of that."

For Sheila, the following days dissolved into a blur of classes and time spent with Dan. While she still slept and showered in the dorm, she did little else there. Dan wanted her with him every possible moment. She had never felt so cherished.

Once she told the other students on her floor about her plans, they wanted to throw her a little bachelorette party. But Dan was against the idea, so she declined the offer. Dan frequently pointed out to Sheila that she was better than the other girls, especially Liz-Liz, who he felt was a particularly bad influence. Sheila knew he was wrong about that, but whenever she tried to argue with him, Dan took her disagreement as a form of rejection, and he would sulk. Consequently, to keep the peace, Sheila reduced her contact with her dorm mates to a bare minimum.

One day, after a phone conversation with JD, Sheila decided to broach the subject of her family during her lunch break at Dan's apartment.

"I talked to JD today."

"Oh? What did he want?'

"He didn't want anything. I'm the one who called him. I just wanted to touch base and see how everyone was."

"I don't know why you want to set yourself up for more abuse from your father. Why can't you just let it go?"

"I can let it go if I have to, but I'd like us all to be speaking again in time for the wedding. I mean, it's going to be pretty awkward at the church if we all give one another the silent treatment."

"Church? What church?"

Sheila chuckled. "Dan! Clear Creek Christian. Where else do you think we're getting married?"

"Who said anything about our getting married in a church?"

Sheila stared at him. "I've always dreamed of getting married in my home church. That's where my parents were married. That's where I've attended services every Sunday of my life. If not there, then where?"

Dan sighed. "Sweetheart, it doesn't make sense for us to have a big church wedding. Surely, you can understand that."

"No, I can't. Why shouldn't we?"

He spoke in a measured, patient tone, as if addressing a child. "Sheila, you and your dad aren't speaking. My parents wouldn't want to make the trip. And we have next to no money. It would be much wiser to be married at the courthouse. Then, we won't have any extra wedding expenses. I'd rather save that money for our education instead of throwing it away on flowers and cake for a bunch of people I've never met and will never see again."

Sheila's shoulders slumped. Dan's reasoning made sense, but she was still disappointed. "It's just that I've always pictured a beautiful church wedding," she whispered. "I can't imagine it any other way."

"Honey, don't be stubborn about this, okay?" Dan's voice was pleasant enough, but his eyes seemed to turn steel-hard. "We aren't in a position to spend money foolishly. Besides, your dad probably wouldn't even come. This way, it'll be *our* day. It'll be all the more special because it's just for us."

Like most of her friends, Sheila had dreamed for years of her wedding day. Now to have it reduced to a justice of the peace and two signatures on a license was overwhelmingly disappointing. She'd expected to make sacrifices in order to get a college education, but having to forgo a traditional church wedding had never crossed her mind. Fiercely willing herself not to cry, she asked in a low voice, "Can I ask my brothers to come? I want someone from my family to be there."

"Sure. Go ahead and ask, but don't get your hopes up. The way your old man keeps those boys under his thumb, I'd be very surprised if they had the nerve to attend."

Determined to put on a good front, Sheila managed a weak smile. "I'll call JD tomorrow to let him know what's going on. Have you looked at the calendar? What date would you like for our anniversary? Better make it a date you'll remember!"

"The sooner the better, as far as I'm concerned. Your six-week scholarship term is almost over. Let's get married next Friday. We can go to the county clerk's office this week to apply for our license and check out all the details. I also need to stop by Reynolds Heating and Air-Conditioning and see about getting you that receptionist job."

Sheila nodded resolutely.

"Good," said Dan. "I've got to dash now. I'll meet you here after the last afternoon session. I love you, Sheila. We'll have a great wedding day, I promise." He put his arms around her waist. "And one other thing, Mrs. Gray. The wedding night will be even better." He kissed her neck before releasing his grip.

"Bye, Dan. See you later."

On her walk back to campus, Sheila thought more about her wedding dreams and tried not to be depressed. Obviously, she had been too caught up in fairy tales and girlhood notions. Still, she wished she could have arranged to have more friends and family present for her big day—including Mrs. Parks, of course. But she still didn't have her former teacher's new address. Why hadn't she heard from her yet? It wasn't like Mrs. Parks to forget a promise.

CHAPTER 8

The following Friday afternoon, JD and Spencer met Sheila and Dan at the courthouse. When Sheila realized her father hadn't come with her brothers, she was almost relieved. She dreaded another confrontation like the one they'd had at the farm. That had been the first time in her life she'd stood up to anyone, let alone her father. The experience had shaken her to the core.

For the courthouse ceremony, Sheila wore her best dress, and Dan wore the only sport coat he owned. JD and Spencer were dressed fairly casually, too, so everyone felt at ease. They gathered in a local judge's office, and the proceedings took less than ten minutes. Sheila marveled that she didn't really feel any different after such a life-changing event. She wondered when the reality of being married would set in.

"Spence and I want to treat you two to a nice lunch," said JD as the four of them exited the building into the bright summer sun.

"Oh, how nice," said Sheila, and she glanced at Dan to see his reaction. "But you boys don't have to do that. You're our guests. We should be taking you to lunch."

"We want to," added Spencer. "It'll be our wedding present to you. We didn't really know what kinds of things you needed."

"We'd love to accept your invitation," Dan said. "The last thing I want is to take Sheila away from her family."

Sheila breathed a sigh of relief. She desperately wanted to share more of her special day with her loved ones.

"I think the bride should pick the spot, don't you, Dan?" JD said.

"Sure," Dan replied. "Whatever my wife wants is fine with me."

They all chuckled at his response, especially JD and Spencer, who also looked a bit startled at the sound of someone referring to Sheila as "my wife."

After a nice lunch at Sheila's favorite Italian restaurant, JD drove to the campus so Sheila could move her things out of the dorm and not have to lug it all to Dan's apartment herself.

The previous day, she had said her farewells to her dorm mates as they were heading home. Because Dan had insisted that she stop spending time with most of them, only one or two still felt close enough to her to question the wisdom of her marrying Dan so quickly. Liz-Liz kept her promise to say nothing more about the mistake she was convinced Sheila was making, but all the mascara in the world couldn't hide the sadness in her eyes when she hugged her roommate good-bye.

Outside Dan's apartment, JD pulled to the curb and turned off the engine.

"Would you two like to come up to see the place?" Sheila asked her brothers tentatively. It seemed strange to invite people into someone else's home, yet she felt an obligation to offer.

"No, thanks," answered JD, opening his door. "We'll let you two get settled in first." He went around back to open the trunk while everyone else exited the car.

Sheila's brothers hugged her and shook hands with their new brother-in-law. Then Dan grabbed Sheila's suitcase and her book bag and started up the stairs to the apartment. Sheila took the pillow and sleeping bag she'd used in the dorm. Once her hands were full, JD stuck something in the outside pocket of her purse.

"What are you doing?" Sheila asked.

"Never you mind," JD answered. "You just get on up there with that husband of yours. And one more thing. You call me anytime, okay? If you need anything at all, you just let me know."

Sheila thanked her brother, then turned and climbed the stairs to her new life. Once inside, she set her things near the dresser they'd purchased at a yard sale for her and Dan to share. She stood in the center of the room, feeling suddenly ill at ease in what was now her home.

Dan took his young bride in his arms. He kissed her forehead and then each eyelid before touching his lips to hers. He hugged her closer to him, and within minutes, the two young lovers were entwined on the mattress that would serve as their marriage bed.

Sometime later, Sheila snuggled against Dan's side and exhaled a long breath. He turned to face her, throwing his leg over her body as if to capture her. "Now, Mrs. Gray. Was that a sigh of satisfaction or disappointment?"

Sheila kept her eyes closed, but her face broke into a grin. "Oh, Mr. Gray, I'm not disappointed. Not at all. You're lookin' at one very satisfied woman."

"Yeah? Well, I'm not lookin' at enough of her," he said as he whipped back the sheet that covered them. "You're mine now, and I want to feast my eyes on my prize."

Sheila felt herself blush as she tried to retrieve the sheet, but he pushed it out of her reach and pinned her shoulders to the mattress. He raised himself up to gaze long and full at Sheila's body, and then he started kissing her again. "Now, my love, let's make sure that we're getting this marriage thing down right, shall we? You know what they say: 'Practice makes perfect.'"

On Monday, after her weekend honeymoon in the apartment, Sheila caught the bus to start her new job at Reynolds Heating and Air-Conditioning. The owner, Mike Reynolds, had interviewed her a few days earlier. He'd agreed to meet with Sheila as a favor to Dan but ended up hiring her on the spot, saying that he could tell she was organized and a fast learner.

Within a short time, the newlyweds fell into a comfortable routine. Dan continued his part-time work with the student newspaper and registered for his fall semester of classes. Sheila worked full-time at her job and spent the evenings and weekends putting a feminine touch to the apartment's décor.

Almost as if to make up for not getting married in a church, Sheila mentioned several times to Dan that she'd like to find a local congregation and start attending on Sundays. Since she and her father weren't on speaking terms, Clear Creek Christian was out of the question—not that they could have gotten there, anyway, since they didn't have a car. Acquiescing halfheartedly to her suggestion, Dan checked the yellow pages for the churches with the most impressive ads. He explained that since friendships and career connections were often made with fellow worshippers, it was only logical to choose a place where the members were people of influence. He indicated two churches he was willing to try.

But mapping out the locations and looking up bus routes, as well as making note of the times that various classes and services were held, fell to Sheila. Within the first several weeks of marriage, she'd managed to get them to both churches, but the worship styles were so different from what Sheila was used to, she didn't suggest going back. Dan seemed perfectly fine with that.

One evening before catching the bus home from work, Sheila stopped at Goodwin's Department Store and splurged on a set of new curtains for their living room. Dan had been hanging an old blanket over the window at night, but Sheila wanted something light and pretty. Excited to show Dan her purchase, she nearly ran the entire block from the bus stop to their apartment. When she reached the top of the stairs, the door opened before she could turn the knob.

"Where have you been?" Dan demanded.

"Hi, Dan. What's wrong?"

"You should have been home thirty minutes ago."

"I stopped at Goodwin's after work. See? Look at these curtains I found for the living room. They were even on sale."

Dan barely glanced at her purchase. "Don't you think I deserve to know where my wife is? Do you plan to start running all over town without telling me?"

Sheila's eyes widened. "I'm sorry. I didn't know you'd be upset. I tried to hurry, but I really wanted to surprise you with these curtains."

"How did you pay for them?"

"JD gave me some cash during the summer and then again when we got married. I hadn't spent any of it, so I thought I'd use part of it on some new things for the apartment."

"You mean, you've been hiding money from me? I had no idea you were the kind of girl who'd do something like that."

Sheila closed her eyes, trying to stop the flood of fear and confusion rising within her. Why was Dan so angry? What had she done wrong? No one had taught her anything about fulfilling the role of a wife. Now, it seemed she'd gotten off to a bad start and had upset Dan somehow.

As calmly as her racing heart would allow, she explained, "I wasn't hiding anything. I just wanted to surprise you. I'm sorry. Really, I am. You can have the rest of the money. Do whatever you want with it. I just don't want you to be upset with me." Tears spilled down her cheeks.

Dan rubbed his face and sighed. "Okay, Sheila. It's all right. Let's just get a few things straight. I expect to know where my wife is at all times. If you're not going to be home at the regular time after work, I want you to call and let me know what's going on. And if you have extra money lying around, you need to tell me about it. Men have better heads for financial matters. I need to make the decisions about how we spend our money."

Sheila nodded. "Whatever you say. I just didn't know. I'm sorry. I'll try to do better."

Dan put his arms around her and kissed her cheek. "Okay, honey. Now let's just forget about this and put up your new curtains."

Once Dan's classes started in the fall, time passed quickly. Sheila continued to work all day at the office. In the evenings, she cooked, cleaned the apartment, and often typed Dan's papers while he studied. Occasionally, if Dan had a night class, one of her high-school friends would stop by for a visit, or she would go to dinner with JD and Spencer; but Dan made it clear that he preferred for her to remain home alone.

By Christmas, Sheila had reconciled with her father. Nothing as dramatic as a joyous reunion had taken place. The event had happened in a matter-of-fact way when Spencer and JD had come to take her to dinner one evening and her father had been in the car with them. Neither had apologized. They'd simply picked up their distant relationship where it had left off. Still, Sheila felt better knowing she could visit the farm again.

By spring, Sheila was using her occasional evenings at the Laundromat as an opportunity to resume writing. She'd missed the gratification of expressing her thoughts on paper, and stretching her creative muscles again felt good. Besides, she planned on starting classes in the fall, and she figured the practice would give her an edge.

She said nothing to Dan, however, knowing he might prefer her to guard her free time so she would always be available to do library research or typing for him. While it was important to Sheila that she meet all of Dan's needs, and she didn't want anything to interfere with that, she was also confident that he would be just as supportive of her when it was her turn to attend college in a few months.

One week before Dan's graduation, when Sheila returned from work, Dan greeted her at the door. "Hi, honey. Don't bother putting your purse down. I'm taking you out to dinner tonight."

"What? Why?"

"Because I want to, that's why. Can't a man take his wife out on a date once in a while?"

"Sure, I'd love that. I'm just surprised you want to spend the money."

"Well, you work hard all week. You deserve a break now and then. Besides, we have something to celebrate."

"We do? Something besides your upcoming graduation?"

"Yes, but it's a surprise, sweetie. I don't want to tell you just yet. I'll explain over dinner. Now, let's go."

Sheila followed Dan out of the apartment and down the steps. She soon realized they were heading toward the Chinese restaurant where they'd had their first date. They made small talk as they walked and as they sipped tea while waiting for their food.

Finally, when their entrees had been served, Sheila could stand it no longer. "Dan, please! You have to tell me what this is all about. The curiosity is killing me."

Dan smiled broadly as he took her hand. "Honey, I'm really excited about this. I could hardly wait to tell you, but I wanted the time to be right. I know you'll be as thrilled as I am."

Dan's enthusiasm was so infectious, Sheila grinned back at him without knowing why. "Go on," she urged him.

He squeezed her hand. "I've been offered a graduate assistantship in the English department at Indiana University. I can assist with undergrad classes and work on my master's degree. Isn't that incredible?"

Sheila squealed with delight. "Oh, yes! That's wonderful. Congratulations, honey. I'm so proud of you! Now we'll both be in school next year."

Dan's smile faded. "Sweetheart, I don't think you understand. This is a chance for me to get my master's degree right away. It's a real break for us."

"I know. I think it's great."

"But, my dear, we won't be able to afford to have *both* of us in school at the same time. They'll pay me a stipend and give me a discount on tuition, but I won't make enough for us to live on, especially since we'll need to buy a car so I can drive to my grad-school classes. You'll need to postpone going to college until I'm finished with the master's program."

The full implication of Dan's news quickly eroded Sheila's thrill at the prospect of being college students together. "I see," she said, looking down at her steaming cup of green tea.

"You're only nineteen years old," Dan pointed out. "You have plenty of time for college. I have to get my master's degree eventually, anyway. This opportunity will put me ahead of the game. With you working full-time and having no tuition of your own to pay, I can take extra courses and try to finish early. Besides, I'll be so busy with school, you'll have more time to yourself. Maybe you could even start doing some writing of your own. You know, keep your skills up."

Sheila knew his points were valid. He had to get his master's degree sooner or later. Right now, he was still in school mode. The momentum of moving directly from Brissenden's undergraduate program into the master's program would be an advantage. Yet, it also meant her dream that had seemed finally to be within her grasp was still eluding her.

She looked at him pleadingly. "It's just that I had *so* counted on going to school this fall."

His expression was almost stern as he replied, "Sheila, remember that I'm the head of the house. Your role is to support my decisions."

Sheila wondered why doing what God expected of her left her feeling as if she'd been punched in the stomach. Even so, she said, "Of course, Dan. You've been given a wonderful opportunity. I'll do whatever I can to help."

"Good girl. I knew you'd see the logic of the whole thing. I won't let you down, honey. You can count on me."

That fall, Dan's graduate program at IU kept him away from home most evenings. Sheila continued her work at Reynolds, taking on more and more responsibilities. Her boss credited her natural talent for organizing and told her the office had never run better. Sheila also worked hard on Dan's behalf, continuing to type his papers and often going to the library to do research for him while he was in class.

Whenever she had a moment of free time, usually in the evenings or during her lunch hour, Sheila wrote and studied writing guides to keep up-to-date on new trends. Each time Dan talked about his coursework, she listened intently, absorbing minute details from summarized lectures. And, as always, she read voraciously. In fact, books were her closest friends.

Dan still discouraged her from spending much time with anyone else. That bothered her, even though she didn't really have a lot of free time for socializing. She was also bothered by the fact that Dan had started coming home with lottery tickets very often now.

"I don't know what you're so worried about," he said when she expressed her concern. "This new lottery program lets us multiply our non-jackpot-level prizes up to five times. Last week, someone in our office won ten thousand dollars. Ten grand! That's a lot of money for a very small investment. Don't worry, honey. I know what I'm doing."

A few weeks later, he came home with $200 in winnings, waving it triumphantly in her face. She had no choice but to ignore the worry that nibbled at the back of her mind.

A year into Dan's master's program, Sheila finally found the nerve to show him a short story she had spent weeks writing, then struggled to perfect. Considering how many hours she put in at the office and how busy she kept herself in helping Dan, he expressed shock that she had found time to write at all. He read the story while Sheila fixed dinner.

When he returned with it to the kitchen, Sheila looked up from stirring a pot of barley soup. "Well? What did you think?"

His jaw seemed to tighten as he said carefully, "It's not bad, honey. Really, it's not. Of course, it's not professional work. But, considering your background, it's really quite good."

Sheila swallowed. She had hoped for a more enthusiastic response, but she knew she had to respect Dan's appraisal. He was far more of a professional than she was.

"As a matter of fact," Dan continued, "I read recently about an annual short-story contest in *Redbook* magazine. Why don't we enter your story?"

Sheila's spirits soared. "Do you really think we should? I mean, do you think it's good enough?"

He smiled but didn't quite make eye contact. "As your husband, I'm not the most objective critic. But what the heck? Let's send it in and see what happens. If they like it, great. If not, at least you'll know where you stand."

The way Dan was focusing on her for a change made Sheila feel good. On her lunch break the next day, she picked up a copy of *Redbook* at a nearby drugstore and found a blank entry form for the short-story contest inside. When she returned to the office, she photocopied her story. That evening, while Dan was at class, she carefully completed the entry form and addressed an envelope to *Redbook*. She enclosed the manuscript, along with a self-addressed stamped envelope so she could be notified of their decision and receive a list of the top hundred finalists. Then she tucked her own photocopy between the pages of her high-school yearbook, right next to the picture of her accepting the Golden Quill writing award.

The next morning, as Dan was passing the kitchen table on his way to the door, he picked up the envelope addressed to *Redbook*. "Hon, do you want me to drop this in the mail for you? I'm going to the post office, anyway."

"That would be great, thanks. I want it to be on its way as soon as possible." Sheila gave him a grateful smile. "I'm going to be thinking positive thoughts all day."

Dan kissed her cheek. "That's fine, but don't get your hopes up too much, okay? If this doesn't work out, I don't want you to be disappointed."

"I know. I won't be."

Dan picked up the envelope and stuck it in his briefcase. "Okay, then. I'm off. I'll see you tonight."

Two weeks later, Mike Reynolds called Sheila into his office. "You've done a great job for us," he told her. "The place has never run so smoothly. You're young, but you've got a good head on your shoulders. I appreciate all your hard work, and I'd like to make you our office manager. The promotion will include a nice salary increase. I know you have aspirations of doing more with your life, but I want to keep you here at my company as long as I can."

For a moment, Sheila was speechless with shock. Then she stammered, "Uh…thanks, Mike. I…I like it here, and I appreciate working for you. Of course, a promotion would be wonderful."

"Great! I'll raise your salary two dollars an hour. Does that sound fair?"

Sheila was thrilled. An extra eighty dollars a week would go a long way toward her college fund. "That sounds very fair. Thanks again."

Sheila couldn't wait to share the good news with Dan. He was already at home when she burst through the door that evening. "Dan! Guess what. I got a promotion and a raise! Mike said I'm doing a great job and he wants to keep me and he's going to pay me two more dollars an hour. Can you believe it? I'm now the office manager. Isn't that wonderful?" She scarcely took a breath as she babbled with excitement.

Dan laughed. "Whoa, lady. Slow down a minute. What are you telling me?"

Sheila drew in a deep breath and then repeated her news, slowly and clearly.

"Congratulations," Dan said. "I'm proud of you. I know you work hard, and it's paying off. That's quite a feather in your cap."

Sheila nodded. "I feel good about it. Oh, I know it's not like a big important job, but, still, it's nice to know Mike appreciates what I do." She dropped her purse on the table and sat in one of the four wooden chairs around the table in their tiny kitchen. "Besides, it'll be nice to have a little extra money."

Then she spied, propped between the salt and pepper shakers, the self-addressed envelope she'd included with her manuscript submission to the *Redbook* contest. "Hey! What's this?" She quickly tore open the envelope.

"I didn't have a chance to tell you it came in today's mail," said Dan. After a slight pause, he asked, "What does it say?"

Sheila scanned the letter briefly, then dropped it on the table, her stomach twisting into a knot of despair. "I didn't even make the first cut. My story wasn't included in the top hundred finalists."

"I'm sorry," Dan said. "I was afraid something like this would happen. Remember how I told you not to get your hopes up?"

"I know. You were right. Still, I thought the story was good. I tried really hard, and I spent a lot of time on it. I can't believe it was so poor that it didn't even make the top hundred. I'm embarrassed I even entered the stupid contest. Maybe Daddy was right all along. I'm not college material, and because Mrs. Parks was fond of me, she was biased."

"Now, Sheila," Dan said, reaching down and patting her arm. "Don't let this be too big a disappointment. You should feel good about your promotion at work. College isn't for everyone, and neither is being a writer. You're my wife, and you're Reynolds's office manager, and you do a super job at both of those things. Remember, there's no shame in knowing your limitations in life."

Sheila scooted her chair away from the table, stood, and held her arms out. The thing she needed at that moment was to be held and comforted. Dan came to her rescue. She put her head on his shoulder as a few tears escaped. "I love you, Dan. What would I do without you?"

Dan soothingly rubbed her back. "Don't worry, my love. I'll always take care of things."

CHAPTER 9

When the sting of rejection subsided after her short story had failed to make even the first cut of the writing contest, Sheila pitched in with renewed enthusiasm at Reynolds Heating and Air-Conditioning. As the new office manager, she was given autonomy over many workplace functions and was responsible for supervising three employees. In spite of her naturally reserved nature, Sheila went out of her way to establish a good rapport with the three women who reported to her.

She concentrated the rest of her energies on her support role at home. After each full day at work, she handled all the household chores so that Dan could be free to study for his classes and make progress on his novel.

One evening, after they'd finished dinner, Dan studied as usual while Sheila cleaned up the kitchen and washed and dried the dishes. She had just hung the dish towel on a rack over the sink when Dan came back into the room.

"Could you do something for me?" He laid a textbook on the counter. "Colonial literature is a snore. Read the Jonathan Edwards sermon and that essay by Ben Franklin. Pick out some key phrases and type them up for me. Then I'll have something to say if I get called on. Meanwhile, I'd really like to log an hour or so on the novel."

"Sure," she said, picking up the book. "Anytime you want me to take a look at the novel or help you with revisions, I'd be glad to do that, too."

Dan frowned. "Sheila, while I appreciate your willingness to help, you must understand that doing a little research or typing up key phrases is very different from real writing. Let's just have you stick to what you're better equipped to do, okay?"

Hurt as much by his tone of superiority as by what he'd said, she simply nodded. She spent the rest of the evening on the couch, carefully going through Dan's reading assignment, while Dan worked on his novel at an older computer he'd bought secondhand from a colleague.

Following work the next day, Sheila accompanied Dan to the Bloomington campus. He dropped her off at the library to do some research for him while he went to his night class. After spending two hours looking through books and making notes, Sheila stood in the library foyer to wait for Dan. A notice on the bulletin board caught her eye. It read, "IU literary magazine seeks part-time editor. See Dr. Samuel Gold, office 206, English Building."

Sheila finished copying down the name and office number just as Dan pulled to the curb. She hurried to the car and, even before her seat belt was buckled, started telling Dan about the ad she'd seen. "It's for a part-time editor position with IU's literary magazine. Do you know Dr. Gold? He's the contact person. I thought you might be interested."

"Yeah, I've had Gold for a couple of classes," Dan replied. "Hmm. Editing that publication shouldn't be any great challenge. Besides, it might be a good way to get in tight with some of the faculty. I'll check it out tomorrow."

The idea that she might have done Dan a favor made Sheila glow. She stuck the paper with the scribbled information into Dan's shirt pocket and gave him a peck on the cheek. Then she settled back in her seat to hear all about Dan's class. He often told her about discussions that took place in his class. It made Sheila proud to hear how much more insightful Dan was than his peers. By his account, he won every classroom debate, hands down.

After breakfast the next morning, just as Sheila was about to walk out the door, Dan said, "I may get home late tonight. I'm going to see Dr. Gold about that part-time editor position. He may want me to begin right away."

Sheila was about to warn him not to count on anything, but she caught herself. "Okay. Good luck, hon. I'll see you tonight."

On the bus to work, Sheila said a little prayer that Dan might get the editing job. Although she knew her husband was smart and talented, a nagging thought kept darting through her mind about why this job prospect was so important. Sheila realized it wasn't so much because they needed the money. It was more because Dan needed the validation the job could bring. However, for reasons that were unclear to her, it seemed no one else could see Dan's strengths.

When Dan returned home that evening, at the usual hour, Sheila turned to greet him while drying her hands on a kitchen towel. "Hi, Dan. How was your day?"

Instead of responding, he dropped his briefcase by the door and slumped into a chair at the table.

After a moment, she asked, "Did you talk to Dr. Gold?"

His face reddened, and his mouth twisted. "Yeah. I never realized before what a complete idiot he is. I told him how I'd worked as both an editor and an adviser for the campus newspaper at Brissenden College and that I'm familiar with every aspect of putting a publication together. I explained that I've written features, sold ads, and have even done layout and design."

Sheila pulled out a chair and sat. "Wasn't he impressed?"

"He claimed that their literary magazine is quite different from a student newspaper—some nonsense about how it comes out quarterly and publishes only a small selection of the hundreds of submissions received. And how, since the university sponsors the magazine, there really isn't any need for outside advertising." He swallowed. "I assured him I just wanted him to know of my experience in the publishing field, and that, even though I understood we were talking about apples and oranges, I still felt certain I could do a good job as editor. I told him I was halfway through the master's program and intended to get my doctorate in creative writing."

Sheila took his right hand with both of hers. "You seemed like the prime candidate to me."

Clenching his jaw, Dan said, "Yeah, well, the catch is, I have to include samples of nationally published features or literary articles with my application." He pounded the table with his left fist.

"So, maybe right now, you should concentrate on writing those articles instead of working on your novel," Sheila gently suggested.

"No!" Dan bellowed. "You've got to understand, that's just what arrogant jerks like Gold would like to see me do. Once they attain their lofty positions, they enjoy manipulating others. I never should have taken your advice to talk to him in the first place."

Sheila drew back as if she'd been slapped. She felt terrible that her well-intentioned assistance had backfired. "I'm sorry, Dan. I really am. I was just so sure you'd be hired on the spot."

He calmed down a little. "Look, I realize you didn't know any better. Actually, on the way home tonight, this incident helped me come to an important decision. A few years ago, I read a great book called *Become Famous, Then Rich.* Thinking again about the principles it outlined helped me realize that I should forget about taking on another part-time job. Instead, I need to start churning out the pages of my novel. That'll be the ticket to the good life for both of us."

Still feeling guilty for causing Dan such frustration, Sheila was grateful for the silver lining he'd found. "Okay, hon. I'll keep taking care of things around here. You just concentrate on your novel."

After that, Sheila spent her evening hours fixing dinner, doing the dishes, and completing other household chores while Dan worked on his novel. However, as he neared the completion of his master's degree, he found it necessary to spend more of his time writing term papers and preparing for final exams.

One night several weeks before his graduation, Dan returned home in one of his dark moods that Sheila had come to dread. She quickly brought him a bottle of diet cola and set it on the table. "Rough day, hon?"

He eyed the soft drink. "Are we out of beer?"

She sighed, then went to retrieve a can from the fridge. In her opinion, Dan was turning to alcohol far too frequently these days. She remained firm in her refusal to buy it for him at the supermarket, but he merely brought home six-packs himself and then complained about her stubbornness when she refused to develop a taste for it. Being brought up by a father who didn't believe in drinking had left its mark on her.

Dan opened the beer, took a long swig, and set down the can with a thud. "I cannot *believe* the morons I have to deal with at that school."

Sheila frowned. "I'm so sorry. Was it one of your students? Or did you have another run-in with Dr. Gold?"

"Neither. The students weren't any worse than usual, and I'll never waste any more of my time with Gold. No, I went to see Parrett, my adviser, to ask about doctoral programs in creative writing. That's why I left the apartment so early this morning."

"I see," Sheila said carefully. "Did Dr. Parrett give you any helpful leads? Or did he mainly push IU—which, of course, is what he's expected to do?"

Dan snorted. "How he can call himself an *adviser,* I'll never know. His advice is worthless. At least he recognizes that I'm a good student who does a good job in the classroom. But, concerning my potential, that bozo is so dense, he doesn't realize I'm gifted at creative writing. 'It's not your strength,' he claims."

When Sheila heard the part about Dan being a good student, she was pleased that her hours of doing research and typing papers had contributed to Dan's academic success. But his comments about his adviser were unsettling.

"I even told him about the novel I'm writing," Dan added, "including how I've been working on it for three years and that a couple of agents are already interested in it."

Sheila gasped. "Really? You never told me about the agents. That's wonderful!"

Dan had started to raise the beer can to his mouth again but suddenly stopped in midair. He blinked. "I didn't? Well…I've been so busy with finals and everything, I probably forgot. Anyway, here's my point. That fool Parrett had the audacity to say he doesn't think a doctorate in creative writing is a realistic goal for me. Imbecile!" Dan's breaths came short and fast as he shook his fist. "You have no idea how much I wanted to give him a wake-up call this morning, right in the kisser."

Alarmed at Dan's agitation, Sheila stepped behind his chair and started to rub his shoulders. "No wonder you're upset. Will you launch a complaint against Dr. Parrett?"

"Nah. Wouldn't do any good. The best revenge I can think of will be signing my novel in the college bookstore while throngs of people wait for my autograph. I'm so positive that will happen, I can taste it."

Sheila gently moved her thumbs in little circles at the base of Dan's neck. "So, what's your next step?"

"I've decided the heck with that birdbrain Parrett. What has he ever written? He's a teacher, not an author. I can find out on my own what I need to know. In fact, I went to the library today before teaching my morning class and investigated several doctoral programs in creative writing. I found five of them at Midwest universities. When I've been accepted to a program in Michigan or Iowa, that'll show everyone."

During the following two weeks, Sheila helped Dan organize his materials and submit applications to all five of the programs he had researched. Although Dan didn't have the support of Dr. Parrett, he managed to find another professor who agreed to write a letter of recommendation for him. To satisfy the requirement of proof of his published work, Dan used a copy of a short story he had written. Sheila was surprised to read Dan's note including information about its publication. She didn't know the story had actually been published. That must have happened before they'd met, and he'd forgotten to tell her about it. But, not wanting to make his dark mood worse, she didn't press him for details.

After mailing the applications, Dan told Sheila they should prepare themselves to settle in for a long wait. Instead, within two weeks, he began receiving envelopes in the mail from the schools where he'd applied. Sheila knew better than to open correspondence addressed to Dan, but his scowls and general grumpiness after four envelopes came back told Sheila all she needed to know.

Dan's last hope rested on a small university in Wisconsin. He assured Sheila he was certain he would be accepted there. Four weeks after he mailed the applications, an envelope with a Wisconsin postmark was waiting in the mailbox. Sheila set it on the counter for Dan to see. When he got home, she busied herself in the kitchen so he wouldn't think she was watching.

With shaking hands, he tore open the envelope and unfolded the single sheet of paper enclosed. He scanned the page for several seconds before he threw the letter on the table and pounded it with his fist. Then he sat with his head in his hands for several minutes.

Sheila found herself almost afraid to breathe. She held very still at the sink, lest she make some noise that would upset Dan even more.

Finally, he let out a big groan. "It's so unfair! Why won't those academic know-nothings admit I'm gifted? I don't want to be just another part-time college 'instructor.' I deserve to be famous." He moaned again and leaned even farther forward in the chair. "I can't wait for the day when I'll show all the people who've ever sneered at me—or, worse, ignored me—how wrong they were."

Deeply touched by Dan's emotional agony, Sheila was at his side almost immediately. "I'm sorry—so sorry," she breathed into his ear. Then she bent and covered the back of his neck with little kisses. "You've worked so hard. You *do* deserve better treatment. One day, all those people who underestimated you will realize their mistake."

He responded by sitting up and pulling her into his lap.

As Sheila snuggled in his arms, she remembered the decision she'd made before they were married to be whatever Dan needed in his life. Now was certainly the time for her to comfort him in a way that no one else had the right to do. She nibbled on his earlobe. "Dinner's ready. Why don't you get washed up now? I have a great idea for dessert."

However, in spite of her best efforts in the following days, nothing Sheila did seemed to lift Dan from his depression. Yes, five Midwestern universities had turned him down. But what about schools in other parts of the country? She was willing to move with him wherever necessary in order to see his dream fulfilled. The trouble was, during the past two years, she'd learned that Dan's writing and career were matters of extreme sensitivity. She needed to weigh her words carefully whenever she brought up those subjects.

However, the Saturday one week before Dan's graduation, Sheila could contain herself no longer. She was fixing breakfast when Dan shuffled into the kitchen, still groggy from sleep.

"Good morning, hon," she said. "I hope you're hungry. I made pancakes."

Dan grunted a reply as he took his place at the table. Sheila poured him a cup of coffee, and once he was settled with all he needed to eat and drink, she took her seat across from him. She concentrated on making her question seem like a casual conversation. "By the way, have you thought about applying for a doctoral program for next year? You know how quickly the summer goes."

Dan stopped his fork halfway to his mouth. He hesitated only briefly before placing it back on his plate and looking Sheila directly in the eye. "I've been giving that a lot of thought," he said. "I've decided not to continue in school right now. I've just been offered a position as an adjunct instructor at IUPUI, the shared campus of Indiana University and Purdue, and I'm going to take it."

Sheila was stunned. Dan was giving up on pursuing his doctorate? Had she really heard right? "But, I thought…I mean, you always said…."

"We've both worked and scrimped and sacrificed the whole time we've been married. It's time for us to take a break and enjoy ourselves. Heck, we're still living in my college apartment. I know how much you want a home of your own. I've decided to put off my doctorate so that we can buy a house."

Sheila frowned. "But this…this isn't what we planned."

"So? Life doesn't always proceed according to plan. I like teaching, and I want to complete my novel. Your working full-time and my teaching part-time will be the perfect arrangement."

"But we don't have enough money saved for a down payment on a house."

"Of course we do, Sheila. We'll use the education fund. You're doing well at Reynolds, and you're secure there. There's no need for you to go to college. If you want, later on, you can pursue an education. But, for now, I want us to have a home. You know you'd love that, too."

Sheila's mind raced to process all the information being thrown at her. Of course, she would love a home of her own, but what about Dan's doctorate? Why was he letting himself be discouraged after only five schools had turned him down? She'd heard enough enthusiastic reports of his academic successes to know that he was more than qualified, even if he'd had the bad luck to get blackballed by a few arrogant people in academia. But the most important question of all was, if she and Dan spent her education fund on a house, would she ever get to attend college?

"I just don't know," Sheila finally said. "It's all so sudden. Can we really afford a home of our own? I've...we've worked so hard to save that money...."

Dan's face took on a crestfallen look. He stared at the pancakes growing cold on his plate. "So, you don't think I can make it as a teacher and a novelist, after all? I should have known you didn't really believe in me."

"Honey, that's not true. That's not what I mean at all. I do believe in you. I've always believed in you."

"It sure doesn't sound like it. You're afraid to invest in a home or to let me pursue my goal as a novelist. It sounds like you think I can't put you through school later. Whatever happened to your belief that the husband should be the head of the home? A supportive wife would trust that her husband knows what's best, and shouldn't question his decisions."

"I'm sorry. Again, that's not what I meant. I'm just shocked, that's all. I need some time to get used to the idea."

"Well, Sheila, I'm afraid you'll have to get used to the idea *now*," Dan said in a disapproving tone. "I've already accepted the teaching assignment, and I haven't applied to any more doctoral programs. I thought you'd be happy. Frankly, I considered it somewhat of a sacrifice on my part. I really thought you'd be thrilled to have a home of your own. I guess I don't know you as well as I thought I did. Are you saying you're not interested in being a professor's wife?"

"No, of course I'm not saying that!" Sheila sighed. "I'm merely trying to make sense out of this sudden change in plans. I'm just a little confused, that's all."

"Look," said Dan sternly. "I've explained it very clearly. I've decided against pursuing my doctorate right now. I want us to establish a home of our own. I think it's time. It's not as if you need to further your education just to work as an office manager. What part of that is difficult for you to understand? Do you think you know better than I do what's right for us?"

Dan's irritation had Sheila so flustered, she couldn't think of a reasonable response. It took her back to the many times in her childhood when she'd felt the same way after her father had confronted her about something. "No, hon, that's not what I think. Of course, you know what's best. I *will* be happy to have a house. It was just such a surprise, I didn't quite know how to take it."

"Do you mean it, Sheila? I don't want you to be second-guessing this decision after the fact."

She stifled a sigh. "I mean it. I want to support you in any way I can. You're my husband, and I love you."

"Great," said Dan. "I've made an appointment with a real-estate agent for us to look at houses later this afternoon."

In July, two months after Dan's graduation, they moved into a two-bedroom brick ranch in Brissenden. Sheila continued her full-time work at Reynolds Heating and Air-Conditioning, and Dan reveled in his new identity as an "Indiana University Professor." His academic schedule of teaching two basic writing courses allowed him ample free time to work on his novel. He joined a writers group and talked to Sheila each evening about the friendships he was developing with his colleagues.

Sheila yearned to go with him to the writers group, and she dropped fairly obvious hints about her desire, but Dan never mentioned the possibility of her accompanying him to a meeting. However, when he came home after each session, he made sure to recount the high points of the discussion and to tell Sheila how much everyone loved his work. He also continued to rebuff her occasional requests to take a look at his novel.

Sheila tried to maintain her enthusiasm about Dan's writing, but her confidence in him was beginning to erode. Having to deplete her education fund to buy them a house was still a sore subject, as Dan's promise that she could go to college had been a big reason she'd been willing to marry him so quickly. And even though her rejection letter from *Redbook* magazine had convinced her to stop writing, she'd never totally given up on her dream of earning a college education.

Dan's increasingly strange behavior was making her wonder if he was really her knight in shining armor, after all. Back when Liz-Liz had mentioned the insecurities she'd observed in Dan, Sheila had considered her roommate totally off base. But now, after noticing cracks in his carefully constructed veneer of confidence, Sheila found the assessment much easier to swallow. The thought even occurred to her that maybe Dan was so desperate to prove himself to the world, he hoped that by surrounding himself with talented people, he would maximize his chances for success. Maybe he thought that the talent—or at least the prestige—would rub off on him.

In spite of her growing doubts, Sheila decided she had little choice but to continue helping her husband in every way she could. After all, when she'd vowed "till death do us part" in front of the judge, she'd meant it.

In November, four months after the move into their house, Dan came home from work unusually excited. "Guess what? We're invited to an open house for Tim Malone."

Sheila frowned. "Tim Malone? Do I know him?"

"No, of course you don't know him. He's a colleague of mine. But you're still invited, by virtue of the fact that you're married to a university professor who works in the same department."

"Is it his birthday?" Sheila asked.

Dan rolled his eyes. "No. For heaven's sake, no one would do anything that hokey. He's just published a book. This party is an invitation-only event—held at a country club, no less—to celebrate with him and to help promote the book."

"Sounds lovely. When is it?"

"Two weeks from Saturday. Make sure to buy something new to wear—something really sophisticated."

Sheila laughed. "I wonder how many wives have husbands who tell them to go shopping. What's wrong with this picture?"

"I'm not kidding around, Sheila. This is important to me. Tim and I are good friends, and this party will give me a chance to talk to him about getting my novel published. His agent will probably be there. Maybe even his editor. This could be a big break for me. I want everything to go perfectly."

"Do you really think you might meet an editor there? How exciting!"

"It's possible. Since Tim and I are close, I'm sure he'll introduce me around. It should be a good chance to network with some bigwigs."

"Okay," Sheila told him. "Tomorrow after work, I'll start looking for a dress. That way, I'll have plenty of time to exchange it if you don't like it. This is going to be fun, isn't it? We haven't been to a party in ages. I can hardly wait."

When the night of the big event finally arrived, Dan paced nervously from room to room, stopping every few moments to scrutinize his appearance in the mirror at the end of the hall. To Sheila, he looked almost as though he were going to a costume ball dressed as The Writer. He wore every clothing cliché in the book—a turtleneck sweater, a corduroy jacket with leather patches on the elbows, and a pipe hanging out of the upper pocket of his coat, even though he didn't smoke. He'd replaced his contact lenses with a set of horn-rimmed glasses, and he hadn't bothered going for a haircut. He looked very Bohemian.

Sheila came into the living room just as Dan started to make another lap around the house. On her feet were strappy black heels. The hem of her long-sleeved black velvet dress hung just above her knees. She'd showed him the dress after bringing it home from the store, and he'd approved of the purchase, but this was the first time he'd seen it on her.

She noticed his gaze moving from the bejeweled clip holding most of her hair up in a flirty cluster, to the tendrils cascading down her neck on the sides and back, to the scoop neckline that highlighted Sheila's slender shoulders, to the side slit showing a discreet flash of thigh.

As Sheila did a slow full turn in front of Dan, he whistled his approval. "Honey, if this party wasn't so important to me, I'd take you right here and now, and we'd forget all about leaving the house."

"Why, thank you, sir," Sheila replied with a shy smile.

"Yes, siree, I'm looking forward to getting back to our own bedroom after the party." He encircled Sheila's waist with his arm and drew her closer to him.

"Now, don't mess me up," Sheila scolded him gently. "I've worked hard on this look. We'd better go before anything starts to get undone."

Instead of letting go, Dan moved his hand to the back of her head, pressed her face to his, and kissed her hard. Then he let her go. "I can kiss you whenever I want," he said. "You're my wife, remember?"

"Dan! Now I have to redo my lipstick."

He pulled a tissue from a box nearby and wiped his mouth. "It was too dark, anyway. Use a lighter shade this time. Meanwhile, I'll get your coat. We don't want to be late."

On their way to the prestigious country club in Indianapolis where Tim Malone was a member, Sheila decided that Dan's excitement had made him overreact to an innocent comment that must have sounded like an order from his wife. This would be a long evening if she didn't find some way to help him lighten up. She began chattering nonstop about the good time they would have and the beautiful neighborhoods they were passing through.

Soon they reached the club and pulled under the portico. The young valet took their car, but Sheila noticed his sneer before he drove off.

Dan must have seen it, too. "One of these days, we need to upgrade from this rusty bucket of bolts," he murmured.

Sheila stiffened. She couldn't bear to think how Dan might sabotage his chances at this party with his foul mood. It was up to her to get his mind off his troubles. When Dan took her arm for the short walk to the door, she snuggled against him and whispered, "This is really going to be fancy, isn't it?"

That comment seemed to help him return to a happier frame of mind. "Better get used to it, honey. If everything goes well tonight, we'll be throwing a party like this for me in no time."

Sheila giggled at the idea that they might host such an affair, since she and Dan so seldom socialized. "It almost seems as if the evening is happening to someone else, doesn't it?" she said as they entered the doorway.

They checked Sheila's coat before stepping into the room, at which point one of the servers mingling in the crowd came by with a tray of champagne flutes. Dan took two glasses and handed one to Sheila.

She eyed it warily.

"Here!" Dan hissed. "Don't make me look unsociable."

She acquiesced to his demand, but after taking one small sip to satisfy him, she merely carried the glass around to look the part. Maybe she *was* stubborn, but she would rather reserve her calorie consumption for food and beverages she actually enjoyed. And, given Dan's all-night access to complimentary champagne, she knew she might just have to be the designated driver when they left.

Although Dan spoke to several people as they maneuvered their way across the room, only one or two responded to him. How puzzling! It almost seemed as if most of the guests didn't recognize him. Sheila wondered how that could be.

Dan led Sheila to a spread of elegant canapés, where they proceeded to fill their plates before locating an empty table. Sheila sampled the smoked salmon first. "Oh, my goodness. I didn't think I liked seafood, but this is absolutely delicious."

Dan dipped a second steamed shrimp into a dollop of cocktail sauce and popped it into his mouth. "Incredible."

While they continued to enjoy their feast, Dan filled Sheila in on all the major players present. She had often heard him speak about his colleagues, but this was the first chance she'd had to meet any of them.

Suddenly, Dan stood as a man passed by their table. "Ken, I'd like you to meet my wife. Sheila, this is Ken Cummings. He's a professor at IU–Bloomington."

The man stopped and stood awkwardly before extending his hand to Sheila. "It's a pleasure to meet you, Mrs.…I'm sorry, but I don't recall your last name."

"Gray," Sheila answered softly. "Dan and Sheila Gray."

"Very nice to make your acquaintance," Ken said. "Well, I'm afraid I've got to dash. My wife's waiting for me." He darted off into the crowd.

Dan seemed unfazed by the exchange, but Sheila was quite taken aback. During Dan's graduate assistantship, he had talked to her on several occasions about his friendship with Ken Cummings, yet the man had hardly seemed to recognize him. Sheila stared at Dan for a long time, but apparently he was too busy scanning the room to notice.

After finishing his second glass of champagne, Dan suddenly took Sheila's hand. "There's Tim. Let's go. I want to introduce you to him."

They weaved through the crowd into the next room, where a man held court in the middle of a circle of people listening with rapt attention to his banter.

As Dan led her closer, Sheila held back a bit. "Let's wait awhile," she whispered. "He seems preoccupied now. Maybe we shouldn't interrupt."

"Don't be silly," Dan told her. "Tim won't care. We're friends. He'll be glad to see me."

Still steering Sheila by the elbow, Dan approached the edge of the circle around Tim and gently eased into the middle. "Excuse me, Tim. I'd like you to meet my wife. Sheila, this is the man of the hour, Tim Malone."

Tim stopped mid-sentence. Sheila noticed a hint of irritation cross his face. She smiled sweetly and extended her hand. "How do you do, Mr. Malone?"

"Very well, Sheila," answered Tim, taking her hand and raising it to his lips. "My, what a beautiful wife you have, Gray. What on earth does she see in you?"

Everyone laughed, even Dan, but Sheila was not amused. She started to pull her hand away, but Tim held on to it. "You're absolutely lovely. But where is your drink?" He gestured subtly, and a server instantly appeared.

"Oh, I'm fine, thank you," Sheila responded, wishing she hadn't left her glass on a table in the corner. "I've already, uh, had some champagne."

"But I insist," he said, taking a flute from the tray in the server's hands. "It's my party, and I want you to have a marvelous time."

"Oh, we are," Sheila assured him. "Aren't we, darling?" She turned toward Dan, wanting to include him in the conversation.

"I didn't say a word to him, now, did I?" Tim asked. "You're the one I'm interested in."

Dan chuckled along with the others as he stepped closer to his wife. "It's a great party, Tim. I've been meaning to call you and arrange to meet for lunch. I'm about two-thirds of the way though my novel, and I thought maybe you could put me in touch with your people."

Sheila felt her face flush at Dan's abrupt entrée to the subject of his novel. She hoped Tim would be kind to him.

"Put you in touch with my people?" Tim asked in an exasperated tone. "Now, there's an amusing thought. You've missed your calling, unless your book is a comedy."

Feeling terribly embarrassed for her husband, for whom it was obvious Tim Malone had no respect, Sheila took Dan by the arm and started to move to the edge of the circle.

"Oh, don't *you* go, pretty lady," Tim insisted. "Get rid of him and come back, won't you?"

Sheila walked on. "Of all the nerve!" she murmured to Dan. What do you see in *him*?" She felt her blush deepen and could hardly bear to look at her husband. When she finally did, she was amazed to see that he was smiling.

"That Tim's a real card, isn't he?" Dan shook his head. "What a kidder."

"I didn't find him the least bit funny. He was arrogant and rude."

"Oh, Sheila, you read him all wrong. We're friends. He was just kidding around in front of the crowd. Besides, he's too busy to talk tonight. We'll have lunch sometime next week."

"Busy or not, he had no right to talk to you that way. He's a jerk."

"To tell you the truth, he's probably a little jealous of me," Dan said. "You know, lots of people would love to have my position at IUPUI. Don't worry. He'll get over it. I'll buy him lunch, and everything will be just fine. Just don't let him see you angry like this, or it will spoil what I've got going."

Once they were back at their table, Sheila mulled over the events of the evening. Things just didn't add up. According to Dan, many of these people were his closest friends, yet not one person had approached them with a greeting or had asked to share their table. It was as if no one even noticed them, despite the fact that Dan was practically jumping out of his chair to greet people as they passed. The few who did stop clearly weren't interested in having a conversation.

Sheila had another momentary flashback to Liz-Liz's assessment of Dan. *"He's just a wannabe, Sheila. He's trying to convince you he's somebody special, because, if he can make you believe it, it might actually come true."*

Sheila rubbed her forehead to dispel the memory. Even so, she couldn't stop wondering whether Liz-Liz had struck a chord of truth regarding his talent as a writer. He'd been telling her for years that he was gifted, and Sheila had sacrificed all her dreams to enable him to pursue his quest. She couldn't bear to think that her investment in him had been misguided. Yet it occurred to her now that she had never heard another person praise Dan's abilities. Not even one. Everything she knew about Dan was based on what he'd told her himself.

As Dan stood and motioned a server over for another glass of champagne, Sheila set her shoulders resolutely. She knew it didn't really matter what the truth was. She'd committed herself to Dan, and she'd long since bypassed any other option. Good, bad, or indifferent, she was Dan Gray's wife. His success—or his lack thereof—was as close as she was going to get to a writing career.

CHAPTER 10

"And that, Mrs. Parks—Laureen—is what I've been doing with my life for the past fifteen years," Sheila said at the end of her two-hour reminiscence. "Turns out I only thought I was destined to be a writer. I'm sure I've been quite the disappointment to you."

"Yes, you have," Laureen affirmed. "But, far worse, you've been a great disappointment to yourself. I've got only a few months left to live, so I don't have time to sugarcoat anything I say. Can you handle straight talk from someone who truly cares about you?"

Sheila stared into her empty coffee mug. Almost like a fourth grader being upbraided by her teacher, she nodded.

"It's pretty easy to see what's going on here," Laureen began. "You grew up in a patriarchal home where Bible verses were taken out of context and used to reinforce male control over your life. With no mother or sisters to give you any other perspective, you lived a life in which men—your father and your two older brothers—made the majority of decisions in the family. Naturally, you assumed that was the way it worked in all families. Going to college was supposed to be your chance to break free from that environment and discover healthier ways of living, but Dan came on the scene and kept the same pattern rolling for you. He was older, male, and domineering, and he convinced you he was looking out for your best interests. So, you allowed him to start making decisions for you...and your life."

Laureen shook her head in disgust. "I blame myself. I should have kept closer ties with you, been there to advise you and encourage you. The only reason you were able to convince your father to let you go to college in the first place was because I kept pushing you. You needed an older female influence in your life."

"You had your own obligations in Texas," Sheila said softly, still keeping her eyes averted. "I know that's why I never heard from you."

"What? You never heard from me? I wrote to you several times. After getting no answer from *you* all summer, I planned to call your home to see what was up, but then I got my initial cancer diagnosis and went into that chemo brain fog so common among cancer patients." Laureen shook her head. "Still, I should have done more."

"I had no idea you'd been fighting cancer for fifteen years!" said Sheila with a gasp, forgetting she was going to reiterate that she'd never received any letters.

"Not exactly. There was a long period of remission in between. But that's neither here nor there. We need to keep focused on today. The question is, what can we do to salvage this situation before I run out of time…or before *you do?*"

Sheila frowned. "I'm afraid I don't follow you."

"That manuscript you submitted to the *Redbook* contest—you kept a copy of it, did you?"

"Well…yes. As I mentioned, I stuck it inside my high-school yearbook along with the rejection letter."

"Could you dig it out?" Laureen asked. "I want to see it."

"What? Right now?"

"Yes." Laureen nodded. "I'd like to take it home with me to read. I want to get a sense of the level of your skills when you stopped writing. If, for all these years, I've had an exaggerated impression of your talent as a writer, then I'll drop this whole matter. But if I feel that my original gut instincts were right, then you and I are going to need to talk further."

"About what?"

"About how we can make up for fifteen years of lost time, that's what! If you had stayed on the track you set for yourself back then, by now you'd be a college graduate and a successful author. Who knows? Maybe you would have finished a graduate degree, too."

"But I couldn't swing it financially," Sheila pointed out. "By the time I looked into scholarships, it was too late to apply for the fall semester, and Daddy refused to give me a penny toward college. When Dan promised I could go to school after we married and I had worked a little while, I thought that was the solution."

"There were other ways." Laureen shook her head again. "I could kick myself for not following up on your progress."

"Well, it doesn't matter now," Sheila said. "It turned out I just wasn't meant to be a writer."

"Nonsense!" Laureen snapped. "Find me that manuscript!"

Obediently, Sheila rose from her chair. Laureen followed her into the front hallway. Sheila opened the door of a storage closet and began pushing boxes from side to side. "I haven't looked through this stuff in ages," she said.

A few minutes later, she located the box marked "Brissenden High." Murmuring "Let me see here," she lifted the cardboard flaps and rummaged through concert programs, faded pictures, autograph books, and even a crumbling, dried-out corsage. The yearbook was at the bottom. "Okay, here it is. *The Argonaut* from my senior year."

"Is the story inside?" asked Laureen.

Sheila flipped to the middle of the book. "Yes. And here's the self-addressed stamped envelope I included with my original manuscript. It came back to me with just the rejection note from *Redbook,* so I put my photocopy of the story inside and hid it away in here."

"Wait a second." Laureen reached out her hand. "Let me have that book, please." She studied the spread where the envelope had been tucked. "Why did you decide to put your rejected manuscript on the page featuring a picture of you receiving the Golden Quill award?"

Sheila shrugged slightly. "I don't know. I guess it was kind of a two-edged sword. If I ever looked at the manuscript and its rejection slip, then I would also see the photo and be reminded that, at least once in my life, I *had been* an award-winning writer. But, on the other hand, if I ever looked at the photo and started thinking of myself as a real writer, the rejected manuscript would remind me that I'd given it a shot and hadn't been good enough to make it."

Laureen put the envelope into her purse. "We'll see about that. But, for now, I need to get going. I don't want to infringe on your birthday any more than I have already. And besides, I have some errands to run."

That reminded Sheila of Dan's to-do list. "Actually, I still have errands of my own to run," she said, handing Laureen her coat. "But believe me when I say that don't know when I've had a better birthday. I feel as though I've unburdened my soul to someone I can really trust. You helped me melt the years away."

"I'll call you for tea in a few days." Laureen smiled as she put on her coat. "You're still my favorite student, you know. Happy birthday, dear."

Sheila hugged her. "If there's anything I can do while you're—"

"Thank you, but just now, I'm holding my own. I'll keep your offer in mind, however." She opened the door. "As I said, I'll call you in a couple of days. I can find your office number in the phone book."

Laureen made her way to the car, and for the second time that day, Sheila slowly closed the front door and had a good cry.

Dan came home that night with two jumbo cinnamon-apple muffins and a variety pack of flavored coffee pods. "A tasty dessert for the birthday girl," he announced, as though he were presenting Sheila with a mink coat or the keys to a new Corvette.

She accepted the small gifts with a smile. At least he hadn't forgotten, like he did the previous year. However, during dinner, Dan kept his electronic tablet on the table and checked various social-media sites while eating, just as though that evening were no different from any other.

"You'll never guess who I ran into today," Sheila said.

"Hmmm?" Dan responded, his eyes still on the small screen.

"Mrs. Parks."

Dan looked up. "Am I supposed to know who that is?"

Sheila frowned. "You remember—she was my high-school English teacher, the one who got me the scholarship to Brissenden College the summer we met. Come on, you've heard me speak of her a million times."

"Oh, *her*," said Dan, turning back to the tablet. "I thought she'd moved to Arizona."

"Texas," Sheila corrected him. "She's back here now, though. To stay. I ran into her at the dry cleaner's."

"You picked up my jacket?"

"Yes, yes, but that's not what I wanted to tell you. Mrs. Parks told me two really startling things today."

"That's nice," he said, without looking up.

"First, she told me that she has some form of cancer and has been given between four and six months to live." Sheila slowed her words. "It's still hard to believe. But she's so strong-willed, she won't accept any pity."

"Mm-hmm."

"Her husband died some time ago, so she came back to Brissenden to be closer to her friends and relatives during her last months. She was even able to buy back her old house."

"That's nice."

"But the other thing she told me was just as startling," Sheila continued, her enthusiasm returning. "She said that in all her years of teaching, I was the best writing student she ever had. It was her dream that I would one day become a successful author. In fact, she thinks I should consider taking up writing again."

This caught Dan's attention. His head jerked up. "She said *what?*"

"That I should consider trying my hand at writing again," Sheila repeated. "I mean, it's not like I could write the great American novel or anything, but...well, perhaps as a hobby or something. Who knows? Maybe I could try entering another contest."

Dan scowled. "Sheila, I believe you tried that route once, remember?" he said, assuming his lecturer's tone of voice. "Why would you want to reopen old wounds?"

"Because I've missed writing," she said, surprising even herself with the quickness of her response. "And because I don't have anything special in my life."

"Then take up cross-stitching or do some volunteer work for the local homeless shelter," Dan suggested. "Writing just isn't for you, honey. Look at all the years I've been working on my novel, and it still isn't ready. I've got a master's degree in English. You've only got a high-school diploma."

"I'm not saying I'm in your league," she responded, lifting her chin slightly. "I'd be content just having a little fun expressing myself. Maybe I could write some children's stories or a romance."

Dan reached over and covered her hand with his. "No, Sheila," he said sternly. "I don't want you doing this. It will only lead to frustration and failure, like last time. Find something else, but leave the writing alone." He stared at her, without blinking, as if to imply that she had better not disobey him.

She was going to say more, but he squeezed her hand in a painful grip and didn't let go. "Listen to me. *Leave the writing alone!*"

Sheila could almost hear Laureen again, voicing her analysis of Dan: *"He was older, and male, and domineering, and he convinced you he was looking out for your best interests. So, you allowed him to start making decisions for you…and your life."*

Laureen had nailed it. However, after spending two hours unburdening her soul to her former teacher, Sheila had realized that, way down deep, she still had some of the spunk she'd used when trying to convince her father to let her attend the summer writing program. She wasn't going to let that spunk be buried again. Still, she needed to be careful not to tip her hand.

She smiled innocently at Dan. "Well, it was just a thought. Let me brew a couple of those special coffees you brought home, and we'll have the muffins."

Clearly pleased at her compliance, Dan finally released her hand, smiled back, and nodded.

When Sheila arrived at work the next morning, she checked her voice-mail messages, as usual. Five calls were from the previous day, when she'd taken off to celebrate her birthday. The sixth call, however, was from Laureen Parks. According to the automated time stamp, it had come in at 6:30 that morning.

"Sheila, I need to see you as soon as possible," Laureen's message began. "I know that I said I'd call in a few days, but this can't wait. It's urgent. If at all possible, please come out to my home during your lunch hour. I'll have sandwiches and tea ready when you get here. I promise you won't be late getting back to the office."

Sheila's interest was piqued. What could be so urgent? And why did it require being discussed in person at Laureen's house rather than over the phone? Sheila thought about calling back, but she decided it would be nice to have lunch with Laureen, no matter the reason.

The morning passed quickly as Sheila got caught up on various tasks. At noon, she told her coworkers she'd be back at one o'clock, then headed off to see her friend. Nothing in the small town took long to travel to by car. In less than ten minutes, she was standing on Laureen's front porch.

The door opened on the first knock. "Come in, come in," Laureen said. "I'm so glad you could make it."

When Sheila entered, she was enveloped by the gentle scent of lilac perfume. "You sounded so secretive on the phone. What's up?"

"Follow me," Laureen said, leading the way to a formal dining room. "Please, sit down. I hope you're not a vegetarian. I made ham-and-cheese sandwiches. Help yourself to the tea." She nodded at a teapot in the middle of the table.

Sheila could see her manila envelope, her manuscript, and the rejection letter from *Redbook* lying at the other end of the table. She took a seat, filled her cup with tea, and mixed in some sugar.

"Here," Laureen said, returning with a tray. "Please have a sandwich. I don't want you hearing what I have to say on an empty stomach."

As mystified as ever, Sheila accepted a sandwich and took a bite. Nestled between toasted slabs of French bread spread with tangy Dijon mustard were thin slices of deli ham and melted Gruyère cheese. "This is wonderful!" she said. "I'd love to have the recipe." She started to take a second bite, then stopped long enough to ask, "What's this all about?"

Laureen, who had started to eat her own sandwich, chewed methodically for a moment, then swallowed before saying, "There's something rotten in the state of Denmark. I've been playing amateur detective since last seeing you, and the clues all point to one conclusion: We wuz robbed!"

Sheila didn't know whether to laugh at the woman's dramatics or to take Laureen seriously. "Okay," she said, playing along, "how wuz we robbed?"

Laureen held up the manuscript. "As soon as I got home yesterday, I read your story. I honestly didn't know what to expect. I tried to put my mind back to when you were still a teenager and to read the story in a way that would give you the benefit of youth and inexperience. But you didn't need anyone to 'spot' you any points on this one, young lady. The story is superb. I was laughing hysterically by page five and crying like a baby at the end."

Sheila stopped chewing. With her mouth still half full, she said, "You're kidding. I mean, it was just a simple retelling of the Cinderella story."

"Exactly," said Laureen. "But the way you substituted your two older brothers—always teasing you—for the ugly stepsisters, and your cranky old farmer father for the evil stepmother, was hilarious. The Hoosier dialect was right on the money. And at the end, when neighbor Charlie Prince came driving up in a tractor to whisk her off to her farm, despite the corniness, it really grabbed my heart. It's a comedy, a parody, a romance, and a social commentary all rolled into one. I loved it!"

Sheila wasn't quite sure what to say. "You really think it's good?"

"Good? It's fantastic!"

"But I didn't even qualify as a finalist in the contest," Sheila reminded her. "It was rejected in the first round. Maybe your opinion has more to do with our relationship—"

"Our personal relationship has nothing to do with my opinion of this story," Laureen interjected. "I may not be able to *write* stories, but I certainly know how to *evaluate* them. This manuscript is wonderful."

"Are you saying you think the judges at *Redbook* didn't give my story a fair evaluation?"

Laureen's face clouded. "Your rejection had nothing to do with the judges and their evaluation."

Sheila was confused. "You've lost me," she said. "If the judges didn't act unfairly, how was I robbed?"

"I don't believe the judges ever saw this manuscript."

Sheila blinked. "What are you talking about?"

Laureen picked up the stack of pages next to her and handed it to Sheila. "Excuse the Perry Mason flourish, but let me display the evidence," she said. "To begin with, we have a first-rate manuscript that, at the very least, should have made it into the finals." Then she lifted the letter from the table. "Second, we have a rejection letter that isn't printed on *Redbook* letterhead. Instead, we have just a couple of paragraphs typed on plain copy paper, the kind found in any office-supply store. A genuine letter from *Redbook* would have had a logo at the top, a side masthead with an editorial board listed, and probably a watermark from a paper manufacturer in either Boston or New York."

Picking up the envelope, she continued, "Third, the envelope has a postmark from Nyack, New York. That's nowhere near *Redbook*'s Manhattan offices. Oh, sure, this envelope was mailed from New York *State*, but not from the Big Apple itself.

"Finally," she said, "there's the matter of the missing original manuscript. That bothered me right from the moment you told me about it. It didn't gibe with the times. Back when freelance writers used typewriters to create their manuscripts, they would enclose SASEs—self-addressed stamped envelopes—with their manuscript submissions. That way, if an editor rejected a manuscript, the author could get it back and send it elsewhere without having to retype it. Today, of course, with e-mail and online submission forms, pretty much all communication takes place over the Internet."

Laureen slid the letter and the envelope across the table to Sheila. "When you entered this contest, you sent a printed copy, as requested. But it wasn't returned to you in this envelope. And besides all that, another reason you provided the SASE was so you could receive a list of prize winners. You didn't get that, either, did you?"

Sheila was stunned. "Come to think of it, you're exactly right."

"I thought so. Now, I need to ask you something point-blank. Did Dan know you had kept a photocopy of this story?"

"No," Sheila said. "I just put it away without ever telling him about it."

Laureen took a sip of her tea before continuing. "You aren't going to want to hear this next part, but here it is: I believe that your husband destroyed your original manuscript, typed a fake rejection slip, and somehow managed to get it mailed from New York State. He assumed that since you were such a novice at freelance writing, you'd never question the legitimacy of the rejection letter. Unfortunately, he was right. And, to my shame, I wasn't there to tell you otherwise."

"Now, wait," Sheila protested. "I admit that Dan has his faults. But why would he do such a horrible thing?"

"Jealousy is a green-eyed monster, Sheila. Look at the facts: Dan knew of your talent as far back as that summer you attended the college writing program. At first, he encouraged you. But then, I suspect, he recognized talent in you that was beyond his own. His ego couldn't handle it. And so, to protect his fragile sense of self-esteem, he prevented you from going to college, convinced you that you'd been eliminated from the short-story contest, and kept you working at a dead-end job, all to make you think you had no special talents of any kind."

"But his own career has gone far beyond anything I could have hoped to accomplish myself," Sheila argued.

"Not really," Laureen said bluntly. "He's got a couple of degree certificates hanging on the wall...but then, so do thousands of other English teachers. Was he accepted into any of the doctoral programs to which he applied to work toward a PhD in writing? No! Has he ever had a book published? No! Has he ever been invited to speak as a guest lecturer on the college circuit or been interviewed on television or been featured in a major magazine or a national newspaper? No, no, no! He calls himself a writer, but the fact is, he's never written anything of importance in his entire life."

"But he's an English professor at Indiana University," Sheila insisted. "People respect him."

Laureen laughed. "Don't kid yourself," she said. "He moonlights as a freshman composition teacher at one of IU's satellite campuses. He's an adjunct instructor with no rank or status. There are scads of high-school English teachers with master's degrees who pick up a little extra money doing that. The real professors are full-time faculty members with rank and tenure and private offices and big salaries and benefits packages. Sure, Dan likes to drive up to IUPUI and play big-time professor, but, trust me, he's a minnow amid whales."

Sheila put her hand to her head as she tried to clear her thoughts. Then she picked up the papers in front of her, looking at them as though she'd never seen them before. Could her former teacher's suspicions be true?

"I can understand your not wanting to believe that your husband intentionally sabotaged your writing career," said Laureen, softening her voice, "but the facts speak for themselves. For fifteen years, your life has been on hold because your husband wanted to keep you at his beck and call, living in his shadow."

Sheila took a deep breath and then blew it out slowly. Finally, she said, "I think I need to ask Dan about this. He deserves a chance to tell his side. Everything you've said today is speculation. I mean, it's not that I don't think you have my best interests at heart, but this is all just so...."

Laureen raised both hands defensively. "I anticipated you would react that way. Dan has you trained well. You never make a move without clearing it with him. Well, this is one time when you are going to have to make a decision on your own. I suggest we run a test."

"What kind of a test?"

"I'd like you to let me edit this short story of yours. It's very good, but it could stand to be updated a little. I'd then like you to type it into your computer at work—unless you have a computer at home that your husband can't get on?"

Sheila shook her head.

"I didn't think so. Then, we'll send it to a couple of national magazines. If it's as good as I think it is, some editor will want to publish it. Should that happen, then maybe you'll believe that you have talent as a writer. However, if it comes back rejected from, say, three different publications, then we'll throw in the towel."

"Oh, no," Sheila murmured. "Dan would be furious if I was published, and he found out I'd been writing on the sly."

"No doubt," Laureen agreed. "That's why you'll write under a pen name and use my home as your mailing address."

"But what pen name would I use?"

"Do you like the sound of Dove Alexander?"

Sheila smiled. "How did you come up with that?"

"Dove is for the way you are going to fly high once your writing career takes off," Laureen explained. "And Alexander is because you, too, are going to conquer the world—the world of publishing."

Sheila was torn between her fear of angering Dan by directly disobeying his orders and her excitement about submitting her manuscript for possible publication. "You're absolutely sure no one would find out?" she asked.

"Lots of writers use pen names," Laureen insisted. "It's a common practice. And with your mail coming here, no one will ever know about it."

Sheila checked her watch. She had to make a decision and then get back to work. She closed her eyes, took another deep breath, and then, without stopping to think any more about the consequences, blurted out, "Okay, then. I'm game. When should I come back for the edited manuscript?"

Laureen beamed. "I'll have it ready tomorrow. Let's plan on lunch again. And, trust me, this is the right thing for you to do. You need to find out, one way or another, if writing truly is your destiny. I wouldn't put you through this if I wasn't absolutely sure you had an excellent chance of being successful. I need this as much as you do, Sheila. I can feel it in my bones that this is going to work out."

"Let's just make sure my husband doesn't discover what we're up to. Please!" Sheila pleaded.

Back at the office, urgent business kept Sheila so preoccupied all afternoon, she didn't have time to reconsider her decision to submit her manuscript. However, once the day ended and she was driving home, the whole conversation with Laureen over lunch came rushing back. By the time she arrived at her house and walked in the back door, she had replayed all her former teacher's words in her mind several times.

How fortunate that this was one of the two evenings a week when Dan drove to Indianapolis to teach a class at IUPUI. Sheila didn't want to run the risk of his sensing that something was up and badgering her to find out what it was.

She dished up a plate of leftover tuna casserole with a side of snow peas and put it in the microwave. While the food was heating, she went out to the mailbox. No matter how late Dan got in on his teaching nights, he expected his correspondence to be waiting on his desk for him to look through.

"And just like a faithful old dog, I do the fetching for him," Sheila said aloud. She could tell that as a result of her reconnecting with Laureen, she was now reexamining every aspect of her life with Dan. For fifteen years, she had put up with the way he walked over her, making her think she should be grateful to be married to such a highly educated and well-respected man. *Well, it would seem that the big man has feet of clay,* she mused.

The microwave was beeping when she walked back inside. She carried Dan's mail to his office and then paused. Normally, she would simply put the mail on his desk and leave. He didn't like anything in his office to be disturbed in any way. Tonight, however, it suddenly occurred to Sheila that Dan wouldn't be home for another four hours. Another *four full hours.*

She decided to be daring. She hurried to the kitchen and opened the microwave door to halt the periodic beeping. Then, abandoning the plate where it was, she returned to Dan's office. The computer's screen had come to life. She sat in the leather chair and scrolled through various folders on the digital desktop. At first, all she found were personal correspondence files, financial records, student term papers that still needed to be read and graded electronically, and memos and notes about events at school. She had no interest in any of those items. She was in pursuit of bigger game.

Finally, she found a folder labeled "NOVEL" in all caps. She clicked on the folder and then on what appeared to be the main document. A dialog box popped up, demanding a password.

She sat for a moment, pondering how Dan might have chosen a password for his work of fiction. She typed her best guesses—his mother's maiden name, his boyhood dog's name, the street he grew up on—but none worked. This was a waste of precious time. What if Dan came home early and found her at his computer?

Calm down, she told herself. *Think!* She went back into the kitchen, removed the plate of now-lukewarm food from the microwave, grabbed a fork, and took a few bites. It often seemed that her mind produced results more quickly when she found a way to ease the pressure a bit. *Relax. Let the problem meander to the edges of your mind, where your brain can work its magic.*

She was halfway through her supper when she remembered how Dan had reacted to receiving rejection letters from the doctoral programs he'd applied to. "Why won't those academic know-nothings admit I'm gifted?" he'd said. "I deserve to be famous." What was the most important thing in the world to Dan? Sheila knew the answer before she even asked it: That people would recognize his gifts, and that he would become a famous writer.

She scurried back to Dan's office and typed "writer" as a password. It didn't work. She tried "gifted" next. Still nothing. She tried capitalizing the *W* in "Writer." Ditto with the G in "Gifted." More "Password incorrect" error messages. Undaunted, she tried the word "famous." Then she tried it with a capital *F*. Still no success.

Twenty minutes had now gone by. She was wasting precious time. *What could that password be?* She'd been confident that either "gifted" or "famous," or some variation of those words, would be the key. Perhaps in another language? But Dan didn't know any other languages. *Think, Sheila. Concentrate!* If Dan caught her snooping, she was certain he'd do more than shout at her.

Shout. That could be it. To "shout" in typed messages, one used all capital letters. Sheila clicked on the password dialog box again, pressed the caps lock key, and typed "GIFTED." *Nope.* In case she'd narrowed the options too soon, she tried "WRITER." That, too, was rejected. Her stomach sank. She had only one more brainstorm, and if it didn't work, she'd have to admit defeat—for this evening, anyway. She brought up the box one more time and typed "FAMOUS."

Bingo! There it was—Dan's manuscript. His lifelong work and masterpiece. The secret novel he had dedicated himself to working on for more than a decade.

"Let's have a look, mister," Sheila said. As she scooted the office chair closer to the screen, she stopped, waited, and listened, her ears straining to pick up any unusual noise. She heard nothing but the hum of the computer. Okay…safe.

The title was centered about a third of the way down the first page: *The Bohemian Generation.* Beneath the title was the byline, in all caps: *BY DANIEL ALTON GRAY.* That didn't surprise Sheila in the least. No doubt Dan's imagination had already projected those big, bold capital letters onto the cover of his published novel.

From time to time over the years, Sheila had asked Dan to read parts of his novel to her or to let her read it herself. In each instance, he would say it was "too complicated" for her to follow and "too deep" for a person without a college degree to understand. Eventually, she quit asking. Now, she would see for herself just how "complicated" and "deep" it really was.

Sheila glanced at the page count at the bottom of the screen. 337.

Well, at least he's prolific, she had to admit. He had been a busy man, all right. And the book wasn't done.

She scrolled to the second page and began to read the double-spaced text. At the bottom, she paused. Then she returned to the story, read three more pages, and paused again. She squinted her eyes and furrowed her forehead in confusion. What was going on here?

Hastily, she finished the first chapter—all eighteen pages of it—and then skimmed the second and third chapters. At that point, she stopped again, closed her eyes, and slowly shook her head. "It's dreadful," she whispered. "Absolutely dreadful."

To say she was astonished would be an understatement. Either she had no concept whatsoever of what a "literary novel" was, or Dan had spent fifteen years writing something so pathetic, it would never see publication.

Sheila moved on to chapter 4 to see if the writing got any better. It didn't. The dialogue was wooden, the settings were flat, and the characters were nothing more than caricatures of real people. She scrolled to the end of the document. After the final page of text, she discovered a story synopsis. She read it through and shook her head again before closing the document and shutting down the computer.

She returned Dan's chair to the way it had been when she'd walked in, made sure the mail was where she always left it, and turned off the lights. Then, feeling more heavyhearted than ever, she headed to the kitchen again.

She finished her plate of cold tuna casserole, but she didn't taste it. Dan—her Dan—was a fraud. He was a writer who couldn't write. A professor who had nothing to profess. What had Laureen called him? *A minnow amid whales.*

And she—Sheila Davis Gray—was stuck with him. She'd been stuck with him for fifteen years, following a fool's dream. She was the Sancho Panza for a Quixote who was still stuck in a dream world, tilting at windmills of the mind. Dan would never be famous or successful. And she, by association, would suffer his same fate of failure. What a total fool she had been.

She had no emotional energy left even to read or watch television. She went to the bedroom, changed into a granny gown, and crawled beneath the covers, expecting to drop immediately into a deep sleep of exhaustion. Instead, her mind refused to quiet down. No matter how limp and defeated her bones and muscles felt, her brain couldn't quit running through various scenarios of how she might proceed.

She couldn't leave Dan. While the State of Indiana would probably grant her a dissolution on the grounds of an irretrievable breakdown of the marriage, her early training made her resistant to that idea. Didn't the New Testament teach that adultery was the only justification for divorce? She was confident that her Dan would never provide those grounds. Then, there was the question of how she would support herself. She didn't earn enough money at Reynolds to make the mortgage payments and related living expenses—if she even got to keep the house. And if she didn't, she still wouldn't be able to afford rent plus other necessary expenses.

She also couldn't confront Dan, the ruling tyrant of her domain. Yet she couldn't just go on, day by day, pretending she hadn't looked under a rock and found only worms and no treasure. She would have to take some kind of action. But what?

When the sound of the garage door opening signaled Dan's return, it was after eleven o'clock, and Sheila still hadn't been able to doze off. She could hear Dan moving around, probably shedding his coat and going into his office to leaf through the mail. With any luck, he'd stay there awhile and check his social-networking sites. She had no desire to have him near her.

But luck wasn't running with her tonight, for she soon heard his approaching steps in the hallway and then a slight stumble when he entered the dark room. She knew in an instant that he'd gone out for drinks with some of the older students or another faculty member. He enjoyed being the big-time "professor" and would even pay the tab if people would hang out with him. She dreaded nights like this one.

She could hear him taking off his clothes, letting each item drop on the floor for her to pick up in the morning. *Please, please, just be drunk enough to want to go right to sleep.*

When he got into bed, she could smell the alcohol on his breath. When he reached out to find her in the dark and pulled her body against his, she realized with despair that he'd had just enough drinks to put him "in the mood."

She went rigid. He shook her a couple of times, but she pretended to be asleep. Undeterred, he began pulling upward on her flannel nightgown.

"It's late," she mumbled, trying to sound as if she had just awakened. "Let's wait until morning."

"I'm ready now," he said, his speech slightly slurred.

"Get some rest, Dan. You've worked hard all day."

He gave the nightgown a final upward tug. "I've worked hard, and I want what's mine." He rolled clumsily on top of her, almost knocking the wind out of her.

Sheila couldn't believe what was happening. He had never been this aggressive with her before. *This isn't lovemaking at all,* she thought. *It's legalized rape.* At the first thrust of pain, she gave a small shriek, but it only irritated him, and he increased his forceful movements. She knew, given his present state of mind, that any resistance would turn out badly. So, she tried to make her body go as limp as possible and used her imagination to escape to a more pleasant place in her mind.

Thankfully, it was all over in just a few minutes. Dan rolled off to his side of the bed and was snoring almost immediately.

Sheila had never felt so dirty. Carefully, she climbed out of bed, tiptoed to the bathroom, and locked the door. Then she turned on the fan for ambient noise and cleaned herself with a wet washcloth. She really wished she could have taken a shower, but that would have been too loud.

The thought of going back to bed with Dan was almost intolerable, but what choice did she have? He'd let her know many times before that her place was in his bed, not on the couch. As she stood barefoot on the cold tile floor, waves of revulsion swept over her. How had she allowed herself to become trapped like this? When the flood of tears finally started, she grabbed a handful of toilet paper and sobbed almost uncontrollably into its softness. Never before had she realized how violated a wife could feel after being with her own husband.

After she managed to stop crying, she blew her nose and recognized a change starting to take place inside her. The victim mentality was slowly transforming into fierce resentment. And although she didn't know what or how, she certainly needed to do something different. She couldn't go on like this. Not after all she'd learned today. Not after all she'd endured tonight.

Dan was still snoring when she slipped back beneath the sheets. Eventually, she drifted into a troubled sleep, from which she suddenly awoke with a jolt. It was still dark outside; the digital clock on the bedside table read 3:00. She didn't know if she had been dreaming or if her subconscious had simply been running rampant. It didn't matter. The fact was that, in the dead of night, a plan of action had come to her.

Afraid that she might not remember all the details if she fell asleep again, she eased out of bed once more, wrapped her bathrobe around her, and shoved her feet into her slippers. She left the room and made her way to the kitchen, where she turned on the light above the stovetop. Then, leaning against the nearby counter, she started making notes on the pad she normally used for grocery lists: *Book study...writing study... discussion times...lunchtimes...two evenings per week....*

She moved the pen rapidly, not worrying about getting her thoughts in logical order but more concerned with not leaving out any element of her plan. By the time she had filled an entire page, she was smiling. Yes, this would do nicely. She folded the paper and tucked it inside her purse before returning to bed.

Her mind now at peace, she relaxed and was confident she'd soon fall fast asleep. Goodness knows she would need the slumber. If today had been an eventful day, tomorrow would be even more so.

CHAPTER 11

When Sheila arrived at Laureen's home for their meeting the next afternoon, she was greeted by a mouth-watering aroma she soon learned was a loaf of sourdough, fresh from a bread machine. Laureen served the still-warm slices alongside a spinach salad topped with dried cranberries, crumbled feta, toasted almonds, and a citrus-balsamic vinaigrette.

"You really are spoiling me," Sheila complained teasingly after her first bite. "Nuking leftovers at the office just doesn't have the same appeal anymore."

Laureen smiled as she passed the butter. "All I ask is that you don't stop my fun. It's not often I get to fix a meal for someone else."

"You've got a deal," Sheila said, grinning. "Now, I have some news. Yesterday, you said you'd been playing amateur detective. Well, last night, I joined the game. While Dan was in Indianapolis teaching his evening class, I snooped around on his office computer."

"You naughty girl," said Laureen, her eyes twinkling. "Tell me everything."

"It took me a while to figure out the password to unlock the document, but I finally was able to access his precious novel," Sheila explained.

"And it was as dry as dust."

Sheila raised her eyebrows. "How did you know?"

"It had to be, based on everything you've told me," Laureen said. "If he'd written anything worth reading or publishing, he'd have made a name for himself a long time ago. He's in denial. He's one of those non-writers who continually tells himself that his pages need 'just a little tweaking' or 'some minor editing,' when, in reality, what they need is a fireplace match."

"I thought that if I read far enough into the manuscript, it would improve." Sheila stabbed a forkful of salad. "But, if anything, it got worse. I had to give up. If I'd read any more, it would have put me to sleep, and Dan would have caught me in his office."

Laureen laughed conspiratorially. "So, his promises of making the *New York Times* Best Sellers list and earning a bazillion dollars and buying you a mansion are all just so much smoke?"

Sheila nodded. "And then he had the gall to come home tipsy last night and—" She caught herself when she remembered who she was talking to.

"Don't worry, dear. I've got the picture. And, to be honest, I'm not at all surprised. A man who would use his wife in the ways you've described...well, such treatment is bound to reach into the bedroom, too."

Sheila didn't know how to respond. Talking to Bev, Lexie, and Sherry at the office was one thing, but her former teacher?

Laureen went on. "Throughout the years, I've enjoyed studying the Bible as classic literature; I also consider it to be the ultimate rule of faith and practice. Of course, in the classroom, you never heard me say anything about my beliefs. I didn't feel that it was the time or place. But now, I *do* have something to say to you about the unhealthy twist I suspect you've been taught concerning a few Bible verses—for example, Ephesians five, verse twenty-two: '*Wives, submit yourselves unto your own husbands.*'"

Sheila wasn't surprised to learn that her former teacher was a woman of faith. There'd always been a special tranquility to her demeanor. "What do you mean, 'unhealthy twist'?"

"Remember when we studied Dostoevsky's short stories and briefly discussed the merits of various English translations from the Russian? I'm talking about how some scholars think that the bygone Victorian era unduly influenced Garnett's work and that modern versions are better."

"I do remember," said Sheila. "It was the first time I'd ever thought about how important a translator's role can be in literature."

Laureen smiled. "The principle applies to Bible translations, as well. For instance, in the original Greek, verse twenty-two of Ephesians five has no verb. It simply says, 'Wives to your husbands.' In order for the instruction to make sense, English translators have to borrow a verb from the previous verse, which tells Christians to 'submit to one another.' Therefore, *submit* means the same in both verses. In other words, submission should be mutual. Does that make sense?"

"It sure does."

"Do you also remember learning that the culture and the historical period in which a book was written are key to understanding the author's message? Well, in the Ephesian culture, the concept of submissive wives was nothing new. *All* wives were subject to their husbands. Those who read those words might have thought, *Well, duh!* What *was* new, however, was the teaching of *mutual* submission."

Sheila wrinkled her brow in thought. "But doesn't the Bible say that the husband is the head of the wife?"

Laureen took a bite of her salad before continuing. "That happens to be the very next verse in the Ephesians passage. The problem, again, is cultural understanding. Today, being the 'head' means being the top dog, the big cheese—someone who lords it over others. But in the first century, the Greek word for *head* meant one who assists; someone who is an enabler, in the best sense of the word. So, the verse actually says that a husband should focus on helping his wife become a complete and fulfilled person." She gazed into the distance with a grin. "Like my Herbert did for me." Then her smile faded, and she looked at Sheila again. "But I can see quite clearly that Dan has never fulfilled that role in your marriage."

Sheila reached into her purse for a tissue, then wiped her eyes.

"Oh, my dear!" Laureen exclaimed. "I didn't mean to upset you. I just felt it was something you needed to know. Please, let's move on to a more pleasant topic. I've got your manuscript edited and ready for you to retype."

"You do?"

Laureen pushed a manila folder across the table to Sheila. "I even went so far as to find a market. I want to try the fiction editor at *Accent Female*. It's a classy, sassy, brassy online magazine, and I like its cutting-edge approach to women's issues. Your story is just off-beat enough, and possibly satirical enough, to grab their attention. The contact information is written on the folder."

"I appreciate that, and I'll get right on it," said Sheila. She peeked inside the folder before closing it again. "There's something else I want to talk to you about."

"Fine," said Laureen, buttering a slice of bread. "You talk, I'll nibble."

"Something you said yesterday and something Dan said at dinner on my birthday came together in my dreams last night," Sheila began. "It was an epiphany. A light went on in my head, and everything became so logical and practical, I actually had to get out of bed and write it all down."

She fished inside her purse again and retrieved her notes. "The other night, I told Dan that I wanted to start writing again. He said there was no sense in my trying because I had only a basic high-school diploma, whereas he had a master's degree in English. And, obviously, if, with all his education, he hadn't been able to get his book finished and published yet, what chance did a minimally educated person like me have?"

"How kind," said Laureen, chomping viciously into her bread slice.

"But then," Sheila continued, "I remembered you saying that lots of people have multiple English degrees and still aren't anything special. That concept finally registered with me last night. *Education* isn't measured by the number of abbreviations that follow your name. It's *what you know.*"

She paused to put the final bite of bread into her mouth and wash it down with a few quick sips of orange pekoe tea. Thus fortified, she looked straight at her former teacher. "You said I was your best student. Well, I want to assume that role again. I'm not nearly as interested in acquiring a college diploma as I am in getting an education. For as long as your health allows, would you be willing to let me drive out here two nights a week—while Dan is away teaching his evening classes—as well as on the occasional lunch hour, to be mentored by you? Would you be my teacher again, this time as a private tutor, editing my writing and telling me what books I should read in order to perfect my craft? You're the smartest, best-read woman I've ever known. If I could absorb even a small portion of all the knowledge you have stored inside your mind, I believe I'd be able to move ahead far more quickly than I would without your help."

Laureen beamed. "You make it sound as though I'd be doing you a favor, but working with you in this way would give me a reason to continue getting out of bed each morning, which is becoming more and more difficult. As this sickness advances, I need motivation to keep me going. Oh, yes…yes, indeed, I would love to have you spend as much time here as possible. In fact, I'm going to do two things before you leave today. First, I'm going to give you a key to this house. You can come over and use my computer or help yourself to my books whenever it's convenient for you. And, second, I'm going to give you a novel that you can start reading today. I'll be right back." She stood and left the room.

Sheila polished off the remainder of her salad while she awaited Laureen's return.

When the older woman reentered the room, she was smiling. "Here. This is the perfect book for us to start reading and discussing."

Sheila accepted the proffered volume and looked at its title. "*Martin Eden* by Jack London," she read aloud. "I remember reading *The Call of the Wild* and several of London's short stories in your class, but I don't think I've ever heard of this book."

Laureen nodded. "Do you see how the title character's initials spell out the word 'me'? This book is a thinly disguised autobiographical novel that tells the story of how Jack London became the most popular writer of his day—without any college degree."

"But how did he become a success with no formal training?"

"The same way you will," Laureen assured her. "He found a librarian in Oakland, California, who told him what books he should be reading. Her name was Ina Coolbrith, and she served as his mentor the same way I'll serve as yours. Later in life, when he needed other advisers, they came along. They always do. Trust me, talent will out. Start with me now, and when the time comes, other mentors will enter the scene. You have a date with destiny."

Sheila glanced at her watch. "Oh, no! I totally lost track of time." She leaped to her feet. "I'll just stay late at the office tonight to catch up on my work. I wouldn't trade our visits together for anything. I love you for believing in me this way." She picked up her purse and the manila folder. "I let you down once before, but I swear it's not going to happen again."

"No," Laureen said solemnly, "it's not going to happen again."

Two weeks later, Sheila called JD and told him she would be stopping by the farm for a few minutes on her way home from work, although she didn't explain why. Now, as she took the turnoff and headed up the rutted, unpaved road leading to the familiar farmhouse, she had a sense of seeing the place with new eyes.

Certainly, the Davis family farm had never been a thriving enterprise; but in the years since Harold's death, the place seemed to have become sorrier and more weather-beaten than ever. The barn roof sagged, the flower beds surrounding the house were devoid of any vegetation, the fields were strewn with rusty discarded machine parts, and the corral's gate was missing several planks. Poor JD.

Literally "poor JD," thought Sheila, as she recalled the series of events that had led to this state of dishevelment. When their father had died, he'd left a stack of unpaid bills for JD to deal with. Sheila had not been named in the will as one of the inheritors of the farm. At first, her feelings had been hurt. But then, the family lawyer had explained that a second mortgage after two bad harvests, plus a long-term loan for a new tractor and combine, had made the debts amount to more than the total worth of the farm. If foreclosure ensued, Sheila wouldn't be named in any of the legal action, since she wasn't an heir. Small compensation, but it had been good news for Dan. He wanted nothing to do with the Davis family's financial problems.

Sheila's brothers had worked hard to keep the place running. A couple of good years had enabled them to pay off some bank notes. JD had married a local girl, and a year later they had a baby. Spencer, still living in the family home, had begun to feel that he was crowding the newlyweds, so he turned the farm operation over to JD while retaining his half of ownership. Spencer joined the army with the intent to serve four years, see a bit of the world, save his money, and then return to Brissenden and either buy out his brother or sell his share of the farm to JD and get a place of his own.

After a year of duty at Fort Knox, Spencer married a young woman from Kentucky. They settled into a small apartment near the base. Not knowing where he might be assigned, Spencer decided that he and his wife should wait to start a family until after his discharge. Two years into his hitch, Spencer's armor unit was deployed to Afghanistan. Three months later, Spencer was killed in a roadside bombing.

Spencer's body was flown home to Indiana and given a military funeral in Brissenden. The shock of his loss emotionally devastated both his siblings, but for JD, the financial repercussions were equally devastating. Spencer's widow, Winona Clark Davis, announced to JD that she was going to have the farm assessed. As Spencer's spouse, she automatically inherited his half of the holdings. She wanted her share in cash. Either JD would pay her off, or she would arrange for the farm and its goods to be auctioned, after which they would split the proceeds.

No amount of reasoning, cajoling, or bargaining would sway her. Finally, JD had been forced to take out new mortgages, borrow from friends, and sell whatever wasn't nailed down in order to pay off Winona. In the subsequent years, he hadn't had a spare nickel—or a spare minute for anyone or anything. It had been work, work, work. Creditors were constantly breathing down his neck.

Sheila's heart sank as she looked at the drooping scene before her eyes. Once again, a series of regrets raced through her mind. *If only I had looked harder for a way to finish college and get a good job, I would have the money now to help JD and his family. If only I'd come back to live on the farm instead of marrying so young, I could have helped keep the place up.*

Well, there was nothing she could do about the past. But, thanks to Laureen Parks's reentering her life, Sheila now realized that no one had more control over her own future than she did. And today, she was taking an important step in the right direction.

As she got out of the car, JD's daughter, Emily, rushed outside to meet her. "Hi, Aunt Sheila!"

Sheila opened her arms to give the girl a hug. "How's sixth grade? Earning straight A's and breaking all the boys' hearts?"

Emily didn't blush. She was used to the ritual. The two linked arms and walked up to the house. "Mom is still working at the factory, and Dad is out in the field, but there's coffee if you want some."

"Thanks, sweetheart, but that's okay," Sheila said as they climbed the porch steps. "I'm stopping for only a minute. I'm on a treasure hunt and could really use your help."

Emily looked puzzled but ready for a game.

Sheila headed upstairs, Emily on her heels, and paused at the door to her niece's bedroom. "Mind if I go in?"

Emily frowned. "Uh, it's not exactly neat."

"It never was when I lived in it, either," Sheila confessed with a wink. Then she pushed open the door and went inside.

"What are you looking for?"

"Buried treasure," Sheila quipped. "I'm going to show you something I bet you've never known about. It's a secret chamber." Sheila crossed the room to the closet. She pulled the string to turn on the overhead light, then got down on her knees, moving aside clothes, shoes, and other items as she felt her way along the wooden floor. After a moment, she grinned. "Gotcha!" she said triumphantly.

Emily leaned closer and watched as Sheila wriggled a shortened floorboard, then pulled it up.

"Ta-da!" Sheila reached inside the space beneath the floorboard and retrieved a small box wrapped in aluminum foil. "See? Buried treasure, just like I told you."

"What's in the box?"

"The key to my past...and my future." Sheila gently peeled away the foil, revealing a small velvet-covered jewelry box. "This won't seem like much to you, but to me, it's a genuine treasure." She opened the box and sighed with relief at seeing what was inside.

"It's a necklace," said Emily.

Sheila only nodded, having suddenly lost her voice in a moment of unexpected nostalgia.

"Is it yours?"

"Yes," Sheila whispered. A little louder, she added, "It's been buried here, along with everything it stood for in my life, for more than fifteen years. But now it's time to bring it out again."

"Is it valuable?"

"Maybe not so much in dollars, if that's what you mean," said Sheila. "But to me, it's priceless." She fingered one of the charms. "This little feather quill was intended to remind me of the statewide writing contest I won my senior year of high school, earning me a scholarship to a summer college-level writing program. And the little book and the tiny clock were to remind me that I was supposed to *stay* in college and continue to learn more and more about writing so that I could one day become an author."

"Did Grandpa give you the necklace for graduation?" Emily asked.

"No, honey. Your grandpa wasn't too keen on girls going to college, and he certainly didn't understand my love for writing. This necklace was given to me by my high-school English teacher, Mrs. Parks. She's the one who entered my essay in the contest that earned me the scholarship for summer school at Brissenden College."

Emily seemed genuinely puzzled. "Then why did you hide your necklace under the floorboard all these years? And why didn't you ever become an author?"

Sheila paused, still a bit shaken by JD's recent revelation that right before their father had died, he'd confessed to burning all the letters Mrs. Parks had sent Sheila from Texas.

Sheila closed her eyes. If only she had found out in time.... But no, she couldn't change the past. All she could do was move forward.

She opened her eyes and looked at Emily. "Because I made a mistake, sweetheart. I let other people make decisions for me. I thought I was too much in love with your uncle Dan to wait to get married—plus, I believed him when he promised I could go to college if I would postpone enrolling long enough to work to put him through school. So, at the end of that summer, I came back to this room and hid my necklace—and my dreams—all at once."

"Why'd you come back for the necklace now?"

Sheila smiled. "Because sometimes you get a second chance to correct your mistakes. After being away for years, my former teacher moved back to Brissenden recently, and I've been going to her house a couple of times a week. We've been reading books together and talking about authors and literature. She's helped me start writing again."

"Ugh." Emily made a face. "You were out of school for years, and now you're going back for more?" She shivered.

Sheila laughed. "It's more fun when you go to school because you *want to*," she assured her niece. "But all this is a big secret. I don't think Uncle Dan would understand it any more than you do, so let's just keep this between us, okay?"

"No problem." Emily nodded. "Want me to help you put the necklace on?"

"That would be nice," said Sheila. She handed the necklace to Emily, then leaned her head forward while the girl fastened the clasp. When she was done, Sheila looked up and announced, "That necklace is on to stay. The only way it'll come off is if I'm dead."

Then Sheila opened her purse, removed a ten-dollar bill from her wallet, and handed it to Emily. "Here. Put this in the empty jewelry box and hide it under the floorboard. From now on, that secret hiding place belongs to you and your treasures."

CHAPTER 12

For Dan Gray, the twice-weekly drive from Brissenden to Indianapolis was its own version of a good news/bad news joke. The good news was, it gave him an hour of solitude so he could think about his writing, his teaching career, his wife, and his future. The bad news was, there was little else worth thinking about.

Dan Gray was at loose ends. He was a man without a game plan. Day after day, for far too long, he had been going through the motions yet making no progress.

A quick glance in the rearview mirror showed him a face with obvious signs of heavy drinking and inadequate sleep. Perhaps on Lee Child, Joe Hill, or Dan Brown, some gray hairs at the temples and a few crow's feet around the eyes would impart a seasoned look. On Dan Gray, however, they were simply glaring indicators of an aging failure.

He made a quick self-assessment. The PT Cruiser he was driving was the oft-clichéd bucket of bolts. His sport coat had frayed sleeves, and its lapels were terribly out of style. His tie had a stain, his watch had been purchased at a discount store, and the faux diamond stud in his left earlobe looked like some unmatched accessory stuck in the side of a Mr. Potato Head.

Who was he trying to kid?

Well...himself, for one.

For years, he had been telling himself that his big break was just around the corner...that his moment in the sun was pending...that fate was set to deal him a winning hand. And, when that happened, all his emotional baggage would be shed like a caterpillar's cocoon, and he would come forth as something magnificent—not only worth beholding, but also with wings for rising above the grief and humiliation and frustration he had known all his life.

He couldn't remember a time when his peers had treated him with respect, much less revered him. His own mother used to make a big fuss when she introduced his older sister, Tiffany, to anyone, listing all her accolades and accomplishments; whereas Dan's introductions were a succinct, unenthusiastic "our son." In grade school, he was always one of the last to be chosen for sports teams.

During his junior-high years, he would drop by the elementary-school playground because he liked being called "one of the big kids" by the fourth and fifth graders. He would tell them lies about being on the football team *and* the honor roll. Once, when a nine-year-old boy with thick glasses dared to suggest that Dan was exaggerating his accomplishments, Dan had beaten him up. Not only had it had felt good, but it had also increased his prestige among the elementary-aged kids.

In high school, Dan was the invisible man. It wasn't that the other students were cruel to him in any tangible way. Far worse, they seemed to look right through him. He was never nominated for a class office or sought out for club membership or invited to dances or encouraged to audition for a school play. It was as if he weren't there.

So, to compensate, Dan sought a place where he could be "seen." He offered to help his former seventh-grade teachers by tutoring slow readers after school. It paid nothing, but it gave Dan a sense of superiority to be given an empty after-hours classroom where he could literally play school.

And it would have lasted longer than one year if that crybaby Lindsay Gardner hadn't complained to the principal that Dan was mocking her stutter. He had been banned from the junior-high campus after that. However, Dan had a long memory, and he knew how to carry a grudge.

During his senior year, Lindsay started high school as a freshman. Dan shadowed her for weeks until, one day, she failed to close the combination lock on her locker. When the hall cleared, Dan stole everything of value from the unsecured locker and trashed everything else. Revenge never tasted so sweet.

Women thought they were so special, but he always managed to show them who was *really* in control. He had been doing that successfully with his own wife for fifteen years. But now, he didn't know what had happened. She certainly wasn't his air-headed, spineless, do-as-she-was-told Sheila anymore. Instead, and quite disturbingly, she was showing signs of being a woman with a dream. And women with dreams were dangerous. They started taking risks, started showing independence, started rebelling against those in authority over them....

Between his troubles at home and his lack of progress at work, Dan was feeling invisible again. The full-time faculty members at Indiana University's extension campus in Indianapolis never stopped by his office to chat. He wasn't invited to faculty parties, readings, or the social and academic outings. When he applied to the faculty chair and the dean for a position teaching upper-level literature courses, his letters went unanswered. Semester after semester, he was assigned to teach basic composition courses. What he needed was an ally, a sponsor, an angel—someone in the department who would open doors for him, give him some breaks.

And now, as he drove, he reviewed his progress with one such possible person. Her name was Dr. Imogene Cunningham. At least eight years his senior, with teeth that needed to be straightened and prematurely gray hair that needed to be tinted and styled, she was no beauty. Yet she possessed certain keys that could unlock doors for him. Dr. Cunningham held a PhD in linguistics and was already tenured. And she was as angry about life as Dan was, although for different reasons.

Whereas Dan was happy to be part of the IU faculty in Indianapolis, he had heard that Dr. Cunningham had long desired to teach at the main campus in Bloomington. She had been lobbying for a transfer for years, but to no avail. Dan had heard rumors: "*Without a man, Imogene just doesn't fit in with the Bloomington crowd"; "Her field of study is so narrow, she simply doesn't have the visibility as a speaker and a writer to add genuine prestige to the Bloomington English faculty."*

A couple of times in the past few weeks, Dan had tested the waters very cautiously and had not been altogether displeased with the outcome of his efforts to woo Dr. Cunningham.

He had noticed a mention in the faculty newsletter that Dr. Cunningham had been asked to read a paper on Old English poetry at a linguistics conference, so he had dropped by her office with a small vase of carnations, along with his congratulations. She seemed genuinely surprised by the special attention and reacted as if no one had ever cared two cents about her research prior to this. Dan eased into a chair and coaxed her into telling him about the paper. He acted totally enraptured by her explanation, despite his failure to understand 90 percent of what she was talking about.

It wasn't that Dan was altogether ignorant of classic literature. In fact, one of his favorite maxims was from *The Prince*, written by Machiavelli and published in 1532. He hadn't read the actual book, of course. But he'd come across the quote somewhere, and he liked it: "Everyone sees what you appear to be, few experience what you really are." Dan was confident that if he gave Imogene Cunningham a good look at what he appeared to be, then publishing success would soon be within his grasp.

A few days later, Dan managed to be in the coffee line right behind Imogene, and he insisted on paying for her latte. They sat and chatted for fifteen minutes. He mentioned he was writing a novel and hinted that he wanted some professional input.

She immediately expressed interest. "I envy you," she confessed. "If you're successful in getting that novel published, and it makes any splash at all, you'll get plenty of attention from the powers that be. That's where the focus is today—on the contemporary writings, not the classics and the antiquities. I hitched my wagon to the wrong star...put my eggs in the wrong basket...threw in with the wrong crowd...choose your favorite idiom."

Dan shook his head. "Surely, you'll receive the recognition you deserve one day," he said, trying to sound as earnest as possible. "If you could find the time to read part of my novel and give me your feedback, I'd appreciate it tremendously. With your background in language and your experience as a literary analyst, I could only benefit from any suggestions you might make."

A light went on in her eyes, and Dan could pretty much guess what she was thinking: If she would become Dan's editorial adviser, it would be a small step toward becoming his coauthor. And if the novel were salable....

Imogene smiled warmly. "Bring me the manuscript the next time you come to campus."

So, today, he had a printout of the book with him. If she liked it—and what did a classics professor know about modern novels to dislike?—then Dan would form an alliance with her. He'd be willing to share authorship of his novel if she would do what she could to get him admitted to the PhD program and arrange for him to start teaching some classes that would be more impressive on his résumé than "Basic Composition."

And if it turned out that he had to provide "other" services to please her...well then, he could even do that, as long as the lights would be turned off. *He* certainly would be.

A slow smile formed on his lips. Yes, there was hope on the horizon. It reminded him of Nellie in *South Pacific*, who sang about being stuck like a dope on hope.

"Yeah, Nellie," said Dan aloud. "Me too, sister."

The two evenings a week when Dan was in Indianapolis, teaching his classes and then usually going out for drinks with his cronies, Sheila continued to meet with Laureen to discuss the books they'd read, as well as receive help on her writing.

At their first meeting after Sheila retrieved the necklace from under the floorboard, she'd showed it to Laureen, expressed regret about why she'd hidden it, and explained what had compelled her to start wearing it again. "Your gift means the world to me, and I wear it every day now. Of course, when Dan sees it, he'll blow his stack at me for breaking my promise to throw it away. I'm postponing that moment as long as possible. So, for now, when my clothing necklines aren't high enough to cover the charms, I wear scarves," she explained.

Laureen's eyes twinkled mischievously. "I totally understand, my dear. Remember what Christ said about casting pearls before swine? He warned that the pigs may trample the pearls under their feet, *'and turn and tear you to pieces.'*" She chuckled. "Not that I'm calling anyone a pig, mind you."

One warm May evening, after several weeks of their get-togethers, Laureen and Sheila held their session on the sunporch at the back of Laureen's house. "I want to try something a little different this time," she announced as she poured Sheila a glass of iced tea. "We've been talking about individual books for a while. Now, I'd like for us to discuss recurring themes in the literature we've read together."

Sheila set down her glass and leaned forward, ready for the challenge.

"The Bible says in Genesis, *'It is not good for the man to be alone.'* With that as a starting point, let's talk about *alienation* as a theme. In what ways have the authors whose works we've been reading for the past four months treated this issue?"

To Sheila, this type of discussion was as much fun as competing on a quiz show. If Dan had respected her abilities more, the two of them could have been having talks like this for years. Now, eager to spill all she'd been storing inside herself during the past twelve weeks of reading, discussing, writing, and questioning, she jumped right into her response.

"Some authors create situations of physical alienation just to see how their characters will respond," she began. "For example, *Robinson Crusoe* and *The Swiss Family Robinson* and even that Jules Verne novel *The Mysterious Island* featured people abandoned in alien environments."

"And what was a common message of those books?" Laureen asked.

"There probably were a lot of them, but what struck me most was the fact that humankind does not adapt to an environment the way animals do. Instead, we force the environment to conform to our wishes and demands. For example, if a dog were abandoned on a South Seas island, he would start shedding his coat and would learn to eat the food available on the island. However, Robinson Crusoe chopped down the trees to make himself a home. He planted his own garden, dug canals, burned off fields—he modified the island, not himself."

Laureen nodded. "So, you're saying that, even when forcefully alienated from society, humans will replicate a form of that society?"

"Yes, exactly," Sheila confirmed. "You referred to Genesis a moment ago. Well, I think that humankind has taken the command to '*fill the earth and subdue it*' to full measure. These authors were suggesting that, whether nature likes it or not, we will make an effort to dominate our surroundings. In fact, that's what kept those characters from going insane when they were totally isolated from the rest of humanity. They worked and created and changed the world they'd been dropped into."

A refreshingly cool breeze drifted through a window screen, teasing the wisps of hair on Laureen's forehead. She brushed her eyes clear of a strand and asked, "But what about other forms of alienation?"

Sheila grabbed a gingersnap from a nearby tray. "Several of the novels we read together proved that a person doesn't have to be lost on a deserted island in order to be isolated. Winston Smith in *1984* and John Savage in *Brave New World* were both totally out of sync with their societies. They recognized that while technology can aid human endeavors, it won't replace such universal needs as dreams, ambition, and love."

Sheila poured herself more tea from a tall pitcher as she continued talking. "Jack London's novel *The Sea-Wolf* was another example of alienation. Humphrey van Weyden was wealthy and well-read, but when he was shanghaied, he found himself in a desperate fight for survival on a ship of seal hunters. He was in a society he couldn't relate to or change the same way Crusoe did his island. He discovered the darker side of human nature."

Laureen tented her fingers. "What lessons can we draw from the extremes in novels of this kind?"

Sheila considered the question a moment. "I think I see a pattern," she began. "In *The Island of Dr. Moreau,* by H. G. Wells, the main character tried to change the island's animals into humans, but the experiment failed miserably. In *Tarzan of the Apes,* by Edgar Rice Burroughs, a man tried to become like the animals. In the long run, that, too, proved unsuccessful. However, the lesson in Robert Louis Stevenson's *Dr. Jekyll and Mr. Hyde* is that humans have two natures—one of them humane, the other barbaric and animalistic—and that, by enhancing the one and taming the other, we have a chance to be united in a wholeness that makes us first at home with ourselves and, second, at home with others. To achieve that is to beat alienation on all levels."

Laureen smiled in approval. "I agree. Very well done, my dear." With a wink, she added, "Would you prefer an A-plus or a gold star?"

Sheila grinned. "Another gingersnap, actually. I'm really into creature comforts these days."

Laureen nodded at the tray of cookies. "Take two, then. They're small. Now…let's pick up where we left off last week in Jane Austen's *Pride and Prejudice.* I suspect this is going to be a topic you will identify with strongly."

CHAPTER 13

The next evening, Sheila warmed up some leftover pot roast, potatoes, and carrots. Dan ate two full plates, finished off the last piece of cherry pie, then told Sheila to make coffee because he would be up late grading papers.

Sheila had just finished loading the dishwasher when Dan returned to the kitchen for his coffee. "What an imbecile," he mumbled under his breath.

"What's that?" Sheila asked, knowing he wanted her to inquire.

"Oh, nothing," said Dan, picking up his coffee mug. "Just this moronic student of mine. She argues with me about everything. Her most recent paper is the stupidest thing you can imagine."

"Didn't she complete the assigned reading?"

Dan smirked. "Oh, she completed it, all right. She just has no idea what the story was about or what the author was getting at."

Sheila added a squirt of gel detergent to the dishwasher. "What was the story?"

Dan waved a hand dismissively. "It's nothing you'd know. It's called 'The Yellow Wallpaper.' It's about a woman who's insane, but this idiot student of mine doesn't understand that."

Sheila closed the dishwasher door, pressed the start button, and turned to face Dan. "Oh, really? You mean, your student doesn't think the main character is actually insane?"

"Hmmm...yeah," said Dan. "The woman in the story is completely bats, but my student thinks she is only—and here's the gist of her quote—'depressed because her creative talent has been suppressed and she isn't permitted to express herself.' Creative talent? Give me a break. This girl wouldn't understand creative talent if it jumped up and bit her in the butt." He turned to leave.

"Actually, she's right."

Dan continued a few steps, then suddenly whirled around. "What did you say?"

"I said, your student was right. She understands the story perfectly."

Dan seemed amused. "You *agree* with her?"

Sheila shrugged. "That story is about a woman who has a deep desire to be a writer. Her family and the surrounding society frown on that kind of activity by a mere *female*, so she has to hide her notebooks of writings. She lives in complete fear of being discovered. Still, she can't suppress her need to be creative. She's terrified, but she's certainly not crazy—not until her husband keeps insisting that she take naps in the room with that awful wallpaper."

Dan looked thunderstruck, as if wondering how his mousy Sheila had the chutzpah to challenge *him* on a matter of literary interpretation. "What the heck is this?" he demanded. "Unless you've actually read 'The Yellow Wallpaper,' you wouldn't have any idea what the story is about."

"Ah, but I *have* read it. Three times. Once in Mrs. Parks's class in high school, once during my summer course at Brissenden College, and once again just a month ago, during a visit with Mrs. Parks at her home while you were in Indy. I love that story. I've even read several other works by Charlotte Perkins Gilman. She's an amazing writer. Her stories speak to me."

"Why? Because you're nuttier than a fruitcake, too?"

Sheila didn't rise to the taunt. "No, Dan. Because I know what it's like to have a burning desire to write and to have every man in your life try to keep you from doing it."

Dan shook his head. "Geez, you *are* nuts."

Sheila lifted her chin slightly. "No, I'm not nuts, Dan. But I am mad. I'm starting to become really angry about all the years I wasted…about all my missed opportunities as a writer."

Dan glowered. "You know full well that you had your chance at writing, and that it just wasn't something you—"

"I never had a real chance," she inserted. "You promised me the chance to finish college. You told me I could study English. You knew that was my dream, but you never let me pursue it."

"You have a house and a—"

"I didn't ask for a house. I asked for a college education and the chance to pursue a writing career. Those were my dreams, my goals. You never understood me, and that's why you can't understand the woman in that story, either." She leaned back against the refrigerator door. "Do you know who I had a crush on when I was growing up? Who would you guess? Some movie actor or rock star? No, not me. I was in love with John-Boy Walton. I used to watch reruns of *The Waltons* every night on cable. And do you know why? Because John-Boy wanted to be a writer. That's all he ever talked about or dreamed about, and, I'm telling you, I understood that. I understood that *completely*!"

Dan stood with his mouth slightly open, seemingly oblivious that the coffee was cooling in his cup.

"I even bought a bunch of Big Chief tablets so I could write stories longhand, the way John-Boy did," Sheila continued. "I wrote about damsels and knights, about detectives and crooks, about rich people and paupers. I even wrote about Indiana dirt farmers. But I hid all my tablets in the back of my closet because my father didn't believe girls should entertain silly notions such as wanting to become writers."

Dan frowned. "Get a grip, Sheila. This is just—"

"I *am* getting a grip, Dan. Thanks to my meetings with Mrs. Parks, I'm getting a real grip on what my life is supposed to be. I'm reading good books and discussing things I should have been talking about for years. I'm way behind, but I'm starting to catch up."

She paused momentarily to get her breath, then charged ahead again, as though unable to stop herself. "But do you know what is scary about the whole thing? Do you know what is—yes!—what is driving me crazy? It's the fact that I've started to do a little writing again, but I'm having to hide all my tablets at my office because I'm terrified you'll find out and make me stop. I'm not crazy, but I sure am paranoid. So, don't try to tell me that you can say for certain the woman in that story starts out being insane. She doesn't! She starts out sane and gets *scared senseless*. I understand that. She and I are both—"

Sheila stopped abruptly and began to tremble, suddenly aware of what she'd just done: raising her voice to Dan, chastising him, and revealing to him all the anger she'd suppressed for more than a decade.

Dan's eyes had gone steel-hard. "I knew all along it was a mistake to let you meet with that Parks woman," he said sharply. "I never should have allowed it. Well, your defiance is going to stop. You *will* get yourself back in line—and fast! Your duty to me—your husband, the head of this home—is to help advance my career. Never forget that."

Sheila watched as rage contorted his face. *Dear Lord, what have I done?*

"And another thing: Nobody plays power games with Dan Gray. Especially not an uneducated writer-wannabe." Dan set his coffee mug on the table and clenched his hands into fists.

Sheila burst into tears and ran to their bedroom, but she couldn't lock the door in time.

The next morning, Sheila arrived at work nearly half an hour late, something totally uncharacteristic of her. No amount of makeup could have masked the puffiness on the right side of her face or the haze of purple around her eye.

"Girl, what happened to you?" asked Sherry Lopez.

"Sorry I'm late," said Sheila, managing a half smile. "I slipped in the shower."

Sherry came closer. "Slipping in the shower busts your butt, not your face. Did Dan do this to you?"

"It was a home accident," Sheila insisted. "I'm fine."

"Did you see a doctor?"

"I called Urgent Care," Sheila lied. "They said I could come by on my lunch hour, so I'm going to do that if it gets any worse. I'm sure I'll be fine, though."

Sherry snapped her fingers. "Your mention of Urgent Care just reminded me that your teacher friend, the one you said is fighting cancer, called here first thing this morning. She asked if you could come to her house as soon as possible. She wouldn't explain why."

Sheila gasped. "Oh, dear Lord, no! She must need to be taken to the hospital. I've got to get to her right away. Cover for me around here, will you? I'll call you...later."

Sheila dashed for the door, debating whether she should call 9-1-1 to have an ambulance meet her at Laureen's house. No, it would be better to assess the situation first. Maybe she would rush Laureen to the hospital herself. Her thoughts were a blur as she raced to rescue her friend.

She swerved into the driveway, jerked to a stop, and leaped from the car, not taking the time to close the door behind her. She fumbled in her purse for the house key Laureen had given her, but before she could fish it out, the front door opened. Laureen stood in the doorway, smiling.

"You're...you're all right?" Sheila said, trying to catch her breath.

"My goodness, yes," said Laureen. "Whatever made you think—oh, my word! What happened to your face? Come in here. Sit down."

"You're okay?" Sheila asked again.

"I'm fine. But you look hurt. Come on in. Let me look at you."

"Wait a second," said Sheila, still wondering what the emergency had been about. She returned to her car, closed the door, then slowly walked back to the house. "I had a message at my office that you needed me to get out here to you *immediately,*" she said. "I thought you were ill or hurt, or...."

Laureen rolled her eyes upward. "I'm so sorry, my dear. What I said was that I'd like you to come to my house as soon as you could, but

I didn't mean to make it sound like an emergency. I do apologize if I frightened you. But what about you? What happened to your face?"

"Dan and I had a fight last night," Sheila said flatly. "I don't know what got into me, but I accused him of lying when he'd promised I could go to college. I also criticized his ability to interpret literature. I ran to our bedroom, and he came after me. We started screaming, and I think I scratched his cheek. The next thing I knew, he backhanded me in the face."

"He struck you?" Laureen asked, sounding aghast.

"Yes, but I think I hurt him, too. It was crazy. I can't believe I really dug my nails into his cheek, but I remember seeing blood on my hand, so I must have. I was scared and wasn't thinking straight. Him either. As soon as he hit me that one time, he stopped. He spent the night on the couch and was already gone when I got up this morning."

Laureen hugged Sheila like a mother comforting her child. "This is getting out of control," she said softly. "We need to keep you away from that man."

Sheila gently pulled back. "I wish it were that easy. I've already thought about it, and I don't have many options. I'm sure Dan will come in tonight, probably with flowers and candy and an apology. We'll try to put it behind us."

"Don't you think we should call the police?"

"No," said Sheila. "They'd see Dan's scratch and my puffy, black-and-blue face, and then one of us might get arrested. It's not worth it. I don't think Dan is violent. He just reacted instinctively to being attacked."

"If you *ever* feel you need to get away from him, you can come here and stay as long as you want," Laureen told her. "Is that understood?"

Sheila smiled and nodded. "Understood."

"Good, good. I worry about you."

"And I worry about you. That's why I rushed out here. But if you aren't ill, what did you need to see me about?"

"Oh, yes, *that*! Follow me, please." Laureen led the way to the sun-porch and motioned for Sheila to have a seat. "My mail arrived early today. That's why I called your office. Something came for Dove Alexander...and it wasn't a large return envelope."

Laureen retrieved a white business envelope from an end table and handed it to Sheila before sitting in a nearby chair. The return address on the envelope was from *Accent Female* in New York City.

Despite the pain and the swelling, Sheila's eyes widened. "What... what do you think...?"

"Open it!" Lauren urged her. "The suspense has been driving me up the wall."

Sheila tore open the envelope, slid out the letter, and gasped. "Oh, my goodness! It's a check for four hundred dollars! Here, you read the letter. My hands are shaking too much."

Laureen took the letter and read it aloud.

Dear Dove Alexander:

We were greatly impressed with your short story and plan to run it in our October online issue. Enclosed is our payment of $400. We hope to receive additional stories from you in the near future. Thank you for your submission to Accent Female.

Kindest regards,
Dixie Trumbull
Managing Editor

Sheila remained silent for what seemed like a full minute. Finally, she looked up at Laureen. "Four...hundred...dollars," she managed.

"To be published *this October*," said Laureen, looking dazed, herself. "On the World Wide Web."

Both women lowered their gazes again to the message now open before them, printed on *Accent Female* letterhead. Neither knew quite what to say. Everything was silent again for another moment.

Then, an uncharacteristically sarcastic, almost sinister, laugh started coming from Sheila's throat. "Oh...oh, my. This is just too wonderful for words," she said between chuckles. "Four hundred dollars. *Four hundred dollars!* I can't wait to wave this letter under Dan's eyes tonight and show him how wrong he's been. He is going to die...just die."

"No!" Laureen cut in, clearly alarmed. "Dan must know nothing of this. Don't you understand what this means? Are you not grasping the full implication of this situation?"

"It means I can write...."

Laureen shook her head vigorously. "No, no! Think about it in the bigger picture. This acceptance letter and check prove that what you wrote fifteen years ago was an excellent story. And that, in turn, *proves* our suspicion that your husband never actually mailed your submission to the contest. It proves that he sabotaged your career, Sheila. He lied to you. He's used you all these years to help himself get ahead when, all along, *you* were the one who should have been going to college and pursuing a writing career. He's a mean-spirited, small-minded man."

Almost as a reflex, Sheila raised her hand to her bruised face.

"He's dangerous," Laureen said. "And scared."

Sheila looked at her quizzically.

"Yes, *scared*," Laureen affirmed, answering the unasked question. "He's scared that you'll somehow discover your real talent, become successful, and reach a point where you no longer need him. He's scared that you'll see through his façade of a big-shot professor and an up-and-coming novelist. He can feel big and important only if he keeps you small and dependent."

"But I hate him for doing such a terrible thing to me," Sheila said. "I want to hit him where it hurts—right in his pride."

Laureen patted Sheila's hand gently. "I understand that. Truly, I do. But you're going to have to bide your time. If you go home tonight and show him this letter and the check, he may send you packing. What would you do? How would you live? He has a master's degree; you have only a high-school diploma. He has the upper hand for the moment. Even if I took you in, my days are numbered, as you well know."

"Actually, I *have* thought this issue through," said Sheila. "I came to the conclusion that the only thing I have going for me right now is a steady job."

"Yes. And, along with that, you have a house payment and a car payment and other expenses. Remember, whatever contracts you've signed with Dan, you're equally obligated to pay. He may not earn much to supplement your income, but he brings in enough to keep you two afloat. You're not financially ready to go out on your own. Besides, there's another problem."

"What's that?"

Softly, Laureen said, "I'm your biggest fan—you know that, my dear. But the story you just sold was penned fifteen years ago. You haven't written anything new since then, except for a few exercises we've done during our sessions. Before you start announcing your success as a writer, I think you'd better write another story and submit it for publication. If that one sells, too, then you'll know you've got what it takes."

Sheila thought that over for a second. "I see your point. I'm not worried, though. I can write another story—an even better one. I've already come up with an idea." She paused before continuing. "But I want to ask you something. You said I should have been the one who went to college and worked on a writing career. Do you...do you think I could write many stories? A novel, even?"

"I'm completely convinced of it," Laureen said with an emphatic nod. "I won't live to see it happen, unfortunately, but, yes—one of these days, if you're given the opportunity and enough time, I have no doubt you'll write a novel. A really *good* novel."

"That's always been my ultimate dream. But what do I do meanwhile?"

Laureen smiled conspiratorially. "I wasn't married to a businessman all those years without learning a thing or two about money," she said. "You're going to need to open your own checking account at a bank in a nearby town. You can put it in your legal name, but be sure to register it as 'DBA Dove Alexander.' That means 'doing business as.' Then, you can deposit any checks you receive for your writing into that account. Dan will never know. Bide your time. Save your money. It may take a while, but eventually you'll have enough cash saved to enable you to go out on your own."

Sheila glanced at her watch. "Let me just leave the letter and check here until lunch," she said. "Then I'll pick you up, and we'll drive over to a bank together. I doubt I'll be able to think straight today. I'm feeling totally overwhelmed. My head is spinning. This has been too much to process all at once."

"You'll handle it," said Laureen. "Just don't tip your hand in any way to Dan. Let him think that it's still his ball game...for now."

True to form, Dan came in that night with flowers and a sweet treat—instead of candy, however, it was a frosted banana-nut loaf. He began to deliver a grand speech about how he wanted to protect Sheila from the agony of additional failures as a writer, but after the first three lines, he paused in obvious surprise because Sheila was nodding as if in full agreement.

"I'm sorry, Dan," she said, filling the silence. "I don't know what got into me. Sometimes, I just feel really insignificant when I think of how far ahead of me you are in your education. The whole reason I was trying to do these book studies with Mrs. Parks was so that I'd be a better conversationalist at your faculty parties. I don't want to be an embarrassment to you."

Dan smiled with obvious approval. "Oh, sweetheart, I'm not embarrassed by you. I appreciate your efforts. I can't tell you how relieved I am that you've returned to your senses. However, from now on, I'll do the literary interpretations for us, okay?"

Sheila giggled innocently. "Okay. It's a deal. From now on, I think I'll just watch television with Mrs. Parks. Books are a bit too heady."

Dan beamed. "Good idea. How about making us some coffee while I cut this cake?"

Sheila smiled, then winced at the pain around her injured eye. Inside, however, she was feeling fine. *"Bide your time,"* Laureen had said. Yes, she could do that. Meanwhile, she would continue to read and discuss literature with Laureen, and during her lunch hours at the office, she would start writing that new story. As Dan cut the cake, Sheila thought of how symbolic that act seemed. *One day, Dan, you will learn that you can't have your cake and eat it, too.*

Within three weeks, Sheila had completed the first draft of her new story. Several times during their evening sessions, Laureen had asked to see parts of it, but Sheila had begged off, telling her that she wanted to do more touching up in certain spots before showing it to her. However, today was going to be "reading" day.

Sheila had observed a steady decline in her mentor's health. Laureen's skin had taken on a yellowish darkness, her eyes were deeply sunken, and even her movements were more labored and obviously painful than they'd been just a few weeks prior. Knowing that the third Thursday of the month was Laureen's scheduled check-up day, Sheila had volunteered to drive her to the clinic and back again, taking off the entire afternoon as personal time she had accumulated.

On the drive back, Sheila asked, "Would you like to stop somewhere for a salad or maybe a bit of pie and coffee?"

Laureen closed her eyes and leaned against the headrest. "Let's just go home, please."

Sheila didn't need to ask if the doctors had said anything more about the advancement of her cancer. Once they arrived at Laureen's house, Sheila helped the woman into her favorite easy chair. "I'm sure you're exhausted after today's outing," Sheila said. "I'm going to make a sandwich, put it under plastic wrap, and leave it in the refrigerator for whenever you get hungry. I'll leave your cell phone right here next to you, in case you need to reach me for anything."

Laureen attempted a smile. "I'll be fine. I like to ease back in this chair and take a nap in the afternoons. Would you please cover me with that afghan?" She nodded at the knitted throw that was draped over one arm of the couch.

Sheila gladly did as requested, then went to the kitchen, made a sandwich, and left it in the refrigerator, as promised. When she returned to the living room, Laureen was already asleep. The routine poking and prodding by the doctor, never a pleasant experience, had worn Laureen out.

Sheila tiptoed to the hallway and retrieved a manila envelope from her tote bag. She laid it on the table beside the easy chair, and then locked the front door on her way out.

As she drove off, she wondered how her mentor would react when she read the new story. Sheila had titled it "Surrogate Mother," and she knew that by the end of page one, Laureen would recognize herself as the main character.

The story told of a young woman who wanted to be a painter but had little to no encouragement from her family and friends. Then, under the guidance of an older woman, along with regular sessions of girl-talk at private "tea parties," she developed her talents as an artist. The story ended with the young woman receiving marvelous reviews for her first gallery show. The collection's centerpiece painting was a portrait of the older woman who had been the young woman's mentor…and the painting was marked, "Not for Sale…Absolutely Priceless."

Sheila hoped that her story would communicate to Laureen Parks not only her desire to give a blatant tribute to her teacher, but also that Sheila was back on track to fulfill her destiny as a writer. She would continue producing stories and selling them to leading magazines, and, with time, she would also write a novel.

Unfortunately, Laureen probably wouldn't live long enough to see Sheila's first published novel. It was obvious her life clock was winding down. Sheila suspected that by now, the cancer had spread to key organs. Nevertheless, any success Sheila enjoyed would be the direct result of the love and guidance of Mrs. Laureen Parks.

"I love you, Mrs. Parks," Sheila whispered as she pulled into her own driveway, ready to play, once again, the role of a clueless wife.

CHAPTER 14

The following week, Laureen arranged to go on hospice care, and during the two months that followed, she declined rapidly. She virtually stopped eating or doing anything else except for meeting twice weekly with Sheila. Those times seemed to cheer her, as if mentoring Sheila was the only thing keeping her on this earth. Sheila wondered whether the tribute she had written about Laureen had given her friend the renewed vigor needed to hang on a little longer. Something, at least, had been keeping her alive against all odds.

In fact, Laureen had loved "Surrogate Mother" so much, she'd persuaded Sheila to submit it immediately to the editor of *Fulfillment* magazine. Although Sheila knew it would likely be several more weeks until she received any kind of response, she found herself becoming more anxious by the day. The story represented not only an act of love and honor toward Laureen but also the acid test of whether she could repeat her earlier success. Fluke? Lucky break? Genuine talent? Time would tell. Her career and her future were riding on the success or failure of this story.

One blustery day in early October, when Sheila returned to work after her lunch break, she found a voice-mail message on her phone. It was Laureen, sounding weary yet somehow animated. "Sheila, I realize today isn't one of our scheduled meeting times, but would you please stop by after work? The visiting nurse will be gone by then. Let yourself in as usual with your key. I love you, dear. See you this evening."

Just then, Mike Reynolds came to Sheila's desk and unloosed a handful of papers. "Good news, bad news," he said with his characteristic toothy grin. "I hate to dump this on you, but the hospital is having an emergency with their temperature-control system. If we get our bid in first, we might land the whole job. Big bucks. Need you to get on it right away."

"Ah, job security," she said in mock delight as she automatically started sorting through the disheveled pile of paperwork. "Who's running it over to the hospital once it's ready? You or me?

Mike checked his watch. "I'd prefer to take it myself, but it'll depend on what happens at the job I've got scheduled this afternoon. I'll be over at Clayton Jordan's house installing a new heat pump. Call my cell when you've got the paperwork ready. I'll let you know then if I can take it over."

Sheila gave a two-fingered salute. "Aye, Cap'n. I'll be in touch as soon as possible."

"Thanks." Mike headed for the back door. "Don't know how we'd run this place without you."

Under her breath, she said, "Lord knows I'd like to give you a chance to find out."

Between the rush job for the hospital bid and the other tasks Sheila had already planned for the day, she stayed busy right up until five o'clock. When Bev and Lexie called, "We're outta here," Sheila looked up and realized it was time to lock the doors and leave. She hurried through her end-of-the day routine in order to get to Laureen's house as soon as she could. She didn't want to keep her friend waiting. Besides, her visits with Laureen were keeping *her* going, too. Heaven forbid that Dan should ever suggest she spend more quality time at home with him.

As she pulled into Laureen's driveway, she smiled at the sight of the tidy little yard, now dotted with bright leaves—red, yellow, and orange. The surroundings were almost as welcoming as was the person living there. Sheila got out of the car and hurried to the door, pulling her key from her purse on her way.

As usual, Sheila knocked as she opened the door. "Helloooo! I'm here." She stepped into the darkened living room, where a hospital bed had been set up. The home aide must have closed the drapes that afternoon against the sun's glare so Laureen could nap.

As she approached the bed, Sheila said, "What's up? Any special reason...?" Then she stopped.

Laureen made no response to the sound of Sheila's voice. Her eyes having grown accustomed to the dimness, Sheila could now see Laureen lying completely still.

Sheila felt for a pulse but couldn't find one on her friend's neck or wrist. The truth of what had happened punched her almost as hard as a physical blow. The most important person in Sheila's life was now gone. Whatever had been keeping Laureen Parks alive had finally lost its protective power against the cancer's curse.

Sheila gently stroked Laureen's wrinkled face as tears trickled down her own cheeks. Then she knelt by the side of the bed, laid her face on the mattress, and sobbed. She cried for the loss of her dear friend, for the mother she never knew, and for the fact that Laureen had died alone. Finally, with her emotions spent, she slowly rose to her feet. It was then that she noticed, clutched in Laureen's hands, an envelope and a piece of folded stationery.

She picked up the items, opened the paper, and discovered it was a letter addressed to Dove Alexander, with *Fulfillment* magazine listed on the letterhead. Sheila's heart began to pound as she quickly scanned the message. It was an acceptance for her story, "Surrogate Mother." Inside the envelope, she found a check for $1,000.

"No!" she said in joyous disbelief, momentarily forgetting she was alone. "We did it!" She quickly scanned the letter again. "Yes! We really did it! We sold it!"

Hearing no response brought her back to reality, but it didn't totally extinguish her joy. "And you lived to see it, didn't you, dear teacher, dear friend?" She glanced heavenward. "Oh, God, thank You for that. This never would have happened without her." Once again, she had to stop and read the letter. No, it wasn't a mistake. Still, what a moment of mixed emotions: her greatest triumph and her severest loss, both here, now, this day, this instant.

But what should she do next concerning her writing?

"Do?" she could imagine Laureen saying just now. *"Deposit that check in the account we opened, and then get started on a new story. Now!"*

Sheila leaned over and gently kissed her mentor's forehead. "I'll never forget you." She refolded the letter, slid it inside the envelope along with the check, and tucked the envelope into her purse. Laureen had hidden the other letter that had come from *Accent Female*, but Sheila had forgotten to ask her where it was. Too late for that now.

She picked up the phone and called the hospice nurse.

Oddly, the funeral itself did not depress Sheila. Laureen had made all the necessary decisions well in advance about the casket, the burial plot, the tombstone, the obituary notice, and even the closing up of her house. The mortician and a local real-estate agent stepped in immediately and followed through on everything per the precise instructions she had drawn up.

At the viewing, several former students of Laureen's came to pay their respects, and Sheila actually enjoyed the opportunity to catch up with them on news, to see pictures of her former classmates' homes and children, and to compare notes about jobs, hobbies, and travels.

More than one person asked, "And what about your writing, Sheila? Do you still do any of that?" She nearly burst with the desire to share how she'd sold two short stories to two leading woman's magazines, but she forced herself to "bide her time," remembering Laureen's admonition. Instead, she smiled demurely and said, "Well, Mrs. Parks and I had been meeting occasionally to talk about literature. I did a little writing for fun. She was trying to get me interested again. But you...what hobbies are you into these days?" That would usually suffice to switch the subject away from her.

Dan hadn't shown up for either of the two days of viewing, but he did make an appearance at the funeral home for the actual memorial service. He even wore one of his suits, although it looked tight on him and was sadly outdated. He didn't bother to drive out to the grave site for the final blessing and interment, but Sheila was gratified that he'd made an effort to acknowledge the loss she felt and to show a modicum of respect for her mentor.

During the ensuing days, Sheila was shocked to discover how truly alone she now felt. At work, there were no more phone messages from Laureen. On Tuesday and Thursday nights, she had no place to go. If any ideas for stories crossed her mind, she felt no motivation to start working on them because she had no one to discuss them with.

She considered forming a bond with one of the other women at work, but a quick glance around the office told her that the idea was a lost cause: Sherry was chewing gum and reading a fashion magazine targeted toward teenagers, Bev was spending her lunch breaks doing cross-stitch while talking on a Bluetooth ear hook to her sister about swapping babysitting duties so that they each could join a bowling team, and Lexie was making yet another trip to the bathroom due to morning sickness...and she wasn't even married.

Sheila could just imagine the reaction if she were to announce, "Hey, any of you girls want to get together a couple nights each week to talk about Tolstoy, Dickens, and Hemingway? I'll order pizza. It'll be a blast." Yeah, right.

Even her private time at work was no longer a special pleasure. Her computer's hard drive housed three short stories she had started, but what was the point in finishing them? Who would read them, critique them, or suggest revisions?

At home, Dan offered no sympathy. If anything, he made matters worse, always talking about his "colleague" Imogene and her lectures and her papers and her...whatever.

Gradually, Sheila morphed into a lethargic, glassy-eyed automaton. She somehow managed each day to go through the motions of getting up, making breakfast, driving to work, typing, filing, returning home, making dinner, washing the dishes, and then going to bed before starting the cycle all over again. But she had no energy, no goals, no purpose, and no motivation. Although she'd known that Laureen was a mainstay in her life, she'd never realized just how *much* the woman had become the focal point of all that Sheila valued and of all that made her happy.

One lunch hour, on a whim, Sheila drove to Laureen Parks's home, now locked and secured. She parked in the driveway and let her mind recall the nights of tea and cookies and laughter and intense discussions. She mentally played back the scene of how they figured out Dan had never submitted her short story to the *Redbook* contest, and then how, all these years later, they had finally managed to sell that story.

"Oh, Laureen, you never should have come back into my life," Sheila lamented aloud. "My ignorance was my bliss. Now, you've ruined everything. I've gotten a taste of education and of writing success, but only enough to let me know what I'll be missing for the rest of my life. I've got fourteen hundred dollars in the bank. That's more money than I've ever had just to myself in my entire life. Yet it isn't even enough to buy a better car." She banged her fist on the dashboard.

"I can't go anywhere or do anything. I'm stuck again. You left me too soon. Six more months, another year, and, sure, I might have been ready to go out on my own. But not now. You taught me college-level English classes, but I have no degree to prove it. You got me writing again, but I've never sent anything out that you hadn't first blue-penciled and carefully copyedited for me. I'm *not* a solo act."

She lowered her head onto the steering wheel. "I've got just enough money, just enough education, and just enough success to make me absolutely miserable. It would have been better if *I* would have died of cancer and *you* would have gone on living."

Although she didn't consider herself suicidal, she knew she had lost her will to live. She'd read enough stories to know that women *could* die of heartbreak. That wasn't a fantasy. Humans had the capacity of becoming so severely maudlin, they would literally lose their appetite for life and for all that went with it. In time, they would either starve to death or become so vulnerable to normal viruses that they would succumb to an illness as minor as a common cold. Sheila now saw that as her destiny. Without a will to live, there was no way to continue. She would even welcome death. She had tried to succeed and had lost. Life had beaten her.

Methodically, she put the car in gear and drove ten miles to a nearby town. As if shutting down a business, she started going through the phase-out stages of her life. She withdrew all the money from her secret account. She purchased a money order made out in her brother's name for $1,400. She drove to the post office, bought a pre-stamped envelope, and wrote on it the address of the Davis farm. She begged a sticky note from the mail clerk and wrote a quick memo to JD, informing him that the money was to be used to reduce some of his family debts. He was not to call her about it or ever mention this matter to Dan. She signed it, "Your loving sister, Sheila." That would more than pay him back for the times he had given her money when she was in college and then first married.

She pushed the envelope through the outgoing mail slot before driving back to Brissenden, where she stopped by the public library and returned a stack of classic novels she had been carrying around in her car, all unread and all owing overdue fines.

When she arrived back at the office, she sat at her desk and powered up her computer. Once the screen came to life, she began to erase the vestiges of her vainglorious dreams of becoming a hotshot author. She dragged "Farm Girl," "The Worm Turns," and "Two Old Friends" to the trash icon. Click, click, click...gone to the eternal abyss of cyber hell.

She sat back. *Okay, no loose ends. Dove Alexander is now a nonentity.*

With luck and a little time, maybe the same would soon be said of Sheila Gray.

Days passed. Nothing could stir Sheila from her doldrums. Her office mates invited her out to lunch. She declined. No appetite. Despite her admonition, JD had called to thank her for the generous check and had invited her out to the farm to spend an evening visiting with him and his family. She passed on that, too. No desire for anything.

Only one tiny interest still burned with the remnants of a spark of life. She called the real-estate agent who had been given the caretaking responsibilities for Laureen's house and explained, "Laureen Parks was a friend of mine, a dear friend. She wanted me to have thirty books in her collection. I'd like to go in and get them. Can I meet you out at her house, please?"

"Oh, no, that would never do," the agent said bluntly. "Until the attorney receives our inventory of all belongings in the home, and the probate hearing has taken place, no heir can have access to her property."

That response was deeply disappointing. Sheila wanted the books. More than that, she just wanted a chance to walk back into the house while it still smelled of orange pekoe tea and lilac perfume and old leather chairs. But now, even that small privilege was denied her.

As the days went by, she could actually feel herself getting weaker. She decided she needed to tell Mike to start looking for a replacement office manager. She knew a day was coming when she simply would not get out of bed. Dan wouldn't be able to threaten her enough. Sherry wouldn't be able to coax her enough. Nobody would be able to inspire her to continue to *exist* in this do-nothing, go-nowhere life of hers.

Then, ironically, on the morning of Halloween, it was as if heaven provided Sheila Gray with one last golden opportunity to make good on her vow not to let her late teacher down. Just after ten o'clock, the phone on Sherry's desk rang. Sheila could hear Sherry say, "Yeah, she's here. I'll transfer you. Just hold a sec." Then Sherry turned around to face Sheila. "It's for you. Long distance. Someone from New York City."

"You handle it, okay?" Sheila pleaded, not even bothering to look up.

"I can't," Sherry said. "This woman didn't ask for the office manager. She asked for you by name. She wants to talk to Sheila Gray, and she sounds like she's in a huff."

Reluctantly, Sheila accepted the transferred call. "Sheila Gray. How may I help you?"

"Well, for one thing, you can help me be sure I've got the right Sheila Gray," said a raspy woman's voice with an obvious East Coast accent. "Are you also known as Dove Alexander?"

Sheila's heart stopped beating for an instant. "Who...who is this?" she demanded. "Who are *you*?"

"First things first," the woman said. "I'm going to ask you once again, honey: Are you, or *are you not*, also known as Dove Alexander?"

Sheila glanced around. Everyone else was busy talking on the phone or typing at a computer, but she couldn't risk exposure. "Uh...please stay on the line a moment," she said, putting the woman on hold without waiting for a response. She went into Mike's private office, closed the door, and picked up line three. "How did you get that name?" she demanded.

After a slight pause, the unidentified woman said, "And nice to meet you, too, lady."

"How do you know about Dove Alexander?" Sheila again asked.

"So it *is* you, eh?" said the woman. "Well, I know about Dove Alexander because I'm the nice lady in the Big Apple who sent you a fat check for a thousand bucks not long ago. Judith Hardy. Ring a bell?"

It rang a bell—cathedral sized. "You're Judith...? The...you're the...?"

"Editor in chief of *Fulfillment* magazine. Is that what you're trying to get out? Yes, ma'am, the one and only. But what's with *you*? Did you join a witness protection program or something? My assistants and I have spent nearly two weeks trying to track you down."

"How...?"

"There are ways," said Judith Hardy, "but the most important thing is, I seem to have finally found you."

Sheila couldn't help herself. "Tell me how you did it."

"You cashed the check we mailed you," Judith explained. "You signed your real name before you signed the pen name. The phone number for Dove Alexander listed on your manuscript is disconnected, so we turned to the Internet. One of the many Sheila Grays we found was listed as office manager at Reynolds Heating and Air-Conditioning in the same area code as the discontinued number. Glad I finally found you. It's been a real wild-goose chase."

"Sorry about that," said Sheila. "That phone number belonged to a friend of mine. She died recently. You just shocked me when you mentioned my pen name. Only my friend and I knew anything about Dove. It's...well, it's kind of a long story."

"In which I have no interest whatsoever, to be quite frank with you," said the editor. "I'm calling you about an assignment. You interested?"

Sheila blinked. "I'm sorry. I didn't catch that."

"I love your style of writing," Judith explained, "and I've got a plot here that is just perfect for my Christmas issue, but the author who was going to write it for me up and broke both arms and a leg in a car accident, if you can imagine. We're in emergency mode here. It pays three large. Can I throw it your way?"

Sheila felt very dense. "I've had several rough weeks since my friend died," she began, "so maybe I'm not tracking well today. You're saying you want a short story written?"

"Bingo. And I want *you* to write it. Three large."

"Three large what?"

There was a pause. "Three large *what?* Three thousand dollars. A buck fifty a word for two thousand words. Deadline's November fifteenth. Appearance in the online Christmas issue, this year. Dove... Pigeon...Skylark...any byline you want on it, honey." The editor waited a second, then added, "Look, sorry about your friend and all, but can I count on you to write this story for me or not?"

"Excuse me," said Sheila, shaking her head slightly. "Is this for real? You're offering me three thousand dollars to write a short story for the Christmas issue of *Fulfillment* magazine?"

"It takes you a while, but eventually...."

Sheila raked her fingers through her hair. "I'm sorry, it's just a bit overwhelming. And I'm flattered beyond words. And I thank you, I do. I mean, *really*. But I'm just not that good. I've only sold two short stories—"

"Two!" Judith interrupted her. "Who got the other one?"

"Who? Why, uh, *Accent Female*, for their October issue. But it was just a little thing I once—"

"Never again, you hear me?" thundered the editor. "If you've got any other stuff, it comes here first. I see it first. I've got the money to outbid the others. Are you hearing me on this, Dove?"

"It's Sheila," she said, still dazed. "And, yes. That is—"

"Good. Very good. Now, here's the gist of the new story. It's Christmastime back in nineteen forty-two in some Midwestern town. Ohio, Indiana…hey, maybe even right there in Bristletown."

"Brissenden," Sheila corrected her, scarcely realizing how she was being drawn into the conversation.

"Okay, whatever. Any little Villeville, USA, burg with a snowy December and a crèche scene on the courthouse lawn and the carolers walking down the sidewalk and the Salvation Army bell ringer on the corner, yadda, yadda, yadda. You're seeing this with me, aren't you, honey?"

"Well, yes, but—"

"And then, one night, lo and behold, someone puts an infant in the manger scene when nobody's around. I mean, a for-real, screaming and crying, don't-I-look-like-the-baby-Jesus-Himself little kid. And some passersby hear the kid and call the cops or the mayor or the board of health—any agency at hand—and report an abandoned child. Is this wild or what?"

Sheila pulled the phone away from her head and looked at it momentarily, then put it back to her ear to listen. Who in creation was she talking to? Was this really an editor?

"Still there, sweetheart? Fabulous. Okay, so they bring the baby inside and—quicker than you can say 'Santa Claus is coming to town'—they discover that this kid is Amerasian."

"Is what?" asked Sheila.

Ignoring her question, Judith raced ahead. "And when the town discovers that this kid is half-Japanese and half-American, and it's only been one Christmas since the bombing of Pearl Harbor, well, you can just imagine what happens next, right?"

"Uh...what?" Sheila asked naively, trying to appease the bizarre woman.

"No, no," said Judith Hardy. "That wasn't a riddle, sweets. That was the assignment."

Sheila felt completely lost. "I beg your pardon?"

"I said, that's where you come in, Dove. That's where I want you to pick up the plot and finish the story. Tell me—and my readers—what happens to that little kid and what lessons the town learns about brotherly love and forgiveness and all kinds of holiday junk like that. You know, joy to the world and all that other bull. Something that'll rip people's hearts out, like that story about the old lady you wrote for us. Schlock. Violins and flowers. Three-hankie final act."

Sheila felt the need to call a time-out. This woman was a steamroller.

"Excuse me, but can we pause here for just a minute?" Sheila asked. "I need to be honest with you about something. I'm *not* a professional writer. I don't have any college degrees or special training. Like I said, I've only written and sold two short stories—"

"Do you have to keep bringing that up?" the editor interrupted, sounding genuinely upset. "Look, Dove...Sheila. The people who read my magazine aren't rocket scientists. They are women who like to relax by reading a story. A darn good story. And that, lady, is something you can deliver. I've got zillions of wordsmiths but precious few storytellers."

Sheila needed to explain. "Ms. Hardy—"

"Judith."

"Judith, this friend of mine who died—the one I told you about—well, she *did* have all those college English degrees. She used to copyedit my rough drafts. She made me look better than I really am. And now that she's gone...."

"Now that she's gone, you've got me," said Judith. "If you think your friend was a stickler for precision writing, you'll discover that I'm an outright dominatrix. Behind my back, I'm known as the Banshee of Broadway, the Jackal of Journalism, the Grinch of Gotham, and some other names fit only for bathroom walls. This isn't going to be a walk in Central Park, sweetheart. You'll probably rewrite this bloody story a dozen times before I put my imprimatur on it in the next two weeks. You got game, girl?"

In spite of herself, Sheila felt her heart racing. It was as though someone had tossed her a life preserver just as she was sinking underwater for the third time. She decided to reach out and grab hold. It was now or never.

"Judith," she said, then faltered a moment. "Judith, it's been a hard couple of weeks for me." Again she paused and cleared her throat before continuing. "I was beginning to think that I had no reason to go on. It's been that bad for me. I don't know why I should be telling you this, except to say that, if you'll work with me, I'll write for you. I swear I'll do the very best I can. I need this. I really need this. So, I'll try. I swear I'll really, really try."

"I believe that," Judith confirmed. "Okay, grab a piece of paper and a pen. I'm going to give you an e-mail address. By tomorrow afternoon, I want you to send me a four-page summary of where you plan to take the story. I want a title, a couple of opening paragraphs, and then a summation. Tomorrow, no later than 3 PM."

"Yes. Yes, count on it," Sheila promised her. "Count on *me*."

When Sheila returned to her desk, she decided to type a quick note to herself about the story Judith Hardy had just assigned her. She had written the first line when she remembered the three stories she'd started—*and then had deleted*!

In a near panic, she clicked on the icon for the recycle bin to see if the documents were still there. Her stories were gone. Erased. Wiped out forever. *Serves you right for giving up on Laureen's dream—my dream,* she scolded herself. *I'm just glad she doesn't know how foolish you've been. At least, I don't think she knows....*

Well, she'd better get Judith's story outline into some tangible form before she lost that, too. No use crying over spilt milk, as her father used to say. As she typed, she happened to notice that the office's automatic backup software was sending a recently changed file to the cloud.

The backup software! She might still be able to recover her files.

She launched the program's interface box, quickly located the most recently saved versions of the three deleted files, and clicked "restore." Within two minutes, "Farm Girl," "Two Friends," and "The Worm Turns" were safely back in her private writing folder.

"Welcome back, you little darlings," she whispered. First, Judith's call, and now the retrieval of her lost stories. In spite of the skeletons, Draculas, and other death-themed decorations her coworkers had draped around the office for Halloween, this day had become a life-affirming turning point for her.

"Hey," she called out to her office mates. "Somebody offered to buy me lunch last week. If the offer's still open, I'm in the mood for pasta."

By the time Sheila got home that night, she was a new woman. Dan had already left to teach his class at the Indy campus, and that was fine with her. She put on some Michael Bublé and spent an hour giving the house a good dusting and vacuuming, singing along with the lyrics of "My Way" and meaning them. Then she made herself a grilled-cheese sandwich, grabbed a bottle of diet iced tea from the fridge, and sat at the kitchen table to brainstorm.

Time evaporated. When she checked her wristwatch, she was amazed to discover it was nearly eleven at night. There before her, however, was a completed outline of a short story, to be called "The Second Noel." She tucked her notes in her purse, left a wrapped ham-salad sandwich and some potato chips on a plate for Dan, then went to bed. She slept restfully for the first time since Laureen's passing.

Sheila was up and gone even before Dan's alarm went off the next morning. She left him a note saying she had to go to the office early to handle some business with a client. That was the truth, after all—even though the client was *hers* and not one of Reynolds'. She typed up and e-mailed the pages to Judith Hardy and tried to imagine the editor's surprise upon arriving at her office and finding the document waiting for her.

However, Sheila was the one surprised when, by noon, Judith returned the document, vivid with track-changes edits, including strike-outs and even some off-color expletives in the comment boxes. Sheila didn't know whether to laugh or cry.

But she did have the presence of mind to send out for lunch. "Bring me a grilled Reuben from the deli, will you, Sherry? I need to stay here and do some work on a private project."

"Your funeral," Sherry called back as she walked out the door.

Sheila smiled. "Uh-uh. My life."

In the days that followed, Judith lived up to her reputation as an über-demanding editor. Sheila created a different folder for each revision of "The Second Noel." She labeled them "Revisions," "The Return of Revisions," "Son of Revisions," and "Revisions Meet Abbott and Costello." Rewrites begat rewrites *ad infinitum*. But Sheila also made good on her promise to Judith, coming back time and again with better ideas, fresher writing, stronger images, and more powerful dialogue.

Finally, after two intense weeks of innumerable e-mails back and forth, Sheila sent in yet another version. To her amazement, instead of a request for more revisions, a short e-mail arrived from Judith that merely stated, "I O U 3 K."

Sheila exited the office, went to the parking lot behind the building, and punched her fist into the air as she screamed, "Yes!" at the top of her lungs. She then walked back inside, the picture of unflappable stability. The self-satisfied smile, however, could not be wiped off her face.

Sheila e-mailed Judith back, inquiring what she should do about the payment. She'd already told Judith about her "husband troubles" and explained that she didn't want Dan to know about her developing career as Dove Alexander.

Judith came up with the suggestion that Sheila let *Fulfillment* magazine keep the money for her "on account" until she needed it. Then, Judith could have specific checks sent to Sheila whenever she wanted to make a cash draw. Sheila agreed readily to the proposed setup and asked that Judith send her $400 at her office and keep the rest on account for her.

When the cash arrived, Sheila created a special "Hoosier Gift Pack" for Judith to show her gratitude. She got a large box and filled it with some brochures about the pioneer settlement at Fort Wayne, a model of an Indianapolis 500 race car, a Purdue University insulated mug, an Indianapolis Colts pennant, a paperback biography of Larry Bird, a state map of Indiana, and, naturally, a big yellow sweatshirt with large black lettering that read "Brissenden College, Brissenden, Indiana." She included a note that said, "You have just been e-mailed a link to a downloadable MP3 of the song 'Back Home Again in Indiana.'" Then she shipped the whole thing to New York.

Two days later, she received an e-mail from Judith: "Tell the Chamber of Commerce that I was very impressed with its barrage of promotional materials. But no ears of corn? What gives?"

Thus began what was to become a long-running personal and professional relationship between two women who had yet to lay eyes on each other. In the ensuing weeks, Sheila worked on the three unfinished stories she'd kept on her computer at work. Judith continued to butcher her copy, sharpen her word choices, and add dimensions to her characters. Sheila found it to be very different from working with Laureen. It was as though she had gone from freshman prerequisites in basic composition to core classes in a master's program in creative writing.

Additionally, on the phone, by e-mail, and even via occasional video-conference calls, Judith started coaching Sheila regarding the ins and outs of copyrights, literary agents, and other aspects of the publishing game. It was a win-win situation: Sheila was gaining an eye-opening education in how to succeed as a professional writer, and Judith was getting some of the best short stories her magazine had ever published. That the two women genuinely liked each other was just an added bonus.

The activity kept Sheila busy throughout what would have otherwise been a lonely Christmas season. Whenever Dan came home inebriated from free-flowing cheer at holiday parties and went to bed early, she was often still at the office, working on her writing.

By the time Sheila's "Surrogate Mother" appeared in print under her Dove Alexander byline, she had already sold two other stories to *Fulfillment* and was working on a fourth. She had more than $6,000 on account in New York. At this rate, if her luck and talent held, she would be able to break out on her own in about five years.

Five years. Each time she did the calculation, it sounded like a prison sentence. True, it wasn't "life without parole," but it still seemed like she had a long, long way to go. And she couldn't help but worry occasionally about what she would do if Judith ever quit her job or was fired. Would that mean the end of the line for Dove Alexander, too?

Well, she had no crystal ball. But she did have a game plan. For now, that would have to do. *Just give me the grit and patience to gut it out, Lord,* she prayed silently each time she contemplated her future. And, once again, Laureen's words would come to her: *Bide your time, Sheila. It will all come together for you if you'll just bide your time.*

"Easier said than done, dear friend," she mused aloud "Easier said than done."

CHAPTER 15

During the week between Christmas and New Year's, Sheila continued to clock herself out at 5:00 PM and remain at her desk to work on personal writing projects. Late one evening, Mike Reynolds called her direct line.

"Hey, Sheila, glad I caught you," he said, sounding out of breath. "We got ourselves a perfect storm."

"What's up?"

"The furnace went out at Brissenden Memory Care Center this evening. I went to look at it myself, since this happened with the same brand of furnace a couple of years ago, and I thought I could isolate the problem. Turns out it needs a new part."

"You want me to place the order? What's the part number?" Sheila grabbed a pen and a pad of sticky notes.

"I already ordered it. The problem is getting it here in time. The original manufacturer went out of business, so, last time, we got a custom job shop in Detroit to manufacture one for us using the worn-out part as a pattern. While they were at it, they made several units so they could supply other businesses that repair the same brand of furnace."

Sheila put down the pen. "Okay. What do you need me to do?"

"Drive to Detroit tomorrow and pick it up."

"What? That's five hours from here. Wouldn't a next-day shipping service be cheaper?"

"Sure it would. But here's the perfect-storm part: Most of the shop's employees have this week off. The assistant who usually takes care of shipping is out with the flu. There's nobody to box it up and overnight it here until after New Year's. Those old people at the center can't wait that long for heat."

"Will there even be anyone at the Detroit shop to give me the part?"

"Yeah. The owner's a buddy of mine from military days, so he offered to meet you at the office himself and then close up after you leave. I'd make the trip, but I've got a couple of other emergency jobs to handle tomorrow. You know Sherry's on vacation, and Lexie's still on sick leave for severe morning sickness. Bev can hold down the fort while you do this for me. You'll be on the clock, and you'll be reimbursed for mileage and meals, of course. Just turn in your receipts. Can you help me out of this jam?"

"Sure. Give me the address, and I'll leave first thing tomorrow."

"You're the best, Sheila. Just the best."

After getting the information from Mike, Sheila shut down her computer and hurried home. Dan hadn't returned yet from teaching his night class. Once she removed her coat, she listened to the messages on their home answering machine. One was from the attorney handling Mrs. Parks's estate, asking that Sheila call him back on his personal cell phone at her first convenience, even if it was after hours.

She was ending her phone conversation with the attorney when Dan came in the door. "Thank you," she said into the phone. "Yes, I'll see you tomorrow around twelve thirty. Good-bye."

Dan stared at her piercingly. "Who was that?"

Sheila glanced at the slip of paper on which she'd scribbled her notes. "A Detroit lawyer named Martin Pembroke. He's handling Mrs. Parks's estate. Since I'm one of the heirs, he called to verify my mailing address so he could send me a copy of her will."

"Is that all?" Dan asked, his tone conveying suspicion. "Why didn't he just have his secretary follow up with you? And why did you say you'd see him tomorrow? Is he coming here?"

Sheila drew in a long breath before answering. "No, that wasn't all. I'm going to his office tomorrow because, in addition to wanting to verify my address, he also wants to see me in person. I'm driving there—"

"What?" Dan interrupted. "Drive all the way to Michigan just to lay claim to a few dozen books? Is he nuts?"

Sheila fought to remain calm. "He offered to meet with me in Indy next week, when he'll be in town for a conference, but I was just going to tell you that Mike asked me to pick up a custom part tomorrow in Detroit. Since I'll be in the area anyway, I can swing by Mr. Pembroke's office."

Dan narrowed his eyes. "That sounds pretty fishy to me. Mike asks you to go on a ten-hour round-trip drive to a city in another state where you just *happen* to need to see a lawyer? I thought this Parks woman lived right here in Brissenden."

Sheila crossed her arms. "Mr. Pembroke's law practice has always been located in Detroit. After he went to college with Mrs. Parks's late husband, he was their family attorney for nearly forty-five years, even while they lived in Texas."

"I don't need the history lesson," Dan snapped. "Can't he just send you a receipt or something, and then you can go out to her place with a box and get the blasted books? It's a cinch the lawyer's office isn't going to be in the same part of town as the parts shop, so you won't be reimbursed for any extra mileage. A few keepsakes aren't worth putting extra wear and tear on the car and taking time off the clock for a personal errand. You'll probably never even read the books, anyway."

"Actually, I've already read them."

Dan frowned. "What do you mean?"

"Oh, not those actual books," Sheila explained. "Paperback versions of them. The thirty books Mrs. Parks left me are first-edition collector's items. She had an autographed copy of Kurt Vonnegut's *Breakfast of Champions* and an autographed copy of Alex Haley's *Roots*, and twenty-eight other autographed books. She used to go to book fairs, library conferences, teachers' conventions...places like that. She'd add a book or two to her collection every year. They're all in mint condition, and she told me she planned to leave them to me when she died."

"Autographed first editions?" said Dan. "You never mentioned that. You've seen them? Actually seen them?"

"Seen them, touched them, opened them. There's a story behind how she got each one—how she met the author, waited for the autograph, where and when it happened. As we were reading the books, she would tell me about her first-edition copies."

Dan raised a hand, traffic-cop style. "That's the second time you've said that. Are you telling me you've read paperback versions of all thirty of those books?"

"Sure," said Sheila. "We read them together. I'd mark up my paperbacks, and we'd discuss them when we met on those two nights each week when you were teaching in Indy."

Dan's face began to flush. "We talked about that, Sheila. You said you were just going to go out there to visit and watch television with her. Television, Sheila. Not books."

Sheila smiled sweetly. "Well, we tried television one night, and it bored us silly. We went back to reading and writing."

"Writing?" Dan said, nearly choking on the word. "Writing?"

"Yes, writing," she affirmed. "I didn't say anything to you about it because you always got so uptight. But she's dead now, so what does it matter to you? I've hardly written a thing in the four months since she's been gone. Haven't felt like it. She used to read and edit my stories and encourage me. I was really, really enjoying myself. And I was getting quite good at it, too. But now...what's the point?"

A look of enormous relief crossed Dan's face.

"But I want those books," Sheila continued. "I loved that woman like a mother, and I miss her terribly." She paused a beat, then added, "And I'd like you to go to Detroit with me."

Dan snorted. "Are you kidding? Sure, I can see some genuine value in laying claim to thirty first-edition books autographed by their famous writers. Heck, the volumes would look great on my shelves at the university. Or maybe we could sell them on eBay. Who knows how much they might net? And we could definitely use the money. But it will be a cold day in July before I drive clear to Detroit to get permission to pick them up. Especially when those silly books are only four miles away from where we're standing right *now*."

Sheila lifted her chin. "I never ask anything of you. I work and bring home a paycheck. I clean the house and cook the meals and do the shopping and run your errands, and all you do is teach part-time and then hide yourself in your den working on your novel. It wouldn't hurt you to do something for *me* just once."

He sighed with impatience. "It's bad enough that *you're* going to miss at least an hour of work time while you're in Detroit on this Reynolds errand, not to mention the extra fuel it will cost, driving around trying to find the lawyer's office. *I* don't need to lose a day of productivity, too."

"But—"

"Look," he said, his tone now menacing. "That novel of mine is our ticket out of this two-bit town. You're just lucky enough to be along for the ride. When I hit it big, it'll be because *I* wrote a book...because *I* had the talent...because *I* had the determination and grit to stay with it all these years. Oh, yeah, sure—you cook and clean, all right. That's all you know *how* to do. I am the one with the education, Sheila. I'm the one who is a professor. It's me—not you—who is going to lift us to bigger and better things."

He took a step closer to her. "Go to Detroit and make arrangements for picking up your precious books, but don't expect me to go traipsing off on some tribute voyage to that Parks woman. I never liked her, even the first summer you told me about her at Brissenden College. She was a bad influence on you back then, and she's been a bad influence on you this past year. I'm *glad* she's dead. Now maybe you'll get your head out of the clouds. You're a small-town girl with no education who was lucky enough to marry above her station. Be grateful, and leave it at that."

Although Sheila had been getting increasingly clear glimpses of who her husband really was, this outburst appalled, shocked, and enlightened her, all at once. She put her hand to her mouth, not knowing what to say but understanding fully that she no longer had any love left for Dan Gray. Now, while she was still in grief over the loss of the best friend she'd ever had, Dan had hurt her beyond measure with his vicious words—words that not only mocked her personally but also slandered a saint of a woman whom Sheila still held dear to her heart.

Memories came flooding back: warnings from Liz-Liz and Sheila's father…and, later, things people had told her year after year about Dan—things she hadn't wanted to hear and hadn't wanted to believe but now were blatantly obvious. Everyone had been right. Dan was small and cruel and self-centered, and…and completely unworthy of her love and devotion.

She closed her eyes and made a silent vow. *Somehow, someway, I am going to escape you, Dan Gray. Sheila Gray is going to disappear one day and be reborn as Dove Alexander. And then you will never find her again.*

The sky was still dark when Sheila began her trek to Michigan. As she drove off, she was both anxious and excited. She had made very few independent excursions. On the rare occasions when she had ventured away from Brissenden, it had usually been in the company of her father and brothers or with Dan.

Since Sheila didn't have a GPS or a smartphone with mapping capabilities, she had used an online service to research the best route to the Detroit job shop, as well as to Mr. Pembroke's office downtown. Now that she had had time to get used to the idea of such a long trip, she rather liked it. It seemed symbolic, in a way, that going to hear the final wishes of Laureen Parks would be her first real gesture of independence. She looked forward to meeting someone who had been close to Laureen. She expected that Martin Pembroke, who had sounded formal and polite on the phone, would be just as refined and cordial in person, since his decorum did not disguise his sincerity.

Once Sheila merged onto the interstate, she turned the radio off and settled back to enjoy the solitude. Laureen had once told her she would never be able to write her novel unless she had experienced some solitude, and she'd emphasized that there was a difference between alienation and solitude. Well, perhaps so, because Sheila was finding it exhilarating to be away from all that was familiar to her, without someone else making demands on her every few minutes. She couldn't remember feeling this liberated since the day Laureen had driven her to Brissenden for the summer writing program. *How ironic,* she thought. *I'm going to learn about the contents of my best friend's will, and for the first time since her death, I'm feeling truly alive.*

Sheila knew she could never turn her back on writing again. Her work now with Judith was providing more and more satisfaction. And, Judith's no-nonsense, independent attitude was rubbing off. Sheila no longer felt the least bit guilty for keeping her latest writing activities a secret from Dan.

She had finally come to understand that her relationship with her husband was far from what constituted a real marriage. Dan was a toxic person in her life—in fact, he had always been. How could she have been so blind? While she wasn't sure how soon she could become financially independent enough to leave him physically, their emotional separation was undeniable.

Long conversations with Judith had given Sheila a yardstick by which to measure her husband's expectations and behavior. She'd never had such a reference point before. It brought a sense of relief and a strength of conviction. Dan could no longer harass or browbeat her into doubting her own self-worth.

After stopping for lunch along the way and then picking up the furnace part in an industrial section of the city, she located Mr. Pembroke's downtown office. The neighborhood was filled with classic brick buildings. She noticed a mixture of some refurbished town houses, a few carefully maintained office complexes, and a series of completely rundown or abandoned establishments.

Mr. Pembroke's building had been cared for meticulously, and with a great deal of pride, it was clear. Sheila found a parking space less than a block away. After filling the meter to obtain the maximum time allowance, she glanced at her watch. It was only 12:20. Well, now that she'd plugged the meter, she'd better see if the lawyer could meet with her a few minutes early. Besides, in this weather, she'd freeze if she waited in the car until the agreed-upon appointment time.

She walked the short distance to the front door, which read, "Martin Pembroke, II, Attorney at Law." Not knowing whether to knock or to take the liberty of entering unannounced, Sheila hesitantly cracked open the door a few inches. "Hello?"

An elderly man with a thick shock of white hair seemed to materialize out of thin air. "Yes, miss? May I help you?"

"Um, hi," Sheila stammered, suddenly feeling unsure of herself. "I'm Sheila Gray. I have a twelve thirty appointment with Martin Pembroke."

The man extended his hand to Sheila. "I'm Martin Pembroke. It's a pleasure to meet you, Mrs. Gray. Please come in and have a seat. I know you've made a long trip. My administrative assistant is running errands for me, but may I get you something? Coffee? Tea? A soft drink?"

"No, thank you," Sheila replied. "I'm fine. I stopped not long ago for lunch."

She followed the attorney through a reception area into his private office, which smelled of leather and books. A massive cherry desk was centered below a large window. The walls were covered with numerous shelves holding legal reference books. As Mr. Pembroke walked behind the desk to sit in a large leather office chair, he motioned for Sheila to be seated in one of two leather wingback chairs facing the desk.

"Before we begin discussing the provisions of the will, Mrs. Gray, I'd like to verify your identity. No, no, don't reach for your driver's license. Please let me see the necklace you are wearing. I'm looking for a quill, a clock, and a book."

Sheila had to smile. Naturally, she'd be the only one with such a necklace. "You're referring to this?" she said, holding the three charms away from her collarbone.

The older man scrutinized the piece of jewelry through his bifocals, then smiled and nodded. "Excellent, excellent. Now, I'd like to speak openly about Mrs. Parks for a moment, if you don't mind."

"Of course, I don't mind," answered Sheila. "In fact, I've been looking forward to meeting someone else who knew her as well as I did."

"I knew the Parkses for nearly fifty years," Mr. Pembroke began. "Whereas it's true they were my clients, more important, they were also my friends. They were two of the most wonderful people a person could be fortunate enough to find in this world. Both of them were educated and intelligent, yet they never lost the down-to-earth quality that endeared them to others."

"That's certainly how I remember Mrs. Parks," Sheila said softly.

"Not long before her death," the attorney continued, "Laureen Parks called me with instructions to change her will. She sent me a copy of the story you wrote about your relationship with her. It's very charming, and I want you to know that you were just as much a surrogate daughter to her as she was a surrogate mother to you. In fact, when she called me about changing her will, her words to me were, 'Martin, I've just adopted a daughter.'" He smiled warmly. "Mrs. Gray, you brought Laureen tremendous joy in her final days."

Sheila's eyes filled with tears of happiness.

"Now, as to the actual provisions of the will," he went on, "my assistant was ready to put a copy in the mail to you, but, since you were coming here anyway, I thought I would deliver it in person." He handed Sheila a manila envelope. "Would you like me to read the document verbatim as we go over it together, or would you prefer that I just paraphrase for you what it says?"

"I'm fine with you just telling me what it says."

"Very well, then, that's what I'll do," he said. "I believe you're familiar with the set of autographed first-edition novels that Laureen collected throughout the years, are you not?"

"Yes, sir." Sheila nodded. "Mrs. Parks shared stories many times with me about the acquisition of those books. In fact, she told me she was going to leave them to me when she died."

"She has, indeed." He paused slightly before continuing. "Thinking you might want to store them for a while, she left instructions that they be boxed up in archive-quality packaging. I've directed the real-estate agent who's handling the details of her property to meet you there at your convenience so you can take possession of the volumes." He handed Sheila a card. "Here's the cell-phone number where you can reach the agent to set up an appointment. I'm glad to see your interest in the books. Mrs. Parks believed you would treasure those novels as much as she did."

"Oh, yes," Sheila said almost reverently, putting the card in her purse and leaning forward as she prepared to stand and leave. "I'll treasure them always. Having them will almost be like having a part of Mrs. Parks back. Thank you very much."

The elderly attorney cleared his throat. "Yes, hmmm, yes. But, uh, that's not all, Mrs. Gray. There's more, significantly more, to discuss. You see, Mrs. Parks made a rather dramatic change to her will shortly before she died, after she read your beautiful tribute to her. She had great faith in your ability as a writer, you know. It became a matter of utmost importance to her that you should have a chance to succeed."

Sheila raised her eyebrows and settled back in her chair.

"And toward that end," he continued, "Mrs. Parks left you the sum of fifty thousand dollars to facilitate your devoting yourself entirely to the completion of a novel."

Sheila gasped. Surely, she couldn't have heard right.

"It was her intent that the bequest should enable you to take a leave of absence from your job, go away—alone—from your hometown, and have the freedom and the time to nurture your creative ability."

Sheila sat with her mouth open for several seconds. Finally, she asked, "Did you say fifty thousand dollars? For me?"

"Yes," Mr. Pembroke confirmed, "but with strings attached. Most definitely, strings attached, Mrs. Gray."

"But I'm not ready. It's not possible. I'm not prepared to write a novel. I'm just a beginner. I...."

Martin Pembroke interlaced his fingers, put his angular arms on the desk, and leaned far forward. "In the many years I called Laureen Parks my friend, I never knew her to make a foolhardy decision," he said. "She was an impeccable judge of her students and of literature. Therefore, young lady, if Laureen Parks believed in your ability enough to make this provision for you, then write this novel you must."

Sheila's mind raced with conflicting images and thoughts of her job, her house, her husband, and her departed mentor. "Well, I'm not contradicting Mrs. Parks, it's just that...." She stopped, searching for what to say next, then smiled as a thought occurred to her. "Hey, what about this—if I agreed to write the novel at home in my free time away from my job?"

The lawyer looked at her soberly and shook his head. "Mrs. Gray, my client made it crystal clear, both in our conversation and in the official documentation, what her specifications were. It is my job to ensure that those directives are carried out to the letter. If you wish to have the fifty thousand dollars Laureen Parks designated for you, then you must comply fully with the conditions she set forth."

"Of course, I want to honor Mrs. Parks's wishes," said Sheila. "It's just that, well, this is all so unexpected. I never dreamed I'd be able to just take off and hole up somewhere and write a novel. The idea is going to take some getting used to."

"That's understandable," Mr. Pembroke agreed. "Please give the matter serious consideration and then notify me of your plans within ten days. Mrs. Parks left instructions for an alternate use for the money in the event you declined the offer."

He stood. "Again, Mrs. Gray, I'd like to convey how meaningful you made Laureen's last days. She wasn't given to excessive expressions of emotion or affection, but she made it clear to me that your renewed relationship with her had enhanced her life immensely. I'm very pleased to have made your acquaintance."

Sheila did not rise. "May I have ten more minutes of your time?" she asked meekly.

Mr. Pembroke nodded and sat again in his leather chair.

"Mrs. Parks obviously trusted you, relied on you," Sheila continued. "I'm wondering if I could seek your counsel on a personal matter."

The old man grinned graciously. "I've stopped taking on new clients at this stage in my career. But, since Laureen Parks considered you a daughter, I'll think of this as continuing the family arrangement. How can I advise you?"

Sheila smiled, relieved. "Thank you. It's a long story, but I'll cut to the chase. Mrs. Parks was helping me revitalize my writing career, but my husband, Dan Gray, has not been supportive of these endeavors. Mrs. Parks and I worked somewhat under the radar. I made a little bit of money writing under the pen name of Dove Alexander and set up a private checking account in a nearby town using the pseudonym in a 'doing business as' situation. After Mrs. Parks died, and I went into a rather severe depression, I closed the account. But now that I'm writing again for editor Judith Hardy at *Fulfillment* magazine in New York, I've opened a new account."

Sheila removed her wallet from her purse, unzipped a hidden compartment, withdrew a debit card, and traced the embossed account number with her fingertip as she continued. "I'm expecting to receive at least one more check for recent work I've submitted to Judith." She looked up. "If I choose to disappear for a while so I can write this novel, could I turn over to you the management of this bank account while I'm gone? You know, maybe have the checks sent to you so you could deposit them for me? You'd be authorized to access the account in person as well as online. I'd surely be glad to pay you for your time."

The lawyer didn't speak for a moment. Then, he asked, "Are you suggesting that if you told your husband about the account, he not only would be upset to discover you've been writing but also might drain the account for his own use?"

Sheila shivered slightly inside her coat. "He'd have an absolute fit. He gives me no extra spending money, and he considers himself the writer in our marriage, so learning about all this would outrage him. But Mrs. Parks felt I deserved not only the chance to become published myself but also to keep the money, since I wrote the stories."

"Indeed," said Mr. Pembroke. "Indeed, you did. Hmmm, most interesting." He paused in thought for a moment before continuing.

"But what if you decide not to take up the challenge of going away to write a novel? You'd still be able to manage your bank account yourself. Do you want to wait to make the final decision about my involvement in your financial affairs?"

Sheila was surprised by the huge wave of disappointment that washed over her at the thought of ignoring Laureen's final wishes. That disappointment was followed by a chill of foreboding at what Dan might do if he ever found out about Sheila's writing activities and related income. She needed an ally, and Mr. Pembroke would fill that role perfectly.

"Actually," she replied, "I…I feel better already, having taken you into my confidence. I'll let you know very soon what I decide about going away to write a novel. Now that the shock is wearing off, the more I think about the idea, the better I like it. Since I'm already here, let me give you all the information you'd need, and I'll confirm my decision with you shortly."

"All right," he said, sliding a blank yellow legal pad toward her. "I'll have my assistant prepare a formal agreement for you to sign—we could handle that via e-mail—should you decide to accept Mrs. Parks's offer. Be sure to give me your e-mail address. Now, I'll make a business deal with you. I'll manage this little account on your behalf, but I want very specific compensation for my troubles. When this novel of yours comes out, I want a first-edition autographed copy."

Sheila blushed. "I can see why Mrs. Parks trusted you so much, Mr. Pembroke. You're not just a kind man, you are also an encourager. Thank you." She picked up the pad and printed her complete contact information and the details of her bank account, along with Judith Hardy's name, address, phone number, and e-mail. Then she handed the pad back to the attorney.

Mr. Pembroke placed it on a corner of his desk and smiled. "It has been a pleasure doing business with you, Mrs. Gray," he said.

"It was *my* pleasure," Sheila replied, standing. "Thank you for all you've shared with me today. I'll think it over carefully on the drive back to Indiana. I want to do my best to honor Mrs. Parks's wishes. I disappointed her once in my life. I don't want to do that again. I'll be in touch very soon."

She was about walk out the door when Mr. Pembroke said, "If I may...?"

She stopped and pivoted to face him again. "Yes?"

"If you will indulge the advice of an old man—speaking for myself and not as an attorney—follow your dream, young lady, not your fears."

Sheila paused, weighing his words. "Thank you. Thank you very much. I truly value your advice."

CHAPTER 16

Even as she walked to her car, she was already starting to play out various scenarios in her mind. There were countless details to consider in making a decision like the one she now faced. Would Mike Reynolds let her take a leave of absence, or would she have to resign from her job? Where would she go to "get away from it all"? Did she have what it took to write a full-length novel? And the most challenging question of all: What was Dan going to say?

Before she started the car, she pulled out her cell phone, called the real-estate agent, and arranged a meeting at Mrs. Parks's house that evening. Then she headed for the freeway.

During the drive home, Sheila mentally juggled each aspect of the decisions she was facing. Between Detroit and Toledo, she came to the conclusion that leaving her job at the air-conditioning company was no gamble. She could always find office work. From Toledo to Fort Wayne, she reached the conclusion that she would have to get completely away from Dan, JD, Sherry, and everybody else if she would ever stand a chance of focusing all her attention on a full-length fiction project. That would mean making a secluded trip to the mountains or a desert somewhere. Well, she had enough money now to do that.

Somewhere between Fort Wayne and Indianapolis, it came to her that she might be able to use her connection with Judith Hardy and *Fulfillment* to make this a better deal than Laureen had imagined. What if, after she wrote the novel, she was able to sell it to the magazine to run in serialization? Charles Dickens had done that more than a century before. In that way, Judith would have the first Dove Alexander novel for her magazine, and she, Sheila, would have extra money *and* a ton of prepublication publicity.

She was still mulling over all the possibilities when she arrived at Mrs. Parks's home for her appointment with the real-estate agent. Just as Mr. Pembroke had indicated, the thirty autographed first-edition books had been carefully packaged in two sturdy cartons, each one small enough for Sheila to carry herself.

From the outside, the boxes gave no indication of their contents' value. But Dan already knew they were worth a lot of money. Sheila remembered the greedy look on his face when he'd talked about the money the volumes might bring on eBay. Funny, but it was almost as if Mrs. Parks had anticipated such a response from Dan, and that was why she'd had the books packed up so well for storage.

Sheila turned to the agent. "Do you happen to know of a self-storage place near here?"

"If you're thinking about a place to keep these books, you'll want a climate-controlled facility," the agent replied. She looked through her handbag and retrieved a business card. "Here. Some of my clients use this controlled-access place for their more delicate items."

Sheila thanked the woman, then drove straight to the address and rented the smallest type of unit available. With her future so uncertain, she decided to pay for two years in advance. If she could help it, Dan wouldn't have the chance to rob her of these treasures.

By the time she pulled into her driveway in Brissenden, cut the engine, and turned off the headlights, she had made the decision to grab this brass ring. She had nothing to lose. Nothing. If she wrote the book, and it wasn't good enough to get published, she still would have lost no money. And being away from Dan wouldn't be the least bit hard on her. In fact, it might prove to be good for their marriage if, indeed, absence did make the heart grow fonder. She wasn't quite ready to accept the notion that all the time and effort she had invested in her marriage for a decade and a half might have been for nothing.

However, selling Dan on the idea of her going away to write a book might be a formidable challenge. After all, they were still married, and she was still legally bound to her responsibilities for the debts they had incurred for their home, cars, and furnishings. She'd have to think in advance about what to say and also be able to think quickly on her feet when telling him the news.

As expected, Dan was waiting for her as soon as she walked into the house. "When do we get the books?"

Sheila smiled slightly. "Yes, Dan, the trip was a success. Thanks for asking."

"Well?"

"It's a little more complicated than I'd thought," she told him.

"Oh, great. Now I suppose you'll tell me your side trip in Detroit turned out to be a wild-goose chase. I knew I shouldn't have let you try to find that lawyer's office while you were up there on business for Mike. I expected you home hours ago. What happened? Did you get lost?"

"No, Dan. I didn't get lost."

"Then cut the mystery. What did you find out about those blasted books?"

"Oh, yes, the books. They're mine."

"Good," he said, dropping onto the couch and stretching out. "You can pick them up this weekend. But I still say it made no sense to spend extra time and gas on getting information you could have easily gotten on the phone or in an e-mail."

"You already said that," Sheila pointed out. "Actually, the books weren't *all* Mrs. Parks wanted me to have."

Dan quickly sat up straight. "She left you something else?"

"Yes," Sheila replied with a smile. "She left me fifty thousand dollars."

"What! That old broad left you fifty grand? I don't believe it."

"Well, you'd better believe it, because it's true. But there's a catch. There are, as Mr. Pembroke called them, 'definite strings' attached."

"Strings? Such as?"

Sheila's smile broadened as she walked past Dan toward the kitchen. She took her time, savoring the fact that Dan was practically salivating over the idea of some money coming his way. He got up and dogged her steps. Sheila slowly pulled a chair away from the table and sat.

"Sheila! What is it? What's the catch?"

"Mrs. Parks left me the money on the condition that I use it to take a leave of absence from my job and go away somewhere to write a novel."

The color drained from Dan's face. "You can't be serious. That's the most ridiculous thing I've ever heard. It's got to be some kind of joke." His upper lip curled as if the entire idea were an outright impossibility.

"Well, apparently Mrs. Parks didn't think so. Her attorney was very clear about it. After having taught me years ago and then again when she returned to town, she was confident that I have what it takes to become a novelist. And it was her dying wish that I get the chance to prove it."

Dan ran his hand through his thinning hair. "Now, look, Sheila," he said in a patronizing tone. "It would be the height of stupidity for you to leave your secure job, with its regular paycheck and benefits, just to chase the mirage of becoming a novelist. This is the time for logic, not fantasies." Then he blinked as if an idea had just occurred to him. "Hey, what if you kept your job and wrote the book in your free time? Could we—uh, *you* still get the money?"

"Nope." Sheila shook her head. "I already checked that out with Mr. Pembroke. It's all or nothing. If I choose not to take advantage of the offer, the money will go to a wildlife preserve. I stopped for coffee in Muncie and studied the will myself. Plain as day."

By now, Dan was pacing, his hands clenched. "That old biddy couldn't mind her own business, could she? She had to come back here and start filling your head with ideas. Now this."

Sheila glared at him. "I will thank you to speak respectfully when referring to Mrs. Parks. In fact, this is as good a time as any to let you know that I've resumed wearing the necklace she gave me years ago." She pulled the three charms from beneath the neckline of her knit top.

"What? I thought I told you to get rid of that. And you promised to do so!" Dan had the look of a man who realized he was losing control of a situation he'd thought he'd long ago conquered.

"I did get rid of it," she said. "And then recently, I...I dug it up again. I didn't know the bequest was coming, and this necklace was the only tangible item I had from Mrs. Parks. As I said before, she's gone now, so what does it matter to you?" She took a deep breath to maintain her serenity. "Now, speaking of the bequest, you have to agree that this is the chance of a lifetime. I'm sure Mike will let me take a temporary leave. If the book's good and sells to a publisher, I could make some money for us."

"Yeah, right. Like that'll ever happen," Dan sneered. "You might as well get that notion out of your head right now. Just because some crazy lady takes a shine to you, that doesn't mean that you've suddenly become Joyce Carol Oates. It's nothing but the warped dream of a desperate old woman."

Before Sheila had a chance to object to his labeling Mrs. Parks a crazy lady, he added, "Hey, what if you decided to go away but needed only *part* of the money to live on while you completed the book—say, half? I know how thrifty you are. Would we still get the other twenty-five grand?"

Sheila didn't like the larcenous gleam in his eye, but she decided to answer his question. "I guess so. Mr. Pembroke didn't say I had to use all the money. He just said I have to use the money to take a leave of absence from my job and go away until the book is finished. The will is a little more specific. I'm supposed to receive a cash advance, then further support money as needed. And then, upon completion of the book, I get whatever balance is left."

Dan furrowed his brow as if doing some quick mental calculations. "Okay. I'll let you play this little game. That way, when you really find out what it takes to be a successful writer, you won't bother me again with this foolishness. Call Pembroke tomorrow and tell him you'll accept the offer. Give him a list of the bills we have pending. Since you won't be getting a paycheck from Reynolds for a while, I don't want you running out and leaving me holding the bag."

Sheila smiled and nodded her acquiescence. She hadn't mentioned to Dan that she'd already stopped on the outskirts of Brissenden, called Martin Pembroke's office, and left a message confirming her plan to take Mrs. Parks's money and write a novel.

"Thanks," was all she said. In her mind, she could hear Laureen telling her, *Good. Now, just bide your time.*

Sheila slept little that night as her mind raced with ideas of how best to accomplish the monumental task before her. By dawn, she had a plan in place. She decided to go to the desert to write her book. After having spent her life in Indiana surrounded by farmland, she felt that the desert would offer just the kind of minimalist atmosphere she would need to focus completely on her writing.

Sheila got up at 5 AM, showered, dressed, and then left for the office before Dan even started to stir. She wanted to be alone when she phoned Mr. Pembroke to tell him personally of her plans. After unlocking the office and starting a pot of coffee to brew, she settled at her desk. She was fairly certain that Martin Pembroke was of the age and attitude to be an early riser, so she didn't hesitate to call his office at such an hour. She could always leave another message, if necessary, asking him to return her call.

But Mr. Pembroke picked up in the middle of the second ring. She asked if he'd received her voice-mail message, and he confirmed that he had. "Have you settled the matter with your husband?" he asked.

"Yes. I explained the situation to him last night. He has agreed to my going away to write the book, so I'm eager to get started. I thought I'd let you know my plans immediately."

"I appreciate that. And what are your plans?"

"I've decided that in order to concentrate fully and devote myself entirely to my work, I need to get far away from Brissenden. I will begin making arrangements right now with the goal of being ready to leave in one month. If you would, please send half the money to the account I asked you to manage so I can take care of travel expenses, purchase a laptop computer, and set up advance payments for my regular obligations here at home while I'm gone."

"And where is it, exactly, that you are going?" Mr. Pembroke asked.

"Well, I haven't figured that out, although I know that the solitude of the desert would be good for me. However, I doubt I'll know the specific location until I get there. It's going to have to feel right. Besides, it's important to me that no one know where I am. I want to be cut off from every*one* and every*thing* that's familiar. That way, I'll have no distractions."

"Are you sure that's a good idea?" Mr. Pembroke queried. "A woman traveling alone can run into some challenging situations. Perhaps you should leave an itinerary of some sort."

"Don't worry," Sheila assured him. "It's important that I do this my own way. This endeavor is about my personal growth as much as it is about writing a novel. I think Mrs. Parks would approve."

"Very well. As you wish. I'll have the money electronically transferred, and I will hold the remaining twenty-five thousand until the completion of the novel, per Mrs. Parks's stipulation. Once I've obtained a copy of the finished manuscript, the balance will be yours."

"Thank you for everything. I'll be in touch as soon as the manuscript is completed."

When the office opened again after New Year's, Sheila spent the morning in Mike Reynolds' office, working with him on a plan. Their relationship had matured over the years into a close friendship, and so, after his initial shock, Mike agreed this was the opportunity of a lifetime. "Can't say I'm happy about you leaving," he said, "but you know I truly want what's best for you, and I'm happy you're finally getting a break. I can count on you to have everything organized to run smooth while you're gone. And, of course, I'm hoping like mad you'll come back and be our office manager again." His eyes appeared to be getting misty, and he added gruffly, "Don't know how we'll get along without you."

On her lunch break, Sheila checked her account balance online. Sure enough, the $25,000 had been deposited. She stared at the figure on the screen, scarcely believing she had that kind of money at her disposal. She intended to go shopping for supplies that very evening.

During dinner, Sheila let Dan know she would be going to the mall afterward to make some purchases for her trip.

"Don't you think you should wait until you actually receive the money before you start spending it?" he asked in a scolding tone.

"The first half is already in my bank account," she said, then took a sip of tea.

Dan looked alarmed. "I hope you're not going to start blowing that money senselessly. Don't forget that whatever you don't use, we get to keep later."

"Dan," she replied, trying to keep irritation out of her voice. "I have no intention of *blowing* any of the money. There are certain things I'll need to have to make this work. Tonight, I'm going to buy a laptop, a bag for it, and a carry-on suitcase for traveling."

Dan sat silently for several seconds. "Well, I guess those things are necessities. I know just what kind of laptop you need."

"I've already decided on the one I want."

His alarmed expression returned. "What do you mean, you've already decided?"

"For a long time, I've been thinking about how nice it would be to have my own laptop. I've done some research and comparison shopping. The computer store at the mall has just the slim, lightweight model I want."

"Now, Sheila...."

She raised her eyebrows and gave him a stern look, and, to her surprise, he closed his mouth. Sheila didn't believe for a moment that he had given up. It was more likely he'd simply decided to pick his battles carefully until he got his hands on her inheritance. That was fine with her. Soon she'd have a blissful reprieve from domestic conflict.

After giving the matter of her destination a lot of thought, Sheila finally settled on the Nevada desert. During the next few weeks, she worked diligently to make the necessary arrangements, among them ensuring that the transition at Reynolds Heating and Air-Conditioning would be as seamless as possible. She wanted to have everything in place, both at work and at home, complete with detailed written instructions.

Then she turned her attention to her own financial affairs. She had Judith Hardy send her $3,000 from her account balance being held at *Fulfillment* magazine. Since she wasn't certain of her exact destination and didn't want the bother of setting up a forwarding address after she'd decided where to land, she thought carefully about withdrawing the remaining $20,000 of the money Mr. Pembroke had deposited into her bank account. The following week, she purchased a prepaid credit card—or, as she discovered it was now called, a prepaid access card. Then she withdrew the remainder in cash. Knowing that the bank would have to report to the government any cash withdrawals of amounts over $10,000, she made certain to keep under that limit with each transaction.

When she'd picked out her new carry-on bag at the mall's travel store, she'd also bought a money belt for traveling with cash. Then she'd gone to an electronics store and purchased a prepaid cell phone. Since no one would have the new phone's number, she figured she wouldn't be bothered by calls during her seclusion, but she would have the phone to use for emergencies.

After some discussion, Sheila finally persuaded Dan to drive her to the Indianapolis airport. In the beginning, he had been hesitant, but when she'd pointed out how much money it would take to use a limousine service or a cab, he'd acquiesced.

Finally, all the details were in place.

No one made any grand gestures preceding her leave-taking, and that was just the way she preferred it. On the day of her departure, as she was checking her packing list, she turned to her jewelry box and withdrew a key taped to a business card for the climate-controlled storage facility she'd used.

At that moment, Dan walked into the bedroom. "Are you ready?"

Sheila glanced at her watch. She hadn't planned to leave for the airport for another hour. "What's the hurry? We've got plenty of time. I'm not eager to spend an extra hour or more waiting at the airport, are you?"

"Uh, that's something I neglected to mention, Sheila. I'm going to have to drop you off at the terminal entrance. I forgot I had scheduled an appointment to meet Imogene for a consultation while in Indy."

"You're not even going to wait for me to get checked in?"

"Why? Do you need me to hold your hand? You've certainly proven yourself capable of making all the arrangements without my help."

"Dan, I'm going to be away for an extended period of time. I thought you'd want to wait with me at least until I had to go through security."

"This is important," he said impatiently. "Imogene has been invited to do a series of lectures, and she needs my help to put the material together. I might be able to get a coauthorship credit if one of the lectures gets published as an article."

"Oh. Well then, don't worry about *me*. If Imogene thinks it's important that you be there, then you'd better be there and hold *her* hand."

Dan scowled. "Geez, Sheila, don't get all upset about this. I promised Imogene a long time ago I'd help her out. How was I supposed to know your travel plans would interfere? Do you really need me to wait with you at the airport?"

Sheila frowned and tucked the business card inside her carry-on. "No. You can just drop me off. I'll be fine."

As they drove to Indianapolis, Dan reached into his jacket's breast pocket and pulled out a plain white envelope. "I want you to give me my one-in-a-million shot the way you got yours. Here's twenty-five bucks. While you're in Las Vegas, I want you to play it on some wild long shot for me."

Sheila blinked at him in astonishment. "You know I have no intention of going into any casinos. That's not what this trip's about. I'm simply landing in Las Vegas before I head into the desert."

Dan sighed. "Look, I think I've been a pretty good sport about your goofy plan. There are some men who wouldn't stand for their wives to take off on a crazy trip like this. The least you can do is this one little thing for me."

Sheila rolled her eyes. "It's not a little thing, Dan. Once I hit the ground in Vegas, I want to be on my way. My agenda doesn't include room for any gambling stops."

"Why the rigid timetable? You're the one who set up the *agenda,* so why can't you do me one favor? I'm not asking for much. Just play the money on a long shot." Dan turned into the airport's entrance.

Sheila didn't want to part on a sour note, even though they hadn't made any sweet music together for a long time. "Okay," she said, accepting the envelope. "I'll spend this on some slim-to-none chance of making you rich. Are you happy?"

Dan looked satisfied. "Yeah. I'm happy."

He pulled to the curb, leaned over, and gave his wife a quick peck on the cheek. "Good-bye, Sheila. Good luck. Let me know when you're finished, okay?"

Sheila stared hard into her husband's eyes, marveling at the stranger he was to her now. "Good-bye, Dan."

CHAPTER 17

When she was almost to the security line, Sheila stopped at a restroom to retrieve the money belt from her carry-on. She'd decided that keeping her huge wad of cash in the nondescript piece of luggage was better than wearing the belt on her person and running the risk of having it exposed by a scanner or a pat-down. She had no desire to become the target of extra attention by the TSA officials.

Once she was through security, the belt securely fastened again around her waist, she pulled out her cell phone and called New York. Judith Hardy answered herself.

"Hey, girlfriend," Sheila said. "I'm really going through with it. Shall I sing you a couple of choruses of John Denver's 'Leaving on a Jet Plane'?"

"John Denver died in a plane crash, lest you forget," said Judith in her typical New York directness. "Where's Lover Boy?"

"My devoted husband dropped me at the curb so he could keep an appointment with the fair maiden Imogene. Honestly, I don't care. I've got my laptop and my carry-on bag, and I'm ready to go into hiding."

"You sure you don't want to call me every ten days or so, just to touch base with the outside world?"

"No can do," said Sheila. "I warned the girls at work, along with Dan, Mr. Pembroke, and you, that I'm disappearing into the desert for as long as it takes to get the novel written. I owe it to Laureen Parks, and

I owe it to myself. It's going to be pure isolation for me until I type the words 'The End.'"

"Okay, enjoy your tomb," said Judith. "But if you change your mind, you have my number. And don't forget your promise."

"I won't forget. You'll be the first one to get a copy of the finished manuscript. If you like it and you want to serialize it in the mag, I'll be overjoyed. If not, maybe you can rip it to shreds with track-changes, and I'll learn something from the experience."

"Hey, kiddo, I'm proud of you," said Judith, turning serious. "Holding your own against Dan about this…making all these plans… taking such a big leap of faith. You're not the same person you were a few months ago."

"No," Sheila affirmed. "No, I'm not. And I have you to thank for a lot of that change, Judith."

"Whoa, don't kid yourself," said the editor. "I just wanted your stories so I could sell more magazines. *You*, I don't like so much. But your stories? *They're* great!"

Sheila chuckled. "Tease me all you want. I still know how much time you've invested in me. I'll call you as soon as I come out of hiding, okay?"

"Good luck, lady. And, hey, don't forget to have a little fun, too. You're a woman of leisure now. Act like it every once in a while."

"Understood. I'll give it a try."

They said their good-byes, and then, with an hour to kill until boarding began for her flight, Sheila bought a paperback novel in one of the shops, ordered a tall nonfat mocha at a coffee stand, and settled in a vacant chair at the gate. The rich chocolaty drink tasted heavenly and did a great job of warming her on the cold February day.

The novel, however, was boring, with unrealistic dialogue and typecast characters. When she couldn't keep her mind on the story any longer, she closed the book, disgusted. She'd heard the author's name on the news a couple of years before. Involved in a government scandal or something. Well, wherever his notoriety had come from, his fame alone, rather than any writing excellence, must have been what made the publisher expect good sales. The author's skill wasn't much better than Dan's.

"I guess I can look at this as just a good example of how *not* to write my novel," Sheila mumbled to herself. She tucked the book into the side pocket of her carry-on and watched as a mother in the row of seats across from her tried to clean chocolate off the face of a squirmy toddler. As the mom wiped the boy's plump little neck with a damp cloth, Sheila became aware that her own hand was at her neck, toying with her necklace.

After she'd gone to her childhood home to retrieve the necklace from its hiding place, it had been her intention to wear the gift always. But now the custom-made charms increasingly reminded her of her failures instead of inspiring her to strive for success. The quill represented her scholarship award and was meant to help her remember to use her writing talent to earn a college degree. Well, she'd blown that one royally.

The book charm stood for all the great literature that she and Mrs. Parks had studied together when she was in high school. It was also to serve as a symbol of her potential to become an author one day. She didn't need a little charm for that now. The thirty autographed first editions would serve as reminders.

Then, there was the clock face—a symbol of the "good times" that she and Mrs. Parks had enjoyed while working on essays and stories. Sheila smiled. Those recollections were sealed in her memory, no matter what might eventually become of the tiny clock face. Mrs. Parks had also said the clock charm was a warning: *Time* was something that should never be wasted, only *invested*.

Heaviness dropped over Sheila's heart at the reminder of her fifteen wasted years. Although she was now investing her time into writing, there was no getting around the fact that those lost years were gone forever. The charms that had once supplied goals to strive for now had become albatrosses literally hanging from her neck.

What should she do with the necklace now? If she were truly beginning a new life—fleshing out her destiny as well as her pen name—wasn't it time to remove the piece of jewelry? Probably. But it didn't seem right simply to toss it into an airport trash can.

Just then, boarding for her plane was announced. As she gathered her purse, laptop bag, and carry-on, she decided that when the moment was right, she would know what to do with the necklace. Until then, she would focus on the new chapter of her life that was now unfolding.

The flight to Oklahoma City went smoothly. When she arrived, she had an hour until her connecting flight left for Las Vegas, so she headed for Gate 12. She enjoyed the feeling of being able to make her own decisions for a change. It would be several months before she had to worry about waiting on Dan hand and foot again.

Oh! Except for the $25 he'd insisted she place on a long shot for him. How annoying that she hadn't been able to stop him from reaching his arm of control over her from more than fifteen hundred miles away. She'd caved to his insistent request, and now she had to place the bet before she could concentrate on figuring out her desert destination.

Just then, she rounded a corner and noticed a kiosk with a bright yellow sign that read "Flight Insurance." Hmm. Her dad always used to complain about insurance premiums on his mortgaged farm. "The house odds is always with them blasted insurance companies!" he'd say, growling, almost as if the transaction were a gamble.

Sheila stopped at the kiosk and scanned the posted directions. The process looked simple. She filled out the information, including her flight number, and pulled Dan's envelope out of her purse. But then she noticed that the machine accepted only credit and debit cards—no cash. Sighing with annoyance, she exchanged the envelope for her prepaid access card and used $25 of the balance to purchase $300,000 of insurance. She would keep the cash to make up for what she'd just used on the card. The kiosk printed out a copy of her policy, which named Dan as the beneficiary, and then she was on her way again.

"Well, Dan, this isn't exactly craps or roulette, but it's gambling," she said aloud. "So, there goes your twenty-five bucks, *sweetie*."

By the time she reached the gate, the waiting area was already very crowded. She found a seat for herself but had to stack her carry-on items near her feet.

She looked around and noticed a young woman, probably around nineteen or twenty, who was sitting alone, weeping. No one seemed to be making any effort to comfort her or even to find out what was wrong. Sheila watched for several minutes, until she could take it no longer. She hoisted her belongings and went to the crying woman. "Excuse me, but are you all right?"

The young woman looked up. Mascara streaked down her cheeks. "No seats," she said. "I need to get to Las Vegas on this next flight so I can make a connection to San Diego, but there are no more seats. They sold me a ticket for the next flight and then put me on standby, but four other people are ahead of me...and no one is canceling, anyway." She found a tissue in her purse and blew her nose.

Sheila smiled kindly. "What's the rush?"

"My husband is leaving for Korea with the army tomorrow," the woman explained. "We've been married only five months, and he's going to be deployed for a year. He doesn't know I'm expecting. I wanted to tell him myself before he left. The next flight to Vegas is an hour later than this one. That's too late."

"Can't you call him?"

The weeping woman nodded. "Technically, yes. But this is the most important thing that's ever happened to us, and I wanted to tell him in person—especially since he's leaving for a whole year."

Sheila made an instantaneous decision. "Grab your stuff and follow me to the ladies' room," she said.

The young woman looked puzzled, but she yielded when Sheila lifted her arm and nudged her forward.

Once they entered the restroom, Sheila said, "Let's swap boarding passes. I'm in no rush. Really. I don't have any checked bags to worry about. You can take my seat on the flight leaving now, and I'll take yours on the next flight. An hour makes no difference to me."

The woman's eyes widened as she pulled her boarding pass from her open purse and looked at it. "Would...would they let us do that?"

"We won't ask," said Sheila. "We've already shown our IDs at security. You've got a confirmed seat, and so do I. That's all they care about. The flight attendants won't be the same, anyway. So, how about it?"

"I can't believe you'd do this," the woman said. "Do you think it'll really work? Is it legal?"

"You're babbling," said Sheila with a smile. "Follow your dreams, not your fears."

"What?"

"That's something someone told me recently. He's a lawyer, so let's assume that what we're doing is technically legal. Here's my boarding pass. Give me that one." Sheila exchanged papers and noted that the woman's name was Karen Watson.

Looking hesitant, Karen stayed rooted in place. "I want to do this, but I don't know. I've always been naive. You're not a con artist, are you? Oh, please, forgive me. Why did I say that? I'm babbling again, aren't I? I just don't think I have the guts to walk out there and try to pull this off."

Sheila could see that Karen, even though she was married and all, was still very young. She'd need something extra to help her get through this. And Sheila had just the something extra. "Do you believe in good-luck charms?" she asked her.

Karen shrugged and gave Sheila a sideways look. "What do you mean?"

Sheila reached behind her neck and unfastened the clasp of the necklace from Laureen Parks. "A very dear friend of mine gave me this necklace when I was just about your age," she explained. "I had good luck when I wore it, then bad luck when I took it off, then good luck again when I put it back on. Life is set for me now, and great things are on the horizon, so I want you to have it. Look—there are even three little charms. They symbolize how your little one will soon expand your family to three. Wear it. Go join your husband. Get lucky."

Karen allowed Sheila to put the necklace on her. Then she reached into her purse, pulled out Sheila's original boarding pass, and glanced at it. "Sheila Gray. I don't know how to thank you, Sheila."

"Just get on that flight and have a good life. That's all I want."

Karen hugged her before turning to go, then glanced back. Sheila waved her on. "Go ahead. I'll stay in here until you're gone, then I'll come out and wait for the next flight."

Sheila fussed with her hair and makeup for fifteen minutes, then bent down to pick up her laptop. A folded piece of paper lay on top the case. She opened it to discover Karen's printed flight itinerary with handwritten notes in the margin. It must have fallen from Karen's purse when she'd pulled out her boarding pass.

Sheila quickly scooped up her belongings and left the ladies' room, but the flight was gone, and so was Karen. Oh, well. Sheila sighed and then smiled self-consciously. *I planned to be incognito for several months, but I didn't think it would begin with an episode of intrigue. Now I really am incognito. For the next couple of hours, I'm Karen Watson, and after that, I'll take on the persona of Dove Alexander. Who knows? This might wind up being part of my novel's plot.*

She found a discarded copy of that day's city newspaper and read the national news, features, advice column, and comics. She was halfway finished with the crossword puzzle when something occurred to her. If she were truly intent on focusing all her concentration and energy on her novel, shouldn't she banish the outside world *completely*? Yes, while living as a hermit in the desert, she should forgo all modern means of communication. She would "live" in the fictional world of her characters each day—no other distractions or intrusions.

"So long, Beetle Bailey, Jimmy Kimmel, and Facebook," she said, as she stood and symbolically discarded the newspaper in a trash receptacle.

As soon as she sat again, she started thinking about her plan to buy a used car in Vegas. Maybe she would ask her cab driver to recommend a used-car lot with a good reputation. But could she trust a cabbie?

She'd never bought a car on her own. Dan had always taken care of their major purchases. She would probably have to show her driver's license to the dealer and fill out registration papers to match her ID, which identified her as Sheila Gray of Brissenden, Indiana. Then, there was the problem of getting mandatory auto insurance. And, at the end of her months in the desert, how would she dispose of the car? That would take extra time and paperwork, even if she just gave the vehicle away.

She was still mulling over the issue when she heard her flight being called. She tucked her purse inside her laptop bag to combine the two into one "personal item" and then got in line to board the plane, doing her best not to look nervous when she handed Karen's boarding pass to the gate attendant.

Her seatmate turned out to be a college anthropology student on her winter break. She was being met at the Las Vegas airport by a member of a Nevada anthropology club, and from there, they would drive to a location about a hundred miles away to join other students on a field trip. "We get to see pictographs and petroglyphs!" she exclaimed.

"I'm afraid I'm not certain what those are," Sheila confessed.

"Sure, no problem. A lot of people don't know the difference. Pictographs are paintings on rocks, and petroglyphs are carvings. Both were done by early peoples. This will be my first chance to see some *in situ*, and these particular examples are especially rare."

"Do many tourists go see them?"

The young woman looked horrified. "I hope not! They're super delicate and shouldn't be touched or even breathed on very much. And then, when tourists help themselves to nearby arrowheads and pottery shards, they do further damage to the site."

Sheila was puzzled. "How does that harm the rock carvings and paintings?"

"Because artifacts lose their context when you remove the things close by."

Sheila nodded, already trying to think of a way she might use some of that information in her novel. "It sounds like the sites should be well protected."

"The ones at state parks are, yes. But the location our group is going to study isn't. The best protection is keeping their whereabouts a secret. It also helps that our destination is in the middle of nowhere."

"Does that mean you'll have to backpack in?"

The young woman shook her head. "It's not that far from a little settlement called New Promise. The town has a run-down motel where we'll stay. Nothing fancy, but it'll be fine." She paused as a flight attendant arrived to take their beverage orders.

Sheila did some quick thinking. After the attendant moved to the row behind theirs, Sheila said to her seatmate, "Let me introduce myself. My name is Dove. I want to…I mean, I'm a novelist, and I'm looking for an out-of-the-way place, where I won't have any distractions, to write my next story. I figured the Nevada desert would give me the solitude I need, but I wasn't sure how to locate the right lodgings."

The student smiled. "Glad to meet you, Dove. A novelist, huh? That's great! While I'll be studying pictographs by ancient peoples, you'll be sort of, like, writing a monograph about fictional peoples. Get it?" She giggled. "By the way, my name's Meeghan."

Sheila smiled. "Hi, Meeghan." She hesitated a moment, then asked, "Do you think the motel would have a vacancy for me?" At the expression of alarm that crossed Meeghan's face, she quickly added, "I'm not expecting to tag along on the field trip. My goal is to stay inside and write."

Meeghan looked Sheila up and down. "Well, if it's solitude you're searching for, New Promise would fit the bill."

"Wonderful! How would I get there? Would I have to buy a car? Or could I catch a bus?"

Meeghan shook her head. "No buses except charter. That's why a local club member, Alison, is picking me up at the airport. Another guy was going to go with us, but he had an emergency appendectomy a couple of days ago and had to cancel. Hey! Want to ride along with us? We sure could use the help with gas money."

Sheila was thrilled at how everything seemed to be falling into place. She just hoped she was making the right decision. But what could go wrong? Meeghan didn't look like a fraud. Remembering how Karen had expressed hesitation at Sheila's offer helped Sheila make up her mind now. "I'd love to do that. But what if the motel is full? If it's as isolated as you say, wouldn't it be a problem to find lodging somewhere else?"

"I don't think that motel is ever full. But when we land, you could call ahead and find out. I have the contact information here somewhere." Meeghan pulled a folder from her bag under the seat in front of her and riffled through several papers.

When the plane landed, and Sheila and Meeghan entered the terminal, Sheila noticed various news crews milling about, city and state police officers guiding departing passengers away from the gate, and crowds growing in the waiting areas. "Who do you suppose is landing?" she said. "Justin Bieber? The President?"

Meeghan shrugged. "This is Vegas. It could be anybody. Oh, want to stop here for a minute and call the motel?"

Once Sheila had confirmed that there was, indeed, a vacancy for that evening—and for however long she wanted to stay after that—the two women elbowed their way through the crowds like bargain hunters on Black Friday. Meeghan recovered her suitcase from the luggage carousel in baggage claim, and they waited at the outdoor arrival area only ten minutes before Alison pulled to the curb. Meeghan explained the situation to her fellow club member and introduced Dove and Alison to each other, and they were off.

As they headed north past the center of town and then on to the outskirts, Sheila pushed up the sleeves of her turtleneck sweater. "Sure is warm here. When I got up this morning in Indiana, the temperature was in the low twenties."

"Yes," said Alison, "I noticed the big, heavy coat you brought. You'll be glad to have it on some of our chilly mornings, but it got to sixty here in town today."

"Great. I love the idea of warmer weather and seclusion. I also love the sound of the town's name, New Promise. That's just what I'm looking for."

"I wouldn't get too excited about the town, if I were you," Alison cautioned her. "The name's much better than the place itself. You said 'seclusion.' Well, after we go north for eighty-five miles, we'll turn off at Verde Junction and travel another fifteen before we reach New Promise and the seclusion you're looking for. Besides the motel and a few houses, there's a combination mini-mart/gas station/general store. Basically, the only people who go there are archeologists and a few geologists and hikers."

"And the occasional novelist," Sheila added under her breath.

Seated on the sofa in Imogene Cunningham's Indianapolis apartment, Dan Gray pinched the bridge of his nose with his thumb and forefinger. He ran his fingers through his hair and then let out a long puff of air. He and Imogene had spent the last two hours verifying documentation for a paper she was set to deliver in three weeks at the Modern Language Association's Midwest Convention.

The doorbell rang. Dan jumped to his feet. "The pizza and drinks," he said. "Not a minute too soon. My eyes can't take any more reading of the small print in these books."

"Here, let me give you some money," said Imogene, grabbing her purse.

It grated on Dan to have to accept money from her, but he'd given his last twenty-five bucks to Sheila to gamble for him in Vegas. Man, he sure hoped his hunch would pan out. Being broke was for the birds. It was definitely time for his luck to change.

He took the money, went to the door, and retrieved the food and beverages. The delivery boy scowled when Dan put all the change in his own pocket rather than give any of it back as a tip.

Imogene cleared a spot on the coffee table for the pizza as the smells of spicy pepperoni and steamy cardboard filled the living room. Then she picked up the television remote and turned on the evening news.

Her apartment was comfortable, but to Dan, it smacked of the setting for *Arsenic and Old Lace*. Even the way Imogene attired herself was dowdy. She wore plain, functional shoes with thick heels. Her dresses were usually in styles that had been out of fashion for at least a decade. And she kept her hair pinned back in a kind of bun.

The first time they had slept together, it had genuinely stunned Dan to find out that the forty-four-year-old woman had never been intimate with a man before. His intent was to play both sides against the middle. Imogene had agreed to list Dan as coauthor of her research paper, which would give him an academic credit he never would have been able to achieve on his own. She'd also agreed to help him with his novel, eventually, so she was very useful to him. Meanwhile, Dan's wife was still young and attractive, and she was set to come into another twenty-five grand in a few months. So, she had her merits, too…for a time.

The key person in this triangle, however, was Dan himself. He was prepared to use both women in any way necessary, just as long as he would wind up with the academic prestige and the big wad of cash he felt he so deserved.

"And so, a strike by sanitation workers here in Indianapolis was averted," he heard the news anchor say. "We'll be right back with your local weather after these announcements." A commercial for a credit card started to run. Dan went into the kitchen for some plates and napkins.

He was still rummaging around the drawers and cabinets when the news resumed. "We continue to follow the breaking story of the crash of TransUniverse flight fourteen eighty-one from Oklahoma City to Las Vegas today," the anchor said. "As reported earlier, the plane was involved in a midair collision shortly after taking off from Will Rogers World Airport in Oklahoma City. It plunged into an oil refinery, causing an enormous explosion. Firefighters are still battling the inferno."

Dan dropped the plates on the kitchen floor with a crash. Tiny shards crunched under his feet as he bolted into the living room, rushed to grab the remote, and turned up the volume. Imogene grimaced, but Dan stood in front of the screen, mesmerized by the roaring orange flames filling the screen.

"FAA and NTSB investigators are already on the scene," continued the news anchor. "No details yet on the cause of the midair collision. At this point, it's being assumed that all flight crew members and passengers on board flight fourteen eighty-one were killed. We will keep you posted as further updates become available. Turning to news in the nation's capital, the President announced today that—"

Dan flipped to another news channel and then another, but neither of them was running the story at that moment. "Sheila!" he shouted, turning with wide eyes to Imogene. "My wife was on that flight."

Imogene covered her mouth. "No, Dan, surely not." She paused, then repeated, "Surely not."

"The second leg of her trip this afternoon was from Oklahoma City to Las Vegas," he said. "I saw her boarding pass, clearly printed with 'TransUniverse Airlines flight fourteen eighty-one.' That was *her* plane. She's...she's...."

"Dead," said Imogene.

Dan didn't know how to react. He wasn't feeling shock or pain or disbelief. It was more like bafflement. The possibility of something like this happening had never once entered his mind. He had no prepared script for how to handle it. "I...think...I...need...to...call...someone," he said, speaking so slowly, it sounded as if he'd recorded himself on the wrong speed.

Imogene turned off the television and stood. "You can use my phone if you want to call the airport or TransUniverse Airlines," she said softly.

Dan didn't move. He cocked his head to one side, feeling almost as if he had just been asked a difficult question to which he needed to formulate an answer. He couldn't focus on anything in the room. He felt as if he were in a cosmic limbo. "No...uh...no," he mumbled at last. "I need to go home. Someone may be trying to call me there. I…I think I need to go home." As though in a dream, he removed his jacket from the back of a chair and put it on. Then he stepped to the door and twisted the handle.

"Shall I come with you?" Imogene asked.

Dan turned and stared at her a moment. He'd almost forgotten she was there. "What? Oh…thanks, but no. I need to go home now." He turned and left without kissing her or even saying good-bye.

He found his way to his car and got inside but didn't turn on the ignition. His mind was racing. Sheila was almost certainly dead. What, exactly, did that mean? His thoughts turned to money. It occurred to him that she would be worth far more to him dead than alive. But exactly how much money would he receive? And from what sources?

Suddenly animated, he banged open the glove compartment and extracted the pen and pad of paper he kept there to record travel mileage when teaching. He started scribbling figures. First, there was the $10,000 life-insurance policy Sheila had set up through work as a part of her employee benefits package. Dan was the sole beneficiary. Next, there was that inheritance Old Lady Parks had left her, which would most likely now become his, by default. That would be another $25,000, right? And then, most incredible of all, there was the automatic $250,000 of insurance provided by the credit card Sheila had used when ordering her airline tickets on the Internet. She'd already paid off the credit-card bill using money from her bequest, but…. Dan shook his head to clear his thinking. Added together, that was more than half a million dollars! And it would be *all his*! He stared at the sum he'd scrawled on the paper, rechecked his math, and stared at it some more.

Indications were that he was a bachelor again and rolling in money. Unbelievable—absolutely unbelievable! At last, his destiny appeared to be coming in line with his hopes, dreams, and ambitions. He had never been so happy in his entire life. His emotions were spilling over. Tears actually sprang to his eyes for the overwhelming joy he felt at his turn of fortune.

Now he'd show everybody. He'd drive a new car and wear tailored clothes and have all the other trappings appropriate for a person of his rightful social stature. He might even sell their little house and move into a modern bachelor pad in a downtown Indianapolis high-rise. Oh, the parties he could throw now. Look out, world!

He started the engine and backed out of the parking lot. He had to get home and set things in motion. The sooner he could get his hands on all that money, the sooner his new life would begin. But first, on the way home, he'd stop at a convenience store and buy some lottery tickets. He still had the few dollars in change he'd pocketed after paying for the pizza, and it would be foolish not to take advantage of his new run of good luck.

He winked at himself in the rearview mirror. "You da man, Dan," he told himself. "For sure, you da man."

When Alison, Meeghan, and Sheila pulled into New Promise, Nevada, Sheila saw that the town was exactly as it had been described to her: small, desolate, and stark. In short, perfect.

Almost immediately, they turned into the parking lot of the motel—or "Mo," as the half-burned-out neon sign advertised. "'Mo' of what?" Sheila said, and all three of them chuckled.

It wasn't a traditional motel, at least not by Midwestern standards. This was a series of eight or so little self-contained units that resembled cabins. Lights were on in only two of them.

The women got out of the car and headed toward the building marked "Office." Sheila gathered her coat from the backseat, slung her purse and laptop bag over her shoulder, and followed the other two, wheeling her carry-on behind her.

A lanky man of about thirty-five sat at the registration desk, an open textbook before him. Sheila didn't know if he was a real cowboy, but he had the appearance of one—denim jacket and blue jeans, western shirt, boots that needed a shine, longish hair, sun-bronzed skin, and an unshaven face.

Alison and Meeghan thanked Sheila again for sharing the fuel expenses. Then they said good night and left for their cabins.

The man turned to Sheila. "Do you have a reservation?"

"I called from the airport a couple of hours ago," said Sheila. "You said you had a vacancy, but I didn't have time to give you a credit-card number to hold a reservation. I hope you still have a room."

The man rose slowly. He was easily six feet two. "For the right price, you can have the whole place," he said, without the slightest hint that he might be joking.

Sheila stepped closer. "A week will do for starters."

The man handed her a registration form. As she wrote "Dove Alexander" on the line marked "Name," he asked, "You here for that anthropology field trip?"

"Can't tell a pictograph from a petroglyph," she said. "I'm just here to rest, work on my tan, and do a little writing."

The man studied her for a moment. "Fifty dollars for every twenty-four hours you stay," he said. "Fresh towels every day, sheets changed every three days, coffee here on the hot plate around the clock."

Sheila handed him her prepaid access card. "I'd like to pay for the first week. What can I do about food?"

The man accepted the card. "There's a microwave and a mini refrigerator in each cabin. You can buy whatever you need at the store across the street and fix it yourself, or you can have dinner made for you in the back of the store. There's a little café, but it doesn't open for breakfast or lunch, except to sell fruit and microwavable sandwiches."

Sheila nodded. "Do you work here every night?"

"I work here all the time. I own the place. Name's Derek Mason." He handed her a key attached to a large red tag imprinted "#10."

She thanked Derek and stepped toward the door. Then she paused, turned back, and lifted her eyebrows. "You an anthropology student?"

He looked puzzled a moment, as if he suspected she was mocking him. But when she pointed to the open textbook on the counter, he said, "Nah. Although, living here, I *have* learned the difference between a pictograph and a petroglyph." He nodded toward the book. "That's a psychology text. Just a hobby." He closed the tome with a thump, as if indicating the conversation was closed, too.

Sheila nodded, then left the office and took her things to cabin number ten. While it wasn't fancy, the dwelling was neat, clean, and functional. "Not the Ritz," she said, "but not the rats, either."

Then she yawned. Her long, eventful day was catching up with her. She put on her pajamas, double-checked the door lock, and pulled down the bedcovers. After brushing her teeth, she decided everything else could wait until morning. Slipping between the sheets, she told herself, "I'll sleep like the dead."

CHAPTER 18

It was still dark the next morning when Sheila opened her eyes. The digital clock on the nightstand read 5:15. *This three-hour time difference is going to take some getting used to,* she thought.

She lay in bed for twenty minutes but was too excited to fall asleep again. She got up, showered, dressed, and pulled her damp hair up in a ponytail. Coffee! She had to have some caffeine before doing anything else. As tired as she'd been the night before, she hadn't slept as well as she'd anticipated. At some point during the night, she'd been awakened by the sound of howling dogs.

Remembering the proprietor's comments about round-the-clock coffee, she put on her coat and headed for the motel office. Halfway across the dirt-and-gravel parking lot, she noticed a scraggly pine tree next to the office, silhouetted against brilliant bands of gold, yellow, persimmon, and hot pink above the hills. The dawn's shimmering beauty nearly took her breath away. She was going to enjoy desert sunrises, that was for sure.

As soon as she opened the office door, she could smell freshly perked brew, but no one was behind the desk. She filled a Styrofoam cup, added sugar and creamer, snapped on a lid, and returned to her cabin.

She was eager to start outlining her story's plot, but she first wanted to get the lay of the land in her new surroundings—and she wouldn't be able to do that on an empty stomach.

She took off her coat, then hoisted her carry-on to the bed and quickly unpacked the rest of her belongings in between taking sips of coffee. She stowed her clothing in the dresser and closet, stashed her travel toiletries in the bathroom, and set up the laptop on the small desk. Then she grabbed her purse, put her coat back on, went outside, and crossed the road to the store. There wasn't a vehicle or a pedestrian in sight.

A chime sounded as she opened the door, and she heard a voice call out, "Mornin'." Behind the counter sat a heavyset woman who looked to be in her sixties.

"Good morning! And what a beautiful day it is." Sheila nodded in the direction of the eastern sky.

"Yep. Most days here is beautiful. What can I do for ya, darlin'?"

"Well, first, I need some breakfast."

"Coffee's over next to that wall…."

"Thanks. I already had coffee at the motel, but I guess I do need a second cup. I'm still a little groggy from jet-lag and those noisy dogs yowling in the night."

The woman grinned. "Them wasn't dogs, hon. We got coyotes 'round here. You'll get used to 'em. But ya said ya wanted breakfast. What'd ya have in mind?"

Still shuddering at the mention of coyotes, Sheila asked, "Do you have yogurt? Fruit? Muffins, maybe?"

"Got all that over in the grocery section. Plastic spoons for yogurt are in that cup above the cooler. Anything else?"

"As a matter of fact, yes. I wanted to travel light, since I wasn't sure where I was going to end up, exactly. So, I need sunglasses and sunscreen. Oh, and shampoo, conditioner, hairspray, toothpaste, mouthwash…all the things they don't let you carry in large quantities in your carry-on bag. Do you have those?"

"Sure do, hon. Personal-care stuff in the center aisle, on the left." The woman paused for a moment, then said, "Sounds like you're gonna stick around here for a while. If ya ever need somethin' I don't normally carry, I can see about orderin' it. Sometimes, them antsypology and rock-hound folks have me do that."

Sheila smiled. "I'm not in either one of those categories. I plan to spend most of my time writing."

"Writin'? Do tell. What'cha writin' about?"

Sheila felt herself blush. "I...I'm writing a novel."

The woman let loose a long, loud belly laugh. "I guess I'd better watch my p's and q's, or I just might end up as a character in that book!" Then she stood and extended her hand across the checkout counter. "The name's Gracie. Gracie Evans."

Sheila shook her hand. "Very pleased to meet you, Gracie. I'm Dove Alexander."

"Dove? Ain't that pretty! Never heard a prettier name 'round these parts. Sounds real peaceful and sweet. I'll bet that suits ya to a tee. I can tell all about people just by lookin' at 'em. I've been out here a lotta years, and I've seen all kinds, ya know."

"I'm sure you have," said Sheila. "And I'm sure this must be an interesting place to call home. This is my first time in the Southwest. I'm eager to learn more about it."

"Ya stick around, honey, and you'll learn about all kinds of things." Gracie winked.

Sheila made her way through the store, putting the items she needed in a shopping basket. Meanwhile, another customer came in to purchase a large soft drink and a tank of gas.

When he went back outside, Sheila approached the counter with her purchases.

"Now, let's see what ya got here, hon," Gracie said. She rang up the total for Sheila. "Will that do it for ya?"

Sheila nodded. "I'm sure I'll be back as soon as I find out what I've forgotten. But, before I do anything else this morning, I'll go on a walk and think through my story characters while I explore the desert. That should help me clear my head and put my thoughts in order so I can start writing when I sit down at the computer."

"Goin' on a walk by yourself, are ya? Well then, did you bring a good insulted water bottle?"

Sheila shook her head, stifling a smile at Gracie's mispronunciation.

"What about a shirt with long sleeves?" Gracie continued. "A hat? I got some dandy broad-brimmed ones over there." She nodded to the side.

"Thanks, but I'm not going on a real hike. Just a leisurely walk so this beautiful scenery can inspire my writing."

"That's all fine and handy," said Gracie, "but sunburn don't recriminate on what'cher doing out there. Look, hon. I can hear it in yer talk that you're not from around here. I can see it on yer winter skin, too. It's as white as a sheep."

Sheila had managed to keep a straight face through the rest of Gracie's charming malapropisms, but now, caught off guard, she laughed. "Oh, Gracie! I don't think you mean I'm as white as a sheep."

The woman made a pensive frown. "Nope. You're right. I meant you're as pale as a goat. But I got another concern." She glanced at Sheila's feet. "I s'pose tennis shoes is okay if ya stay on the trail what goes on up towards them Pixargraphs. But hikin' boots is always better to protect 'gainst rattlers and king snakes."

Sheila stared at her. "Snakes?"

"Sure, hon. If ya don't know it, them hills're infatuated with dangerous critters. Yep. Snakes, scorpions, poisonous spiders, cougars, coyotes...ya never know what might be crouchin' in the shade by the rocks or them Mormon Tea shrubs."

"Th–thanks for clueing me in," Sheila said. "I guess I have a lot to learn about survival out here."

"The trick is to plan ahead. Survival out here—well, I guess for life in general, too—is 90 percent mental. The other half is by the grace of God."

Forty-five minutes later, fortified inwardly with breakfast and outwardly with sun-protective gear, Sheila ventured forth on her first desert stroll. She pulled her cell phone out of her pocket and turned it on so she could record her thoughts and also call 9-1-1 in case of an emergency—such as an encounter with those snakes or coyotes.

On both sides of the hard-packed trail of reddish earth grew clumps of the Mormon Tea bushes Gracie had mentioned. Ahead, a gentle dry breeze rolled a few tumbleweeds along. Later, a hawk flew overhead, and then Sheila saw a couple of jackrabbits darting among the desert foliage.

The breathtaking scenery and the silence soothed her spirit. Maybe the effect was heightened because she was so far away from the stress of living with Dan. Whatever the reason, her peaceful surroundings simply felt good. Now she could concentrate on the cast of characters who would populate her book.

When she returned to the motel, she was ready for another cup of coffee. This time, when she entered the office, the proprietor was sitting behind the desk. "Good morning, Mr. Mason," she said.

"Mornin'," he replied. "Just call me Derek. No one around here stands much on formality."

"Okay, then. Derek it is."

He returned his attention to the book in front of him.

Sheila poured herself a coffee and stirred in the usual additions. Instead of returning to her cabin immediately, she hesitated. Gracie had joked about ending up as a character in Sheila's novel. Maybe Derek was a candidate too. "So," she said, "how long have you lived in New Promise?"

Derek looked up. "Why?"

"Just curious. No, wait. Maybe I'm with the census bureau. Don't think of me as a stranger in town. Think of me as your advocate in Congress."

That made him smile. "Are we still part of the United States way out here?" he asked.

"We sold you to Mexico," she answered, "but the check bounced."

"That I can believe," he said. "Who'd want this place?"

"Me, for one." Sheila took a sip of coffee. "So, really, how long have you lived out here?"

Derek looked her in the eye. "Some days, I think it's been forever." He glanced down at his book, then looked up again, as if he'd suddenly remembered his duty to be hospitable. "Did you find everything in your cabin okay? I forgot to tell you last night that Wi-Fi service is available for an extra charge."

"Thanks, but I'm not interested. I came here to get away from it all." Sheila chuckled. "And I do mean *it all*."

Derek looked concerned. "Should we expect the sheriff to show up anytime soon?"

She laughed. "Oh, I'm not on the FBI's most-wanted list or anything. I'm a novelist. At least, I want to be. I live in a small town in Indiana, but I've been given a once-in-a-lifetime chance to devote myself to writing a novel. I left everything behind to come as far away from the Midwest as I could. My plan is to stay completely cut off from the outside world until I finish the book."

"So, you'll just rely on TV news to make sure the world's still in one piece?"

"Not even that."

"But think of all the information you'll be missing. Earthquakes, stock-market tumbles, plane crashes...doesn't that bother you?"

Sheila set her cup down and dramatically covered her ears with both hands. "It's just a distraction. Besides, I can always go back and catch up on things later when the book is finished."

"That's pretty unlikely, isn't it?"

"Look," she said, picking up her coffee again. "I know it may seem a little silly, but it's really important for me not to be distracted from my goal. I won't ever get another chance like this one, and I don't want to blow it. And, speaking of my writing project, I guess I'd better get to it."

"Okay. Coffee's on all day whenever you need more." Derek bent over his book again.

Dan didn't wait for official confirmation of Sheila's death from the airline or government authorities. He immediately leaped into action on his own. The morning after the crash, he phoned Sheila's office. Sherry Lopez answered. When Dan told her of Sheila's death, Sherry actually screamed. That only annoyed Dan.

As Sherry gushed words of sympathy, shock, and sorrow, Dan kept counterpointing with questions about the insurance company that the heating and air-conditioning business had used to insure its workers. He finally pried out of Sherry that it was called King's Monument Life and that the local agent was Alan Garinger, who kept an office on Montgomery Street. Dan hung up on Sherry as she was still spouting her condolences. He found Garinger's office number online and dialed.

When the insurance agent answered, Dan got right to the point. "Mr. Garinger, my name is Daniel Gray. My wife, Sheila, was killed in the plane crash in Oklahoma yesterday. You may have seen it on the news. Your company is carrying a ten-thousand-dollar policy on her."

After a brief silence, Garinger said, "Mr. Gray, I'm sorry for your loss. I had no idea anyone from Brissenden was on that flight. How tragic. I didn't know your wife personally, but—"

"What I am wondering," Dan cut in, "is what needs to be done to process the claim. Do you require an official death certificate, or what?"

"Process the claim?" said Garinger, as if surprised by Dan's eagerness to talk business when he should be in a state of grief. "Well, yes, we would need an official death certificate. In the case of an airplane crash or a train wreck or a similarly tragic event, the NTSB coordinates the official paperwork. I can handle that for you. It will probably take about a week."

"Good," said Dan. "I'd appreciate any personal attention you can give to this matter."

"This was a policy you bought from one of our agents?"

"No, it was through my wife's job," Dan explained. "Reynolds Heating and Air-Conditioning." Dan heard the click of computer keys on the other end.

"Yes, I have it here," said the agent. "You're right—a ten-thousand-dollar policy on the life of Sheila Gray was taken out six years ago by her employer."

Dan grinned. "So, uh, how soon do you think you can get the check mailed out to me?"

The pause that followed lasted so long, Dan thought he must not have been heard. He started to repeat the question, but Mr. Garinger responded softly, "Were you aware, sir, that Mrs. Gray—that is, that your *wife* came into our office last spring and revised the beneficiary on this policy?"

Dan was momentarily confused. "She what?"

"She revised the beneficiary," the man repeated. "The full amount—all ten thousand dollars—goes to her brother JD Davis. I see here that my administrative assistant was the witness on the Change of Beneficiary form. It's legal and official. If you'd like to come down and—"

Dan jabbed the off button and threw the phone across the room. Then he stormed down the hall into their bedroom, grabbed Sheila's framed photo from the dresser, and smashed it to the floor, stomping on it three times for good measure. He unleashed a volley of vile words denouncing the deceitfulness of women in general and his wife in particular. He pulled open drawers containing her clothes and threw them at random, ripping most of the items in the process.

After ten minutes of an all-out tantrum, he barged into his study and did an online search for Mrs. Parks's lawyer. He was hampered at first by the inability to remember the man's exact name. Brokenpew? Penbreaker? Finally, he stumbled upon a site where he could search for Detroit attorneys grouped according to their legal specialties. He chose "Estate Planning" and then clicked on "Wills." On the resulting list, he recognized the name of Martin Pembroke. He punched the number into the phone in his study.

An office employee answered and then kept Dan on hold for nearly five minutes before the lawyer finally picked up. "Martin Pembroke here. I understand that I'm talking to Mr. Daniel Gray. May I assume you are the spouse of Mrs. Sheila Gray?"

"I *was*," said Dan, still peeved about having been kept on hold so long. "She's dead. She was one of the passengers on that TransUniverse flight that went down yesterday into an Oklahoma oil refinery."

"No!" said Mr. Pembroke with a horrified gasp. "That can't be."

"It's true," said Dan, "and I blame you and your client Laureen Parks for what happened. It was you who filled Sheila's head with the crazy idea of flying off to Timbuktu so she could write a novel. Now she's dead. Satisfied?"

"Oh, Mr. Gray, I am just heartsick over this news," said Mr. Pembroke. "Surely, you can't believe that I intended any harm to befall your wife. She was charming...absolutely delightful. She had a marvelous future ahead of her."

Dan snorted. "*Had* is the right word, lawyer. You got her on that plane, it went down, and she's dead. Her future is now null and void."

"I just do *not* know what to say to you," Martin Pembroke uttered in a more restrained voice. "This is a terrible tragedy. I'm so sorry for you... and for her."

"Well, being sorry isn't going to bring her back," said Dan, turning pragmatic. "I've got to think about my own future. That's why I'm calling."

"I'm sorry...what was that?" Pembroke asked.

"Sheila told me that Mrs. Parks left her fifty grand," Dan said. "You gave her half of that bundle to set her up for this trip, so you still have the other half."

"And your point would be...?" The lawyer's tone had become positively icy.

"I'm her only heir," Dan responded flatly. "I want you to send the balance of that money to me. *Today*."

"That simply isn't possible."

"Okay, then, I'll give you a couple of days to handle it, but I expect you to get on it right away. I want to see that money in my account before the end of the week."

"Mr. Gray, you need to get one thing straight. If the plane crash that killed your wife happened only yesterday, it is far too soon for anyone to make claims on her estate. A death certificate must be issued first. While it is true that *death in absentia*, or presumption of death, is typically declared in disasters such as the one you described, it still takes several days for the process to be completed. And, in addition to that, I'm afraid you completely misunderstood me. It isn't a matter of timing. It's a matter of directives."

"Don't bury me in legalese, mister. Just send me the money."

"That's not going to happen," the attorney said with finality. "The directives in Laureen Parks's will were very specific. The money was to be given to Sheila Gray *only*. It was to be used to provide a time of retreat for her so that she could write a novel. In the event that Mrs. Gray chose not to use the funds for this purpose, the money was to be given to a charitable organization, as designated in the will. Once I receive confirmation that your wife is dead, I will send the balance of the funds to that organization."

"That money belonged to my wife," Dan yelled into the phone. "And I'm her rightful heir!"

"Wrong. That money belonged to Laureen Parks, to be used as she designated. You, sir, do not fit into the picture in any way. I will contact the proper authorities, verify that your wife's name was on the flight manifest, and obtain a copy of her official death certification. And then I shall fulfill the directives of the will. You needn't call here again. Our business is concluded."

This time, the phone was hung up in *Dan's* ear.

Dan didn't realize how tense he was until he heard the pencil in his hand snap in half. *Strike two*, he thought. *This isn't going at all the way it's supposed to. What else can go wrong?*

A sharp knock on the front door startled him. He rose slowly, went into the hall, and peeked through the peephole. Two men stood on his porch. He opened the door.

"Daniel Gray?" asked a man in a police uniform.

"Yes."

"May we come in?"

Dan found himself moving aside to let the men enter. The second man was wearing a clerical collar, and Dan got a glimpse of an official emblem on his upper sleeve. They advanced through the hallway to the modest living room. Dan motioned for everyone to be seated.

The man in the clerical collar spoke first. "I'm Reverend Bruck, chaplain with the Brissenden Police Department, and this is Officer Santos." He hesitated briefly before continuing. "We're sorry to have to bring you this terrible news, Mr. Gray. As you may know, your wife, Sheila Gray, was aboard TransUniverse flight fourteen eighty-one. Perhaps you've heard that it was involved in a midair collision yesterday and landed in an oil refinery, where it exploded and is still burning in spots. Emergency responders do not believe that anyone on board survived." He paused, as if to give Dan a moment for the news to sink in.

Dan looked at the man blankly. He already knew that Sheila was dead. But it occurred to him that perhaps he ought to appear a little saddened at the news. He glanced down at the floor and then thought of a question. "Does anyone know the cause of the collision?"

"That's still under investigation," said Officer Santos. "Although the remains of the aircraft are pretty badly burned, the authorities are trying to locate and identify the bodies now. It might help if you could tell us what your wife was wearing."

"Wearing?" said Dan, squinting as he struggled to remember. "Geez, I don't know. Let's see. She had on a blue turtleneck sweater, I remember that. And tennis shoes. They were new. And blue slacks...no, wait. She was wearing jeans."

"Did she have any tattoos? Special dental work? Plastic-surgery markings?" asked Santos.

"No tattoos," said Dan, "but she had a small scar on her left knee from when she got caught on some barbed wire at her father's farm when she was eleven. I've got a picture of her in our...."

He paused mid-sentence, remembering what he had done to that photo and to their bedroom. He'd rather not let the authorities lay eyes on the resulting destruction. "I've got a photo of her here in my wallet," he said, reaching into his hip pocket. "Yeah, there you go. She had brownish hair."

"What about jewelry? A wedding ring, for example?" asked Santos.

Dan nodded. "Sure, she had on a wedding ring. An engagement ring, too. Plain yellow gold, one diamond, small cut. Oh, and something else. She always wore a necklace. It was gold and had three little charms, in the shapes of a quill and a book and a clock. It was a keepsake from one of her high-school teachers. She had it on night and day. And she also had a wristwatch. It was one of those inexpensive kinds that you can get at big-box stores, with just a plain brown leather band."

Santos was taking notes of everything Dan said.

Reverend Bruck asked, "Will you be all right, Mr. Gray? Is there anyone you'd like to call to have come stay with you during this time?"

Dan shook his head.

"Well, here's my card if you need to talk with someone about what you're going through. Forgive me, but, due to the extent of the explosion, it may take a while for the bodies to be located and identified, and some...well...." The chaplain cleared his throat. "We're sure this has been a terrible shock." He stood and gave his card to Dan.

Officer Santos also handed Dan a card. "And here's mine, in case you can think of anything else that might be of help in identifying your wife's body. As more is learned in the investigation, someone will be in touch. Again, we're sorry for your loss."

As soon as the men left, Dan closed the door and exhaled in one long, slow breath. He needed a beer or two to relax. Maybe then he could think more clearly about what to do next.

CHAPTER 19

Seven days after arriving in New Promise, Sheila stopped by the motel office following her early walk to pay another week's rent in advance.

"Well, if it isn't the happy wanderer," Derek greeted her. "How are your jaunts going each morning?"

"Great," she replied. "The scenery is always spectacular, and the exercise feels fantastic. Sort of offsets sitting at the computer all day. I'm making good progress on my story outline. I was right about the desert being what I needed."

Derek wrote out a receipt and handed it to her. "So, how'd you come to wind up here, of all places?"

Sheila took a deep breath while evaluating the pros and cons of sharing her story with Derek. She wouldn't be dishonest with him, but neither was she ready to tell him much more than she'd already explained.

"Well," she began, "as I told you, I needed a place to hole up and write a novel. My seatmate on the airplane was coming here for an anthropology field trip, and when she told me about New Promise, it sounded like just the secluded place I was looking for. Now, what about you? Did you grow up in this area?" She hoped he wouldn't evade the question this time.

Derek shifted his weight. "Nope. Moved from the East Coast eight years back."

"Do you have relatives here?"

"None," said Derek with a wry grin. "Ours wasn't what you'd call a close-knit bunch. If I'd had family here, it would've been the last place I'd have headed."

Sheila found herself smiling back at him. She noticed that when he grinned, his eyes conveyed mixed signals, as though, like herself, he was a person of hidden stories.

"I don't suppose you'd be interested in sharing a picnic lunch with me one of these days," he said. "I mean, you have to stop and eat every so often, anyway, and getting away from the computer for a little bit once in a while would do you good. We could get sandwiches at Gracie's and eat them outdoors. By noon, it should warm up into the sixties."

Sheila wasn't sure how to take Derek's invitation. Was he coming on to her? Or was he simply looking for some sociable conversation in this lonely place? She decided one lunch together couldn't hurt. "Okay. You're right about the benefits of breaks, as long as I don't take them too often. But a picnic?" She glanced out the window at the rocky terrain. "Those jackrabbits out there look none too plump. Wouldn't the smell of food attract unwelcome visitors?"

Derek smiled again and inclined his head to the north of the building. "I was thinking of that picnic table under the pine tree. Most animals stay away from people—during the day, at least. I'll bet you've never been on a picnic in February before."

Sheila laughed. "You're right again. How about next Saturday?"

Dan's frustration at JD's receiving the insurance money that Dan had counted on getting was assuaged slightly when he was notified he would soon be paid $300,000. Sheila had apparently taken out a flight-insurance policy and had named Dan as the beneficiary. He was beyond annoyed that she had done such a thing without clearing it with him first. His meek little wife had certainly changed during the past few months, and it was all the fault of that meddling Parks woman.

Of course, he was thrilled at the flight-insurance bonanza. Who wouldn't be? But he couldn't figure out why in the world Sheila would stiff him the $10,000 from her job-related policy and then arrange for him to get thirty times that amount from an air disaster. It simply made no sense.

Unless.... Unless she somehow had a sixth sense that the plane was going to go down, and she knew it would make Dan a prime suspect in case it was found to be sabotage.

But when he learned that the policy had been purchased at an airport kiosk in Oklahoma City, and that the premium had cost an even $25, his mind went back to the moment he'd let her off at the airport door. He'd given her that twenty-five bucks and had insisted she bet it for him in Vegas. He remembered how she'd resisted, saying she didn't want to take the time to go into a casino. But he'd pressed her until she'd finally agreed. So, she'd apparently found a way to place the "bet" without setting one foot inside a casino. More proof of rebellion against him. Again, he placed the responsibility for that squarely on the shoulders of Old Lady Parks.

Nevertheless, even though Dan didn't approve of the act of defiance that Sheila's surprise flight-insurance purchase indicated, he had to admire her cleverness.

When Dan saw Imogene that evening, he told her about the windfall. At first, she gasped in amazement, but very soon a hard gleam shone from her eyes. As if to keep Dan from guessing her true thoughts, she batted her eyelashes a couple of times and tenderly laid her hand on his arm. "Not to make light of your loss, dear, but I *am* glad at your sudden change in fortune. With your new resources and our strategic partnership, we can go anywhere we want to go."

"Yeah, but it still galls me that JD gets ten grand in insurance money that should have been mine. What right did Sheila have to go behind my back and change the beneficiary of her policy? I was her husband. That money should have been mine!"

"But darling, that's perfect."

"Perfect?" he almost screamed. "I lose ten grand, and you say that's perfect? What's with *that?*"

"Think it through," Imogene told him. "Brissenden is a small town. Word is going to get out that you got two hundred fifty grand from the credit-card company and another three hundred thousand from the extra flight-insurance policy. If JD had half a brain, he'd sue you for a portion of his sister's estate. It would cost you sixty-K either to buy him off or to drag it through the courts for five years. Let him have the ten grand. It's a bargain."

Dan considered that for a moment. "Okay. I see your point. That makes sense. It still grates me he'll get that money, but I see what you're saying. It *is* cheap, when you look at the big picture."

"And he doesn't have to keep *all* of that money," Imogene continued.

"Huh?" asked Dan. "How's that again?"

"This is just a suggestion," she said, "but you might want to call your bereaved brother-in-law and spend some time consoling him."

"Are you serious?"

"Let me finish, darling," she admonished him softly. "As a way of sharing your grief, you could suggest to him that the two of you share the cost of a small gravestone, a sort of tribute to Sheila. You could further suggest that the marker be placed somewhere on the family farm, under a favorite tree or by a pleasant stream. Naturally, JD will see the sentimental value of this. You could even have a cleric come out and say a few words, and you could perhaps read a poem."

"Totally maudlin," said Dan with disgust.

"Who cares?" asked Imogene. "You won't pay for a gravesite at a cemetery or for a funeral, and JD will even contribute half the price of the little marker. When the locals hear about what you and JD have done, they'll think of it as something marvelously chivalrous...a fitting tribute to a hometown girl who died tragically."

Dan weighed that idea a moment, then chuckled. "Marvelous! I love it."

"Yes," she said with a conspiratorial smile. "I thought you'd like that. And there's more."

"More?" he said.

"The paper we finished documenting—the one I'll be reading at the MLA conference in a few weeks? I sent it to the editor of *Literary Analysis Quarterly*." Imogene picked up the printout of an e-mail message and handed the page to Dan. "As you can see, it's been accepted for publication in next spring's issue. I put your name first in the authors' listing. That's step one in getting you the academic recognition we both know you deserve."

Dan's chest began to swell. This was the frosting on the success cake.

Imogene continued. "You need to get out of that cracker box you're living in now. Sell it and move here to Indianapolis. Get a high-rise apartment. Hire a decorator to give it a stunning contemporary décor. Image is everything, darling. Oh, and a new car, too. We'll throw a housewarming party after you move in. We'll invite all the English department faculty and a couple of deans, and some area authors and bookstore owners. Even a few local TV personalities. You can let it be known that your article is set for publication in the summer...*and* you can start making it known that you have a novel in the works."

Dan could see himself in such a setting. Posh apartment, plush furniture, luxury car, classy clothes, upscale friends. "Hey, I like the sound of all that."

"The sky is the limit, darling," Imogene assured him. "We'll really show them who the new king and queen of the university campus are. Make your calls, dearest. Contact JD and the insurance companies, then come back tomorrow night around seven. I'll have dinner waiting. It will be celebration time."

"Right," Dan agreed. "I'll bring the bubbly."

Sheila was having great writing momentum. The outline she'd composed that first day had primed the pump quite well, and very soon the characters were driving the plot on their own. By Saturday, she was glad to break for a longer lunch instead of eating her normal salad or sandwich at the computer. She closed her laptop and walked to the office.

"Hi," Derek said when she came in the door. "Ready for a picnic?"

"You bet. I'm starved."

Once they'd purchased their sandwiches and soft drinks, Sheila and Derek sat at the outdoor table next to his office and enjoyed casual conversation while they ate in the shade of the pine tree. Sheila was amazed at how many things Derek was interested in and informed about. He could talk about books, nature, even cooking.

"So, you've actually made Baked Alaska?" she asked. "Almost everyone has heard of the dessert, but I've never in my life met anyone who's really made it."

"I didn't say it was edible," said Derek with a laugh. "I just said I made it. Believe me, it wasn't all it's cracked up to be. At least, not my version."

"Still, that's quite an undertaking. You must be very competent in the kitchen."

"I do okay." He smiled. "But don't take my word for it. How about I cook dinner for you sometime? It probably won't be anything fancy. Depends on how much time I'd have to plan and prep. But I promise it'll be better than my Baked Alaska."

"I'd love that one of these days," said Sheila as she stood. She collected the used napkins, plastic wrap, and empty cups from the table and threw them in the nearby trash can. "Sometime next week?"

Derek nodded. "Sure. Let's make it seven o'clock, a week from tomorrow. Sunday evenings are usually slow at the motel. Come to the office. I live in an apartment in back."

"Then seven on Sunday it is," Sheila confirmed.

That week, as scenes turned into chapters and as the characters grew in complexity, Sheila finally glimpsed more fully the gift of creativity that Laureen Parks had always insisted she possessed. Sure, Sheila often ran into plot problems or couldn't quite figure out the best way to handle a transition or a chapter opening, but if she simply made a note of the issue and soldiered on, it wasn't long before her subconscious presented her with the solution—sometimes in a dream, at other times during the desert hikes that she continued to take each morning.

On Sunday of the following week, she set her cell phone's alarm clock for 6:30 PM so she'd be reminded to pull herself out of her novel's setting and get ready for dinner with Derek.

Now that the month of March had arrived, daytime highs in New Promise averaged in the upper sixties to the low seventies, but nighttime temperatures still got as low as the upper forties. She could tell that the warmth of the day was already cooling, so she turned the wall heater on low and pondered what to wear to dinner at Derek's.

From among the limited number of clothing items she'd brought with her, she selected a dressy long-sleeved pullover shirt in turquoise blue, a lightweight black knit cardigan, and a pair of black jeans. As she removed her sweatshirt and put on the silky top, the turquoise color reminded her of the pair of genuine turquoise earrings she'd been unable to resist purchasing at Gracie's store her first week there—the same day that Gracie had insisted on giving her a complimentary "insulted" coffee mug. Sheila retrieved the jewelry pouch from the dresser drawer where she'd stashed it, removed the earrings, and was delighted to see that they matched the color of her shirt perfectly. With a happy sigh, she put on the earrings and then opened a tube of lipstick. The shade was too pale for her coloring, but it would have to do. She hadn't had the time or the interest to shop for cosmetics in Nevada, especially since Dan wouldn't approve of anything too colorful that she took back home with her.

As she combed her hair, she realized she hadn't had a haircut since before Laureen's death, when her normal schedule had turned topsy-turvy. Now, her hair was growing out into a style she liked better than the one Dan had insisted upon for so many years. Of course, it could use a trim, but maybe she'd keep the new style, even if Dan did grumble. She liked the feeling of making her own decisions.

She grabbed the key to her cabin and stuffed it into a front pocket of her jeans, then glanced at her reflection in the mirror. The turquoise earrings and shirt made her greenish eyes appear a little more turquoise, too. She smiled approvingly. *All things considered, not half bad.*

At 7:01, she opened the door to the motel office and called out, "Hello?"

Derek appeared in the doorway behind the front desk. "Hi, Sheila. Come on back. Dinner's just about ready."

"Good! It smells wonderful."

While Derek hurried out of sight, Sheila stood near the door and glanced around. Derek's residence was sparse but very neat and clean with a calm, relaxing ambience. In addition to the living room, there was a small kitchen, a bathroom, and a bedroom. Sheila noticed very little in the way of decoration, except for a few framed photographs of stunningly attractive desert scenes on one wall and several shelves lined with books on another. She noticed a lot of familiar titles and was again impressed by Derek's eclectic interests.

"I like your place," she said when Derek peeked out of the kitchen. "It seems really comfortable."

"Thanks. I enjoy it. I'm not really into a lot of creature comforts, I guess. I spend most of my free time reading." At that moment, a timer rang. "Oh, the chicken almondine is ready."

During the meal, Derek questioned Sheila about her writing project. She felt comfortable relaxing her guard a little more and shared details with him about her novel's characters.

They were almost done with the main course when Derek suddenly stopped eating and looked intently at Sheila.

"What's wrong?" she asked.

"Why are you here?" he asked. "I know you're here to write the book, but what I'm wondering about is, why *here*—why *now*?"

Sheila hesitated, wondering just how much she could—or should—share with this man. She'd been too gullible about men in the past—well, about Dan, at least. But she also didn't want to turn into a stonyhearted woman who trusted no one. As she looked into Derek's warm brown eyes, she decided that if she told him a brief history of her life, she wouldn't run much of a risk of having her confidence betrayed, even if there were anyone else in this out-of-the way place he could tell it to.

So, she launched into her life story, starting with losing her mother before she ever knew her, then going through high school and winning the writing award, spending six weeks at Brissenden College, and meeting Dan at the summer writing program. She described the sacrifices and compromises that had made up her relationship with Dan.

Eventually, as Derek's facial expressions and occasional, brief comments reflected interest and nonjudgmental concern, she found herself recounting intimate details of the hurts her husband had inflicted upon her over the years. When she talked about Dan's unwillingness to let her work with Mrs. Parks, tears ran down her face.

Sheila was amazed to realize that, for the first time in her life, a man was genuinely interested in not only what she had to say but also, more important, how she felt.

"And so," she finished, "that's how I ended up in New Promise. I only hope that the name rings true for me. I want a new start, and I truly feel like I'm in the right place to see that happen."

Derek smiled. "I'm glad you're here, Dove. I want you to know that you are welcome for as long as you want to stay. And anything I can ever do to help you, I'll do."

Sheila wiped her eyes with her napkin, not feeling the least bit self-conscious. "Thanks. Now, it's your turn. Why are *you* here? You said you don't have any family in the area. Why would a bright guy like you choose to isolate himself out here in the middle of nowhere?"

Derek told her of his lifelong sense of not really belonging and how that had led him to enlist in the army. While he wasn't crazy about the strict regimen of military life, he nevertheless had become close friends with two guys in his unit. None of the three was the least bit interested in making the military a career. In fact, all of them had dreams of starting a business together after they were discharged.

But before their terms of service were up, they were sent overseas to Afghanistan. Tragically, both of Derek's buddies were killed in a rocket attack. Derek sustained only superficial cuts. After that, however, he struggled with depression. He couldn't understand then, and still didn't understand, why his friends had been lost and he'd been spared.

"It's just not fair," he said. "They were really great guys. For the first time in my life, I felt like I was starting to belong somewhere. We had plans. We could have made a bright future. Instead, they're gone, and I'm left here alone. I just don't get it."

"I don't have any answers," Sheila said gently, "but I do know one thing. If you were spared, there must be a reason. Don't give up on finding out what it is."

Derek smiled back at her and cleared his throat. "Okay, enough seriousness. How about dessert?"

"Dessert? Yes! That is, as long as it's not Baked Alaska."

Derek laughed. "Nope. No Baked Alaska tonight. Tonight, we're having cheesecake with a blueberry glaze."

"Yum!" Sheila exclaimed. "Did you know that's my absolute favorite?"

"I had a hunch. I asked Gracie for ideas, and she told me that blueberry cheesecake is your favorite flavor of yogurt, so I figured you'd like the real thing, too."

After Sheila had eaten her entire wedge of rich, silky cheesecake, she pushed her chair back from the table and stood. "That was the most delicious meal, not to mention the best conversation, I've had in ages. In fact, since Mrs. Parks died. I appreciate it more than you know. Thank you."

Derek got up from the table, as well. "No, Dove, thank *you*. I haven't talked about all that for years. After you bury something down for so long, it really helps to let it out. Thanks for listening."

Sheila reached over and patted Derek on the arm. "You're a wonderful man. Don't ever forget that." She nodded toward the door to the reception area. "I need to head for the cabin now. Thanks again for a great evening. I really appreciate how welcome you've made me feel."

Derek opened the door for her and followed her through the reception area to the main entry. "I'll watch until you get into your cabin safe and sound. Good night."

"G'night. Maybe I'll see you in the morning when I stop by for my first cup of coffee."

Derek was not at the registration desk, however, when Sheila arrived with her insulated mug the next morning. But as she entered the store to buy breakfast, Gracie was at her usual spot, eager to hear how the previous evening had gone.

"Well, look who's up at the crank of dawn, just like always. And what'd ya think of Derek's special dessert? I told him how I make sure to keep blueberry-cheesecake yogurt on hand for ya all the time now."

"It was delicious," Sheila assured her. "And so was the chicken almondine he prepared, along with tossed salad, sunshine carrots, and warm rolls. I was very impressed by his culinary skills."

"Yep. And he's a good cook, too. The first time I tasted his grub, ya coulda knocked me over with a fender. Here he is, eking out a foot-in-the-mouth existence in a forgotten corner of the landscape, when I bet he could be a fancy-schmancy cook somewhere down in Vegas." As Sheila headed for the dairy cooler, Gracie raised her voice and continued. "I s'pose you're not too tired to go on yer walk this mornin' like ya do every day?"

"Oh, no," said Sheila, returning to the counter with a yogurt cup, a poppy-seed muffin, and an orange. "Walking will help me puzzle out a problem I'm having with prepositions."

"What? Who tried to preposition you, hon? Was it one of them ant-sypology folks? They usually don't cause no trouble. In fact, the reason they come here is to preserve it."

"No," Sheila said with a grin. "When I was proofreading a scene last night, I caught an overabundance of prepositional phrases. It isn't anything I can't handle after a good walk and breakfast." She paid for her purchases and accepted her receipt.

Derek, who had learned a lot about taxes after buying the motel, had told Sheila she should keep all her receipts of writing-related expenses to claim as tax deductions. The way things were going with the sale of her stories and the promise of a book contract, she might need every deduction she could legally take that year.

"I think my walk will help me sort through another issue, too," she went on. "I unburdened my soul to Derek last night about what I've had to put up with in my fifteen-year marriage. After I went to my cabin, a lot of anger I didn't even know was still inside me bubbled to the surface."

A look of affectionate concern crossed Gracie's face, but before she could say anything, the door-alert chimed, and a family came in for snacks and to use the restroom. The children's chatter soon informed Sheila and Gracie that the family had been visiting relatives in a town eighty miles up the road. For some reason unknown to her, Sheila stayed rather than use the break in conversation as an opportunity to leave.

When the family had gone, Gracie said, "Hon, I been seein' it in yer pritty green eyes that somebody'd done ya wrong. For us gals, too many times, it's a husband or boyfriend. I'm so sorry for yer hurt."

"Thanks, Gracie. I appreciate that. But what do I do with all this rage? Dan has stolen fifteen years of my life! That's a decade and a half I'll never get back. I could have been a successful writer by now. Instead, I'm hiding out on the back side of the desert, putting my life on hold to write my first book. I hate that man. Absolutely hate him! Sometimes on my walks, instead of enjoying the peace of these beautiful surroundings, I find myself thinking of ways to get revenge. It scares me how many methods I can come up with. We writers have good imaginations, you know."

Gracie's look of concern changed to one of alarm. "Oh, now, hon, it's normal to be angry for a spell, but don't hang onto it fer so long that ya get bitter. There ain't nothin' much worse than a spirit of bitterness in a person. It makes yer heart as cold as bone. And the thing is, when ya want to hurt somebody else, you're the one who ends up gettin' hurt the worst. Holdin' on to bitterness is like carryin' around a rattlesnake inside yer shirt. You're hopin' the other person'll get bit, but half the time, they don't even know about the snake you got. Meanwhile, you're dyin' from venom overdose."

"But Dan isn't sorry for how he's treated me. He hasn't apologized to me even once."

Gracie gazed through the store's front windows into the distance. "Ya don't have to wait for no apology," she said softly. "Forgiveness ain't about the person who done ya wrong. It's about you." She turned to look at Sheila again. "As long as ya hold on to a grudge, ya stay in bondage."

Sheila glanced down at her sack with the yogurt quickly losing its chill. "But it isn't fair for him to be let off the hook. He deserves to be punished."

Gracie clucked her tongue. "Child, if I was a writer, I could write a whole 'cyclopedia about bein' done wrong to and holdin' grudges. If somebody hadn't explained it to me a lot better than I'm explainin' to you right now, I'd be a shriveled-up old biddy, probably twirlin' in my grave. But here's the truth. Decidin' to forgive don't say the person's innocent when they're guilty as gin. It don't let 'em off the hook a-tall. It lets *you* off the hook and gives the rascals over to a higher court where God's the Judge."

Gracie opened a drawer and pulled out a dog-eared Bible with a colorful paperback binding. "I read from the Good Book now and then. Don't understand it all, but one thing I do get: God's forgiven me a whole lot more than I've ever had to forgive anyone else. Somewhere in here—don't remember 'zactly where, now—it says that if we don't forgive others, God won't forgive us. And that's one promise I don't want to bet against the house on."

Sheila walked behind the counter, put her arm around Gracie's ample shoulders, and squeezed. "Gracie, I love you for speaking the truth to me. An older friend in my life used to do that, but she died recently, and I miss her terribly. I'll think about what you said. It makes sense. I'm just not sure I'm ready yet to forgive my husband. But I can tell that to God, too, can't I? And ask Him to help me find the strength to let go of my anger?"

"Of course ya can, hon. And don't let it get ya down if it takes ya a while to *feel* like forgivin'. This business of forgivin' ain't no walk in the picnic. It's a process. Ya decide to forgive, and then, like ya say, ya tell God all about it. Don't worry if it ain't no fancy prayer. Bein' honest is what counts. The good Lord can handle yer straight talk about what's buggin' ya. Do what ya can today. Then, tomorrow, see if ya can do it again, plus maybe a little more."

Sheila gave Gracie another squeeze, then picked up her breakfast purchases and started for the door. "Thanks again. I'd better get on my way."

"Ya do that, hon. And be patient with yerself. Home wasn't built in a day."

CHAPTER 20

In the six weeks since the demise of his wife, Dan Gray had gone through a metamorphosis. Under the tutelage of Dr. Imogene Cunningham, he had emerged from his cocoon of obscurity into a world of high visibility. He had sold his house and most of his belongings. After paying off his mortgage, he had pocketed only $13,000 net, but what did that matter? He was rich from other sources.

The first check to arrive had been the $250,000 from the company underwriting the credit card Sheila had used to book her airline tickets. A great deal of that money had been spent before it ever appeared in Dan's account. He was now driving a new cherry-red Mustang. He was wearing tailored clothes, and his hair had been dyed and given a weave to make it appear thicker. His leather items—from wallet to shoes to belt to briefcase—were Gucci. He wore a genuine Rolex watch studded with diamonds, as well as a pinkie ring of onyx and gold with a large solitaire diamond in the middle.

Imogene had found an ideal apartment for him—and he got the impression she was looking forward to moving in with him before long. He didn't mind in the least. The apartment was high above the city in an exclusive building of aging yuppie tenants. Imogene had hired a decorator and was clear about what she wanted the place to look like when finished. Just as Dan was about to protest, she complimented him on his "exquisite" taste regarding fashion and style. He also noticed that the more she focused on sharpening his image, the more uptown she became, herself. In addition to those benefits, the end result of all the redecorating pleased him immensely. The apartment had just enough hardwood and chrome to appear masculine.

Once the second check arrived, Dan was in high orbit. "Life is so very, very good," Dan said, as he lay next to Imogene in his new bedroom. "Every time I look online at my checking account balance and see a six-digit figure, it makes me want to sing 'What a Wonderful World.'"

"You deserve it, darling," cooed Imogene. "And I want to see it continue."

Dan rolled to one side and looked questioningly at her. "What do you mean by that?" he asked.

"I don't want this good life to evaporate, that's all," she said with an adoring smile. She'd had her hair darkened, and she'd shed a few pounds. "Let's face it, the university isn't paying you a pittance of what you're worth. But, until you finish your novel and find a publisher for it, that's the only income you'll have for a while."

Dan grimaced. He liked living this high life, and he didn't welcome any kind of talk that suggested it might not go on forever. He waited for her to say more.

"Right now, you're well established," Imogene continued, in a tone that suggested she was trying to sound subservient. "But the apartment, furnishings, and decorator fees, the new car, your custom wardrobe and accessories, plus the marvelous parties you've been hosting, have cost you two hundred seventy-five thousand dollars. Your car insurance fees are now higher. You'll need to consider holiday tips for the doorman. You need to order a new computer for your home office.... My point is, you can't keep spending indefinitely without some incoming cash flow."

Dan felt as though someone with a straight pin was tiptoeing toward his bubble. "Are you trying to worry me?" he asked, unable to keep anger from edging into his voice.

Imogene reached over and stroked his cheek. "No, sweetheart," she said. "I just don't want your dream world to dissolve."

Dan wrinkled his forehead. "How so?"

"Well, it's simple math," she said slowly, as if to help him keep up with her reasoning. "You got thirteen thousand dollars clear from the sale of your house. Then, you got a quarter of a million from the credit-card insurance settlement. Then, you got three hundred grand from the flight-insurance payment."

"I know all that," said Dan, defensively.

"But you've already spent quite a lot. Plus, once I'm able to snag a private office for you at the university, there'll be additional interior-design expenses."

"So?" said Dan. "That will still leave, uh...."

"I figure around two hundred eighty-five thousand, maybe more," said Imogene.

"Yeah, yeah." Dan grinned. "Lots of dough."

"But drain off rent...car maintenance...insurance...utilities... food...entertainment...clothes...credit cards...hairstylists...." She paused in between each item she listed, as if to give him time to process it.

"What's your point?" Dan demanded, not liking where this appeared to be headed.

Imogene smiled. "Passive income and reserve cash," she said. "That's my point. If you were to put a hundred fifty grand into a mutual fund that paid five percent, you'd earn seven grand every year in interest alone. With your teaching salary of thirty-four thousand, you'd pull in forty-one thousand each year, still have sixty-three thousand dollars of spending money in your checking account, and have a solid-gold credit rating because you'd still have the hundred fifty grand in reserve in those mutual funds."

Dan weighed this line of reasoning. "Let my money make even more money."

"That's the ticket. We'd still have enough liquid funds for a trip to Hawaii or France, and your wallet would be full of green, but you wouldn't see your cash going out with nothing coming in."

Dan saw the logic of what she was saying. The thought of free money appealed greatly to him. He nodded his approval at Imogene's suggestions. "Seven grand a year from the mutual funds for doing nothing?" he mused aloud. "Yeah, that sounds like something I could get used to. You know someone who could help me?"

"We can use your banker," Imogene said. "Banks carry all sorts of mutual funds and certificates of deposit nowadays. You can just pick up the phone tomorrow and make a call, and they'll do all the processing for you. Easy as pie."

Dan settled back into the oversized pillows and smiled. With his money diversified and working for him, he could continue to be "The Playboy of the Western World." He could also devote himself more fully to his novel. And, he'd still have plenty of cash to flash about. What a lucky star he had been born under. Life was so very, very good.

Even though Sheila and Laureen had discussed solitude as a literary theme a time or two, and Sheila had experienced some of it on her long drive to Detroit, it had never been as vibrant a concept to Sheila as it was now. After six weeks of staying sequestered in the desert, she had experienced a radical shift in her whole perspective on life. Each day, she took time to walk alone in the desert à la John the Baptist in the wilderness. Her skin had become tawny and radiant, her leg muscles were firmer, and, in spite of the broad-brimmed hat, her hair was now slightly sun-bleached.

She recalled the chapters in Samuel Butler's semiautobiographical novel *The Way of All Flesh* recounting the many weeks the main character had been imprisoned. Instead of breaking him, the time spent in prison had rejuvenated him. The young man had been forced to stop and assess his life, to set new and better goals for himself. Then, when his sentence was up, he'd been able to leave jail sober-minded and eager for a second chance at life. During Sheila's discussion with Laureen about that section of the novel, Laureen had said, "You've never had enough solitude to see yourself in a proper perspective, Sheila. Until that happens, you won't be able to write your novel. Solitude isn't always alienation. Sometimes, it's self-discovery. And, sometimes, shutting out all the noise around us is what finally enables us to hear the whispers of God."

Laureen had been right about that. Six weeks without access to news and with no communication with her friends and family back home had forced Sheila to look inward—and upward. Her talks with Derek and Gracie had helped her gain a different perspective on the disappointing turns her life had taken. Marathon hours of working on her novel had allowed her the chance to play out scenarios that might have happened, or even should have happened.

Because of this growth in her inner being, Sheila found herself unable to recall much from her former life with any clarity of memory. She could no longer vividly picture her home and its furnishings. Her coworkers at the office, with their frivolous priorities, now seemed like half-forgotten characters from a summer rerun show. JD and the farm, Dan and his silly manuscript, the small town of Brissenden...*everything* seemed part of a bygone era. Only Judith Hardy and Laureen Parks remained dear to her thoughts and recollections—those two noble ladies who had rescued her from the tedium of her existence prior to the creation of Dove Alexander.

In many ways, Sheila dreaded her eventual return to Brissenden. She'd discovered that now, whether her novel ever sold or not, she was larger than her little hometown. She couldn't turn her back on her new persona. She was no longer merely the product of a legalistic home environment; she was a woman able to ponder her faith through the lens of her own life and experience. She was no longer an office manager at Reynolds Heating and Air-Conditioning; she was a writer. She was no longer Dan's maid, cook, and emotional—and sometimes physical—punching bag; she was a woman of independent thought and means.

If only life could be like a story in progress, she sometimes thought. *Just delete the sections you no longer like and write out what you would prefer.* Whenever she pondered that concept, she would add, *It's too bad it can't be that easy*. And that would remind her of what Gracie had said about the process of forgiveness: "It ain't no walk in the picnic."

Sheila couldn't simply delete unwanted sections from her life, but her friends in New Promise were helping her write a new chapter that was more satisfying than she ever dreamed possible. "Thank You, God, for this fresh beginning," she whispered on many a night, just before closing her eyes and drifting off to sleep.

Almost two and a half months after the plane crash in Oklahoma, a DVD arrived in the mail for Dan. It contained a catalog with photos of personal items recovered from the downed TransUniverse flight 1481. Dan was given ninety days to examine the catalog and submit a claim for any items he recognized as belonging to Sheila.

He slid the DVD into his computer. There it was on page ten—the gold necklace that Parks woman had given her. Attached to the smoke-blackened chain were three charms in the shapes of a clock, a book, and the base of a quill pen.

Dan shuddered. Even if the ongoing DNA testing finally identified one of the recovered body parts as Sheila's, such news would not give him the final sense of closure that seeing her necklace in this catalog provided.

Dan closed the catalog, ejected the DVD, and dropped it, along with the cardboard mailer and claim form, in the wastebasket. Automatically brushing his hands, he went to the phone. He hit the first number on speed dial and listened to Imogene's recorded voice requesting the caller to leave a message.

"Hey," he said, "it's me. Remember not long ago you said something about a trip to Hawaii? Well, I think that would be a nice place for a honeymoon. Are you game?"

During the next few weeks, while Sheila was pleased with her progress on the novel, she was distressed by a constant sense of dread. The closer she got to completing her story, the sooner she would be obligated to return home to Dan. She was a much stronger person now, but standing up to her controlling husband wouldn't be easy, especially without the support of Gracie's folksy wisdom.

Gracie made no secret of the fact that her insights were based on what she'd discovered in the "Good Book" and from what certain people in her past knew about the Bible. That piqued Sheila's interest. Whereas the older woman would never be mistaken for a Bible scholar, something about the way she found God's mercy in daily life soothed Sheila and made her want to find that same mercy. It was different from anything she had ever experienced growing up. So, when Gracie presented her with a paperback copy of the *New International Version* of the Bible that had come in a recent order, Sheila accepted it in the spirit it was given.

One evening after a full day of writing, her thoughts returned to Gracie's comments that morning about King David telling God his honest expressions of frustration. Since Sheila's upbringing had given her the image of God as a cosmic enforcer, she would never dream of saying anything that might provoke divine retribution. How could David be so blunt with God and escape being struck by lightning?

She picked up her new Bible and flipped through the pages. Somewhere close to the middle of the Psalms, the word *"tumbleweed"* caught her eye. She'd never noticed that term in the Bible before. She read the entire sentence—all of Psalm 83:13: *"Make them like tumbleweed, my God, like chaff before the wind."*

Immediately, she thought of Dan, curled up like a ball and rolling along the reddish desert ground. She grinned. Then she remembered Mrs. Parks's admonition to look at the context. This verse was talking about God's enemies. Well, Sheila wouldn't go that far in classifying her husband, but she was amused at the image, nonetheless.

She flipped ahead in the Bible, until the first two verses of Psalm 142 grabbed her attention: *"I cry aloud to the LORD; I lift up my voice to the* Lord *for mercy. I pour out before him my complaint; before him I tell my trouble."*

There it was again—David telling God his complaints and troubles. Why had she not noticed that before, back when she used to glance in the Bible now and then? A translator's note explained that David had written the psalm while hiding in a cave as he fled for his life.

Sheila didn't fear being murdered when she returned home, but, again, she worried that her newfound sense of confidence might not be able to survive Dan's controlling, abusive nature. What should she do? Gracie would urge her to be honest with God. But, as Sheila closed her eyes and tried to form a prayer using "thee" and "thou," she'd been taught in her childhood, she struggled. *God, I want to tell You how I feel, but I don't know what to say.*

When she opened her eyes again, her gaze fell on verse 3 of Psalm 142, and its words seemed to leap off the page. She read them aloud: "'*When my spirit grows faint within me, it is you who watch over my way.*'"

As Sheila continued to lift more of David's words as her own prayer, a sense of peace filled her soul. She closed the Bible and poured out her heart to God with a freedom she had never felt before. She'd already asked God to help her forgive Dan, just as Gracie had suggested, but this was a deeper conversation from the most profound part of her heart. When she was done, she knew without a doubt that God had heard every word. While she still wasn't comfortable at the thought of going back home, she sensed that God would take care of her, no matter what happened.

As the weeks went by, her friendship with Derek continued to develop through casual conversation whenever she came to the office for coffee and to pay her weekly rent, as well as during their occasional picnic lunches.

One day, Derek again invited Sheila for a Sunday evening dinner. This time, he prepared a succulent stir-fry of shrimp and broccoli seasoned with orange segments and jalapeños, all served over steamed rice.

"When you first told me what you were making, I was afraid to try it," Sheila confessed. "But the melding of flavors is wonderful! And the amount of spicy heat is just right. I'd love to have the recipe before I leave tonight—if you're willing to share it."

"Sure thing," Derek said. "And it's low-fat, so you don't need to worry about walking off extra calories tomorrow morning." He took another bite of the shrimp. After a minute, he put down his fork and said, "Dove, speaking of your walk, I'm worried about your safety. You've cut yourself off from all communication with the outside world, but that isn't always the wisest thing to do, especially in desolate terrain."

"Don't worry," Sheila assured him. "I carry a cell phone with me."

"But you told me you didn't want any outside distractions."

"I don't. Nobody has the number. I mainly use the phone's voice-recorder feature on my walks to capture ideas about my novel that come to me. But I also carry it so I can call 9-1-1 in case of an emergency."

Derek shook his head. "Dove, Dove. This rural area doesn't have any professional emergency responders. They're just community volunteers. When a call comes in, they have to leave their jobs—if they're able to. Out on the highway, response times are a little better now than they used to be, but if you got bitten by a snake or attacked by a cougar on the trail, you'd probably be dead before anyone showed up."

Sheila blinked. "So, what am I supposed to do? Hide in the cabin all day?"

"No, of course not," Derek said, his voice softer now. "I'm just... well, concerned, and I have been for some time. Do you have the motel's phone number saved in your contacts?"

"No."

"Then I'll give you my business card before you leave so you can program it in. And why don't you give me your number, too?"

"Why? So you can call me in an emergency, and I can come rescue you?" A smile teased the corners of her mouth.

Derek ignored her second question. "I'd feel better having your number in case you ever failed to return from a walk, that's all."

"Okay. But I don't have it memorized. I'll have to look it up and bring it when I come by for coffee in the morning. Good enough?"

Derek nodded. "Good enough."

After a dessert of glazed Bundt cake, Sheila stayed to wash the dishes, while Derek dried them and put them away. Then he brewed a fresh pot of coffee. "Now, don't tell me how you like yours," he said, grinning. "I remember. Cream *and* sugar."

Thanking him, Sheila accepted her cup, sat on the couch, and sipped the warm, creamy brew. Then she set the cup on the coffee table and picked up a large textbook. "What's this?"

"That's the same psychology text I was reading the night you first arrived."

"And it's still holding your interest? What do you find so fascinating in here?"

"Almost everything," he said. "It sheds light on the essence of humanness...the frailties, the quirks, the fears, all the things that result from heredity and life experiences that shape our personalities and form the roots of our problems."

"*Our* personalities? Are you trying to say that *we* have psychological problems?"

Derek laughed. "You make it sound like there's some distinct group of people out there fitting that description. It's not like that. There's often only a very fine line between 'normal' and 'abnormal' behavior. Sometimes, it's just a question of degree. Lots of people I know fit the criteria for a specific personality disorder, but they lead full and productive lives. They wouldn't be easily identified as having psychological problems, but their distinctive traits are described in this book."

Sheila looked at him quizzically. "Could you give me an example?"

"I've got the perfect one. In fact, I bookmarked the page so I could tell you about it. I'll read a list of criteria, and you tell me who it reminds you of, okay?"

Sheila handed him the book. "Go ahead."

"All right." He flipped to a section. "First, I'll read the general description, followed by some of the individual criteria. 'A pervasive pattern of grandiosity in fantasy or behavior, a strong need for admiration, and often a lack of empathy for others. This condition begins in early adulthood and is present in a variety of contexts.'"

Sheila pursed one side of her mouth, then said, "I think I already know who it is, but keep going."

"Don't get ahead of me, now," Derek cautioned her. "Okay, here are some of the corresponding characteristics. 'The individual has a grandiose sense of self-importance and exaggerates personal achievements and talents, expecting to be recognized as being superior. Such a person is preoccupied with fantasies of unlimited success, power, and brilliance and believes he or she is special and should associate only with other special or high-status people. Said individual requires excessive admiration and has a sense of entitlement. This person will take advantage of others to achieve his or her own ends. He or she is often envious of others or believes others are envious of him or her.'" Derek looked up. "Well? Remind you of anyone?"

"Yes. It's Dan, to a tee."

"That's exactly what I thought. Even though I've never met the guy, I recognized his symptoms just from hearing you talk about him."

Sheila shrugged. "So, what's all that mean? Are you saying he's psychotic or something?"

"Whoa!" Derek put up his hand. "That's not what I'm saying at all. I'm simply suggesting that it sounds like Dan has what this textbook calls 'narcissistic personality disorder.' It's not all that uncommon. In fact, lots of folks exhibit one or two of those behaviors. But, when someone exhibits several of them, it often indicates a personality disorder."

"Okay," said Sheila. "But what causes a personality disorder?"

"In Dan's case? I wouldn't know. It could be anything. Figuring out the *why* is what makes the study of psychology so interesting to me. We all could benefit from a better understanding of why we think and feel the way we do. In fact, that's how I became interested in the field of psychology."

"Really? And how did that happen?" Sheila sipped her coffee.

"After my service in Afghanistan, I went into a depression. It was a long time before I realized I was suffering from post-traumatic stress disorder."

Sheila frowned. "PTSD?"

"Yeah. Like I told you, when I came home in one piece without my two closest buddies, I started having all kinds of problems. My body was whole, but my mind was fractured with flashbacks, nightmares, wrestling matches with guilt. I couldn't sleep, couldn't concentrate on anything, and I started isolating myself more and more. Finally, I came out here to try to find the perfect escape. I thought I was nuts. I just wanted to bury my head in the sand."

"Obviously, you didn't."

"No, not literally. I bought this place for a song. While cleaning up one of the cabins, I found some discarded college textbooks. Studying a couple of the psychology volumes helped me understand why I felt the way I did. At last, I could give a name to my problem, and I knew that other people had suffered from it, too. That's when I started to get a new perspective on things."

Sheila leaned back against the armrest of the couch. "So, you're over it now?"

"Not fully. Maybe I never will be completely healed from it. But I'm in the process. And, more important, what I've learned about psychology has helped me be a support to other people who are hurting."

Sheila smiled at Derek. "You've sure been a tremendous support to me. Being able to stay here, becoming friends with you and Gracie, having a chance to work through many of my own issues...I can't begin to tell you how much that all means to me. I've become a different person. I feel stronger every day. You and Gracie have listened to me and talked to me in ways no one ever had, except for Laureen Parks."

Derek grinned back. "I'm glad. You may not realize it, but you've helped me a lot, too. For a long time, I've needed someone to talk to."

"You've been lonely out here, haven't you?"

"Yeah, in a way. But most of it was self-induced. I can see now it was a mistake. I need to be around other people. Through the years, I've helped a few others—some other vets and even a couple of shady characters who were friends of Gracie's. They got into some legal trouble and came to my motel to hide out. The thing is, I think I could do a lot more if I got a degree. My dream is to set up some kind of clinic out here to help vets who have PTSD. This is the perfect place to guide someone through the process of intense introspection."

Sheila sat up straight and clapped her hands. "Yes! Do it!"

Derek laughed out loud. "It's not quite that simple, Dove. Even before investing in a clinic, I'd need to earn a bachelor's degree, then a master's, complete three thousand hours of supervised experience, and pass a certification exam."

"Well, then," said Sheila, "you'd better sign up right away for an online degree program."

Derek chuckled again. "You make it sound so simple. Do you really think I could do it?"

"Absolutely. There's no doubt in my mind. I believe it's your destiny." She stopped for a moment, frowning in thought, before she grinned with excitement. "You're eligible for the GI Bill, aren't you?"

"Yes."

"Then that settles it. Please pull your head and heart out of the sand and dust them off."

"But think about how long it would take. Do you know how old I'd be before I got my degree?"

She nodded. "Just as old as you'll be if you don't pursue your dream."

"But I don't have any idea where to start. I mean, what schools offer degrees online?"

"Just do an Internet search."

Derek looked down at his coffee mug. "Actually, I'm not really good at online stuff. I mean, we haven't had Internet access out here that long, and I just never needed to figure it out before." He glanced up at Sheila again. "I don't suppose you could show me."

Sheila thought a minute. She'd been determined to stay isolated from the outside world so she wouldn't be tempted to lose her concentration on writing the novel. But helping Derek find the right online program wouldn't distract her from her goal. It was the right thing to do. She stood. "Sure, I could. Let's get started."

Derek stared at her for a second, then said, "I guess you're serious. Well, fine. Let's see what you can find out."

Sheila first checked out the Web site for the Department of Veterans Affairs to learn how Derek could sign up for the GI Bill. Then she helped him narrow his choices of online universities and look at each institution's course offerings.

Finally, Sheila turned to him. "Are you ready to sign up?"

"Now?" asked Derek. "Before I get really serious, I'll need a laptop. As you can tell, this computer is ancient. It's been okay for bookkeeping and motel correspondence. I hadn't seen the need before to invest in an upgrade."

"Why don't you drive into Vegas tomorrow and get that laptop? I can watch over the registration desk so you won't have to pay anyone to cover for you. Please, no arguments. I'll be here by eight forty-five so you can leave by nine. Okay?"

One Friday afternoon, the phone in Dan's apartment rang. He picked it up.

"Hello, hubby," said Imogene. "Do we have any plans for the weekend?"

"Not that I know of," Dan replied. "Why?"

"My professor friend Dr. Foxworth has invited us to a little dinner party she's having on Saturday evening, and I think we ought to go. Would you enjoy that, dear?"

"You're friends with the elusive Morgan Foxworth?" Dan asked, hating that his voice ended almost in a squeak. "I didn't know that."

Imogene seemed to hesitate slightly. "Well…yes, although she didn't give us much advance notice of the event. I didn't want her to think I was too eager to accept, so I said something to the effect that you and I might be flying to Chicago for dinner and a musical this weekend. I said I'd check to see if you'd made any definite plans yet. I figured it wouldn't hurt to make her squirm a little."

Dan laughed. "Good thinking. How did she react?"

"She got red in the face and apologized for the last-minute invitation. She said it was a complete oversight on her part, and that she'd love to have us and hoped we could make it."

By now, Dan was practically salivating at the opportunity to rub elbows with Morgan Foxworth and her hip crowd. "Of course, I'd love to go. Morgan's close to the dean and some of the most influential people on the Bloomington campus. Do you think any of them will be there?"

"Perhaps." Imogene's tone was as smooth as silk. "It's hard to say. But if you'd like to go, then I'll accept."

"Oh, yes, do. I need—I mean, it might help both our careers."

"All right. I'll let Morgan know. But don't worry about exposure, darling. Didn't I get your name published first on our article?"

"Yes, you did."

"Just remember," she purred, "as long as you stick with me, I'll make sure you get all the publishing credits you need. We make a great partnership, don't we?"

"That we do, dear wife. That we do."

True to her word, Sheila showed up at the motel office at 8:45 the next morning. The housekeeper, Carmen, getting ready to head for the cabins with her cart, laughed when Sheila booted Derek onto the road. Sheila spent the rest of the day at the front desk with her laptop, working steadily on her novel and fielding occasional phone calls.

When Derek's dusty pickup finally pulled into the motel parking area, the sun was low on the horizon. Sheila left the office to welcome him.

"Help me with some of the smaller boxes, if you could," he said as he got out of the truck.

"What'd you do, buy out some store?" Sheila teased.

"Hey, going to Vegas to upgrade my computer was your idea," he said. "I figured while I was in town, I should combine the trip with a supply run. But my first stop was a public library so I could research the best kind of laptop for my needs. A librarian helped me look up the latest recommendations from online computer magazines and the *Consumer Reports* Web site. When I got to the warehouse club, I found a great deal on one of the recommended laptops and picked up an extra software package. The saleswoman strongly recommended that I get a couple of flash drives, too, for transferring files at the library or whatever. After that, I got the rest of my supplies. Then I needed a bite to eat and had another couple of stops to make." He grinned. "You know how it goes."

Sheila nodded. "Okay, here's the last of your purchases. Looks like a five-year supply of coffee filters. I'm going back to the cabin now for a snack and to finish up the scene I was in the middle of when you pulled in. See if you can go online tonight and sign up for a degree program. I'll check back later." She closed her laptop and left.

Around eight o'clock, she returned to the office. Derek was standing at the registration desk, scowling at the screen of his new laptop.

"Uh-oh," Sheila said. "Trouble?"

Derek looked up at her with bleary eyes. "I just spent an hour trying to figure out how to start loading the new software the saleswoman talked me into buying. I don't think I have enough energy left to finish that tonight, let alone register for college." He gave her a pleading look. "Is there any way you could help me out?"

"No problem," Sheila assured him. "I was the computer expert at Reynolds Heating and Air-Conditioning. We'll get this software in place and then tackle the college-registration process."

Within half an hour, Derek's laptop was fully functioning, and before another hour had elapsed, he was a full-fledged first-year college student.

Sheila walked around the end of the registration counter and picked up her jacket. "Congratulations! Now nothing can stop you from accomplishing your dream."

"I hope not," Derek replied in a worried tone.

"What's the matter now?"

"I'm not so concerned about the general psychology class, but English composition one-oh-one scares the daylights out of me." He made a face that morphed into a grin as he looked at Sheila. "Hey! How about a trade? I'll proofread your novel, and you can look over my English comp homework."

Instead of smiling back, Sheila bit her lip.

"Did I say something wrong?" asked Derek.

"I don't know how I'd feel about having someone read my story."

He looked surprised. "Hey, sorry. It was just something I said off the top of my head. I didn't mean to put my nose in where it doesn't—"

"No, please," she interjected quickly. "It's not that. I'm...well, just nervous about what people—anyone—will have to say about what I wrote. I mean, I know I'll have to show it to someone, sometime, but having you ask just now to see it made me suddenly realize that 'judgment day' is coming. Wow. That's actually kind of scary."

"I've got an idea," Derek said. "Why don't you just talk to me a little bit about your story? Then, if you feel comfortable enough, someday soon, you can share some of the chapters with me."

"Well, it's kind of three stories crisscrossing together," she began slowly. "I've titled the book *Hearts of Bronze*. The three couples in it are not golden-hearted angels, or even silver-hearted heroes. But they aren't flint-hearted people, either. They're kind of in the middle, the way bronze is a useful but not precious metal. These people are trying to make their way in this world, but they have their share of disappointments, lost dreams, setbacks. The book is about how they just keep pushing ahead as best they can."

"Is it a romance?" Derek asked as he started to power down his laptop.

Sheila considered that a moment. "There's romance in it. But it's more about relationships, learning to trust people, learning to grow emotionally, even spiritually. One of the couples is a pair of newlyweds in their early twenties. Another couple has recently divorced, and both are discovering it was the stupidest mistake they ever made. The last couple is two people who knew each other in high school, got married to other people, and were successful in their own ways but now find themselves single again after the deaths of their mates. They've met again after thirty-three years apart, but they don't know if they're still the same people they were when they last saw each other."

Derek closed the laptop and slid it under the counter. "Man, are you sure you don't need that book to be proofread by a psychology student?"

Sheila laughed along with him. "On second thought, you might be right," she said. "Besides, I've already told you so much about my life, letting you read the novel shouldn't be a big deal to me." She grabbed one of the new flash drives still lying on the counter. "Okay. When I get back to the cabin, I'll put the first five chapters on this and bring it right back. I'm still working out a tricky scene in chapter 6, so I'll give you more chapters later. Anyway, if you find time this week or next week to read them, let me know what you think."

At one o'clock in the morning, Sheila was jolted awake by her cell phone. At first, she thought she'd set the alarm incorrectly, but when she tried to hit snooze, she realized someone was actually calling her. She panicked momentarily. Had Dan somehow found out her number? But then her eyes focused on the screen, and she realized the caller's area code wasn't from Indiana. She pressed the button to answer. "H-hello?"

"More!" Derek said.

"Wha—? What are you—"

"Lend me your laptop or transfer more pages to my flash drive. I can be over in a minute. Please! I can't stop reading this story of yours."

Sheila moaned. "You've got to be kidding. It's the middle of the night, Derek. Go to bed."

"Not until I find out what Aimee decides to do about Gil's proposal and what Jedidiah is going to do about that business merger."

"You've actually started reading the book?"

"Started and finished what you gave me," he affirmed. "I need more pages. Now!"

She groaned again. "Oh, all right. You can borrow my laptop tonight. I'll put the rest of my chapter drafts in a special folder on the desktop called, um, 'Chapters for Derek,' and while you're reading, you can even comment directly and save the changes. My originals won't be affected. Give me five minutes to do that now, and then you can come get the laptop. After that, I'm going back to bed!"

With Derek reading parts of her novel and then commenting on the characters and the overall plot development, Sheila found extra motivation to keep churning out both new and revised pages. It made the following days and weeks fly by with amazing speed.

Finally, Sheila completed her novel. That same week, Derek finished his first online college class and earned three credits toward a bachelor's degree. The celebration dinner they shared with Gracie that night at the café in back of the store may have been nothing fancier than pork picadillo served with Mexican red rice, pinto beans, coleslaw, and tortillas, but it might as well have been a royal banquet.

For Sheila and Derek, it was graduation day—a stepping off into a new and promising direction for each of them. New Promise, Nevada, had finally lived up to its name.

For Gracie, it was an opportunity to celebrate two people she had grown to care about deeply. She raised her lemonade glass in a toast: "To the three of us—insufferable friends to the end!"

CHAPTER 21

Dan Gray was in the middle of the ten-song medley he'd been perpetually humming for weeks. It began with "I'm Sitting on Top of the World," segued into "What a Day for a Daydream," and next moved seamlessly into "Pennies from Heaven."

He surveyed his university office and smiled broadly. He now had a black leather office chair, a burnished-wood desk with a new laptop computer at dead center, a Persian rug, original artwork on the walls, a flat-screen television, and a credenza with a coffeemaker, bookcase, and array of wireless computer accessories.

Imogene had succeeded in using her influence to wrangle the private office, and she had been the one to furnish and decorate it—with Dan's money, of course. Students coming for appointments were impressed, and Dan enjoyed the increased amount of respect it earned him. Yes, image was everything, and he now had the look, the package, and the prestige he had craved all his life.

Dan eased into his chair, shot the cuffs of his professionally pressed Oxford shirt beneath his Armani suit jacket, lifted his gold Cross pen, and posed for the mirror across the room. He grinned and started humming the next song in his medley, "Everything's Coming Up Roses."

And that's when his office phone rang.

He let it ring three times. No busy man ever picked up right away.

"Good afternoon," he answered. "Professor Gray speaking. How may I help you?"

"Dan? What gives? I called our home phone, and a recording said it was disconnected. Didn't you save back some of that money I gave you to pay the bill?"

Dan blinked. "I think you have the wrong number. Who were you trying to reach?"

"I was trying to reach *you*. I'm getting ready to come home. Can you meet me at the Indy airport on Tuesday?"

Dan pulled the phone away from his head and rapped it twice against his palm. Surely, static on the line was making him hear strange things. He lifted the phone to his ear again and said, "Who is this? What is this about?"

"Are you serious? It's me, Sheila. I've finished my book, and I'm getting ready to come home. I need you to pick me up at the airport on Tuesday."

Dan's stomach recoiled as if it had just been punched. His eyes opened wide in shock. Was this a sick joke? A ruse by a student? Or could it be...? "You...you're dead."

The woman chuckled. "Hardly that, Dan. Just on furlough for five months. And it was super. I made some new friends, got a great tan, walked off a few pounds, and, best of all, finished my novel. I'll fill you in when I see you. So, Tuesday, right? I'll book the flight and e-mail you the details of my flight number and scheduled arrival time."

Beads of sweat formed on Dan's forehead. Feeling dizzy and lightheaded, he tightened his grip on the phone, leaned forward on his elbows, and cradled his forehead in his free hand. "Sheila is dead. Sheila is dead."

After a moment of silence, she asked, "Have you been drinking, Dan? Why are you talking like this? I expected you to be happy about my return, if for no other reason than to have someone do the housework for you again. What's wrong with you?"

Dan took three deep breaths in an attempt to steady his nerves. He flexed the fingers of his free hand several times, trying to restore the blood circulation. "My wife is dead. *Dead*. She died in a plane crash. I don't know who you are or what this is about, but my wife is dead."

"That's crazy," the woman said in an angry tone. "What have you done? You didn't lose our house, did you?"

"I didn't lose it, I sold it," Dan replied, then shook his head. Why had he said that? Who was he even talking to?

"Sold it! That's a joke, right? I mean, you're kidding. Tell me you're kidding, Dan. I've been gone only a few months. How could you have sold our home? What kind of trouble have you gotten us into? Talk to me!"

Dan felt completely disoriented. Was he having a nightmare? Was he being secretly recorded for one of those reality TV shows? What was going on?

Finally, he managed to say, "You…you sound so much like Sheila. How are you able—"

"Daniel Gray, stop clowning around. I want some answers. How did you lose our home? What did you do with the money I left with you? What's happened in the time I've been gone? Give me answers!"

"You can't be Sheila. You can't be. She died in a plane crash. Sheila is dead."

There was an exasperated sigh. "That's the second time you've mentioned a plane crash. No, I did not die from a plane crash or anything else. I am alive and well, here in Nevada. In fact, I'm probably in better health now than I've been in for years. Start from the beginning and tell me what happened to our house."

"You're a fake," said Dan, slowly regaining his composure. "Sheila's dead, and I have proof. I have all the proof."

"Proof? Look, Dan. I don't know what your game is here, but I'm your wife, and I sure as shooting am not dead. You have a mole on your left buttock. When we were dating, you took me up to your crummy apartment, got me out of my clothes, and then messed up your 'spontaneous' seduction by pulling out a condom. Would anyone else know these things?"

Dan swallowed hard. He couldn't speak.

The woman raged on. "You bought my wedding ring out of a catalog a couple of years after we got married, remember? We once argued over the symbolic meaning of the short story 'The Yellow Wallpaper.' Does that ring any bells? And you threatened to sell my collection of first-edition autographed books—the ones I inherited from Laureen Parks—on eBay." She paused, as if to allow time for everything she'd said to register with him. "Shall I continue, or are you getting it through that thick skull of yours that it's me, the real Sheila?"

Dan could deny it no longer. "Oh, dear God! It really is you, Sheila. But…but how? Your boarding pass was scanned. They found your necklace in the wreckage."

"Boarding pass? Necklace? What are you talking…?" Then, as if memories were rushing back and she finally grasped what might have happened, she said in slow, clear tones, "At the last minute, I swapped boarding passes with someone else and took a later flight. Are you saying that the plane I supposedly left on crashed? Is that what you're saying?"

"It was all over the Internet and on TV. How could you not know? A midair collision…ground impact with an oil refinery…no survivors. You…you died in that. Uh, you…." He recognized that he was babbling, but he couldn't help himself. It was like being in an episode of *The Twilight Zone*. How could any of this be true?

"Seriously? Wow. Won't JD be surprised when I show up on his doorstep next week?"

"No!" Dan almost screamed. "You can't do that!" Suddenly, he was hyperventilating.

"Can't visit my own brother? Don't be ridiculous. He'll be relieved… excited."

"We—he spent the money," Dan said, thinking quickly.

After a moment, she said, "What money? What are you talking about?"

"Your life-insurance policy," said Dan, trying to think logically and speak deliberately. "At your job. You named him beneficiary, not me. He got the money. He and I spent some of it on a grave marker in your memory, and then he used the rest of it to pay down some of his loans."

"Wait a second, here," she said. "Insurance money? Oh, my goodness! I bought flight insurance with the twenty-five bucks you gave me, and you got a huge payoff. This is all starting to make sense. You're worried about having to return all that money when I show up in the flesh in a few days."

"You can't do that," Dan said, not bothering to veil his desperation. "I…I'm not able to return the money."

"Why not?"

"I've been spending."

"Okay. That I can believe. What kind of money are we talking about?"

"A lot."

"Be more specific. And keep in mind I have ways of accessing your IRS records, Dan. For one thing, I know our accountant."

Dan licked his lips. Haltingly, he said, "More than half a million dollars."

"That's way more than I was estimating," she said, sounding impressed but also caught off guard. "When you sold the house, that couldn't have cleared you more than fifteen thousand."

"Thirteen and change," Dan said.

"All right. That's on top of the policy I bought at the airport. But, even added together, that's only about half of the amount you mentioned. Where are the other funds coming from?"

"You bought your ticket with a credit card," said Dan. "That added an extra two hundred fifty thousand dollars of life insurance."

She gave a low whistle. "We're rich."

The sound of "we're" made Dan's heart go cold. It also emboldened him. Dead or alive, little Sheila was not going to start dictating how he would spend *his* money.

"Hold on a minute," he interjected. "The money is mine, Sheila. I'm the beneficiary. It's changed my life. I've got a new car, a high-rise apartment, new clothes. And I...well, actually...I've remarried."

He heard a gasp and a thump, as if she had fallen against something or had sat hard on something.

After a moment, she said in a raspy whisper, "You remarried?" Then her voice became distorted with tears. "Remarried? You didn't even grieve over me, Dan? Fifteen years together, and you didn't even grieve over losing me? Did...did I mean so little to you?"

"Sheila, Sheila, Sheila," Dan chanted, falling comfortably into the patronizing tone he typically used with her. "You need to understand—"

"I understand all I need to understand, you weasel," she snapped, her voice stronger than he'd ever heard it. "And that is, you never loved me. You never supported me. You never worried about my needs, my goals, my passions. It's always been about you. You drained me dry—which is a terrific bit of irony, Mr. Literary Expert, because, after spending nearly half a year in the middle of a desert, I've never felt more refreshed."

"Now, Sheila—"

"I'm not finished! I'm in shock, but I'm also seeing things more clearly than ever. Your selfish actions have released me, Dan. I'm now morally free. I kept my vows, but—what? You're now in bed with another woman?" Her voice thundered over the phone like a locomotive gathering steam. "It's probably that Imogene Cunningham, isn't it? And you know what? I'll bet you were sleeping with her even before you thought I was dead. Our marriage is certainly over. But you're the one who severed it, not me."

"But, Sheila, you know that I've—"

"I want my half," she broke in defiantly.

Dan restrained himself. He didn't want to misspeak. To give himself time, he decided to pretend he hadn't heard her correctly. "I'm sorry?"

"No," she said. "No, you're not. Unless you're sorry that I'm not really dead." She waited a beat, then said, "I won't ask for my half of the house sale, but if you expect me to stay 'dead,' it's going to cost you two hundred seventy-five thousand dollars."

The air went out of Dan's lungs. "You…you can't really—"

"Do whatever you have to, Dan, but pull together two hundred seventy-five grand for me, in cash, and have it ready in three days."

"But, Sheila, the money's invested in—"

"Three days, Dan. Three days, or I'll prove to the insurance companies I'm alive and well, and then you'll have to give back *all* the money."

The line went dead.

Sheila dropped her cell phone and collapsed next to it on the bed. Her plunge from the euphoria at having completed her novel to the shock of learning she was now husbandless, homeless, and "lifeless" had taken less than five minutes.

How had this nightmare started? Her mind replayed the scene at the airport in Oklahoma City again and again, like an endless video loop. Spying Karen Watson, the weeping military wife. Swapping boarding passes with her. Giving Karen the necklace with the charms. Catching a later flight. Fighting her way through the crowds and the confusion at the Las Vegas airport.

How could her act of generosity have gone so terribly, terribly wrong? She had planned for her second phone call to be to Mr. Pembroke to inform him she was now eligible to receive the remaining $25,000 of Mrs. Parks's bequest. But now she wasn't sure what to do. She needed to talk to Derek right away.

It was still early afternoon in Nevada. She stood and glanced out the cabin window at the searing July day. A caravan of SUVs had just pulled in, and hikers in khaki shorts were heading toward the motel office to register.

Sheila flopped onto the bed again, fighting with her emotions, willing herself to wait until after the busy dinner hour before bothering Derek. Eventually, lulled by the hum of the air conditioner, she drifted into a troubled slumber.

From seven until eight o'clock that warm evening, under the lone shade tree outside the motel, Sheila did all the talking. Derek sat at the weathered picnic table, looking as if he didn't dare to interrupt, as Sheila paced, waved her hands, gestured with her cell phone, ran her fingers through her hair, and occasionally even stomped her foot on the ground in frustration.

"And that's how it happened," she finally summarized, dropping in exhaustion onto the bench beside Derek. "I phone my husband to share the news that I'm ready to come home, and he tells me I have no husband, no house, no life!"

"I remember hearing about that plane crash," Derek said. "Of course, I had no idea you were supposed to be on that flight."

"Yeah. If it hadn't been for some wild twist of fate...." Sheila slumped forward, moaning, her head almost to her knees. "It's all so unbelievable!" she said. "I've been erased, and Dan's sitting back in Indy, playing the life of the fat cat."

Derek blinked, as if wondering whether he should stay quiet or try to offer some kind of consoling words.

Then Sheila sat erect, sighed, and added, "I guess my outrage at being victimized for fifteen years took over."

"What do you mean?"

"I told him I wanted half the insurance money—two hundred seventy-five thousand dollars. In cash. I told him I wanted it in three days, or else I'd come back to life and force him to return it all to the insurance companies."

First, Derek grinned. Then he started chuckling. And then he began to guffaw, nearly falling off the picnic bench.

"What?" Sheila demanded. "What's so funny?"

"It's marvelous!" said Derek, trying to catch his breath. "I'd have given anything to see that guy's face. You hit him where it hurts—right in the wallet. How were you able to think on your feet so fast?"

"I wasn't trying to be clever," Sheila said, perplexed. "I was just angry that Dan was benefitting from my loss. Life insurance is intended to help with expenses after a person's death, right? Well, this time, it's the 'dead' person who needs financial assistance, since I've lost my home and can't return to my job." Then she smiled wryly. "I guess my reaction must have shocked Dan. I've never talked to him like that before."

"Well, your response was perfect," said Derek, wiping his eyes. "If, as he seemed to indicate, he really has spent a ton of that money on a car and an apartment and clothes and other stuff, you've just cut him off at the knees, lady. He's already spent half, and now you're taking the other half. Oh, geez, I'm still cracking up over this. Wait till he tells Billie Jean the news!"

"Imogene," Sheila corrected him. And then, suddenly comprehending the humor of the scenario she had concocted, impromptu, for Dan Gray, she, too, began to giggle, then chuckle, and then howl with laughter, which only set Derek off again. It was a full five minutes before the two came up for air.

But Derek's smile gradually faded into a worried expression. "I'm glad we can see the funny side to this," he said, "because if you have to play dead for the rest of your life, you'll have some serious strategizing to do."

At that moment, they noticed Gracie crossing the road. "No wonder I got yer recorded voice instead of yer real one," she hollered to Derek. "Out here to enjoy the sunset?"

"Actually, Dove's just gotten the shock of her life—or of her death, I guess I should say."

"Huh?"

Having vented to Derek for most of an hour, Sheila was able to give a succinct version to Gracie, although, for some reason, she left out the part about demanding half of Dan's insurance windfall. Instead, she emphasized how relieved she was that she would never again be subjected to his abuse.

Derek added, "I was just telling her she needs to strategize about how to live the rest of her life as a 'dead' person."

"Tell ya what," said Gracie. "I can hear a lot just by listenin'. Sun's going down, and the café's closed, but come on over, and I'll serve us up some iced tea so we can help ya figure out what to do next. Don't want no monkey gettin' throwed into the works."

When the three were seated, Derek took a sip of his tea, then set the tall glass aside and said, "Okay, I hate to start with a checklist, but I think we need to assess where things are now."

The two women nodded their agreement.

"First, the good news," he continued, addressing Sheila. "You've got your novel done, and, in my opinion, it's a winner. You're also set to rake in—"

Sheila silenced him with a kick under the table, then looked at Gracie. "I...I've just come into quite a bit of money," she explained, not quite meeting Gracie's gaze.

"Yeah," Derek picked up. "And you're out of an awful marriage, through no fault of your own. That means you don't have to go back to Indiana if you don't want to."

"So," said Gracie, her eyes narrowed in thought, "Dan's hopin' you'll just bury the hammer and shut up 'bout him bein' a bag o' mist?"

"Y-yes," Sheila said in a low voice.

"Second, the bad news," Derek went on. "If you stay dead, you'll have to sever all ties with most of the people you care about. You won't be able to see your brother again, or your coworkers, or, sure as heck, Mr. Pembroke, which will also mean forfeiting the rest of Mrs. Parks's bequest. With Pembroke being a member of the court system, he'd have to report you if he ever found out you were still alive."

"But," said Gracie, raising a hand to interrupt, "there's no reason to call him, anyhow. If, for all this time, he thought she was dead, he's done given away the rest of that money to the charity that Miz Parks's last will and estimate said it was supposed to go to if Dove didn't finish her book. Right?"

Derek smiled. "Good thinking, Gracie. Point taken."

"Uh, not to wake you from your dream," said Sheila, "but, well, I'm not actually dead."

"Oh, shoot, girl," said Gracie matter-of-factly. "I got friends who can fix that for ya."

Sheila flinched.

"Gracie didn't mean 'shoot' in a literal sense," Derek hastily explained. "She meant she still has some 'acquaintances' in Vegas who could provide you with documents: a new driver's license, birth certificate, Social-Security number, perhaps even a passport."

"More 'n that," Gracie insisted. "If ya want to make sure Dan never finds ya, there's some sawbones down in Vegas who does cuttin' on showbiz folks to keep 'em lookin' young. Hippie laws keep their mouths shut, and if you got enough green to slip 'em, they don't even need a reason for givin' ya a whole new puss. Even yer own kin wouldn't recognize ya. It's expensive, but sounds like that ain't an issue with ya no more."

"Plastic surgery?" said Sheila. "A new birth certificate? And what are 'hippie' laws?"

"Them laws that keeps your medical stuff private."

"Oh. You mean HIPAA? Okay, that makes sense. But...who would I be?"

"Who you are already," said Derek. "Dove Alexander, short-story writer and novelist. Make a few facial changes, get some hair dye and a different wardrobe, and throw in a western accent or a southern drawl, and *voilà*!"

"Become Dove for real?" said Sheila. Shivers ran down her spine. "You mean, like they do with people in a witness protection program? A total identity makeover? Could I really pull that off?"

"Remember, we've never known you as Sheila Gray," said Derek. "You've already been living your new identity here for five months. Of course, you can pull it off."

"Yeah, but there's a couple of flies in the joint," cautioned Gracie. "Ya know how Dove said she asked that Pembroke feller to manage her bank account? Well, I'm bettin' when he thought Dove kicked the bucket, he probably called that editor woman in New York and told her Dove was dead and not to send any more checks. So, what'll happen if Dove picks up the phone and says, 'Howdy, Lady Editor, I ain't really dead'?"

"Here's an idea," Derek put in. "I'll call Judith Hardy, swear her to secrecy, and then explain that Sheila Gray isn't really dead, and that, in fact, Sheila herself will call her half an hour after I hang up. Now, if I know anything about how people climb ladders—and, having been in the military, I know all about ascending ranks—this woman is going to be only too happy to have her star short-story writer return to life. Dove's stories sell magazines, remember. And when magazines sell, editors have job security. My guess is, she'll be eager to join in our little conspiracy."

Sheila nodded. "I like that idea, but for a different reason. "Not only is Judith Hardy my friend as well as my editor, but she's also well connected to publishing circles in New York. Maybe she can get a literary agent to represent me. You know, handle the sale of my novel...if it's marketable."

"*If* it's marketable?" Derek said, shaking his head.

"Yeah," Gracie added. "From what Derek, here, tells me after readin' yer novel, bein' a good writer ain't just a fig leaf o' yer imagination."

Sheila reached both arms across the table and placed one hand on Derek's hand and the other on Gracie's. "You realize, don't you, that you're more than just my friends now? You're also my family. I have no one else." Then she stood, teetered slightly, and had to steady herself against the table's edge. "My brain is swirling. I'm going to head back to my cabin to do some praying. This has been a day of shocks and surprises for me, but at least I haven't had to face it alone. I'm truly glad you're both in my life. Thanks for standing by me. Oh—and I'm going to go online and read all about the airplane crash I supposedly died in. Then I'm going to think through everything we've talked about so I can come up with a plan."

Gracie smiled affectionately. "Just don't think so hard ya end up with a conclusion of the noggin," she cautioned her.

That night, long after her talk with Derek and Gracie, Sheila sat at her laptop and read about a newly licensed pilot who had misjudged his small plane's instrument readings at the airport in Oklahoma City. The tail of his aircraft had sliced through the right wing and horizontal stabilizer of the Vegas-bound passenger jet Sheila was scheduled to be on. The badly crippled liner spiraled into a petroleum refinery below, and the resulting explosion burned for days. It was assumed that the bodies of four passengers never found had simply vaporized in the intense heat.

Sheila blew her nose for the umpteenth time. If only there was a way to assuage some of the guilt she felt for having sent Karen Watson to her fiery death, however inadvertently. When she'd done an online search for Karen's name, she'd found an interview with Karen's mother. Since Sheila had used Karen's boarding pass on the later flight to Las Vegas, and Karen's boarding pass to San Diego was never used, everyone assumed Karen had disappeared at the Vegas airport. Perhaps abducted. Her family was desperate for answers.

Sheila stared out the window at the rising crescent moon. In three days, she'd have plenty of money, but it felt as if her windfall had been paid for by the misfortunes of others. Yes, it was Dan's greed for the good life that was to blame for her needing to stay dead. And even if Sheila didn't take a portion of the insurance money, it wouldn't bring Karen Watson back to life. But if Sheila could think of some way to honor Karen's memory, she might feel better about the whole situation. She lifted her face to the star-sequined sky and prayed, "Dear God, show me what I should do next."

After a moment, she opened a new document on her laptop and began typing ideas. What if she could pass some of the money on to Karen's mother? And why stop there? She ached to do more for JD than she'd done already. And dear Laureen Parks. She had believed in Sheila all along. Surely, Sheila could find a way to honor her memory, too.

Stopping frequently to do Internet searches, she typed notes and ideas and various dollar amounts until the first pale rays of dawn streaked across the eastern horizon. Then she stood, went to the closet, and took down her carry-on bag from the upper shelf. After unzipping it, she felt inside an inner pocket for a business card with a key attached. At the same time, her fingers also ran across a couple of folded papers.

She pulled out all the items. The card and key would give her access to her first-edition books in storage. One of the papers turned out to be the boarding pass with Karen Watson's name, and the other was the flight itinerary that had fallen out of Karen's handbag at the airport.

As Sheila looked at the items, she frowned in thought. She would need Derek's help in executing her plan, but he wouldn't be awake for a few more hours. She placed the papers, card, and key on the desk, returned the carry-on to the closet, and got ready for bed. She'd talk to Derek when she went to the office later for coffee.

She didn't know if she'd experienced the "conclusion of the noggin" Gracie had warned about, but right now, she was too exhausted to think any longer. She climbed into bed, and without any needed lullaby, Sheila Davis Gray was out like a light.

CHAPTER 22

After Sheila ended their conversation, Dan sat rigid for a full minute, trying to comprehend what had just happened. Then, as his rage grew, his hands began to shake. How dare Sheila turn on him like this? She'd been so perfect in her role as the submissive wife. But ever since that meddling Parks woman had inserted herself back into Sheila's life, Dan had suffered for it. Now, this outrageous demand. Well, he wasn't going to stand for it. He deserved—yes, *deserved* the lucky break that Sheila's death had brought his way. He would simply take control of Sheila as he'd always done in the past. He wasn't about to permit a ghost to ruin his new life.

But when Sheila called the next day to give him detailed instructions for the money transfer, she didn't allow him a chance to get the upper hand. Speaking forcefully and rapidly, she informed him that since it was now the weekend, she would be generous and give him three *business* days to liquidate her portion of the funds. Dan was to have the cash ready, in hundred-dollar bills, by Thursday of the coming week. Sheila would send someone to Dan's office to pick up the money. To prove that she was still alive, the messenger would produce a note in Sheila's handwriting, accompanied by her wedding band and the cheap engagement ring. "I have no use for any reminders of you now," she said in a disgusted tone.

She also informed Dan that she had procured the contact information of all three life-insurance companies, plus that of Indiana's

Attorney General. Additionally, she had the Twitter handles of investigative reporters at several Indianapolis television stations. If Dan didn't follow her instructions to the letter, she wouldn't hesitate to come to Brissenden in person and prove to everyone that she was still very much alive. "You have until Thursday morning," she told him. "And the countdown begins at one minute after midnight."

He gagged and then choked out, "Now, see here, Sheila," before realizing the connection was dead.

With the wind taken out of his sails, Dan called his banker, Doug Barcalow, and told him he needed to liquidate all the mutual funds he had set up just a few months earlier. Doug expressed more than a little surprise. "Why do you need to make such a radical move?"

"Just get everything ready, in cash, by next Wednesday evening. That's all you need to know," Dan said before hanging up the phone.

So, the banker did as he was told, and Dan also did as *he* was told. He was in his office Thursday morning when a man who introduced himself as Derek Mason opened the backpack he'd been wearing and pulled out Sheila's handwritten note and wedding ring set.

Dan examined the items. He tried to hold the note steady enough to read. It was her handwriting, all right, although where the firm, self-assured manner of communicating had come from, Dan wasn't sure. Sheila certainly was no longer the demure little mouse he'd been able to control so well for so long. And what part did this cowboy Mason have to play in her life?

Although it made no logical sense, Dan felt an old jealousy stirring. "So, you're the bag man, eh?" he said with a sneer as he put the rings and the note in a side drawer of his desk.

"No," said Derek, eyes narrowed à la Clint Eastwood. "I'm the hit man. The bag man couldn't make it, so they sent me in his place. If you don't have the money, I'm supposed to kill you and then leave."

Dan assumed the man was making a cynical joke, but when Derek kept a straight face, Dan decided not to chance playing tough guy with the stranger. "It's all here," he said, lifting a briefcase and setting it on top of his desk.

Derek looked at him with emotionless eyes. "I'll be the judge of that."

"What, you're going to sit here and count it?"

"Every dollar." Derek opened the briefcase and, for the next twenty minutes, counted the stacks of bills, transferring them one by one to the backpack. The entire time seemed an age to Dan, who feared Imogene might "pop in" at any moment for a quick visit.

"Okay, it's all here," Derek finally said as he zipped the backpack closed and stood.

"Sheila told me she was still in Nevada," Dan said quickly. "I tried calling her cell phone back, but she didn't answer, and her voice mail isn't set up. If I need to get in touch with her, how can I do that?"

Derek looked him in the eye. "I can't think of a single reason you should ever get in touch with her again." Then he turned and walked out of the office.

Up until that moment, Dan had hoped desperately that it was all going to work out in his favor. But it hadn't. And he was now running on financial fumes.

During the next few days, he converted his checking account to cash, pawned his Rolex watch, and gathered all the available money he could find around the apartment. It totaled slightly more than thirty grand.

Then he told Imogene that he needed a couple of days of "research time" for his novel and would be leaving for Chicago right after teaching his class that afternoon. She begged to go along, saying they both could cancel their classes for a few days, and she could do some shopping while he was doing research. *Shopping?* Right! As though he didn't have enough money problems already.

He explained that he needed the time alone, and besides, he wanted her to cover for him by teaching his classes so that the students wouldn't fall behind. It was a smokescreen, but she accepted it, and that was all that mattered.

Dan put on his lucky shirt, the one that had seemed to bring him his best lottery wins. Then he caught I-65 North and drove as far as Lafayette. He pulled off for a bite to eat before getting back on the expressway and taking it to I-94, which led him to Michigan City and the *Golden Lighthouse,* a riverboat casino resort on the Indiana shore of Lake Michigan. It was nighttime when he arrived, but that meant nothing. People gambled round the clock.

Dan checked his money belt and found that his cash was still secure. "From a small acorn comes the mighty oak," he mused philosophically. As he crossed the parking lot, he could see myriad lights twinkling in the inky sky overhead. He felt good about that. His lucky star was up there, just now, shining down on him.

When he entered the hotel attached to the riverboat casino, he stopped at the bar and ordered a drink to fortify himself. It wouldn't be long now before he'd be sitting with a sack of cash. It was his fate, his destiny...his *right*! "Bring it on," he said under his breath.

Just inside the main casino, Dan paused at a vintage one-armed bandit and dropped in a quarter. He pulled the slot machine's handle. It came up three bells, a cherry, and a pirate flag. Ten quarters fell into the metal trough. Dan smiled and retrieved his winnings. A good omen, for sure.

He went to the cashier's window and bought $5,000 of chips of various denominations. He decided to start slowly and not take big chances or make any grand-scale wagers. He went to the roulette table. There was a simple side bet of red or black, he knew. His odds were fifty-fifty. The payoff was modest, but the risk was minimal. He put $100 on black. The croupier spun the wheel and dropped the ball...and it came up black. Dan received $100 in winnings. He decided to let it ride. The wheel moved, the ball dropped...and it came up black again. He now had $400 on the table.

Wow! In three minutes, he had won $300. Oh, and an extra $2.25 in quarters. It was happening just as he had planned. "Shine, lucky star. Just keep on shining," he whispered.

He moved his winnings to red and added enough chips to make it $1,000. He jiggled his other chips in his right hand, somewhat haughtily. He was liking this.

The wheel spun, the ball dropped...but it came up black again. The croupier raked Dan's thousand dollars in chips off the table.

Dan flinched slightly, then did some mental calculations. Well, it was really only a $700 loss, because the other $300 had been the gaming establishment's. Not so bad. And the reason he had lost was obvious: His color was black, not red. He needed to stick with his sure bets. He put $1,000 in chips down on black, smiling as he did so.

The wheel spun, the ball dropped...and it came up red. His chips were raked away from the table. Dan stood there, puzzled. He tried to use logic to understand what was going on. After a few seconds, it came to him. Yes, he had been right to assume it was time to switch to red. Only...well, he had done so one turn too soon, and now he was out of sync with the board. He would have to get back on track.

He put down $2,000 in chips, this time back on red. He was pretty sure that was due up again. The wheel spun, the ball fell...and, yes, indeed, it did come up red. The paymaster added another $2,000 to Dan's winning spot on red.

Okay, yes. Now he was rolling. Now he had the system down pat. He moved his winnings to a black square and put down the rest of the chips in his hand. *What would that be?* He tried to calculate it in his head. *About ten thousand in total cash. Or am I still down a little?*

The wheel turned, the ball bounced several times, and it finally settled...and came up red. One quick sweeping motion removed all Dan's chips from the table.

In an immediate reactionary move, he balled his fist and hit himself in the forehead. *No, no, no!* he admonished himself inwardly. *It was still on the black momentum.* He'd moved once too soon again. He needed to get this system down pat. *Think!* he told himself. *Think!*

Maybe another drink would help. He ordered a whiskey sour and started sipping it, trying to puzzle out his next move. Halfway through the drink, he quickly lifted the glass and drained it. Then he marched back to the cashier's window, pulling money from his belt as he went. "Another five grand in chips," he ordered the man behind the cage screen. "Half in five hundreds and the rest in hundreds."

The man exchanged the money for chips. Dan turned resolutely back toward the roulette table. Even a baby could win a pile of cash at fifty-fifty odds. He just needed to stay calm, think clearly, and bet wisely. Yep, that was the ticket. Just bet wisely.

Derek Mason had flown from Las Vegas to Indianapolis, but since he couldn't risk carrying a backpack filled with thousands of dollars in cash through airport security, renting a car was part of the plan he and Dove had worked out for his return. And while in the area, he would use the car to run a few special "errands" on her behalf.

After purchasing an inexpensive backpack and then getting the money from Dan, Derek drove to Brissenden. With the aid of the rental car's GPS system, along with additional directions Dove had written for him, he located the farm of JD Davis. He pulled in just after seven in the evening, went up to the front door, and knocked.

"Help you?" asked the man who opened the door. He looked as if he feared Derek might be trying to collect on an unpaid bill.

"Are you Mr. JD Davis?" Derek asked.

"Why?"

Derek smiled slightly. He'd given Dove the same response when she'd asked about his personal life the morning after she'd arrived in New Promise. He understood the man's natural tendency toward caution.

"Mr. Davis, my name is Randolph Christensen, and I'm with Allied-Jefferson Life Insurance," Derek said smoothly, following the scenario he and Dove had worked out. "Our company has now settled all the final claims for the TransUniverse air disaster five months ago. We've discovered that you are the closest surviving blood relative of one Mrs. Sheila Davis Gray. Here is the final settlement payment for you." He pulled a white envelope from his pocket.

JD scrutinized Derek's western attire. "You say you're an insurance agent? I've already received a death benefit from insurance she had where she worked."

Derek shook his head. "I don't know anything about that. This is just a cash settlement from our company to you." He extended the bulging envelope.

JD frowned as if he smelled a rat. "If you got yourself a summons to serve, just say so," he demanded. "It doesn't look like a check inside there."

Derek nodded. "You're right, it's not a check. It's ten thousand dollars in cash. All yours. I'm going to leave it out here on the porch and drive away. There's no catch. It's your money. Good day to you, sir." Derek set the envelope on a little table next to a rocking chair and then walked back to his car.

Seated behind the wheel, Derek watched as JD gingerly opened the screen door and inspected the envelope. When he saw the contents, his eyes widened, and he yelled toward the car, "Hey! Don't I have to sign a receipt or something?"

"We trust you," Derek called back. "Good-bye, Mr. Davis." He started the engine and drove off.

At two o'clock in the morning, a security guard employed by the *Golden Lighthouse* was trying to reason with Dan. "Look, mister," he said. "I'm going to help you find your car, and then you need to take the hundred bucks my boss returned to you and go find a motel someplace. You're in no condition to make a long drive anywhere tonight. Where'd you say you were from?"

Dan, bawling, refused to stand. "All of it," he wailed. "I lost every bit of it."

"Yeah, yeah, I know, pal," said the guard. "It happens that way sometimes. Just tell me what your car looks like, and I'll try to help you find it in the lot, okay?"

"I need to get back on that boat and—"

"Easy, pal. Easy does it," said the guard. "You and that boat have parted company forever."

Dan allowed the man to pull him slowly into a standing position. On his feet, Dan felt himself waver slightly. "You don't understand," he said, sniffing loudly and wiping his nose with his sleeve. "I'm an important man back in Indianapolis. I can't go back home without my money. My wife expects to go to…to go to…." In his drunken haze, he couldn't quite remember now exactly where Imogene was expecting him to take her, but he knew it was someplace overseas.

"My wife has big plans," Dan finally said.

The guard nodded, put one of Dan's arms around his shoulder, and then started walking him toward the parking lot. "She'll forgive you, partner," he said, in a tone that hinted he knew full well she wouldn't. "Now, help me find your car. Can you remember what color it is? What make or model?"

Derek checked out of his Brissenden motel early the next morning, went to a local café for breakfast, and was in the office of the Superintendent of Schools for Johnson County by nine.

"How can I help you, Mr.…?" asked Dr. Jim Holmes.

"Smith," said Derek as he sat across the desk from the superintendent. "Smith will be fine."

Dr. Holmes raised an eyebrow. "Very well, Mr. *Smith*. What can I do for you?"

"Are you familiar with the reality television program *Secret Millionaire*?" Derek asked.

Dr. Holmes nodded. "It's one of my wife's favorite shows. Millionaires assume secret identities to find people they believe deserve a cut of their fortunes. Everyone's led to believe that the TV cameras present are there merely to film documentary footage."

"That's right," said Derek. "Well, think of me as a representative of one of those benefactors."

Dr. Holmes raised both eyebrows now. "Oh, really? I'm afraid it looks like you forgot your camera crew, didn't you? Now, see here, Mr. *Smith*. I don't mean to be rude, but—"

"Do you recall a faculty member named Mrs. Laureen Parks?" Derek cut in. "She taught high-school English in this town about sixteen years ago."

"Mrs. Parks? Oh, yes, indeed," affirmed Dr. Holmes. "Wonderful woman. She died just last year and is buried in the Brissenden Cemetery."

"So I understand," Derek said. "In fact, one of her former students—someone who wishes to remain anonymous—desires to set up a memorial scholarship fund in her honor. It would seek to recognize high-school seniors who show talent as creative writers, and the money would be used toward a college summer program in writing. I have a printout of all the requirements and parameters. I also have twenty thousand dollars in cash to help establish the fund. My client wants you to handle the details. Is that something you'd be willing to do?"

The superintendent paused, clearly astonished. "This is on the level?" he finally asked.

Derek reached into his denim jacket and withdrew a brown envelope sealed with a button-and-string clasp. He tossed it on the desk in front of Dr. Holmes. "If you can have your assistant come in here and witness a receipt for this twenty thou, I can be on my way."

Dr. Holmes unwound the string, opened the sturdy envelope, and dumped the contents on the desk. He stared at the stacks of cash for a full minute before hitting the intercom button on his phone. "Darlene?"

"Yes, Dr. Holmes?"

"Come in here for a moment, please. And bring a pen."

Dan was still in a deep sleep at one o'clock on Wednesday afternoon when the telephone jolted him awake. He found himself lying on a bed in a nondescript motel room, but where it was located or how he'd gotten there, he could not recall.

He groaned and held his head as he sat up and moved his legs to the floor. The blasted phone was on the opposite side of the king bed. It would probably be easier to walk than roll across the mattress to reach it. He painfully stood and felt needles shoot through his head. By the time he got to the phone, it had stopped ringing. He swore and pressed zero.

"Front desk," said a young woman. "How may I help you?"

"This stupid phone just woke me up," Dan groused. "Where am I?"

"You're calling from room forty-three," the woman informed him. "And as a matter of fact—"

"No, no," Dan interrupted her angrily. "Where in blazes am I?"

There was a slight pause, and then the young woman answered, "You're in room forty-three of the Hug-a-Bye Motel on Highway Thirty, just outside of Plymouth. My records show that you checked in at three thirty this morning. You paid cash for one night's lodging. However, checkout time was noon. If you'd like to stay another night, please come to the front desk and make financial arrangements immediately. Otherwise, we ask that you vacate the room within twenty minutes so that our housekeeping staff can prepare it for the next guest."

Dan hung up without another word. His clothing smelled like cigarette smoke, he had a terrible taste in his mouth, and a quick rub of his hand across his face gave evidence of stubble.

Blinking his burning eyes, he looked down at his money belt under his waistband. He opened it and found a twenty and a five. *But of course,* he mused. *Of course, it would have to be that.* The exact amount he had given Sheila to gamble for him.

His clothes felt sweaty from having been slept in. He still had twenty minutes, so he undressed, then staggered into the bathroom, where he found a bar of soap and small bottles of shampoo, conditioner, and mouthwash. He gargled with the mouthwash, then stepped into the shower and turned the water on hotter than he normally liked it. He scrubbed his body, then washed and conditioned his hair before switching the water to cool. The temperature change shocked his body into a more alert state.

After he'd stepped out of the tub and toweled off, he looked in the mirror and was jolted by the image staring back at him. It wasn't so much the growth of beard he wasn't used to, but his artificial weave had gotten tangled when he'd washed his hair. Too late, he remembered he wasn't supposed to do that. He retrieved a pocket comb from his pants and worked as best he could to pull the weave from his natural hair. It left him looking old, balding, bearded, and hungover.

He went back into the small bedroom and sat naked in a chair. How, oh, how was he ever going to explain all this to Imogene? First, he had given away $275,000 to his "dead" wife, and then he had lost another $30,000 in one night of gambling.

She would kill him…if he didn't kill himself first.

He had no choice but to go home. He didn't have enough money for another night in a motel. Did he even have enough money to buy himself some lunch, or would he need it all for gasoline for the drive back to Indy? Plymouth was, what, nearly three hours north of Indianapolis?

He slowly put his clothes back on, left the key card on the dresser, and went out to his car. The fuel gauge indicated the tank was more than half full. That would help. As he left the parking lot, he saw a sign advertising fried chicken two miles up the road. "Fried chicken for lunch," he told himself, "and crow for dinner."

Derek left Brissenden by ten in the morning and covered a lot of ground in the next several hours. He paid attention to the radio sometimes, but he mostly thought about Dove. The solitude gave him time to assess their friendship. During the five months they'd known each other, their relationship had never crossed any lines of impropriety. After all, Dove had been a married woman.

Then, even when they'd both learned that when the court declared her dead, her marriage ceased to exist, they still hadn't moved toward romance. He realized that they weren't in love with each other. They were in "like." They really, really liked each other. They'd become confidants, close friends, trusted buddies. It was obvious neither of them wanted to ruin that bond by pushing it in a direction toward which they had no natural inclination. Dove was like a sister or a cousin to him. She was family, in an odd sort of adoptive way, closer than any of his blood relatives had ever been to him. He knew he could always count on her. And he would protect and help her for as long as she needed him.

As daylight faded, he decided to spend the night in St. Louis and then drive on to Oklahoma City the next morning. He had one more important "errand" to run there for Dove.

Dan stopped at a mini-mart near Anderson. He bought a disposable razor, then went into the men's room, locked the door, lathered his face with liquid soap, and gave himself a shave. He combed his hair toward his forehead in an attempt to cover some of his bald spot.

"You've still got one ace up your sleeve," he told his mirrored face. "It's where you should have concentrated your efforts all along. Finish the novel. That's the real ticket to fame and fortune. Sixteen years of sweat and toil, and now, it's payoff time. Just keep up the playacting until the novel gets sold, and then everything will be back to normal. Even better than normal, in fact."

He went outside, put ten bucks of premium gas into his Mustang, and then started the last leg of his drive back to Indianapolis.

If he could convince Imogene that their status quo still existed, he would be okay. He just needed a little more time to finish the novel, and then they'd be on Easy Street. Sure…sure, it was that simple. *Just fake it till ya make it.*

Derek arrived in Oklahoma City late Thursday afternoon. He programmed the address Sheila had given him into the GPS system and followed its directions to an established subdivision.

Along with giving him the address she'd found online, Sheila had sent with him a printout of the Internet article she'd discovered about Karen Watson's disappearance. Derek's next mission was to call Karen's mother, Irene Grzegorczyk, who was interviewed in the piece. He glanced down at the article and practiced pronouncing the surname using the phonetic key the reporter had provided in parentheses: Greg-*gor*-check. He hoped that pronouncing her unusual name correctly would prevent the woman from thinking he was a cold-calling salesman.

He drove past the home for one block before pulling to the curb. Then he picked up a manila envelope from the front seat and walked casually toward the house. If he had any doubts about its being the correct residence of Irene Grzegorczyk, he would simply return to the car and leave.

The neighborhood looked quiet, and the yards seemed empty. No barking dogs. Perfect. Derek stepped quietly onto the front porch. To his immense relief, he saw a small decorative plaque above the doorbell that read "The Grzegorczyks." He turned to the left and placed the zip-top bag at the base of a brick porch column where it wouldn't be visible from the street. Then he retreated to the car.

He picked up the news article from the front seat and called the number for Irene Grzegorczyk that Sheila had written in the margin. After four rings, it went to her voice mail.

"Hello, Mrs."—Derek glanced quickly at the pronunciation guide—"Greg-*gor*-check. I'm calling with information about your daughter, Karen Watson. Here's where you can reach me." He recited the cell phone's number. He knew he risked receiving a call back from the woman, even days later, after he'd concluded his business with her. Any mother desperate for news about her missing daughter would do the same thing. It was for just that reason he'd brought Dove's pre-paid phone with him and had left his personal cell phone back in New Promise with Dove.

Another benefit to having Dove's phone with him was that he knew, even before Dan told him, that Dan had tried to contact Sheila.

Within three minutes, the cell phone rang.

Derek answered. "Hello?"

"I just received a call from this number," a woman said. "Do you really have information about my daughter?"

"Yes, ma'am, I do."

"Who is this?"

"That isn't important for now," said Derek. "I'm just a messenger."

"Please...who is this? What do you know about Karen? Where is she? We've had prank calls in the past. Please, don't do anything cruel."

"Ma'am, I'm not a prank caller," Derek said. "And I'm sorry to have to give you this news by phone, but Karen was killed in an accident the same weekend she disappeared."

He heard a wail, followed by a long series of denials: "No, no, no, no!"

Derek had read enough in his psychology books to expect a reaction like this. He pressed on quickly. "I'm truly sorry, ma'am. I really am. I never knew your daughter, but a friend of mine did. She asked me to call you and tell you not to keep hoping. It's hard to give you this bad news, but it's even harder for you to go on thinking your daughter might return someday."

"Who are you to tell me my daughter is dead?" Mrs. Grzegorczyk screamed. "You aren't with the FBI, or you would have identified yourself. This is just your idea of a sick joke. I am going to hang up on—"

"I have proof," Derek interjected.

The woman was quiet, except for her anxious, heavy breathing. After an extended silence, she said, "You...you can prove what you've said?"

"Yes, ma'am, I can. I have two ways of verifying it to you."

After a momentary hesitation, clearly fearful of hearing the worst, Mrs. Grzegorczyk said, "All right. What is your proof?"

"If you're not already sitting down, then please do so," Derek cautioned her, "because this is going to be a shock."

He could hear the sound of chair legs scraping against a floor.

"I'm listening," she said.

"Let me ask you a question. Did you know the reason why your daughter was making a trip to see her husband in San Diego?"

"Yes," the woman responded. "To say good-bye before he left for Korea."

"Yes, well, true. But is that *all* she said the trip was about?" Derek pressed her. "Did she confide in you, her mother, that she was pregnant and wanted to give the news to her husband in person?"

Mrs. Grzegorczyk drew in a sudden breath. "No one knew about that except...."

Derek waited a moment to let that information settle in with her before he continued. "I also have her boarding pass to Las Vegas, as well as her flight itinerary with handwritten notes in the margin. Now, after we hang up, I want you to go to your front porch. At the base of one of the support posts, you'll find a manila envelope."

"What? What do you mean, on *my* porch? Did you put it there? Are you close by? Why can't you meet me face-to-face if you truly do have knowledge of what happened to my daughter?" Her voice dwindled to a moan. "Who are you working for? Oh, I just don't know what to believe anymore. None of this makes any sense."

"Ma'am, I regret that I can't meet with you personally," said Derek, "nor can I tell you who I'm a messenger for. I can only say that your daughter died instantly, and she was not mixed up in anything illegal or wrong. She simply died in a tragic accident."

"But why haven't the authorities—"

"Please!" Derek cut in. "I know this is hard for you, but I'm not able to explain any more. Let me finish telling you about the envelope. Inside it, you will find Karen's boarding pass and flight itinerary I mentioned earlier. You'll also find a sizable amount of cash."

"Cash? What cash?"

"The person I represent wants you to use the money in any way you see fit to honor Karen's memory," Derek explained. "You can buy a tombstone with her name on it or make a donation to an orphanage or set up a scholarship. Whatever you decide will be all right. It's a token of my friend's admiration for Karen."

Mrs. Grzegorczyk began to cry harder. "Please, can't you tell me who you are or who sent you? I need to know more. Don't leave me hanging like this."

"I'm sorry, ma'am," Derek said again with heartfelt sympathy. "Trust me, I know what it's like to lose someone you care deeply about. I've been there myself. In fact, the day Karen was killed, someone else was killed, too. This whole ordeal is about the death of two women, not just Karen. I have to go now, ma'am. You have my deepest sympathies."

The only sound was of Mrs. Grzegorczyk's sobbing. After a moment, Derek simply ended the call, then adjusted his rearview mirror so he could see the porch behind him. Soon, he saw the front door of the Grzegorczyks' house open. A crying woman stepped out and glanced at the posts. Then she retrieved the envelope Derek had left and hurried back inside.

Derek sighed. He'd finally completed the most bittersweet of all his errands for Dove. He readjusted the mirror, started the car, and headed for the on-ramp to Interstate 40 to begin the final leg of his long journey home.

Dan's bluff lasted until the moment he entered his apartment. Imogene took one look at his ridiculous hair, his rumpled clothing, and the two shaving nicks on his right cheek and surmised that something was wrong.

"What in the world happened to you?" she demanded. "You look like something the cat dragged in. And why haven't you called me back? I must have left you a dozen messages. Where have you been, and why do you look so absurd? Did anyone see you when you came in just now? You're a mess!"

Dan didn't know which question to try to respond to first. He wondered if he should stick to the story about doing research in Chicago for his novel. Did he really look that bad? He opened his mouth to speak, but she never gave him a chance.

"Listen," Imogene said. "I need some answers. I called Doug Barcalow at the bank today to arrange for a withdrawal from our government securities mutual fund so we could order my new car. He informed me you had closed out that fund...as well as all our other funds. He thought I'd known about it."

Dan felt the blood start to pound in his ears. "Yes, well, you see—"

"Then, this morning, I opened our closet safe to get some spending money, and everything was missing. You're the only one besides me who knows the combination. What's going on here, Dan? Where is our money? What have you been doing? Explain. And make it good!"

Dan tried to elbow his way past her to get to the bar, but she grabbed his arm and spun him around.

"No booze!" she declared. "Out with it, Dan. What's going on? Where is our money?"

Dan lowered his gaze to the floor and said in a hard voice, "She took it from me."

Imogene turned her head to one side. "Who? Who took it from you? What are you talking about?"

Dan looked up at Imogene. "Sheila's alive."

Imogene squinted at him a moment in an expression of absolute outrage. Then she pulled back her hand and slapped Dan hard across the face. It sent him stumbling backward, but Imogene moved forward, pursuing him.

"Don't talk to me as though I were some kind of idiot," she raged. She grabbed his slumped shoulders and shook him violently. "Where is all that money? Answer me!"

Dan dropped to one knee, holding up his hands in a posture of defense. "I'm not lying. Sheila's alive. She's been hiding out in the Nevada desert for the past five months. She called me last week. She didn't even know she'd been declared dead."

Imogene knelt and grabbed Dan's face in her hands. He grimaced as her manicured nails dug into his cheeks.

"You're talking nonsense, Daniel, absolute nonsense," she said. "Her scanned boarding pass proves she was on the doomed flight. You saw her necklace in the catalog of recovered personal effects. What happened is, you've let someone con you, you fool!"

"No, no, it's real," Dan insisted. "She talked to me on the phone. I recognized her voice. There was some kind of mix-up of boarding passes. She threatened to come back here and ruin everything unless I gave her half of the insurance money. So...I cashed out the mutual funds and paid her off."

"You saw her?" asked Imogene. "You actually saw Sheila?"

"No, not in person," said Dan. "She sent a representative to pick up the money. Some tall guy dressed like a cowboy. He had a note from her and her wedding ring set. I recognized her handwriting. And those were her rings, all right."

"You idiot!" screamed Imogene. "You actually fell for something like that? Faked handwriting...an actress's voice on the phone... cheap discount-store rings? Couldn't you smell a sting like that a mile away? You actually gave half our money to some con artists? You moron!" She slapped Dan again, harder this time. "You complete idiot!" She hit him again and again with her fists.

Dan steeled himself to endure the pain until her anger was spent. He wasn't ready to admit he couldn't find some way to recoup at least some of their losses. And someday he'd make Imogene pay for treating him like this.

"You've ruined my life!" she shrieked. "This will turn me into a laughingstock with everyone. How could I ever have imagined you were anything but a second-rate, witless, bumbling fool?"

"But I...I can fix things," he managed to say between blows.

"You've fixed enough already," Imogene spat, landing another punch. "There. That's for my lost trip to Paris." She landed a double punch. "That's for taking away my new car." She rained more blows on him. "Somebody needs to beat some sense into that empty, empty skull of yours."

Finally, when she had apparently tired of beating on him, Imogene went into their bedroom. She came out seconds later and threw a pillow and a blanket at Dan. "Sleep on the couch!" she commanded. "I can't stand to look at you."

She returned to the bedroom and slammed the door on Dan Gray.

CHAPTER 23

Although Sheila had come to appreciate the isolation of the desert, she found that she also missed Derek while he was gone to Indiana. During the day, she and Carmen took care of the motel. In between hospitality duties, Sheila kept busy with phone calls and e-mail correspondence with Judith Hardy in New York. But in the quieter evenings, she missed the companionship she had grown to cherish. Her friendship with Derek had illustrated what it meant to have a soul mate. It seemed there was nothing they couldn't discuss. Finally, she'd learned what it was like to be respected by a man. It felt good.

On the evening Derek was scheduled to return to New Promise, Sheila cooked a special dinner in his kitchen as a homecoming celebration. She didn't think he'd mind, since he'd given her permission to fix meals for herself there while she ran the motel in his absence.

She kept an ear out for the sound of his pickup. He'd planned to drop the rental car in Vegas, retrieve his truck at a friend's place, and then drive home. When she heard the pickup stop outside, she hurried to the door. "You did it!" she exclaimed. "I'm so glad you're back."

Derek laughed as he grabbed his duffel bag and the backpack. "*We* did it, Dove. You did the hard part. I just carried out your plan."

"You won't believe everything I have to tell you," she said as they went inside. "Put your bags down and come to the table. I made a welcome-home dinner for you. I hope you'll like it. So, what did Dan say?

Did he act like a jerk? How about JD? How did he seem? Is he okay? Wait till you hear my news."

Derek grinned and put up his hand. "Whoa, slow down. We can take all the time we need to catch up. I promise to listen to all your news, and I won't skip a single detail in sharing mine. But first, I have to get something else from the truck."

When he returned to the office, he set two boxes on the registration desk. "Here are your books from that storage place, all safe and sound." He walked around the end of the counter, pulled open a drawer, removed a small box cutter, and handed it to Sheila.

With a gasp of delight, Sheila slit the packing tape of the first box and opened the lid. Each book had been sealed in an archival plastic bag. She lifted one out and held it up. "These treasures remind me of how much Laureen Parks invested in launching the career of Dove Alexander." She grinned as she replaced the book inside the box. "And soon, I'll have my own first edition to add to these contemporary classics. I'm amazed at everything that had to happen to make my writing career a reality. Dan tried to destroy it. Daddy burned all the letters Mrs. Parks had sent me from Texas, so it's a wonder she and I became friends again later in life. Yet, despite all that, I'm a published writer, and I've just finished my first novel. I wonder where I should keep these books now."

"You can build a library room, if you choose to," Derek said. He picked up the backpack and beckoned for her to follow him into the kitchen. Then, unzipping the pack, he asked, "Ever seen more than a hundred sixty thousand dollars in raw cash before?"

Sheila looked inside and gasped. "Oh, my goodness," she said, her tone subdued, almost reverential. "It's real?"

"Must be," said Derek, "'cause I've been spending money all across this vast country of ours. Go ahead, touch it. It feels good."

Sheila started to reach for a bundle of bills, then stopped herself. "No, that can wait. Close it up and set it aside. We're going to eat this little banquet I've prepared while we catch up on news, and then we can turn to business later. Sit down, sit down. Start talking. I want to know every detail of the trip, even if it takes all night."

During the meal of breaded pork chops, scalloped potatoes, and sautéed mixed vegetables, Derek shared the specifics of his trip. When he described the condition Dan was in, Sheila shook her head. "How could I have been so stupid?" she said. "I can't believe how I let him control me all those years. Liz-Liz was so right about his deep insecurities. If only I had listened to her."

"Don't be too hard on yourself, Dove. Remember, you were just a kid when you met Dan. You were a naive little farm girl looking for her first love. Plus, you thought you'd found a way to go to college, eventually. It's not like you'd taken 'Marriage Prep 101' or anything. You basically just jumped into it blind."

When Derek described his meeting with Sheila's brother and the look of awe on JD's face when he saw the money, a lump formed in Sheila's throat. She was thrilled to have been able to help her brother, but an arrow of sadness pierced her heart at the realization she might never see him again. However, the knowledge that she had left a legacy for Laureen Parks in Johnson County cheered her, and her eyes grew misty when Derek recounted his interaction with Irene Grzegorczyk.

Finally, Derek leaned back in his chair. "Okay, Dove. You said you had lots to tell me. You're up."

Sheila beamed. "You aren't going to believe everything that happened while you were gone."

"Shoot, after becoming friends with you these past several months, I'll believe just about anything!" He stretched his arms. "Too much time in the car. I feel fidgety. You mind if I clear the table while you talk? No, seriously, let me do this." He stood and picked up their plates, then carried them to the sink and started running hot water. The scent of lemony dish soap filled the little kitchen.

"Well," Sheila began, "Judith and I have been in touch regularly ever since you paved the way by warning her I wasn't dead after all. She wants me to keep detailed notes so I can remember everything when I write my autobiography one day. She's a hoot, I tell you. You'll love her when the two of you meet in person."

Derek said nothing as he rinsed a dinner plate, but he raised one eyebrow and looked pleased.

"But that's not the exciting part," Sheila continued. "What's exciting is that I sent her the book manuscript. She read it through in one sitting, and she loves it! I've already signed the agreement for serialization. Isn't that great?"

"It is. But something occurred to me on my long drive back home," Derek said. "For five months, she thought you were dead. How will she bring Dove Alexander back to life for your readers?"

Sheila grinned. "I asked Judith that very same question. See why you two need to meet?"

Derek flicked some soapsuds at her.

She dodged them, laughed, and then continued. "When Mr. Pembroke called Judith to tell her of my demise, the magazine had just gone to press with one of my stories, and it was too late to make the announcement. Then, Judith wasn't sure she should spill the beans to the public, after all. She wondered if she could find another writer who could take on the Dove Alexander byline and keep the 'phenomenal ride' going for the magazine. She thought about a book publisher in the last century, Edward Stratemeyer, who had hired ghostwriters to produce the Nancy Drew, Dana Girls, Hardy Boys, and Bobbsey Twins stories under the pen names of Carolyn Keene, Franklin W. Dixon, and Laura Lee Hope. That had worked rather well for Stratemeyer. So, even though she thought I had perished in a horrible plane crash, Judith wasn't ready to put Dove Alexander into the grave quite yet."

Derek quickly wiped his hands on a dish towel, slung the cloth over his shoulder, and stepped to the table. He covered one of her hands with his still-damp ones and patted it. "I'm very glad you're not in the grave yet. And that's marvelous news about your novel. I knew the story was great. Didn't I say so? I'm really happy for you."

"And that's not all," she said, nearly sliding off the edge of her seat in her enthusiasm.

"Don't keep me in suspense," he said, letting go of her hand. "What is it?"

"After we got the serialization agreement all worked out, Judith showed the manuscript to one of her publisher friends in New York."

Derek stepped back and leaned against the sink. "And?"

"And he wants to publish it!" she screamed, jumping up from the chair. "Can you believe it? My contract should be here any day now."

Oblivious to the dish towel falling to the floor, Derek grabbed her in a hug and whirled her around once before setting her back down. "Of course, I believe it. I knew you could do it. I knew it!"

Sheila began to pace the little room as she filled in details of how she'd confided in Judith about her plans to become Dove Alexander officially—from the plastic surgery to the new ID. Judith had promised to become her accomplice and confidante.

After Derek finished the dishes, they moved to the living room.

"This is just like a dream," Sheila whispered. "But don't pinch me, 'cause I'm lovin' it."

"You deserve every bit of happiness you get," Derek told her. "Don't ever doubt that."

"The same goes for you, you know. Good things are coming your way, too, Derek. I'm certain they are."

"They already have, thanks to you. I have a friend I wouldn't trade for anything in the world who has given me the courage to go after my dreams. I couldn't ask for more."

"There's something else I haven't told you, Derek. While you were gone, I finalized arrangements with a cosmetic surgeon in Vegas. I leave in four days for my pre-op consultation, and the surgery will be a week after that."

Derek studied her face intently. "Are you absolutely sure about this, Dove? It's a huge step. Once you have the surgery, there's no going back."

"Yes, I know. I've thought it all through. This is the only way. It has to be a new beginning, in every sense. Gracie insists on being my caregiver when I get back. I'll stay in her home for several days during recovery. But will you be with me for the surgery? I won't be able to drive myself back."

"Of course. You can count on me. I wouldn't have it any other way. I'll always be there for you."

Dan had been relegated to a fate worse than death. After a week of banishment from their bedroom and the cold-shoulder treatment from Imogene, he was given his marching orders—but not the ones he'd expected.

He assumed that, one day, Imogene would inform him she'd hired a lawyer and would be serving divorce papers on him, and he needed to leave their fancy apartment. That would have been bad. But what she announced to him instead was something very different and infinitely worse.

"Daniel, we are stuck with one another," she said to him matter-of-factly one morning. "We have a lease on this apartment for another five months at four thousand dollars per month, a sum neither of us can afford alone. If we default and break our lease, the landlord will merely sue to get a judgment to garnish a portion of our salaries. That will humiliate us both, and it won't save us any money. As such, we are going to have to go on living here and meeting those payments until the lease is up."

Imogene paused while her words weighed on Dan.

"We can sell the jewelry and the high-tech toys you bought, and get whatever the market will bear," she added slowly, as he winced at the thought of his electronic gadgets and other playthings being taken from the apartment. "In time, you'll have to get rid of your new car, too, even though I know it's been paid for."

"But if it's already paid for, couldn't we…?" Dan tried to argue, then froze when he saw the glare in his wife's eyes.

Imogene continued, "And you are going to have to take on a second job."

Dan looked at her in complete bafflement. "Second job?"

"I called an acquaintance of mine who's vice president at a community college here in the city," said Imogene. "It so happens they need someone to manage their learning resource center. You'll be helping students with remedial reading and teaching basic computer skills, reshelving books in the library, helping to decorate bulletin boards...that sort of thing. I e-mailed your résumé two days ago and have a form for you to sign to send them your transcript. You have an interview with HR at one o'clock this afternoon. Be sure to wear your new blue suit and that nice pinstripe tie."

Dan nearly choked. "Remedial reading! Basic computer skills! Bulletin boards! Are you kidding? I'm a university professor."

"No, you're not," Imogene said coldly. "*I* am a university professor. You are a part-time adjunct instructor. I have a doctoral degree, *you don't*. I have tenure, *you don't*. I have a record of academic publications, *you don't*. You are an unpublished non-PhD, Daniel. And in the world of academia, there is nothing lower. So, you will continue to teach your two classes of freshman composition at IUPUI, and you'll start working twenty-five hours a week at the community college. Oh...and I will manage all of our finances."

In the weeks that followed, Dan experienced a form of public education that made him cringe every time he had to show up for work. The people he taught in the remedial classes were nothing like his students at the university. Some were sleep-deprived single parents who seemed too overwhelmed by life to focus on improving their reading skills. Others had recently been released from prison and were still adjusting to life on the outside. English was not the first language of a good percentage of those in his classrooms, and Dan was forced to choose simple words and to speak slowly and clearly. All too often, his students failed to turn in their homework assignments.

Then, there were the enrollees who considered it their duty to harass their teacher. They called him "Teach," "Bud," "Mack," "Dude," "Baldy," and any number of other disrespectful nicknames. When he admonished them to call him Professor Gray, his request garnered a round of whistles, catcalls, and whoo-hoo-hoos.

And, as if that torture weren't bad enough, Dan found himself battling another constant problem. He started seeing Sheila everywhere he went. If he stopped by the mall, he'd see a woman with Sheila's hairstyle, and he'd rush over and stand in front of her, only to discover it wasn't Sheila. Walking down the street, he'd be following a woman with a figure just like Sheila's, so he'd run ahead, grab her arm, and be faced with a total stranger staring wild-eyed at him. He saw Sheila at the coffee shop, the drugstore, driving in a car next to him on the freeway, walking a dog in the park, checking out books at the public library.

Dan could not accept the fact that Sheila was dead and that he'd been duped out of his money by some con artists. He knew Sheila's voice, her expressions, her phrasings, the rise and fall of her sentences as she spoke. She had told him things no one else could possibly know. It had been her...surely.

He'd looked at her wedding band and engagement ring. She had told him it would be a sign that the messenger she'd sent had really come from her. *But, face it,* he concluded, *how many men really ever look closely at their wife's wedding rings after they purchase them?* He hadn't paid attention to Sheila's ring set ever since he'd bought it for their second anniversary to quiet her nagging. Now, he couldn't even remember which catalog he'd ordered it from—Sears? Penney's? Maybe Imogene was right. It was probably a generic set found on the finger of a bazillion women.

But, that voice...it still haunted him. A man couldn't live with a woman for fifteen years and not know the true sound of her voice, could he?

When at last he had started to think that maybe Imogene was right, that maybe he had been suckered—and maybe a private eye had somehow learned all those personal things he thought only Sheila would know—he suggested they call the police and report it.

Imogene looked at him like he'd grown a third eye. "And just what will you say to the cops, Mr. Wronged Citizen? Will you say that you paid off your ex-wife so you and she could continue to bilk the insurance company? Don't be an even bigger idiot than you already are, Dan. The money is gone, and we can't do a thing about it."

From that moment on, Dan knew he would spend the rest of his life in academic hell unless one of two things happened. The first solution had two parts: 1) if he could find Sheila and prove to Imogene that she was alive, and 2) if he could then talk some sense into Sheila so that maybe she would give him some of his money back. That only increased the frequency of "Sheila sightings" Dan experienced.

But time was beginning to convince him that he would never see Sheila again because, in reality, she probably *was* dead. And even if she were alive, she'd never give him any money. No, the Sheila who had talked to him on the phone had *sounded* like his Sheila, but she had not acted like his Sheila. That woman had been strong, brassy, demanding, calculating—a completely different person. To that end, Imogene might be right about her not having been the real Sheila. That was food for thought.

His second and only other escape ticket was the publication of his novel. His hatred of working at the community college resource center had driven him to write like a madman to complete his sixteen-year project. He started getting up early in the mornings to write. He used his lunch hours to proofread previous days' pages. He stayed up late at night making notes about plot and characters. Soon, very soon, it would be done, and then it would be his chance to claim his titles of professor, lord and master of his household, and literary lion of the Midwest.

Finishing the novel now became Dan Gray's total obsession.

Four days after Derek returned home, Sheila borrowed his pickup and made the two-hour drive to Las Vegas for her pre-op appointment with the cosmetic surgeon. The receptionist handed Sheila a clipboard with forms to fill out and sign, and then she asked for a piece of photo ID.

As Sheila retrieved her driver's license, she hesitated. "A friend told me that this entire procedure, including my identity, is totally confidential. Is that right?"

The receptionist nodded. "Absolutely. Not only do HIPAA laws protect your right to privacy, but our clinic also specializes in serving clients who must keep their cosmetic work absolutely confidential. We even provide a list of suggested responses you can use when explaining your absence from work or other responsibilities during the recovery process. Right now, I just need proof that you are who you say you are. And when you return next week for the surgery, we'll need to check your ID again so we can be confident of matching you to today's lab work." She smiled encouragingly.

After Sheila completed all the paperwork, she was escorted to a consultation room, where the surgeon questioned her in detail about what she wanted to change and how she wanted to look. They discussed eyelid surgery, cheek implants, under-eye bag removal, and other procedures. A computer program allowed Sheila to see how each option would affect her appearance. She became confident that with the surgery, a new hair color, and contact lenses to intensify the green shade of her eyes, no one would ever mistake her for Sheila Davis Gray.

After she signed the surgery consent form, she made her appointment for the following week, and a technician drew blood for some labs.

When she returned to New Promise, Derek talked seriously with her about how plastic surgery often affected patients psychologically—usually in very positive ways, but not always. She listened but still felt sure she'd made the right decision.

In spite of her confidence, however, Sheila slept little the night before her surgical appointment. Images from throughout her life kept flashing through her mind like a slide show. She saw herself as a small girl running through the fields of her family's Indiana farm. She visualized her first time on the school bus with her big brothers in the seat behind her. She pictured the scene of the senior awards program at Brissenden

High School and Mrs. Parks at the microphone. Finally, after tossing and turning for what seemed like hours, she got up and walked to the bathroom. She turned on the light and, after letting her eyes adjust to the brightness, studied her reflection in the mirror, touching every inch of her face with her fingertips.

It's all about change, she thought. *I'm a work in progress, in every sense of the term, and I always have been. I've been scared a lot of times in my life, but I've managed to make it this far. Nothing's going to stop me now. I'll be okay. I* am *okay.*

After that, Sheila felt calm and drowsy. She turned off the light and went back to bed. Within minutes, she fell into a deep sleep.

Early the next morning, Derek gave last-minute instructions to Carmen's father, Fernando, who had agreed to manage business at the motel while Derek was in Las Vegas. The older man had helped Derek in the past whenever he was between jobs.

Fernando watched as Sheila and Derek got into the pickup outside the motel office. "Do not worry," he told Derek. "Carmen will help me take good care. *No problema.*"

During the two-hour journey, Sheila asked Derek how his online classes were going. She knew he was a star student, finishing assignments at a good pace and going beyond the course requirements. But she hadn't had a chance to get a recent update.

"Actually, I'm surprised at the progress I've made," he said, pulling into the left lane to pass a tractor-trailer. "I was worried I'd been out of school too long to keep up with everything. But one of my professors even sent me an e-mail yesterday, praising my efforts. That sure was nice."

When they reached the surgical clinic, Derek stopped under the portico to let Sheila out before he parked the truck. "You okay?" he asked. "It's not too late to change your mind, you know."

Sheila forced a smile. "I'm all right. Just a little nervous, that's all. I've never been in any kind of hospital before, let alone had surgery."

He patted her arm. "Everything will be just fine. And I'll be right here."

She grasped the door handle and then paused. "Derek?"

"Yes?"

"I wouldn't mind you saying a prayer or two while I'm under the knife."

Derek looked thoughtful. "For you, I'll do that."

Sheila learned later that while the surgical procedures were taking place, the wait had been very hard on Derek. After he'd checked into a hotel across the street, he'd returned to the clinic and paced the waiting-room floor. He'd consumed innumerable cups of coffee and tried to read a textbook he'd brought with him, but he wasn't able to concentrate. He'd picked up every magazine on display to try to find something that would hold his attention. The staff even suggested that he walk off some energy in a shaded courtyard behind the clinic, where the splashing sounds of a rock fountain often soothed clients. Nothing worked.

When the nurse finally allowed Derek to enter the recovery area, Sheila was still groggy from the anesthetic. "Hey," he said. "It's about time you woke up. I've worn a path on the floor in the waiting room."

Sheila wanted to respond, but she felt too sleepy to think of a good comeback. And why was Derek looking at her so strangely? "What's wrong?" she whispered. Then she remembered being told she'd be wearing a full face-and-neck compression bandage—the surgeon had called it a facial surgery garment—for the first twenty-four hours. Everything was covered except for her eyes, nose, and mouth. "Do I look like a mummy?"

He smiled. "Almost."

She closed her eyes again. "I can hardly stay awake."

"That's okay, Dove," Derek assured her. "You just rest for now. I'll be here when you wake up."

He went to the hotel late that night and checked out early the next morning to be with Sheila when the surgeon replaced the compression bandage with a stretchy wrap under her chin that extended over the top of her head.

"We'll see you in a week," the doctor said, handing her several printed sheets of post-op instructions. "Everything looks good, but be sure to call us if you have any concerns."

"Will you remove sutures next time?" Derek asked.

"No need," the doctor replied. "We use superglue now, instead. I did apply a couple of butterfly stitches, but those little adhesive strips will wear off on their own in a week or two."

Derek chuckled as he helped Sheila out to the pickup. "Superglue for a super lady," he said.

Sheila managed a tiny smile and murmured, "Let's hope there's something prophetic in that." Still under heavy pain medication, she dozed most of the way back to New Promise.

Carrying a foam wedge that the doctor had prescribed, Derek helped Sheila into Gracie's house, where a bed had been made up for Sheila in the living room. Sheila lay on the bed, her head elevated by the wedge, while Derek arranged a chilled gel eye mask on her face. By the time Gracie popped in later to see how she was doing, Sheila was almost asleep again.

Over the next few days, Gracie, Derek, and Carmen took turns preparing special meals for Sheila, helping her take her meds, and keeping her supplied with chilled gel masks. By the end of the week, Sheila was well enough to move back into her own cabin. She ate microwaveable meals and rested while watching television or reading books from Derek's library.

The following week, Derek drove Sheila back to the clinic. The doctor announced the good news that she didn't need to wear a facial garment anymore and could even start using a little concealer around her eyes. "The swelling and bruising will be greatly reduced in a couple of weeks and mostly gone in two or three months," he said. "As the incisions fade, you'll find you can go anywhere and do almost anything, as long as you're careful not to get bumped. And for the next year, at least, it's vital that you use a potent sunblock." He then instructed her to see the receptionist on her way out to make an appointment for her thirty-day post-op exam.

Back in New Promise, Derek helped Sheila out of the pickup and into her cabin once again. "Gracie wants to come over tonight for the big reveal," he told her.

"Tonight?" Sheila asked. "Can't she wait a week, so I'll look better?"

Derek laughed. "Wait? We're talking about Gracie, remember. Besides, she'll think you're beautiful, even if you do look like you've just gotten beat up."

Sheila playfully threatened him with her fist, and he retreated, whistling, to the motel office.

She had not yet looked at her reflection in the mirror without the chin wrap. Seeing herself with a different face would be hard enough, but she wasn't sure if she could handle the "beat-up" look, too. However, the doctor had said she could start using concealer. That was one of the few cosmetic items she'd brought with her from Indiana. Maybe she could minimize the skin discoloration before Gracie arrived that evening.

Sheila stepped to the mirror on the wall, took a deep breath, and looked straight into her reflection. The woman gazing back was someone she'd never seen before. She flinched slightly at the changes, but after only a few seconds, she noticed a few vaguely familiar features. Sure, the differences were dramatic, but the curve of her lips and the lines of her teeth were the same. She hadn't yet purchased the green contacts she'd planned on or dyed her hair blonde, so her eyes and hair hadn't changed, either.

She carefully applied concealer to the discolored areas and then curled up on the bed with a book about local Native American cultures.

That evening, Sheila was just answering Derek's knock when Gracie arrived at the cabin's doorstep. She took one look at Sheila and let out a shout. "Girl! If I didn't know ya, I wouldn't know ya. I never seen anything like it in all my life—and I still haven't."

Derek smiled. "I agree. Even your closest friends wouldn't recognize you on the outside. But inside, you're the same wonderful person you were the day you arrived here." Then, careful not to touch her face, he put his arms around her and gave her a warm hug.

Never one to be left out, Gracie threw her enormous arms around both of them. "Dove, honey, I'm so happy for ya, I could blow a casket. Yer future now sure ain't what it was. Ya really are a new woman."

When Derek extricated himself from the group hug, he added, "'New woman' is right. I talked with Gracie's Vegas contact earlier today. Your birth certificate and Social Security card are almost ready. As soon as you get colored contact lenses and your face is ready for an ID photo, your driver's license can be made up, too."

Sheila looked at her friends with deep affection. "I don't know how to thank you for everything you've done for me. It's…it's…."

"I know one way," Derek said gently. "Start thinking of yourself permanently as Dove Alexander. Around here, we've never known you as anyone else. It's time you said good-bye to your old life for good."

She closed her eyes and nodded as she mentally said her final farewell to Sheila Davis Gray. When she opened her eyes, she breathed a sigh of relief. Except for her few remaining follow-up appointments at the cosmetic surgery clinic, she would be Dove Alexander for the rest of her life. And what a life it was turning out to be!

CHAPTER 24

For Dan Gray, the end of the academic year the following May was the relief he had been waiting for on a moment-by-moment basis. No longer would he have to put up with the indignity of working in the community college resource center.

He knew that his wife, Dr. Imogene Cunningham-Gray, had actually been dreading the end of the academic year. She'd complained bitterly about the day when she and Dan would have to move out of their lovely high-rise complex because Dan had foolishly lost their windfall.

With most of their fancy furniture and high-tech gadgets already sold, the move to a modest-sized condo on the outskirts of Indianapolis would be relatively easy, at least from a logistical standpoint. But from an ego standpoint, the downward move was going to be absolutely humiliating for Imogene. Her social status at the university had already slumped back to its pre-Dan, pre-wealth days. No one invited her and her husband to parties anymore. Since Imogene hadn't purchased anything new in ages, she no longer received compliments on a new outfit or a new piece of jewelry. And, worst of all, she had nothing to speak about in conversations with her students or colleagues, now that she and Dan were no longer dashing off for trips to Reno, Oahu, Chicago, and other fun spots.

Imogene had once told Dan she'd always believed that if true love and true wealth ever came into her life, she'd be ecstatically happy. That belief had proved to be valid for her. And now that both had been taken from her, she was maniacally depressed. More than once while railing to Dan, she grumbled, "As Sophie Tucker used to say, 'I've been rich and I've been poor. Rich is better.'"

"All I can say to that," Imogene added, "is a hearty amen."

Because she blamed Dan for giving her a taste of the high life and then taking it away, Dan was stunned by her unexpected announcement one morning as they sat at the breakfast table. "I've talked to the dean of our division, and he's told me he'll be able to hire you again in the fall to teach two classes of basic freshman composition," she said, her tone that of a domineering older sister rather than a wife.

Dan nodded as he bit into a slice of wheat toast with strawberry jam. "Good," he said, "but I never assumed I wouldn't be doing that." He smiled with satisfaction as he savored the sweet berry preserves.

"And I've called your supervisor at the community college and told her you'll be signing another contract to return in the fall as the learning resource center director," she continued.

Dan choked on his half-swallowed bite of toast. He grabbed for his cup of coffee and gulped several swallows in an effort to clear his throat so he could breathe again. "You did *what?*" he finally managed to say between gasps. "You know I hate dealing with those stupid lamebrains. I never want to set foot in there again."

Imogene glared at him. "Well, you should have thought about that when you gave away two hundred seventy-five grand to a total stranger and when you lost more than thirty grand at the gambling tables. If it hadn't been for your own stupidity, we'd still have a lease for this apartment, we'd still have our nice furniture and clothes, and we'd still be able to hold our heads up on campus."

He tried to say something in his defense, but she never gave him the chance.

"You know how I hate moving from this place, and I blame you for ruining the fantastic life we had going for us. It's all your fault. I want this life back, somehow, someway. I called Doug Barcalow and had him restore two of our former mutual funds. You're going to work two jobs, and I'm going to continue full-time at the university. We're going to save and invest for as long as it takes in order for us to get back on top. I want a fine apartment again. I want the nice furnishings and the new clothes. And, more than anything else, I want that new car and that trip to Paris you still owe me!"

Dan's stomach roiled. He pushed his breakfast plate away. The very thought of spending years and years working at the resource center made him physically ill. *No, no, any fate but that!*

Imogene crumpled her napkin and tossed it on her empty plate. "I'm off to teach my summer-school class. Make sure you clean this place up while I'm gone, then start packing your clothes for the move. I'll be back around three this afternoon."

With that, she stood, walked to the hallway, picked up her purse and briefcase, and left the apartment. No good-bye kiss or words of farewell. Whatever affection had existed between them had morphed into a state of survival bondage. They were still legally married and slept in the same bed. But, in all other aspects, Imogene was the queen, and Dan was the vassal. She controlled the money and called the shots.

Dan sat immobile at the kitchen table. His wife had just announced his life sentence in prison. He couldn't—he just *couldn't*—go back to that resource center in the fall. He'd jump off a building or stand in front of an oncoming train before he'd sign a full-year contract to work in *that* place again.

"Screw the dishes," he said, suddenly coming to life and jumping up from the table. He made his way to his home office. The lovely dark mahogany desk was still here, but a yellow tag taped to it noted the time later that week when a used-furniture dealer would be picking it up. Imogene had sold it without even consulting Dan.

He sat in the comfortable leather office chair and pulled a flat cardboard box from a nearby packing carton. He lifted the box's lid and removed a printout of his novel. On top were three rejection letters he'd received from publishers. He read them again. They all seemed generic, plain vanilla, nonspecific. No one commented about his characters or his plot or his research or...anything.

He examined the first letter, actually more of a note:

> *Thank you for letting us consider your proposal. We regret that it does not meet the current needs of our planned editorial direction, but we wish you well in placing it elsewhere. Kindest regards...*

Dan crushed the paper in his hand and tossed it into the wastebasket. He picked up the second letter and read it for, what, the hundredth time?

> *Your novel does not meet our current editorial needs, but please do not take this as a reflection of its merits. We are unable to provide personal responses to everyone who contacts us, so please accept our apologies for this standard letter. Best wishes for success at another publisher.*
>
> *Most respectfully yours...*

Dan also crumpled and discarded that letter.

He extracted the third letter from the box and read it slowly and painstakingly, not wanting to miss any nuance of hope or encouragement he might have overlooked on one of the dozens of earlier readings:

> *Thank you for letting Calvin and Fox Publishers review your outline and sample chapters. Unfortunately, we are unable to accept unsolicited manuscripts. We recommend that you seek the services of a reputable literary agent. In this way, you will receive editorial and marketing guidance, which we have neither the time nor the staff to provide. Nevertheless, thank you for considering Calvin and Fox Publishers.*
>
> *Very truly yours...*

Dan studied this letter, allowing its intent to register with him. "Yeah, sure, that's the ticket," he mused aloud. "There's nothing wrong with my novel. I just haven't gotten it into the hands of the right people. If I could just *meet* an editor or a literary agent and pitch my idea one-on-one, then I'd have an 'in' with publishers. It's probably like any other business. It's who you know."

His published colleagues at the college had not offered to introduce him to their agents or editors, so he'd have to figure out how to find an agent on his own. *Where there's a will, there's a way,* he reassured himself. And, oh my, he certainly had the will. The thought of having to return to that resource center filled him with abject horror. He simply had to do whatever necessary to get his novel sold and thus earn a reprieve from such a life sentence.

Hastily, he rummaged through a box of the writing magazines he subscribed to and located the most recent issue of each publication. He took out a pen and a pad of paper to list every writers conference, workshop, and convention being held that summer within a hundred miles of Indianapolis. If their staff included any major-name writers or editors or literary agents, he'd figure out a way to worm himself into the event and get in front of those key people.

He looked down at his novel's cover page with the title, *The Bohemian Generation*. "You and I didn't endure fifteen years of living with that hick farm girl just to be thwarted now," he said to the manuscript, which, by now, he considered a longtime friend. "I'll find a home for you, and you'll become my 'Get Out of Jail Free' card."

In June, Judith Hardy flew to Las Vegas and drove a rental car to New Promise for a week of "working vacation" time. Early one evening, while it was still light but the temperature had started to cool, she set out with Dove on a desert walk. "Did you ever in your wildest dreams imagine you'd get your own pre-publicity tour with your very first book?" Judith asked. "And then a national book tour scheduled for a few months after that, when the book is released?"

Dove smiled self-consciously as she slathered SPF-45 sunscreen on her face. "Never in my wildest dreams did I imagine I'd even get a chance to write a book. Just getting it completed and contracted exceeded my expectations. I owe you a lot for opening doors for me." She plopped her broad-brimmed hat on her head.

"You don't owe me squat," said Judith, following her up the trail. "Our circulation has shot through the roof since we started serializing *Hearts of Bronze*. The whole country is talking about your forthcoming book, and I'm the genius who landed it for *Fulfillment* magazine. You can bet when my contract comes up for renewal, I'll be putting the screws to my publisher."

"Well, I'm still grateful for all your help," Dove said. "And, while I've loved it out here, I'm ready to get back in the real world. It took longer than I thought to heal completely from the surgery."

"You look great, kiddo, trust me," said Judith with a dismissive wave of her hand. "You have a natural, fresh look now, not like those balloon-stretched, masky-faced old socialite broads in New York who get themselves pinned back every three years. Their necks are like bunched layers of cloth holding up a cartoon of someone freeze-framed in a look of fright."

Dove chuckled at Judith's ever brassy way of calling things as they were. "Thanks," she said. "I still surprise myself at times when I get up in the morning and see a blonde-haired, new-faced me reflected in the mirror. It'll probably be that way for a while. I'm okay with it, though. Anyway, what's the agenda you've got planned for us?"

"The whole world is eager to meet Dove Alexander, so we're going to be obliging," Judith answered. "We'll fly from Vegas to New York and do appearances on all the leading networks, all the morning talk shows, and some of the syndicated shows, too. I hope you've studied that press kit info I concocted about you."

"I have," Dove affirmed. "My parents 'died of yellow fever while serving as missionaries in Brazil'—wasn't that part a bit overboard?"

"Not in the least," countered Judith. "It'll make you sympathetic to your fans, and it'll explain why there are no death certificates and other records relating to your parents. We've got to cover our tracks, sweetheart. When you get famous, the scandal sheets start snooping like crazy. Danielle Steele has been accused of everything from having a baby out of wedlock to cheating on her taxes, although not even the slightest bit of proof of either allegation has ever surfaced. You'll need to be on your toes."

"I know the script," said Dove, "and it really sounds like it's going to be a lot of fun. Still, I'm glad you'll be along. I'll probably be a little nervous at first."

"You'll adapt quickly," Judith assured her. "We'll get you out of these blue jeans and into something chic, we'll work more on that Southern drawl, and I'll rehearse you prior to each interview."

"I'm amazed you can get this much time off to spend with me."

Judith laughed. "Look, honey. You're a cash cow to *Fulfillment* right now, so my publisher wants us to do everything we can to give you high visibility. When he heard you'd already started on a second novel and that you were going to let us serialize it, too, he gave me free rein to support your publicity in any way I could."

"That's great," said Dove. She paused, then asked, "Did you do anything about setting up something near…?"

"What? Near Brissenden? Sure, sure, I've got that covered. The annual Midwest regional meeting of the North Atlantic Booksellers Association is being held at the Indianapolis convention center in three weeks. Your book's publisher, Calvin and Fox, always has a booth where people can buy new books, get autographs, take promo photos…that sort of stuff. You're this year's headline attraction. We'll sit at the table and meet folks for a couple of hours, and then I'll get you out of there."

"What then?"

"We'll take a rental car down to Brissenden," said Judith. "No driver, just us two girls. We can sashay by your brother's farm, go by the house you had with Dan, and then even skirt by the office building where you used to work. One last farewell look, but no meetings or talks with anyone. You're clear on that, right?"

Dove nodded to show her understanding. "Yes, I'm straight on that. But I also want to drive by the home where Mrs. Parks used to live. I just want to see it all, for memory's sake."

"I'll let you do the driving," said Judith. "In New York, we use the Subway and cabs. I didn't even get a driver's license until I was twenty-eight. Never needed one before that. We'll have to drive back to the Indianapolis hotel that same night. You're filming two interviews for local TV shows the next morning, and you've got a radio call-in show that afternoon. We'll catch the red-eye back to 'The City' at ten o'clock that night."

"It sounds great," said Dove. "We'd better start back now. Derek's a good cook, and he doesn't like his supper guests to be late."

Judith raised an eyebrow as she and Dove turned around. "Hey," she said conspiratorially, "speaking girl to girl, what's his story? When I first checked in, I couldn't help but notice how handsome he is—so tall and muscular. He's got a great sense of humor, he has manners, and he isn't full of himself. Why hasn't someone grabbed him up already?"

Dove smiled as she gently chucked Judith on the shoulder. "You sound personally interested."

"Don't kid yourself, girlfriend. I *am*. He's like Mel Gibson and Brad Pitt wrapped in one. I can't believe he's never been married. And, I mean, you two, all this time out here alone…?" She waved her arm at the desert landscape, leaving her hand extended in the direction of the motel.

Dove shook her head. "You forget that we both thought I was still married," she reminded Judith. "Besides, it wasn't like that with us, even from the start. We've always been just friends. When I first got here, we both needed someone to talk to. Derek never had a good relationship with his family, then he lost two good buddies when the three of them were in Afghanistan, so things just kind of piled up on him, emotionally. He's okay now, though. He's got his motel business, and he's working on a college degree in psychology. He's never asked me for a penny, but I bought him that new pickup truck for his birthday last month. We're like kissing cousins. We love each other, but we're not 'in love,' if you follow me."

Judith was starting to sound a little out of breath. "Do you know how many unattached *normal* men there are in New York?" she said. "The last ten dates I've gone on have been with 'artists' who were flat broke, construction workers whose view of the world did not extend beyond sports, actors who were bisexual, and male models who were more in love with themselves than they could ever be with a mere woman."

"That bad, eh?" said Dove, wincing. "Well, I don't know what you're looking for in a man, but Derek is more of a free-range maverick than an uptown metropolitan. He likes the Grand Ole Opry more than grand opera, and I don't think he even owns a suit and tie. I can tell you this, though—if you're looking for honesty, manliness, a good listening ear, and a decent cook who isn't afraid to wash the dishes when it's his turn, then Derek's the guy."

"And what about me?" asked Judith.

"What do you mean?"

Judith stopped on the trail and pointed to herself. "If he were to ask you what I'm like, what would you say? Be honest."

Dove paused a moment, then answered with directness. "I'd tell him that you are confrontational, dogmatic, argumentative, and blunt... when you work as an editor. But, as a friend, you're viciously funny in your own way, sophisticated but not snobbish, and as loyal and dependable as a seeing-eye dog, only better-looking...somewhat."

Judith feigned a kick at Dove, who jumped out of the way and hurried up the path again.

Judith followed. "What do you think? Should I, maybe...?"

Dove grinned. "Why not? You're my two closest friends. If I could get you together, we'd all come out on top. Yeah, go ahead. Flirt a little. Talk his talk."

"And what is his talk?"

"For the past few years, he's been reading westerns," said Dove. "Stuff like Zane Grey, Tony Hillerman, and Louis L'Amour. That's for relaxation. He studies psychology and likes to talk about what motivates people to do what they do. He cooks a bit as a hobby. He enjoys horseback riding, but he also likes pickups. He can communicate in Spanish on a basic level, and he studies local pictographs and petroglyphs of the ancient peoples who used to populate this region."

Judith crossed her eyes in vexation. "Well, how fortunate," she said. "I just happen to be up to snuff in every one of those areas. I can see that this is a match made in heaven."

Dove laughed. "Actually, it's your lucky break," she said. "Derek isn't much of a conversationalist until he gets to know someone. If you open the door to any one of these topics, your natural curiosity as an editor will keep him talking. You'll ask the right questions, he'll respond... and you *know* how people love to have anyone listen to them with rapt attention."

"Okay, then," said Judith. "Let's get to dinner and see what's cookin'." She took two steps forward, stopped suddenly, touched her hair, and asked in a panic, "How do I look?"

"Oh, *please*," said Dove, laughing out loud as she walked on ahead.

With the limited allowance Imogene gave him, Dan lacked the funds to sign up for any of the writers' conferences and seminars he so desired to attend. He tried a couple of end runs by calling conference directors and volunteering to serve on staff as a guest lecturer. But when they asked for his list of publications and for references from other conferences where he'd served on the faculty, he had nothing to offer.

He then tried to pretend he was a reporter wanting to interview some of the celebrity authors, but when they asked him for the names of his editors so they could confirm his reporter status, that hadn't worked, either. Next, he talked to the dean of his division at Indiana University's Indianapolis campus, but he learned that seminar funds were available only to full-time faculty members.

Just as he was about to pull out his hair in frustration, he happened to notice an advertisement on the *Indianapolis Star*'s Web site promoting the Midwest meeting of the North Atlantic Booksellers Association. The ad contained a link to a book fair that would be open to the public on one of the afternoons. Dan clicked on the link and found a feature article related to the booksellers' meeting. It mentioned that one of the publishing companies sponsoring booths would be Calvin and Fox, featuring its new mega-celeb Dove Alexander, author of *Hearts of Bronze,* currently being serialized in *Fulfillment* magazine and soon to be released in hardcover. The article further stated that Ms. Alexander would be accompanied by her editor from *Fulfillment,* Judith Hardy, and an editor from Calvin and Fox named Donna Jean Sumner.

Dan's heart skipped a beat. This event had no admission cost, and Calvin and Fox was the very publishing company that, after reading just his outline and sample chapters, had encouraged him to make direct contact with a literary agent or an editor. Okay, okay. Now, all he had to do was take his entire manuscript to the book fair and get in line for an autograph. Then, when he got up to the table, he could place his manuscript in front of this Dove Alexander and her two editors. He'd make his pitch and leave the manuscript with them. The next thing he knew, his phone would be ringing, and a contract would be in the mail.

Yep, it all comes down to making the right contacts. That's all. He gave a wide Cheshire-cat grin as he closed the browser tab.

CHAPTER 25

The months she'd spent in serious discussions with Laureen about literature paid off handsomely as Dove Alexander took to the airwaves. On a rather snooty cable TV program called *Dust Jackets,* the highbrow host seemed eager to expose the shallowness of this new up-and-comer, Dove Alexander.

The host referred to passages in Dove's novel presented as letters exchanged between the central characters. He asked, "How do you equate the style of the epistolary portions of your novel with the writings of other authors who have employed this format?" He stared at Dove with a triumphant smile, as if expecting her to look at him blank-faced and then ask what he meant.

Instead, she began to talk about Richardson's *Clarissa* as the originator of the epistolary style, Jules Verne's adaptation of it via journal entries in his *Journey to the Center of the Earth,* and the style's reinstitution in more recent books, such as Alice Walker's novel *The Color Purple.*

After the show, Judith told her, "When you put that stuffed shirt in his place, I could barely hold back a cheerleader's yell. Oh, yeah, girl. You're good! You not only made him look like a buffoon, but you also did it with a smile and a soft Southern accent. Proud of ya, kiddo."

During a radio call-in show, a caller challenged Dove regarding all the information about farming she had included in one section of her book. He claimed that using outside researchers took away the originality of a work.

"And to what, exactly, are you referrin', sir?" she asked softly.

He launched into topics related to crop rotation, fertilizer, and even home-canning methods, only to admit, after her responses, that Dove was a walking expert in all those areas. The caller finally said, "When I saw that picture of you on the back cover of your book, sitting there in that frilly dress, I never would have guessed you really knew so much about farm life."

"Well, sir, you shouldn't jump to conclusions like that from now on," teased Dove. "We Southern girls still have our roots in plantation livin', ya know."

Judith continually expressed her amazement at how well Dove always rose to whatever the occasion called for. "It's as if this was your tenth publicity tour, not your first," she said. And it was having a great effect on the public, increasing the book's already-booming pre-sale figures. The public was liking Dove Alexander's novel in magazine serialization, but now the public was also liking Dove Alexander, herself.

One evening after a particularly successful television interview, Dove and Judith returned to the nearby hotel where they had checked in that afternoon. Dove was rummaging around in her overnight bag when Judith, slouched in a chair, said, "All right, sweetheart. Something's going on. You're just as great as ever in public, but you're in your own private world the rest of the time. What gives?"

Dove sighed and plopped on the bed. "It's just no good."

"What's no good?"

"All of this." Dove waved her hand at the comfortable room and then shoved a pillow between her back and the headboard behind her. "Ever since Gracie called me last week, I've barely slept. My conscience is killing me."

"Gracie called you? Look, where I'm from, people don't seem to remember what the word 'conscience' means. But go ahead and tell me what's on your mind."

Dove rubbed her forehead with her thumb and index finger, as if trying to erase some disturbing memory. "I'm okay with taking advantage of my apparent death and assuming a new identity. I didn't do that for the purpose of fraud. It let me escape Dan's clutches and ultimately see what kind of a person he is. I'm truly glad to spend the rest of my life being Dove—writing more books, bringing some joy into people's lives...."

"Works for me," said Judith, as if still not sure where the conversation was headed. "Thus far, we're tracking together. But what about Gracie? Does she regret helping you change your identity?"

"No," said Dove, shaking her head. "Although it would have been better if I could have done it legally—you know, convince the authorities that my life was in danger unless I assumed a new identity. But what's done is done, and I can't see how anyone would benefit by my trying to 'resurrect' my former self now."

"Agreed. So, what's the problem?"

"I never told Gracie where I got my windfall. I guess I knew deep down she'd never approve of my taking life-insurance money when I wasn't dead. Although she doesn't have a lot of formal education, she's one of the most perceptive people I know. That's why something didn't feel right to her, and she finally asked Derek point-blank where my money had come from. As you know, he's antiestablishment and sees nothing wrong with benefitting from the insurance fat cats."

"I'm on his side there," Judith put in. "But Gracie *does* see something wrong with it, and that's why she called?"

"Exactly. She read me the riot act for five minutes straight for stealing more than half a million dollars."

"But is it really stealing?"

Dove sighed. "You and I both know it is. I'm defrauding all three insurance companies by taking money that doesn't rightfully belong to me."

Judith frowned. "It's not like you kept it all for yourself. You gave a big chunk away—to your brother, to the school district for a scholarship in your teacher's name, to the woman in Oklahoma whose daughter died in the plane crash...."

"But the money wasn't mine to give," Dove insisted. "You can call me a conservative Midwestern hick, you can tell me Christian morals are out-of-date. The problem is, you can take the hick out of the village chapel, but you can't take...." She slumped back against the pillow and looked up at the ceiling. "I've learned that when people are in abusive situations for a long time, their thinking patterns change. In order to survive, they adapt to beliefs and courses of action they never would have considered previously." She glanced back at Judith. "I was taught as a girl to be honest in all my dealings. I'm ashamed to see how far I slipped without realizing it. But now I *do* understand what I've done, and I want to make amends."

Judith seemed to weigh that a moment, then said, "You know, this really isn't as *heavy* as you're making it out to be. For one thing, you didn't take the entire five hundred fifty grand. Your ex-hubby made a serious dent in that pot of gold."

"Dan will have to deal with his own guilt," said Dove, "although I'm sure he hasn't lost any sleep over it. But he couldn't have gotten away with the scheme if I hadn't agreed to stay quiet about being alive."

"Okay, okay. But let me suggest something else," Judith continued. "Life-insurance policies pay off when people are dead. And, in case you haven't noticed, one Mrs. Sheila Davis Gray definitely is dead. She has gone down in ashes, never to be heard from again. There's even a marker to her memory on her brother's property. Sheila is dead. D-E-A-D."

"On paper, sure, but not in actuality," Dove countered. "I know it, you know it, Derek and Gracie know it, and even Dan knows it. What Gracie said makes a lot of sense. When she asked why I hadn't told her about the source of the money, I had to confess I didn't think she would have approved. She said, 'And in tryin' to show that scalawag ya ain't no babe in the wool no more, ya let yer common sense go out the wayside.'"

Judith laughed, then quickly sobered when Dove glared at her.

"I've also been very careful," Dove continued, "not to let Mr. Pembroke know I was alive, because he'd be honor bound, as an officer of the court, to expose all that had happened." She thumped the bedspread next to her. "Well, if he was honor bound, why on earth haven't I been honor bound?"

Judith shrugged. "Maybe because everyone hates insurance companies, and you're coming off as a hero in all this. It's time someone stuck it to them."

"But that's where I think differently than you and Derek. I've wrestled with this for days on end, and I've come to a decision. I have a plan, and I'm going to need your help in carrying it out."

"Marvelous," said Judith through gritted teeth. "Just when things were going so well."

Dove reached for her purse on the bedside table and pulled out a notepad and pen. "Give me some guesstimates. How much do you think I'll pull in on the sale of my book—hardbound, paperback, electronic versions, foreign translations, and then movie rights, plus an advance for a sequel?"

Judith raised her eyebrows. "Who said anything about a movie?"

"My agent. She's already been talking with her colleagues in Hollywood. Don't stall. You've been in this game a long time. What kind of money are we talking, here?"

"I can see where this is going, and I don't like it," said Judith. "Please, don't tell me you're thinking of giving all your earnings to the insurance companies. That can't be your plan. Tell me that isn't your plan. Tell me."

"It is my plan," Dove said firmly. "And I've thought of half a dozen ways to go about it."

"Really? I'm almost amused. What—like, you're going to walk into the lobby of each company and say, 'Oh, excuse me, but did someone here happen to drop this envelope containing thousands of dollars in cash?'"

"Don't mock me. I'm serious about this. The guilt is eating me alive."

Judith grimaced. "Okay," she said. "I'll bite. How do you plan to return five hundred g's and make it look natural? You've come up with some good plots before, but this one should be a doozy."

"It's all come down to research," said Dove. "You'd be amazed at what you can find online."

"No, I wouldn't."

"Okay, maybe not you. But speaking in general terms. It's amazing."

"For example...?"

"For example, one of the insurance companies in question paid country-music singer Teddy Doyle and soap-opera star Ginger Esquivel half a million bucks each to do commercials endorsing the company's policies and products. If my book is a huge hit, I could do an endorsement...gratis. I'd sign the contract and do the commercials but never bill the company."

"Well, at least you'd be speaking with the voice of authority," said Judith with a sardonic smile. "If anyone can attest to the fact that the company pays its claims, it's you. I'll give you that."

Dove smiled, then continued. "I also found out that one of the other insurance companies donates half a million dollars each year to Riley Hospital for Children. If I could assemble a portion of that, in cash, I could let the insurance company take the credit for the donation, but I would fund it and say I wanted to stay out of the picture entirely."

"How modest of you. You've really been thinking about this, haven't you, girl?"

"You have no idea. I cannot escape it. But I will. I've got to make this right. My third idea—"

"Okay, stop." Judith raised a hand. "I'm convinced. Speaking personally, I think it's unnecessary and silly and a waste of good money. But I know you well enough to realize you won't give this up. So, okay, you've got half a dozen ways to give the money back. And, yeah, I'll help you. Just do me one tiny favor first."

"Of course," Dove assured her. "What?"

"Earn the money before you start to give it away."

Dove grinned, feeling relief for the first time in weeks. "I'll write night and day until my emancipation is secured."

Several days later, as their flight landed in Indianapolis, Judith leaned over and whispered, "Welcome home, Hoosier."

"Why, whatever are you referrin' to?" Dove whispered back. They shared a quiet chuckle.

A limo whisked them to the hotel. Donna Jean Sumner was already at their reserved suite, which included a fully stocked bar and complimentary Wi-Fi access, to welcome them on behalf of Calvin and Fox Publishers. The company had sent fresh flowers and a large bowl of assorted fresh fruit.

"We need to get to the convention center in about three hours," said Donna Jean. "Do you want me to call room service and order some lunch?"

"Nothin' for me," said Dove. "I'm goin' down to the fitness center for a workout and some steam, then I'll just have some of this fruit when I get back." She was careful to maintain the drawl around everyone except for Judith, Derek, and Gracie.

"Normally, I'd order something ridiculously expensive and highly caloric," Judith confessed with a sigh of lament, "but I think I've got a boyfriend now, so I'd better go down to the torture chamber with Dove and try to do some damage control."

After Judith exhausted herself on the stair stepper and returned to the suite to rest, Dove relaxed alone in the steam room. She pondered the remarkable path her life had taken during the past sixteen months, and suddenly, a scene unfolded in her mind as clear as the day it had happened.

She'd gone to the door of her home in Brissenden and found a birthday card from her coworkers at Reynolds. It had teased her about getting older but not better. She had cried at the truth it forced her to face—how miserable her life was, and how small, insignificant, and even stupid Dan made her feel. His abuse had extended beyond physical harm to thwarting her career, keeping her locked in a dead-end job, and making promises he had no intention of keeping.

If she had one regret regarding all that had transpired in her life since that time, it was the fact that Dan had gotten away with murder—the killing of Sheila Davis Gray. And he'd been paid generously. Sure, it had been a huge inconvenience for him to give her half the insurance money, but he'd still managed to enjoy the other $275,000—plus the proceeds from the sale of their house. With Gracie's help, Dove had forgiven him for the fifteen years of servitude he had put her through. But this latest offense was still unfinished business in her mind, especially now that she had come to terms with her moral duty to return all the money to the insurance companies herself. What she wouldn't give to make him pay!

However, as Dove conjured up inventive ways to extract a pound of flesh, Gracie's voice rose from the depths of her conscience, reminding her that holding on to a grudge was like hiding a snake in one's clothing with the hope that the other person would get bitten. Instead of the intended victim being affected, the "person dyin' from a venom overdose," as Gracie had colorfully phrased it, was the one hanging on to the serpent of unforgiveness.

Dove knew her friend was speaking from personal experience. Gracie's life had been no easier than her own. In fact, it'd been worse. Gracie had explained that forgiveness just gave "the rascals" over to a higher court. Dan certainly fit the description of "rascal." Dove knew that, as difficult as it might be, she needed to follow Gracie's example and forgive Dan for this additional offense.

Dove looked around the empty steam room. The solitude of this little enclosure seemed to be as good a place as any to talk to God about the issue.

Dan arrived at the convention center more than an hour before the doors were scheduled to open to the public. He'd thought that by showing up that early, he would beat the crowds. But he was wrong. People were amassed at every entrance, eager to meet their favorite authors and get their pictures taken with them and have them autograph their books.

Dan rubbed his eyes as he stared at the crowd. It was happening again. He was seeing images of Sheila everywhere he looked. She was one of four women laughing in a small group; she was dressed as one of the ushers inside the glass doors; she was one of the members of the press corps now being let in through a side entrance. Of course, each time, upon a more careful scrutiny, he realized it wasn't Sheila. Dan chastised himself, eager to get past the ridiculous obsession that had been haunting him for a year now.

The doors finally opened, and everyone surged forward. Dan held his precious manuscript close to his chest, fearful it might get jostled out of his hands and scattered. His game plan had been to run football-style through the crowd of women in order to find the Calvin and Fox booth and be first in line. However, when he left the foyer and stepped into the large open arena, he became mesmerized by all the glory of the world of publishing that lay before him.

Here it was—the epitome of success for writers. Huge posters touting new books were hung high on all the walls, and tables filled with giveaways—bookmarks, pens, photos, press kits—were positioned near the most highly trafficked areas. The authors themselves were ensconced in booths adorned by posters of their book covers and flanked by gofers who were only too eager to fetch cups of coffee or supply fresh felt-tip pens for autographing. Posted schedules indicated that by late afternoon, some publishers would even be pouring complimentary glasses of wine for the customers.

Ever since Dan had entered college and started to study English and journalism, he had coveted this life. As he watched adoring fans line up for a chance to meet the authors, he envisioned himself inside one of the booths. He would smile patiently as one person after another told him how much he or she had loved reading his latest book. For two decades, he had imagined and fantasized about such scenes, and now, today, he was going to take the final step needed to make that dream come true.

He forced himself to put his reverie behind him momentarily and to concentrate on the task at hand. He passed from booth to booth until he finally located the Calvin and Fox display. Three people were seated at the table inside the booth. He recognized one as Dove Alexander. How bizarre—even *she* reminded him of Sheila, in certain ways. He dismissed the thought and admonished himself to keep his imagination in check. There was serious work to be done.

The publisher had set up a table piled with promotional booklets containing the first two chapters of *Hearts of Bronze* and prominently featuring the publisher's Web site, where the novel could be pre-ordered. Once fans picked up the booklets, they inched forward in a line toward Dove's table, where they could meet her and get her autograph.

Dan joined the line, picked up a copy of the booklet, and placed it on top of the box containing his manuscript. It wouldn't be much longer now.

Although she had heard it from hundreds of readers already, Dove listened patiently as a middle-aged woman told her how episode ten of Dove's magazine serialization had just devastated her. She had cried for an hour when the character Suzanne had died. But it had been so wonderful that she and her mother had made up before that happened.

While Dove listened, she autographed a booklet for the woman.

"We're so pleased you're enjoying the story," Judith cut in. "Thank you very much for coming by to meet Dove today. And be sure to pre-order the book from our Web site. Next person, please."

The next woman rushed forward and placed her own booklet on the table. "Hi, Miss Alexander. I just love your story. I want to give this booklet to my mother so she can have your autograph. Could you please sign it 'To Janeen Heidinger'? I'm ordering the book for her birthday, so maybe you could add something about...."

While listening, Dove glanced out into the crowd. When she spotted Dan Gray in line, she failed to hear anything else the woman was saying. What on earth was Dan doing in her line? Had he somehow found out who she was? Was he here to try to get his money back? Would he make a scene and expose her?

Absentmindedly, Dove finished signing the booklet and handed it back. "I'm sorry," she said, "but I need a two-minute break. M' back is jest killin' me." She turned to Judith and said, "Judith, dearest, would you come with me to the powder room for a moment?"

Judith looked at her with a puzzled expression, but Dove's sudden glare must have gotten the message across, for Judith quickly agreed. "Sure," she said. "Donna Jean, would you let the folks in line know that Dove will be right back, and could you have someone round up a couple of diet sodas for us while we're gone? Thanks."

The two women ducked out the back of the booth. The moment they were no longer in earshot of anyone, Dove said in a shaky voice, "He's here. I saw him!"

"Who?" asked Judith. "Who's here? Your brother? Your former boss?"

"Dan! He's out there in line."

"You're kidding. Are you sure?" asked Judith. "No, no, I'm sorry. Of course, you're sure. What do you think he wants?"

"You're asking me? How should I know?"

"Because you used to live with him, that's how!" said Judith, her voice starting to rise. "Why would he be here?"

Dove wrapped her arms tightly around herself and started to pace the small area behind the booth. "I don't think he's been fooled. He probably heard me on some talk show and saw right through everything. He's probably going to make a scene and start calling me Sheila in front of everyone...."

"Stay cool," Judith told her. "I've got an idea. Wait here just a second. Don't go anywhere."

In less than three minutes, Judith returned, carrying two ibuprofen tablets and a plastic cup of cold water. Accompanying her was a man in a blue uniform. After Judith handed Dove the water, she gave her the tablets and told her to swallow them.

"This is Joe Dusseau, one of the security guards on duty today," said Judith. She turned to face the man. "Officer Dusseau, we would be very obliged if you would stand close to the Calvin and Fox booth for the next twenty minutes. We saw a guy in line who looked a little tipsy, and we don't want anything ruining our party. He probably just wants an autograph, but I've seen people at affairs like this who hit the free wine a little too hard. We'd like you nearby, just in case."

The security guard nodded his understanding. "I'll stand off to the side," he said, "and if you need any help, just flash me the high sign."

"Thanks," said Judith. She waited until he was gone before she turned to Dove and said, "Okay, we're going to play this straight. Who knows? Maybe Dan and his new wife are just touring the book fair to get autographs. Isn't she an English professor or something? His presence could be just a coincidence. Let's not tip our hand if we don't have to, okay?"

Dove was trembling by now. "I'm not sure I can look him in the eyes," she said. "I'm getting sick to my stomach."

"Stop it!" said Judith. She grasped Dove's face with one of her hands and turned it so she could look directly into her eyes. "Get a grip. Not two hours ago, you told me you'd reached another level of forgiveness with your ex. You said you'd settled your score and given that loser over to God to be dealt with. Personally, I don't know how you did that, but, hey, if I wore hats, I'd tip mine to you. Now, take back the power that was rightfully yours years ago. Donna Jean and I are here by your side. So's Officer Dusseau. Go out there and sign your autograph for him. See this for what it is: He's paying homage to you, at last! Enjoy the moment."

Dove's breathing started to normalize. As Judith released her grip on her face, Dove gradually smiled. "What if...what if he really *doesn't* know it's me? Wouldn't that be a kick?"

"Now you're talking," said Judith. "Come on, let's have some fun."

They returned to the booth, and Judith waved for the next person in line to step forward. Dove resumed her autographing ritual. Step by step, person by person, Dan Gray drew nearer to the front of the line.

Dove refused to look at him, but she could feel her palms getting moist. Finally, Judith gave the nod for him to step forward. Dove took in a deep breath, let it out slowly, and then flashed a winning smile. "Afta'noon, handsome," she said. "Shall I sign this fo' you or fo' your girlfriend?"

Dan stood awkwardly in front of her a moment, then said, "Huh? Oh, oh, the booklet. Yeah, sure, just sign it to me. Dan Gray. Gray with an *a*. But, look, the real reason I'm here is to share something special with you ladies."

He set a cardboard box on the table. Then he glanced at Donna Jean's vendor ID badge before saying to her, "I'm a college professor here in Indianapolis. I've been working for sixteen years to complete this novel. It's high-quality work, I assure you, and I need a publisher. I'd like you to consider it for Calvin and Fox."

He then turned to Judith Hardy, eyed her badge, and said, "You might want to look at it, too, since your magazine serializes novels. It's really first-rate."

Neither woman seemed to know what to say. It had never occurred to Dove that Dan might have finished his novel and would be trying to market it. Who would have guessed that *that* was what had brought him here today?

As Dan stood at the table, Dove noticed his hands resting on the box presumably containing his precious manuscript. Everything she'd suffered from those hands began to flash through her memory. She looked up and saw the familiar steely hardness in his blue eyes. He wore a self-satisfied smile on his lips—the same lips that had minimized her worth and had colluded in taking from her whatever he wanted, whenever he wanted it, whether or not she'd been willing to give it.

Then she suddenly realized that if she'd ever wanted to humiliate Dan Gray in retaliation for all he'd put her through, now was her chance. She knew about his novel's pathetic characters and laughable dialogue. She could slice him to ribbons in front of her fans and editor friends. He'd never see it coming.

"Actually," Donna Jean started to explain, "our company only accepts agented submissions that are—"

"Let's not be too hasty, now, Donna, darlin'," Dove broke in. "Mista' Green just may have a masta'piece here."

Dan smiled broadly. "It's Gray…Dan Gray. Yes, I'm sure you'll be impressed."

Judith looked at Dove as if she thought she was crazy and wondered what in the world was going on.

Dove lifted the top of the box and looked at the stack of printed pages inside. "Well, sir, let me just glance at this a little bit. Do y'all mind if I read a few pages? Maybe Miz Hardy, too?"

Dan beamed with excitement. "No, no, not at all. Go right ahead. I'm in no rush."

Dove lifted out several of the top pages, saying as she did so, "I often like to help Miz Hardy, here, in sortin' through the many, many manuscripts sent to her fine magazine each month. Isn't that true, Judith, darlin'?"

Judith blinked. "Yeah…uh, sure you do. You're a big help…a big help."

"*The Bohemian Generation,*" Dove read aloud from the cover page. "Well, I guess that means the novel eventually winds up in Southern California, doesn't it, Mista' Gray?"

"W-why, yes," Dan stammered, his tone conveying his amazement. "Yes, that's right."

Dove frowned as she read the first, then the second, and then the third, page of his novel. She saw immediately that whatever Dan might have done to the manuscript since she'd sneaked a peek at it the year before had, if anything, only made it worse. Sarcasm sharpened her tongue in preparation for the fatal thrust. Yet....

The people in line behind Dan were starting to grumble. He didn't look as if he cared a bit. Instead, he had the appearance of someone whose whole life was on the line.

Dove put down the pages. What was she doing? She'd already made the decision to forgive Dan. The momentary delight of taking revenge now would quickly morph into permanent regret. What was it Gracie had told her? *"Do what you can today, then tomorrow, see if you can do it again, plus maybe a little more."* Well, it was time to do a little more. For her own sake, she needed to let Dan Gray off the hook for good, and that meant passing up the opportunity to retaliate. If, at the same time, she could also find a way to remove his false hope of getting his novel published, she'd actually be doing him—and editors everywhere—a favor.

She sighed heavily and said, "Dear, dear Mista' Gray. Is this another one of those standard stories about a family that comes to America from some European country, and they all get jobs in the steel mills, and then one of them tries to form a union, but he gets killed in the process, and then his son tries to do the same thing in the next generation, but he succeeds?"

Dan's mouth fell open like the end of a flatbed truck about to be unloaded. He seemed absolutely stupefied that Dove Alexander had just summarized the plot of his entire book.

"Well...yes, basically," he murmured, "but I...that is...."

Dove returned the pages to the box and set the cover back on top. "I'm so sorry, Mista' Gray, but we see that same plot at least ten times a month at the magazine. It has been done to death. Am I right, or am I right, Judith, darlin'?"

"Huh?" said Judith, coming in a beat late. "Oh...oh, yeah...the old steel-mills-and-union plot. I honestly can't tell you how many times I've seen that storyline just this year alone."

Dan appeared beyond being stupefied. "Other writers have actually thought up the same plot? *M-my* plot?" he stammered. "But, uh, I think that, well...once you really got into the book...."

Instead of delighting in Dan's discomfort, Dove realized she actually felt a tiny bit of pity for the miserable man. She smiled sweetly. "I'm terribly sorry, Mista' Gray, but I can tell it's just another chaw on a worn piece of tobacco, as we say in the South. But, here, I can at least sign the booklet for you." With careful penmanship, she wrote:

To Dan Gray. There is no shame in knowing your limitations in life.

Dove Alexander

She handed the booklet back to Dan, who took it but kept protesting. "But my novel has a lot of fascinating twists and turns," he insisted. "The characters come to life as they...."

Judith gave the high sign to Officer Dusseau. The security guard rushed over. "We all need to take turns, my friend," he said as he put his hand on Dan's arm.

"Wait a second!" Dan pleaded. "Just wait a second!" He wrenched his arm free.

"Oh," said Dove, picking up the cardboard box and handing it to Dusseau, "don't let the gentleman fo'get his novel."

Officer Dusseau took the box with one hand and Dan with the other and started to move away from the booth. "Come on, buddy. On your way, now."

In less than a minute, Dan's pleading voice was lost in the din of the crowd.

Dove started to have second thoughts about the little joke she'd made when autographing Dan's booklet. Would he be hurt by it? She searched her heart and could honestly say that revenge had not been her motive. Still, she wasn't very far along on this journey of forgiveness yet and had a lot to learn. She needed to be patient with herself. Then she smiled, remembering something else Gracie had said: "*Home wasn't built in a day.*" How very true.

Judith tapped Dove on the shoulder and beckoned her to follow. Once again, they stepped behind the booth. When alone, they hugged each other.

"Did you see that?" Dove asked. "He didn't recognize me. He honestly didn't know me!"

Judith stepped back a pace and looked her friend squarely in the face. "I got news for you, sugar. That bum never knew you from the start. Why be surprised now? If he'd ever taken the time to know you, he'd have found a talented and loving and gifted woman worthy of his total devotion."

"Thanks," said Dove. "I can't tell you how relieved I feel. If I can fool Dan, I can fool anyone. I can now be Dove Alexander forever."

Judith smiled in agreement. "Hey," she said, "you've had a long afternoon. Why don't I tell Donna Jean to send the rest of the rabble away, and we'll just jump into that rental car and head out to Brissenden?"

Dove considered that a moment, then said, "No, I've changed my mind. Let's forget the trip to Brissenden. Let sleeping dogs lie, as we say in the South." She smiled at her parody of herself. "I can go on the old-home tour sometime in the future if I ever change my mind. Now, I'd actually much rather go back out there and continue to be Dove Alexander."

"Really?" asked Judith.

"Really," said Dove. "Because that's who I am."

ABOUT THE AUTHORS

Dennis E. Hensley holds four degrees in communications, including a PhD in English from Ball State University. He is chair of the Department of Professional Writing at Taylor University, where he holds the rank of full professor. Dr. Hensley is a recipient of the "Award for Teaching Excellence" from Indiana University and the "Elisabeth Sherrill Lifetime Achievement Award for Writing and Speaking." He is the author of 60 books and more than 3,500 published articles, devotions, interviews, columns, and features. He was awarded six medals for service in Vietnam as a sergeant in the United States Army. He and his wife, Rose, have two grown married children and four grandchildren.

Diana Savage has written or contributed to eleven books and has published more than one hundred articles, along with several short stories and poems. She speaks at a variety of venues in the U.S. and abroad and is director of the annual Northwest Christian Writers Renewal conference near Seattle. As principal of Savage Creative Services, LLC, Diana provides professional writing, editing, Web site management, and speaking services. Diana earned her BA degree from Northwest University and her Master in Theological Studies degree from Bakke Graduate University. She has served on the board of directors of four nonprofits, as director of women's ministries at a large West Coast church, and as development officer for a ministry to homeless children and their families.